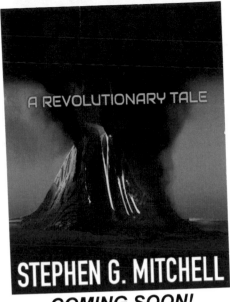

A REVOLUTIONARY TALE

STEPHEN G. MITCHELL

COMING SOON!

Visit http://stephengmitchellbooks.com

A CURE TO DIE FOR

A MEDICAL THRILLER

STEPHEN G. MITCHELL

CREATIVE ARTISTS
Publishing

Creative Artists Publishing
2047 Last Chance Gulch, Ste. #338
Helena, MT 59601
www.acuretodiefor.com

First Edition: July 2011

Publisher's Cataloging-in-Publication

Mitchell, Stephen G. (Stephen Gerald), 1951-

    A cure to die for : a medical thriller / Stephen G. Mitchell. -- 1st ed. --
    Helena, MT : Creative Artists Publishing, c2011.
    p. ; cm.

    ISBN: 978-0-9832060-0-2

Summary: A wonder drug, a miracle cure, and a conspiracy to destroy it.

    1. Conspiracies--Fiction. 2. Cancer--Treatment--Fiction. 3. Pharmaceutical
    biotechnology--Fiction. 4. Genetic engineering--Fiction. 5. Pharmaceutical
    industry--Corrupt practices--Fiction. 6. Detective and mystery stories.
    7. Suspense fiction. I. Title.

    PS3613.I868 C87 2011   2011920071

    813.6--dc22   1103

Cover and book design: Patricia Bacall
Cannastar illustration: Tara Thelen
Cover concept: Chris Sokolsky
Author photo: Jason Savage
Book consultant: Ellen Reid

Printed in the United States of America on acid-free paper.

For Beverly
who made it all possible

CHAPTER 1

A Winter Fire

Like any date with destiny, this one was blind. The letter was an invitation, if you could call it that, from a friend he had not heard from in almost 20 years. Mainly it was a list of reasons why he shouldn't come—which made it all the more compelling. The timing couldn't have been better. Alex Farmer had lost his way and needed to get his life back.

The commuter jet was less than a mile out when the airfield finally appeared through the overcast. The plane screamed out of the sky and touched down on the frozen runway. A December wind moaned softly and blowing snow swirled across the tarmac as the passengers deplaned. It was one of those winter days in Montana when even the cows can't stand it.

Alex headed for the terminal with the other passengers, clutching his jacket to his throat. He was a tall man, 42 years old, who for the past year had walked slightly bent and with a slight limp from the pain in his back—a pain that had returned with a vengeance now that he was off the prescription drugs. Sleepless nights had taken their toll on his handsome features and given him a haunted haggard look. He looked less like a doctor now and more like a sailor too long at sea.

The hospital director in Los Angeles had given him a choice: he could resign his position in the ER or lose his license. That's what sent him into rehab. He was clean and sober for the first time since the accident. He didn't know how long it would last.

Alex stood looking for his ride, shivering at the airport curb with his only luggage, a backpack, slung over his shoulder. All he saw was the snow that blew across the icy asphalt. He didn't think it was possible to lose the feeling in his fingers this fast.

Then out of the colorless day came the grinding sound of an ancient engine and a wreck of an old truck pulled up under the airport canopy. The driver reached across and pushed on a passenger door that creaked open on rusted hinges.

"Alex Farmer?"

He nodded, too cold to speak. Whatever his old friend might look like now, this wasn't him. In fact, as near as Alex could tell, it wasn't a him at all, it was a her who was muffled under so many layers of scarves, sweaters and long johns that the only thing visible under her hat was a shocking mane of hair that fell long and dark around the shoulders of a coat that was almost as worn out as the truck.

He hesitated, his breath coming in small clouds.

From within the shapeless mound of clothing the muffled voice spoke again:

"It's not any warmer in here than it is out there. Probably better if you changed your mind anyway." She leaned back across to close the door.

Alex caught the handle and swung himself and his pack inside.

"I must be out of my mind," he said.

"No argument there."

"I see he sent the limo." She looked at him sharply and he saw in her pale eyes that she had been crying. "Sorry," he said. "So where is he, Maury Bernstein I mean?"

She motioned with her head to indicate the bed in the back of the truck. "I had to bring him into town anyway."

He followed her gaze, rubbed the fog from the rear window with his sleeve, then rubbed frantically again and stared. In the bed of the truck was a body wrapped in a dirty tarp and hastily tied with ropes.

"What...what is this?" he gasped. "Who is that back there...?"

His words were lost in a terrible grinding of gears as the truck lurched forward. Smoke belched from the exhaust pipe and was quickly lost in the flat light as the truck followed the empty road out of the airport.

Badly shaken, Alex asked how his friend had died.

"Hunting accident," she said. "I'm not the one that found him."

"Maury doesn't hunt," Alex said. "He hated guns."

"I didn't say he was the one hunting." Her voice was flat, almost monotone. There was a silence before she spoke as if she were waiting for distant voices to tell her what to say.

"What about the police?"

"Police?"

"Are you saying you haven't called them?"

"This is Montana."

"What the hell is that supposed to mean?" She was concentrating intently on the icy road ahead and didn't answer. "How do you know Maury?" he asked.

"I worked for him at the university when I was there." The truck lost traction and started to slide. She corrected the skid

and said, "Also, I'm his landlord. Now stop bothering me so
I can drive."

THE BEAT-UP TRUCK WITH the bound roll of canvas in
back containing the body of Maury Bernstein pulled into a
driveway and stopped. The sign in the front yard, half buried
in snow, read "Appleseed Funeral Home". The mortuary was
in a huge, gracious, somewhat dilapidated three-story brick
Victorian house with a wraparound front porch, a witch's
hat turret and blacked out windows on the third floor. It was
painted a hideous red color with green and black trim, a color
pallet that made it look like a mansion haunted by colorblind
ghosts. Attached to one side of the house, in front of where
they were parked, was a nondescript flat roofed garage-type
structure that Alex assumed was where they kept the bodies
and parked the hearse.

The driver beeped the truck horn and the garage door
opened immediately and they both got out of the truck. A robust
and extremely overweight undertaker stepped out into the cold
wearing a short-sleeved shirt that fit snugly around his gigantic
biceps. His professionally somber mask gave way to something
far sadder as he came forward to hug the girl. With all the
clothes she was wearing he was unable to get his arms even
half way around her. The smell of marijuana when he brushed
past Alex almost made him gag. It was mixed with something
else he couldn't identify—a sweeter odor almost like chocolate.

"I couldn't believe it when you called," he said. "I still
can't."

"No tears, Otis. We said no tears, remember?" She patted
his enormous back, holding him tightly.

"You loved him too, I know you did," he said.

Standing to one side, Alex said, "I'm going to need to examine the body."

The undertaker, shivering now in his short-sleeved shirt, looked at Alex suspiciously. "What would you want to examine a dead body for, man?"

"Hobby of mine," Alex said.

"He's some kind of doctor," the girl said.

Alex helped Otis load the ice-covered tarp in the back of the truck onto a gurney. The three of them wheeled it through the garage and into the preparation room where Otis heaved the deceased onto a stainless steel table equipped with metal gutters, trays, pans, instruments and tubes. The room was cold as death. Alex tried to lift a corner of the canvas that covered the body, but it was frozen solid and wouldn't budge.

The beefy mortician went to a thermostat on the wall and turned it up. "Why don't we go inside where it's warm while we let him thaw out," he said. "You two look like you could use something hot to drink."

Alex had never been a fan of funeral homes, but this one was so bizarre he didn't know what to think. He stepped through the door to the main house and hot, humid air enveloped him. It felt like he had walked out of a refrigerator into a sauna. The pungent earthy smell of a rain forest filled his nostrils. Potted plants were everywhere, large and small, some with vibrant colors, others with enormous leaves, none of which had he ever seen before. He heard the sound of water rushing over rocks and had an image of himself paddling upstream in a dugout canoe. He could almost hear the screech and cry of birds and monkeys.

It was more of a premonition than he ever imagined.

Otis led the way through the lush foliage, past the display room where different coffins were for sale, and stopped at the kitchen door.

"Cyd, why don't you take our guest into the parlor while I put the kettle on," Otis said. The girl gave him an anxious look. He smiled reassuringly. "Nothing like a nice hot cup of Lipton on a cold winter day, that's what I say."

The air was so humid it was hard to breathe. Cyd started shedding her outer garments. Underneath the bulky clothes she was slender and shapely. Alex was stunned at how young and radiant she looked. He guessed her to be in her late twenties.

Otis came back balancing a tray that held a steaming pot and three mugs. He bent to pour and he and Cyd exchanged another look. "It's just Lipton," he assured her.

Alex blew on his tea and set it back down. "What kind of research was Maury doing when he died?" he asked.

"Why do you want to know? What did he say to you?" the girl demanded.

"Let's hear him out, why don't we," Otis said.

Alex searched his pockets, pulled out a crumpled envelope and removed a letter. He cleared his throat and saw them staring at him intently.

"Dearest Alex," he began, reading aloud. "If I sound desperate it's because I am. This thing is so big and I am in so much trouble. I only have two, maybe three people I can trust. It isn't enough. I can't tell you to come, a friend wouldn't ask that. Too late anyway, I should think. It's getting worse by the day and I need more help."

Cyd and Otis listened with pained expressions. Alex went on:

"I don't want to burden you at a time like this. A former colleague of mine in Los Angeles told me of your troubles and I am so sorry. Such a schmuck, I am. Brought it on myself. Thought they'd want it, welcome it with open arms. How could I have been so naïve? How do you save a world that doesn't want to be saved? It's all about greed, you know, about not rocking the boat. This is a boat rocker my friend, let me tell you. Can you imagine? Revolutionize modern medicine—is that such a bad thing? Ignore this letter, Alex. Don't get involved. I didn't know where else to turn. Forgive me."

"It's signed Maury Bernstein and it came with a plane ticket," Alex said. "You want to tell me what this is all about?"

Otis studied the bottom of his teacup.

"He'd been upset for weeks, not sleeping or eating well, keeping to himself," Cyd said. "I was worried about him…"

Alex winced as he came to his feet—standing up was the hardest part of his back injury—and started to leave the room. A cold wind whistled around the old house.

"Where are you going?" Cyd asked.

"I need to spend some time alone with my friend."

"There's a parka by the door," Otis said. "Put it on if you want."

Alex entered the preparation room hugging Otis's gigantic parka around him. He went over to the canvas-wrapped body on the table and stood looking down. The room was getting warmer, but he didn't notice. Tears began to run down his cheeks.

Otis and Cyd came in an hour later and found him still crying. Alex angrily wiped at his eyes and gave the frozen tarp another tug. The canvas came away stiffly and made cracking sounds as he forced it back. He was so intent on removing the covering that it was a minute before he looked at the colorless face of the corpse. It was Maury all right. The same bushy eyebrow, the same kinky black hair and beard—except that now they were flecked with gray.

Otis put a sympathetic hand on Alex's shoulder. "Sorry, man," he said.

Alex set to work examining the body. He found two bullet wounds in a relatively tight pattern, both in the back. One had gone through the shoulder; the other had punctured a lung. This was something he knew a lot about. The bullets came from a high-powered rifle, fired at a distance, with a great deal of accuracy. One might be an accident; two this close together was murder.

"I'm calling the police," Alex said. "Where's your phone?"

"Better let me do it," Otis said.

"Why's that?"

"It might look better. I'm also the county coroner."

Police officers arrived at the funeral home and stayed for hours. They made careful notes of everything they saw and everything Cyd told them:

It was Betty Littlehorn who had found Maury up on the mountain and brought him back down to Cyd's ranch on horseback. "You get to Betty's place through mine," Cyd said. "She's been riding her horses over my dad's property since before I was born. She knew Maury was staying with me."

The homicide detective turned to Otis. "We're gonna need a complete autopsy."

Otis nodded. The detective was used to the undertaker's somber demeanor and had no idea this case was personal or that Otis had so much at stake.

THE DRIVE NORTH TO WOLF Creek from Helena took an hour in Cyd's old truck. The canyon walls got steeper as the interstate climbed the pass. Then they were on a winding two-lane road that continued northwest, rising steadily as it left the river and the trees behind. The ancient truck sounded relieved as the asphalt leveled out across rolling wheat fields turned white and clean with snow. It was after dark by the time they arrived at Cyd's ranch. The lack of heat in the truck had caused Alex to lose the feeling in his toes.

"You can afford a ranch like this but you can't afford a decent car?" he said.

A long pause. "It runs," she said. "And who says I can afford the ranch?" Another pause. "His lab is in the barn. You want to see it tonight?"

"Morning will be fine," he shivered.

The truck rattled past a cluster of weather-beaten ranch buildings and corrals that Alex could barely see. Inside a windbreak in one of the corrals stood two shaggy horses pulling hay from a round bale with their teeth and munching it lazily. The black gelding belonged to Cyd and the gray-backed dun mare had been her father's horse. Cyd stopped in front of an old two-story log house that was dark and silent. Snow crunched underfoot as they got out.

"All we need now is howling wolves," Alex said. Just then a wolf howled in the night. "Great," he muttered.

"Why are you limping?" Cyd asked as they entered the house.

"Was I limping?"

It was colder inside the house than out. Cyd knelt by the stone hearth to light the fire. It flared quickly and the flickering light cast long shadows over a tall ceiling of rustic log rafters that stretched from the living room to the dining room to the kitchen in one long rectangle. A log staircase ran up one wall and led to the second floor.

Cyd pushed herself to her feet. "The couch pulls out into a hide-a-bed," she said as she headed for the stairs.

"Cyd," he said quietly. "What the hell was Maury doing all the way out here?

"Research."

"What kind of research?"

She stopped halfway up the steps. Again the long pause. "It had to do with transgenics, with the human immune system."

"In his letter he said he was in trouble. Do you know what kind, exactly?"

She disappeared down the hall at the top of the stairs. He heard a bedroom door close softly.

Alex sat on the sofa staring at a crackling fire that offered little relief from the immense stillness that seemed to seep through the windows from the remote land outside.

Heads of dead animals stared down at him from the log walls, eyes glinting in the firelight, unconcerned with what the rifles in the glass gun cabinet next to the front door could do—or had done.

LOUD BANGS AND CRASHES STARTLED Alex out of a restless, freezing sleep. Yellow shadows flickered wildly across the room. Cyd bolted out of her bedroom and down the stairs pulling her coat on over her nightgown.

They ran outside to find the barn on fire. Flames shot from the roof and smoke bellowed from the doors and loft. The horses screamed from the relative safety of their corral. Cyd ran straight into the flames. Alex hesitated before he could bring himself to follow.

Inside the barn the timbers were burning and falling around them. He was blinded by smoke. Burning hay was floating in the air. There were no animals in the barn, only a large metallic room built in the center of the floor under the hayloft. He saw Cyd dart inside the room and he ran after her through the metal door. Inside he could hear glass crashing and breaking. The lab wasn't on fire yet, but it was so hot it was melting the computers. The chemical stench was awful.

Gagging and covering his mouth, he searched and couldn't find her. Then through the smoke he saw her on her hands and knees under a lab table frantically pulling up the floorboards. He lunged forward and hauled her to her feet just as she pulled a briefcase out from between the floor joists. A barn timber crashed onto the roof of the lab and the overhead lights exploded in a sparking shower of glass. They clawed and fumbled their way toward the door. Another timber crashed as they came back out into the burning barn. She fell and the briefcase slipped from her hand and skidded across the ground. She groped for it blindly, her fingers closing around the handle just as he grabbed her up and lifted her into his arms.

Alex burst through the smoking barn door and out into the open air and fell choking to the ground, spilling Cyd into a snow bank. Pain from his back shot through his butt and down the backs of his legs. There was a horrible burning in his eyes and his lungs were on fire. In the distance he could hear the sound of engines. The sound grew louder until a caravan of pickup trucks appeared, barreling down the drive, bouncing over the frozen potholes, their headlights flashing at crazy angles in the dark.

"Don't let them see this," Cyd gasped, holding out the briefcase.

He took it from her and flung it into the bushes just as the trucks skidded to a halt in front of the barn and dozens of men piled out with pick axes and shovels. A big yellow water truck was just behind. The heavy construction vehicle tipped dangerously as it wheeled to a stop in front of the barn, spilling water. Men swarmed the truck and almost instantly had it pumping water on the fire.

Half an hour later Cyd sat on the tailgate of a truck, huddled under a blanket, staring at the smoldering remains of her barn.

Alex checked her pulse and helped her wash her eyes, cursing the fact that he didn't have any oxygen to give her.

A soot-covered rancher, not as tall as Cyd but about her age and barrel-chested as his water truck, came over and put a comforting arm around her shoulders. "It didn't get to any of the other buildings, Cyd. I think you're going to be okay."

She jerked away and glared at him. "How did you know my place was on fire?"

The tiny mouth in his round head smiled patiently. "Whole damn sky was lit up. Good thing one of my men spotted it."

"A fire is easy to spot if you're the one that started it," she said. "Why didn't you just let my whole damn place burn?"

The smile stayed frozen on his face. "Come on Cyd, don't be like that."

She looked like she was going to take a swing at him. "Get the fuck off my property, Ty."

"Suit yourself," Ty said with a shrug and walked away.

"Who was that?" Alex asked.

"My asshole second cousin."

"He lives around here, I take it?"

"He lives everywhere but here and he's not going to live here," she said. "Not if I can help it."

The sun was just coming up as the trucks were leaving the ranch. The moment the last truck was gone Cyd threw off her blanket and ran for the bushes. Alex was puzzled until he remembered the briefcase. Moments later she reappeared holding it to her chest with both hands and heading straight for the house. He ran to catch up.

"I'll just be a minute," Cyd said, backing through the front door while holding the case behind her.

"You want to tell me what that is?"

"It's nothing. Don't worry about it."

Alex lost his patience. "My best friend is suddenly dead, your barn burns down in the middle of the night, you almost get us killed over a briefcase you dig out from under the floorboards of some kind of high-tech lab in a horse stall and you say it's nothing? That I shouldn't worry about it? What the hell is going on here?"

She backed farther away. "Who are you? I don't even know who you are."

"I'm a friend of Maury's," he repeated evenly.

ALEX FARMER, MAURY BERNSTEIN AND a third friend, Joe Angolia, grew up together, but it was Joe alone who adopted the aggressive, streetwise, in-your-face attitude it takes to survive a New Jersey childhood. Alex and Maury didn't need it. What bound the three unlikely companions together was a mutual intelligence that surpassed everyone they knew in school including their teachers.

They came together naturally through the logistical coincidence of growing up on the same block of identical working class row houses in the town of Mt. Ephraim, New Jersey, just south of Philadelphia. And because few bonds are ever forged as quickly, easily or more deeply—and with so little judgment or discretion—as those formed in childhood, they were best friends. Later, after their lives diverged, it would be a bond that would stretch but never break. If they had never known each other as kids and had met in later life they probably would not have been friends at all. But because of that universal common denominator—youth—they would always be.

Alex was easygoing to the point that almost nothing bothered him. He was good at sports, but didn't take them seriously. He had a crooked smile that was so natural he didn't even know he had it, a smile that inspired in girls the urge to either kiss him or slap him—sometimes both at the same time. He had the zero-body-fat metabolism of a runner, a hairline that was already receding and, even then, a doctor's healing hands.

Maury cared only about science, loved chemistry and tried too hard at everything. He was always ebullient, always overly excited about his latest scientific discovery—the typical nerdy Jewish kid with black kinky hair and one bushy eyebrow that ran all the way across his forehead. He had no concern for his physical appearance and went about his disheveled life with the boundless energy of a scientific cheerleader. As far as he was concerned, his body was just something to work in like the mismatched clothes he wore. Alex was so used to Maury's odd combinations of stripes, plaids and clashing colors that he hardly noticed. What he saw was the beauty of his friend's mind. Early in grade school Alex and Joe took on the job of protecting Maury, and as a result Maury did not have to endure the childhood taunts and torments that would normally have been his fate. Maury thought that everyone loved him, not just his two friends, and never suspected why the other kids showed him so much respect.

As for Joe, he stole things. He didn't even have to think about it—he had already found his profession: Joe was a crook. He shadowed the lives of his two friends like a ghost; a wiry little chain-smoking terrier of an Italian with a rasping voice and a hook nose you could use for a letter opener.

While Alex and Maury were getting straight A's, Joe was cutting classes and making other types of friends—the kind they would one day make wise-guy movies and TV shows about. He was every bit as smart as Alex and Maury, smarter than either of them when it came to math. He was so good at handicapping sports that by the time he was seventeen the local bookies wouldn't take his bets anymore because he had won so much money off of them. He had to keep going farther away from home to place his wagers. Finally the word was out for 30 miles around: if a pint-sized kid with a hook nose shows up and wants to make a bet, don't take his money.

So Joe was forced to perfect his other talent: stealing and not getting caught. He didn't care what it was, he loved to steal. Things would disappear from trucks, stores, houses, parking lots and boat docks, and it was as if a phantom had stolen them. No one saw him come, no one saw him go; he didn't exist. The liquidation of his stolen merchandise required that he get to know certain other men whose professional lives were lived in the same shadows that Joe would come to know so well. His fame as a master thief soon surpassed his reputation as a gambler. The old hoods who hung out in the social clubs in New Jersey were very impressed.

Alex admired Joe's talents, his expertise, his enterprise; he admired his balls. In Maury he found true scientific genius. In himself he saw little to appreciate. He felt he was a fake—not a fake in the sense that he wasn't smart, a fake in the sense that he was certain he lacked the creative talent of his friends. He had no idea what he wanted to do with his life. He was good at sports, but so what? Amongst the three, Alex thought that if greatness was reserved for any of them, it wasn't him. What was most amazing was that he didn't resent his friends for it. On the contrary, Maury and Joe were probably the only two people his age that Alex truly admired.

After high school Joe got the inspiration that there was a lot more money to be stolen legitimately than illegitimately and got a job as a runner on the floor of the New York Stock Exchange. It didn't matter that it didn't pay much to start; he had another source of income: the New York bookies didn't know him yet. Alex and Maury were offered full academic scholarships to the prestigious University of Pennsylvania and went off to college together. Maury would never see Joe again. Alex would keep in touch, but many years would pass before they reunited, and by that time they would be in desperate trouble and asking each other for the impossible.

In college Maury grew the bushy black beard that was to become his lifelong trademark. And Alex found something he could finally be serious about—after undergraduate school he was going to go to medical school and become a doctor. The idea suddenly appealed to him: he might be able to help ease some of the suffering he saw everywhere.

They made a strange pair huddled together in the coffee houses off campus—the tall, slim athlete and the short dumpy scientist—intent on endless discussions that revolved around science, chemistry and physics. Had Maury stopped to think he would have realized he loved Alex as much as Alex loved him, but it wasn't something he thought about; he had more important things on his mind. Mainly what he appreciated about Alex was that he was one of the few people intelligent enough to keep up with him during his endless disjointed technical ramblings and diatribes.

So Alex smiled and laughed and coasted his way through undergraduate school while Maury went about proving his genius as a research scientist. When they graduated they went their separate ways. Maury went on to Harvard and eventually earned a PhD in molecular biology. Alex accepted a scholarship to UCLA because he had always wanted to live out west. When he finished medical school he joined the Army where he did his internship and served two tours of duty in Iraq.

After he got out of the service Alex moved back to Southern California and applied for work in the emergency room at Martin Luther King Hospital. On his employment application, under *List any special skills or specialties*, he scrawled, "If it isn't an IED or a bullet wound, I don't know how to treat it." The irony of his personal evaluation escaped the hospital administrators, but this was East Los Angeles and the bullet wound part appealed to them greatly so he got the job and bought himself a condo in Santa Monica. It wasn't until later, after his life had blown up in his face, that he bought the boat.

On his first day at work he met the horny-flighty-beautiful Alicia Mills, a stunning blond nurse with high cheek bones, a quick wit, a sleepy smile and a body that made him weak in the knees. Three months later they were married.

The accident that injured his back and left him in pain happened four years after that. It ruined his marriage and destroyed his life. The fires and explosions in the wake of his growing pill addiction kept getting bigger and louder until, a year later, he was the one that blew up.

By the time he was asked to resign, Alex had worked in the emergency room at MLK for almost 5 years. During that time the city had puked drugs and violence into his ER until he felt like he had lived his entire life in a war zone. Leaving the hospital was a harder adjustment than leaving the military. He figured he had two choices, rehab or suicide, and if one didn't work out he thought he might try the other. Maury's letter reached him the day before he was scheduled to get out of rehab. A trip to Montana to visit an old friend sounded like just the thing.

CYD SNATCHED A BOTTLE OF BOURBON off the table, poured herself a drink into a dirty glass, knocked it back and quickly had another.

"Well…I don't trust you," she said. "I don't trust anybody."

Alex took a deep breath. "I understand how frightening this all must be for you."

The bourbon seemed to relax her. She gestured with the bottle to ask if he wanted a drink. He dismissed the offer with a flick of his hand.

"I thought Maury was going to have a heart attack waiting for you to come, he was so anxious," she said. "I don't know… maybe you're right, maybe I'm just being paranoid. You would be too after all that's happened. The last thing he said to me yesterday when he left the ranch was if he didn't make it back in time I was supposed to pick you up at the airport no matter what."

"Who would want to kill him?"

She shook her head. "Nobody, everybody, who knows? All I know is what Betty said. Somebody shot him."

"Open the briefcase," he said. She didn't move. "I said open it!"

Cyd slammed the case on the table and petulantly dialed the combinations to the locks. The lid popped open and she stared…then began frantically digging inside. "They're not here," she cried. "Where the hell are they?"

"What are you talking about?"

She turned the case upside down and shook it. It was empty.

"What was supposed to be in there?" he said.

Another maddening pause. "His research papers," she said. "The documentation for everything he's done."

"So is this why he was murdered?"

She sat down, put her hands flat on the table, blew out her cheeks and bowed her head. Looking back up, she said:

"You know Rxon, the big drug company?"

He sat down carefully across from her. "The one that's been buying up all the other drug companies?"

"Maury had a research grant from them. His lab was in Missoula at the University there. I worked for him part-time for two years while I was finishing up my master's in plant genetics. Maury was one of my faculty advisors, my favorite. He was close, so close to a breakthrough. Then one day I come in and he's acting all crazy, running around like a madman, stuffing things in boxes and shredding papers."

"What happened?"

"He said he'd heard from somebody at Rxon. A friend of his. He had a lot friends you know; he was a genius." Alex nodded. He'd known long before anyone else what Maury was. "Whoever it was told him they were going to shut his project down. The rumor was that they were going to bury his research, not bring it to market, not even go through the testing to try and get FDA approval. Basically, they were pulling the plug."

"Why?"

"I don't know. All I know is he was scared. We had about a week to phony up some fake research documents before they came to padlock the lab. When they showed up we acted all surprised and angry and indignant and then we quietly left town with the real research. It was a pretty good performance if I do say so myself. That was a little over a year ago."

"And that's when you came up here?"

"Maury needed a place to work where no one could find him or bother him. It was like he was obsessed. I'd just inherited the ranch. I promised my father before he died that I'd keep it no matter what. I grew up here, you know." She looked wistfully out the window at the snow in the front yard where she had played as a little girl. "Anyway, I couldn't even pay the taxes on the place. Maury offered me a full-time job, plus he rented my barn from me. It was enough to keep me afloat. He built the lab with his own money." A stricken look came over her. "What am I going to do? The research—it's gone!"

Alex thought a moment, winced again as he got to his feet, went to the door and pulled on the parka Otis had lent him.

"Let's go," he said.

"Where are we going?"

"I want to talk to this Betty woman who found Maury's body."

THE TRIP TO BETTY'S PLACE was a thirty-minute ride over frozen bumpy roads. Alex sat in silence, buried inside a parka that fit him like a sleeping bag. Cyd turned to study him as she drove, cocking her head to one side.

"What?" he said.

"I never thanked you for saving my life back there."

"I'm used to saving the lives of people who are trying to kill themselves—it's what I do." He couldn't help noticing the splay of freckles that ran across the bridge of her nose and scattered out along her cheeks.

"I mean it. Thank you."

"Don't mention it," he said with his crooked smile. "I needed a ride back into town and I didn't want to have to drive this truck."

For some reason his smile made her angry.

BETTY LITTLEHORN WAS A LITTLE hard of hearing, her concentration was on the hoof she was filing, and the blower on her gas forge was going, so she didn't hear Cyd and Alex come in. Betty was a small, compact woman with a handsome head of short gray hair that looked like she cut it herself. A ring of keys jangled on the outside of her belt. She had no tolerance for fools and even less for wearing makeup. She made her living shoeing and training horses.

Betty looked up, saw she had visitors and ignored them. She finished off the hoof she was working on, went over to her anvil and pounded on a horseshoe with a hammer, sighting down it to make sure it was true. Going back to the horse she lifted its leg again to see if the shoe fit the hoof.

"With you in a minute," Betty said, her mouth full of nails.

"No worries," Cyd said.

A couple more whacks with the hammer and she was satisfied with the fit. She nailed the shoe on, clenched the nails and finished off the hoof with a file; then with one hand on the small of her back she straightened up, unhooked the horse from the cross ties and put him in a stall.

"How you holding up, Cyd?" Betty asked, taking off her leather apron.

"They burned down my barn."

"I saw the smoke. Anybody hurt?"

"Not physically. Betty, this is Alex Farmer."

"So you finally made it," the farrier said, crushing his hand in hers. Alex had never felt a hand so calloused. "Let's go inside, I got coffee on."

Betty led the way out of the shed, past a round pen that was half fallen down, past a rusted creaking hot-walker that was leading a string of horses around in a circle, and toward a house with peeling paint and a roof with several shingles missing.

"I still got six horses to ride so we gotta make this quick," she said.

The inside of the house was a dark, crowded museum of battered cowboy boots, saddles, horse blankets, ropes, chaps, tack and antique spurs and bits, none of which had been dusted since the beginning of time. Betty poured out three cups of black steaming coffee, set them on the kitchen counter top and leaned back against the counter on her elbows.

"So you're him," she said, looking Alex up and down. Betty saw things in black and white, right and wrong, and once she made up her mind about somebody, that was it. "Maury thought a lot of you."

"He never was a very good judge of character," Alex said.

Betty gave him a final going over. "You'll do," she said. "How's your coffee? I cook it with the grains in the pot. Some people don't like it that way."

"It's good," Alex lied.

"I taught him to ride, you know. If it wasn't for me, maybe Maury wouldn't…" Her voice trailed off.

"Can you tell me how he died?" Alex asked.

"I didn't see him actually get shot and I never saw who did it, I was too busy running. We were up on the Dearborn…"

CHAPTER 2

Starry, Starry Night

On a beautiful fall afternoon three and a half years earlier, Sam Seeley was preparing to celebrate his 70th birthday at his sprawling 180-acre Virginia estate located less than an hour's drive outside the Washington Beltway. The invitations read, "Come one, come all and join us for Senator Seeley's birthday!!!" Tickets were $10,000 for organizations, $3,000 per individual. To accommodate the some 1,200 people that were expected to attend, great white party tents, a band shell and an outdoor dance floor were being set up on the sprawling lawn behind the 27,000-square-foot Georgian mansion that overlooked the lawn, the manicured gardens and the dome of a brand new glass greenhouse that gleamed on the bank of the private lake just beyond.

Like a shark is the perfect eating machine, Senator Sam Seeley was the perfect political machine. He was a short, dumpy man who made up for any limitation in size by being overly cruel. He had a big mouth, brass balls, no integrity, no morality and was not burdened with anything resembling a sense of right and wrong. His decades of service to the American people had been devoted almost exclusively to the pursuit of his own self- interests. He'd worn his game face so long it *was* his face: a permanently frozen smile that was not so much a smile as a warning. His legendary public charm was only slightly less legendary than his reputation for being cold-hearted, mean-spirited and bull-headed stubborn.

The Senator stood in his boxer shorts staring out the balcony window of his upstairs bedroom at the army of people scurrying about down on his lawn making final preparations for his party and felt a familiar sense of boredom. He sighed, brushed back his fatherly mane of white hair, took a sip of his cocktail and walked into a closet the size of a bedroom. From his rack of fifty expensive, big-shouldered suits he chose a lighter colored one for today's occasion. From a Gatsby-size collection of shirts he selected a soft pink dress shirt with white collar, then found a festive red and white striped tie to go with it. From his seventy pairs of custom-made shoes he picked out a pair of tasseled loafers. Once he was dressed he adjusted his tie and inspected himself in the mirror. Not only did he look rich, he looked powerful.

Before the party started he had to go outside and deal with his wife's contractor. The man—he couldn't remember his name—had just completed the colossal new greenhouse down by the lake and wanted his final payment. His wife's passion was growing flowers, but that was not why he had let her build her Titanic glass shit-house. He would have let her build it twice as big as long as it kept her off his back. Personally he hated the damn thing; he didn't want to have anything to do with it and had no intention of ever setting foot in it.

The contractor was waiting for the Senator beside the lake next to the greenhouse. A decent competent family man, Jim Toomey had a redneck crew cut and the beefy build of a barroom brawler. He prided himself on his integrity and in always bringing his projects in on time and on budget. Unfortunately, this one was neither. He was on the hook for over half a million dollars and he needed to get paid or the bank was going to take his house. Annie Seeley, the Senator's gracious wife, was a nice lady and he wanted to please her, but all her nervous fussing and constant changes had run the job way over.

He rubbed his hands together nervously and the calluses on his palms made a dry scraping sound. He looked up at the sun glinting off the enormous, gracefully curved structure of double-pane glass and in his mind he examined it for problems. He found none; it was perfect, not a flaw. The greenhouse was divided into separate climate- controlled rooms to create different growing environments and he had installed the plumbing, heating and air conditioning himself to make sure it was right. It was going to be a big feather in his cap, this project, and he figured making the Senator happy would get him a lot more work among what he called "the psycho-rich". He just wanted his money so he could get the hell off this particular job; people in power made him nervous.

He had waited two weeks for this appointment with the busy Senator so he could get paid off and when Sam Seeley finally appeared beside the greenhouse, impeccably dressed in a pink shirt and red and white tie, he was greatly relieved. He stepped forward, extending his hand.

The Senator snorted an inaudible greeting and shook hands, grabbing the contractor's hand by the fingers and squeezing until it hurt.

"Let's have a look around, shall we?" Sam said, turning away before their eyes could meet. "Got a goddamn birthday party to go to." For a short old guy, the Senator was quick. He managed to make it around the corner of the greenhouse before Jim could catch up.

"What's this?" demanded the Senator. He had dropped to his haunches and was sighting down one of the eight enormous walls of hexagon-shaped glass panels set in the complicated curved metal frame that made the eight-sided structure look like a small domed football field. "This wall isn't straight."

Jim Toomey squatted behind the Senator to sight down the wall. Because of the reflections in the glass it looked like it wavered in places—and in fact it did move in and out a bit as it went.

Toomey shrugged. "That's just the nature of glass and metal frame structures," he said.

"It doesn't line up," Sam Seeley said. "I'm not paying for a building that isn't straight. No way." He stood abruptly and started back toward the house.

"What about my check?" Toomey said, calling after him.

"Do it right and you'll get paid."

Jim Toomey watched helplessly as the Senator walked away, a horrible sinking feeling in his stomach.

THE SKY WAS DRESSED IN its finest stars. Music, laughter and the steady drone of party conversation drifted out over the lake that reflected the nighttime sky and danced in a confusion of party lights from the lawn. A thirty-piece orchestra had turned the small outdoor dance floor into a blur of designer gowns. Throngs of Washington's elite ate and drank under the tents, peering at each other's name tags and shaking hands like they were pumping for oil. Drug companies, insurers, hospitals, medical-supply firms, health-service companies, associations of health professionals—their representatives were all here to celebrate the birthday of the man best qualified to represent them and their interests, a man who chaired the committees most important to their well-being.

Before he was the object of all this affection, Sam Seeley was the heir to a vast Montana ranching, timber and mining fortune. Furthermore, he was one of those rare individuals who held both an MD and a JD, meaning he was both a doctor and a lawyer. He had never practiced medicine, but as a lawyer he had amassed a second fortune winning massive settlements in medical malpractice suits. Thirty years ago when he decided to enter politics, the insurers were greatly relieved and welcomed him over to their side with open arms.

The galaxy of partygoers swirled around the Senator as if he possessed the gravity of a black hole. Sam Seeley had the annoying habit of losing interest in a conversation and walking off, often before the other person was finished talking, and the drunker he got the worse it got. His other limitation as a host was that if the number on your last contribution check was not followed by at least four zeros, he could not remember your name. Neither shortcoming seemed to reduce his popularity.

A Middle Eastern man with an unpronounceable company name on his nametag approached with an eager smile. "Happy birthday, Senator!" he exclaimed in perfect English, extending his hand. "My name is Ahmad Hamad al Tayyib. I was hoping at some point we could sit down and I could tell you a little about the energy independent profile of our Wyoming project. My clients will be seeking some regulatory relief from…"

"Yeah, yeah. Talk to one of my aides," the Senator said with a limp handshake, quickly moving on to be immediately swallowed by a crowd of suits from a large health insurer.

A big scratch-golfer with a military haircut and an ingra- tiating University of Texas fraternity boy smile was politely moving people aside with his broad shoulders as he made his way toward the Senator.

"Riley Gray!" Sam Seeley cried, a smile lighting up his flushed face. "Thank heavens." He slipped his arm through the arm of Rxon's chief lobbyist and moved him away from the crowd. "Let's go get a drink, shall we?"

They made their way to the bar where they ordered drinks and stood overlooking the formal circus of party goers that swarmed the lawn below.

"Sam, I need to talk to ya 'bout somethin'," Riley said. "Need a favor."

"Anything," Sam said. "You know that." The Senator didn't have any problem at all remembering the number of zeros on Rxon's contribution checks—it was like counting the stars.

Annie Seeley, the Senator's wife, backed into the shadows and snuck quietly away from the party. Her tiny feet followed the darkened cobblestone path by memory toward one of her musty smelling old greenhouses that would soon be replaced by the big glass-domed new one down by the lake. The moon reflected off the silver of her tomboy haircut and swam in the startling blue of her eyes—eyes that made her elderly face look young.

A dark form waited for her in the starlit greenhouse. Annie switched on the lights and the two women cried with delight when they saw each other. They embraced, surrounded by an explosion of chrysanthemums that filled the old shed with oranges, reds, blues, yellows, pinks and whites that rioted like fireworks all around them.

"Annie, your flowers are gorgeous," the young girl said. "I can't even believe it."

"They're not as pretty as you, darling." A gentle southern breeze, soft and warm, blew through her speech. "I used to be that pretty, but not anymore."

"I could never be as beautiful as you," the girl said. Her hair was as black as Annie's was white.

"I'm so proud, Cydney. A bachelor's degree in Botany from Cornell, imagine that!" She was related to Cyd by marriage only but could not have loved her more if she had been her own flesh and blood. They had a special relationship and a special bond that was grounded not only in mutual affection but in a mutual love of all things that grew from the ground. "And you got through school all on your own. I had to do that too, you know."

A pause. "I did it on a partial scholarship and by waiting tables until I thought my feet were going to fall off."

"Well, now we have to get you on to graduate school."

"I can't afford graduate school. I could barely afford the gas to stop by here. I'm on my way home to Montana."

"We'll ask Sam," Annie said with a resolute nod and an admiring smile. "I swear, when you were a little girl, I'd never seen anyone who could grow things like you could."

"You know he hates my father," Cyd said. "Sam Seeley's side of the family hasn't spoken to my side of the family in three generations. I mean, look at us. We're still meeting in secret because he hates my dad so much."

"You let me worry about that," Annie said confidently. Her parents were tobacco farmers from North Carolina and she knew all about family feuds and what it was like to grow up as the poor relation. "Now you go in the house and wait for me in the library."

It wasn't hard for Annie Seeley to get her husband away from the party. As a politician's wife she knew something about politics. She merely told him that someone important with a lot to contribute wanted to see him in the library and that he had to come immediately. Sam had already talked to everyone at the party that mattered and he was bored to death anyway so he welcomed the distraction.

When he entered the library with Annie on his heels and saw the attractive young woman standing there he almost had a heart attack. For a horrible instant he thought that one of his girlfriends from town had shown up uninvited. He would never divorce his wife, she was the mother of his son and it wouldn't look good in the polls anyway, but that didn't mean he didn't have his own friends. *Money buys happiness, no question about it*, he often thought in regard to the ladies of Washington, DC whose living expenses he subsidized.

He was relieved when he realized he had never seen this particular girl before.

"Sam, I want you to meet your first cousin once removed, Cydney Seeley. Cyd, this is your cousin Sam."

"Charley's kid? You know how I feel about that part of the family. Bunch of dead beat share croppers that couldn't get a job in a slaughter house."

"You know what?" Cyd said. "I'm outta here."

"Wait," Annie pleaded. "Please Sam, look at her. Does she look like anybody you could hate?"

Sam looked. His wife was right, the girl was a knockout. He put his hands on her shoulders and held her out at arm's length to examine her more closely. "I saw a picture of you once when you had pimples."

"How flattering," Cyd said. She felt like Lolita with Humbert Humbert staring at her.

"I only meant that you are very pretty. You should get to know my son Ty."

"There's enough inbreeding in this family already," Cyd said.

"Don't get your back up, now. Have a seat." He motioned her into a wing-backed chair. "Please," he added.

Cyd sat on the arm of the chair.

"She just graduated with her bachelor's degree," said Annie. "Isn't that wonderful? She's a botanist."

"My wife's into flowers," Sam said. "Spends a small fortune, but I've never seen her make a dime from it. What do you do with a degree like that?"

The blossoms that grew in Annie's gardens and greenhouses filled her enormous house year-round. The bedroom, the breakfast room, the library, the French drawing room: in the fall there were always chrysanthemums, in winter amaryllis, poinsettias, narcissus, camellias and azaleas; in early spring flushes of sweetly scented freesias, lilies, snapdragons, Bells of Ireland and forced tulips. Potted plants filled all the nooks. Long stemmed flowers were arranged in magnificent centerpieces for the dining room table and in lavish sprays for the drawing room and pavilion.

"Cyd plans to go to graduate school," Annie said. "She wants to study plant genetics. I thought we could help her out."

"That's what she has a father for," Sam said.

Cyd stood and turned to Annie. "Thank you, but I really have to be going now."

"Not so fast," Sam said. "Sit back down. Where do you want to go to school?"

"University of Montana."

Sam couldn't believe his ears. "That a fact. In Missoula?"

"How did you guess?"

"Fascinating, very fascinating. Maybe we can work something out after all." Sam was amazed that the solution to his lobbyist friend Riley Gray's problem would fall in his lap this easily—and so quickly. "If I did help you, paid your tuition and the like," he said thoughtfully, "I'd expect you to get a job to help pay your way."

"I've always paid my way," Cyd said. "And I don't need any help from you or…"

Sam raised his hand to stop her. "I might even know of a position that's open," he said. "Something in your field, how about that?"

"How about what?" Cyd said cautiously.

"I just heard there's a guy over at the University of Montana that's doing some pretty amazing stuff in plant biotechnology. One of the big drug companies, Rxon, is funding his research. What if I could get you a job working for him?"

"That would be good," Cyd said. She could feel herself getting excited.

"I'll put you in touch with the point man from Rxon. He'll want you to report back to him. Keep him posted on the research, what kind of progress is being made, that sort of thing." He saw the hesitant look on Cyd's face. "They're putting a lot of money into this guy and he has this psychotic obsession with secrecy..."

"You want me to be a spy?" Cyd said.

"They have a right to know where their money is going, wouldn't you agree? Be kept up to speed so to speak. Is that so horrible?"

Cyd hesitated. "I guess not."

"Good, it's settled then. His name I think is Bernstein."

"Maury Bernstein?" Cyd cried. "He's the best in his field. He's the reason I want to go to Missoula in the first place!"

"Yeah, that's him. Well, anyway..." He was done with the conversation and heading for the door. "See my secretary for anything you need. I'll tell her you'll be in touch." He started to close the door behind him, then turned back and smiled. "You keep us in the loop now, you hear?"

When he had gone Annie spun around to face Cyd grinning with delight, two triumphant thumbs in the air.

CHAPTER 3

Weeds in the Attic

The Dearborn River emerges from a mountain in the Scapegoat Wilderness, flows through the canyons and scenic valleys of the Rocky Mountain Front, and out onto the Montana prairie. It was along this river, Betty explained, high up in the trees near the headwaters of the Dearborn, that Maury Bernstein died.

After hours of bouncing in the saddle Maury's butt was raw, but he was too anxious and nervous to care. They had been following a trail that more or less paralleled the winding river and were at a place where the path veered uphill sharply to the right. He watched as Betty left the trail and urged her horse into the stream, crossing at a shallow ford and continuing on up a secondary trail on the other side that wound between the trees—a path that would have been invisible under the snow had his guide not been coming up here most of her life. He followed gingerly behind, leaning forward in the saddle to try and take the pressure off his aching rear end. Under any other circumstance, even though he was a terrible rider, Maury would have been thrilled to be on horseback in the Montana back country in winter. Not today.

The steep trail came out in a clearing and they reined in their horses. Betty Littlehorn took off a battered cowboy hat, wiped her brow with her sleeve and turned in her saddle to check on the miserable looking scientist behind her.

"Your call," she said. "What'll it be?"

"This will do. I need to go on alone from here." Maury kicked at his horse, flailing his arms to make him go. "The rapids you said are just up ahead, am I right? If I'm not back in an hour, call the rabbi."

"As your friend, I have to tell you I don't like it. Whatever it is you're going to do up there, let me come with you."

"I told you before I don't want you to see this. I'll be fine, don't worry. The less you know the better."

"Amen to that," Betty said, watching in dismay as he disappeared over the hill. She took a round tin of chew out of her shirt pocket, put a pinch between her cheek and gum and settled in to wait, spitting occasionally.

Thirty minutes passed.

When she heard the shots she sat up straight in the saddle, gathered her reins and spit out her wad of tobacco. She was spurring her horse to the top of the hill when she saw Maury's horse come racing toward her with its rider slumped over in the saddle. Her eyes grew huge and she kicked her horse into the path of the runaway horse, grabbing its reins and yanking hard. Maury's horse cried out and reared and Maury fell off backwards.

Betty jumped to the ground and bent over his body. Blood was spilling freely onto the rocks, turning them dark red. She tore open his coat, saw the extent of his wounds and was suddenly weak with fear. Maury gagged as blood and foam trickled from his mouth. He grabbed her by the coat, pulled her down to him, pressed a note pad into her hand and began whispering urgently in her ear.

"Understand?" he gasped when he was done giving her instructions.

"Yes, of course," she said feebly.

"So get out of here already. Go…!" His words were gargled in blood.

"No way am I leaving you behind." Betty started to lift him, then gasped as he shuddered and died. She frantically yanked off her glove, pressed two fingers to his jugular and dropped her ear to his nose to listen for breathing. Behind her, from the direction of the river they had crossed, came the faint sound of horses thundering up the trail.

Betty swung onto her horse and with a desperate glance back at her dead friend, took off in the opposite direction. She cut left and right in a slalom course through the trees, flying over unmarked terrain she had ridden a thousand times before. Moments later three riders came pounding up the hill and reined in hard over Maury's body. They jumped off, stripped him of his clothes and searched him from head to toe. When they found nothing one of them, a Native American cowboy with sunken cheeks and a pockmarked face, looked around and saw Betty's tracks leading off into the forest. He pointed in the direction she had gone with a hand that was piously tattooed on the back with a large religious cross. In an instant they were back in their saddles, following her tracks.

Betty had a good head start and she knew exactly where she was going. Again she veered, this time uphill, spurring her horse over loose rock so that she wouldn't leave tracks, climbing toward stone cliffs that towered overhead.

Under one of the cliffs was a narrow slit in the rock, invisible from below, just wide enough for a horse and rider. She ducked inside. The interior of the cave was cold and damp and frozen. Her sweating horse gave off steam and danced nervously over the charred remains of an old campfire. Betty had discovered the cave as a little girl riding her ponies up here and it was a place of grand adventure, her secret hideout she'd named "Hole In The Wall, Too".

She dismounted, breathing hard, and snuck back to the cave entrance to peer out. Far below she saw three cowboys ride by and continue on down the mountain with their rifles across their saddles, looking like frustrated hunters.

She waited until dark before coming out, letting her horse gingerly pick its way down over the loose shale to the trail. From there she turned and headed back up to where she had left Maury. She found him lying stripped half naked, white and bloody in the moonlight. His horse nuzzled at the frozen ground nearby, cold, tired and hungry. The temperature was dropping by the minute.

Betty struggled, finally managing to slide Maury up and over his saddle and get him tied to the stirrups. It was a long trip down off the mountain. She rode in silence, turning occasionally in the saddle to make sure the load on her pack horse hadn't shifted.

It was after midnight when Cyd heard Betty calling from outside the house. She opened the door saying, "Where the hell have you been, I've been worried sick…"

And then she screamed.

Cyd helped Betty wrap the body in a tarp, bind it with rope and lay it safely on a bed of hay in the barn where the cold would preserve it and the wolves couldn't get at it. It was the best they could do for the night. They went in the house.

Betty stood with her back to the fire, warming her hands behind her. Her clothes were stained with blood.

"I don't know what the two of you were up to," she said, "but it got him killed."

Cyd blinked rapidly, covered her face with her hands and burst into tears.

BETTY TRIED POURING CYD AND Alex more coffee but her hand was shaking and she ended up spilling it and had to set the pot back down. It was the first time she had spoken of Maury's death and she clearly wasn't over it.

"Maury wasn't much of a cowboy and he talked funny, but he sure had great tips on how to grow my tomatoes," she said with a forced smile. "Showed me how to change the pH in the water. Talk about improving the taste. I'll get you some to take home if you want."

"No thank you," Alex said. He had the feeling she was holding something back.

"There's not so many of us Jews in town that we can afford to lose one, you know?" Betty said.

"Is there anything else you want to tell us?" Alex said.

"I almost forgot. There is something." Betty began rapidly opening and closing kitchen drawers, fishing around in the back of them until she found what she was looking for.

"Knew it was here somewhere," she said, placing something in Alex's palm.

He looked down, staring at an orange key with a number on it. "What's this?" he said.

"A key to one of the lockers out at the airport. I don't know what's in it and I don't want to know, so don't tell me. All I know is Maury said it wasn't safe anymore out at your place, Cyd, and if something happened to his lab I was to give this to you. I expect it has something to do with why he was killed."

Cyd took the key from Alex, closing her fist around it excitedly.

"You're a good friend," Alex said, giving Betty a kiss on the cheek that startled her greatly. "I can see why Maury trusted you."

"Lot of damn good it did him," she said.

"What are we waiting for?" Cyd said, heading for the door. "Let's go!"

"I'm right behind you," Alex said. On his way out he noticed something on Betty's mantel that caught his eye. Nestled in among her collection of dusty horse show ribbons and trophy buckles was a large pickle jar.

"What in God's name…?" he said, peering closely at a pale curved piece of fleshy sausage, severed at one end and pointed at the other, that was floating in a jar of formaldehyde.

"Pickled penis," Betty said proudly.

Alex's voice caught in his throat. "Whose?" he stammered, all medical objectivity gone.

"Mine," Betty said.

"Yours…?"

Betty laughed as Alex stumbled backward and almost fell over the sofa.

"Don't believe her," Cyd said. "She got it in a pawn shop."

"That's because I had to hock it once when I was short of cash."

BY THE TIME THEY GOT to the airport it was early afternoon. The terminal was practically deserted.

The bank of lockers was against a far wall near the bathrooms. They inserted the key into a locker door with a matching number and the door opened easily. Inside was Maury's lost research. Cyd let out a squeal of delight, looking around quickly so see if anyone had heard her. Alex removed a huge manila envelope that was stuffed with papers, reached back in and withdrew a CD holder. The soft wallet was packed with compact discs, each in a plastic sleeve. Across the face of both the manila envelope and the CD holder Maury had scrawled in marker pen:

Property of Dr. Maury Bernstein

"The lab computers in your barn are toast," Alex said. "Where can I look at these CDs?"

"There's a copy store in town that rents computer time."

"I'll follow you there. We're going to open these files together and you're going to explain to me exactly what it is I'm looking at."

"What do you mean, you'll follow me?"

"I'm renting a car. I'm done freezing my ass off in that thing you call a truck."

"Fine," she said, holding out her hand. "Give me the papers and the CDs then."

"You tend to lose things," he said. "I'll hold on to them. Meet me in the rental car parking lot."

"Suit yourself," she said, walking away. Under her breath he heard her mutter, "Asshole."

Alex rented a red 4WD Jeep. Walking toward it in the rental car parking lot he could almost feel the warmth of its heater. He slid gratefully into the driver's seat and was delighted when the engine fired the moment he turned the key. Waiting for the car to warm up and for Cyd to appear and lead him to the copy store, he pulled some of Maury's papers out of the tightly packed envelope and began thumbing through them. Most of what he saw was mathematical calculations and early lab test results. He shivered because the heater wasn't putting out any heat yet and pulled out more papers. These had more recent dates on them and the tests were headed, "Weeds In The Attic".

What the hell is that supposed to mean? he thought.

The temperature gauge moved off its peg and the heater began to fill the car with warmth. Alex looked skyward, thanked a God he no longer believed in, and hastily stuffed the papers back in the envelope. Just then there was a terrible screeching of brakes and Cyd pulled up behind him. He put the Jeep in reverse and waited for her to move, but she just sat there staring straight ahead. The rear window was still defrosting and he couldn't see out too well so he beeped his horn. When she still didn't move he got out of the car...and the lights went out. Something struck him on the head from behind and he went down face first in the snow.

When he opened his eyes the snow around him was red with blood from a gash in the back of his head. He saw a blur of footsteps running away, heard an engine roar and speed off, felt someone shaking him. He rolled over and Cyd's face came partly into focus. She had a black eye and a bloody mouth and was crying angry tears.

"They took the papers and the CDs!" she wailed. "They're gone!"

"Who...?" He couldn't focus and his head was swimming.

"Two men. They were waiting for me by my truck when I came out. They were wearing ski masks and I thought they were shoveling the walks or something. They wanted Maury's research. When they found out I didn't have it they started hitting me and hitting me until...Oh Alex, I'm sorry!"

He struggled to sit up, reached out and gently touched her battered face. "You're hurt..." he said in a sleepy voice.

"Those papers were the only documented evidence we had of the discovery, the only way to replicate..."

"Who are you again?"

"What...?!"

"I think I'm going to need stitches. How are you with a needle and thread?"

She struggled to get him to his feet. "We need to get you to a hospital."

"Emergency rooms are good. I used to work in one, did I tell you?"

She tried to load him in her truck but he kept turning back toward the Jeep. "Let's take the pretty red one," he said. "I like red." Finally she gave up and tumbled him into the passenger seat of the rental car.

She had read somewhere that short-term memory loss can sometimes accompany a concussion. On the way to the hospital his memory started to come back but in reverse, beginning with his earliest memories.

"...and then I took my little brother up on the garage roof and tied a towel around his neck and told him he could fly and when he broke his arm was when I started wishing I was a doctor so I could fix it..."

"Where is he now, your brother?" Cyd asked, driving as fast as she could while trying to keep him talking so he wouldn't fall asleep.

"Gone. Eaten up by cancer," he mumbled. "Wish now I'd been nicer to him."

The cut on Alex's head took seven stitches. It was almost dark by the time they left the hospital. Alex had a clean white bandage taped to the back of his skull and a splitting head-ache, but at least his memory was back. They got in the Jeep. Cyd started the engine and then sat there, fighting back tears until she couldn't hold them at bay any longer.

"It's all my fault," she said.

"How is it your fault?" He leaned over to look more closely at her eye that was almost swollen shut.

"I blew it, it's over," she cried. "We got the research back and we lost it again!"

"Did you get a look at the men who robbed us?"

"They had on ski masks, I already told you. One of them, I think, had a cross on his hand."

"A cross?"

BACK IN THE AIRPORT PARKING lot a fist was coming at Cyd's face. She turned and it struck her in the mouth and blood came from her lip. She tried to focus and in a terrified blur of pain and confusion she saw a black religious cross tattooed on the back of the hand that was drawing back to hit her again.

"If you don't have it, then where is it?" a voice yelled.

ALEX SAT BESIDE CYD IN the passenger seat of the Jeep in the hospital parking lot with his head feeling like it had been crushed under the wheel of the car. It hurt to speak, it hurt to think.

"Why don't you start from the beginning and tell me what this is all about. I want it all, every detail, right now."

"I've already told you…"

"What does 'Weeds in the attic' mean?"

She was shocked. "How do you know about that?"

"I know," he snapped and a jolt of pain shot through his head. "Now spit it out!"

She hesitated, then jammed the Jeep in gear and drove off without a word.

TEN MINUTES LATER THEY PULLED UP in front of Otis's funeral home. Cyd jumped out and marched toward the front door. Alex started to follow but fell back in the seat with another shooting pain in his head. He tried a second time and this time made it out of the car.

They found Otis in the kitchen warming up a pizza. "You're just in time," he said, turning around as they came in. "I got plenty..." His voice trailed off in alarm when he saw Cyd's bruises. "My God, what happened to your face?"

"He knows," Cyd said.

"We should have told him yesterday," Otis said, craning his neck to look at the bandage on the back of Alex's head. "Were you two in some kind of car wreck or something?"

"We got mugged," Cyd said. "They got Maury's research papers."

Otis let out a breath and sat down heavily. "Everything?" he said.

"Everything."

"This just keeps on getting worse."

"What's your part in this?" Alex asked Otis impatiently.

Otis came to his feet with amazing agility for a man his size. "You're going to want to follow me upstairs."

They climbed an ornate Victorian staircase. On the second-floor landing Otis opened a small door to a much smaller staircase, glanced back over his shoulder to make sure they were still behind him and continued to climb. His shoulders brushed against the narrow walls. At the top of the stairs was another door that opened onto a huge, high-ceilinged attic.

Alex stepped into the room and stood staring in amazement at a massive array of lights that hung down from the exposed rafters. Under the lights were over a hundred plants that were at least eight feet tall, their jagged-edged leaves reaching for the lights. They sat in plastic buckets, their roots suspended in nutrient-rich, oxygenated water—a happily crowded hydroponic jungle looking up at what looked like the landing lights of a hovering spaceship. Narrow pathways wound between the buckets under a canopy of green foliage.

Alex recognized the plants and it made him furious. "You brought me up here to admire your pot garden?"

"Not marijuana," Otis said mildly, "transgenic creations of a most unusual kind."

"Bullshit. I know weed when I see it..." He broke off, staring at a small table in the center of the room spotlighted by a narrow cone of light that shown down on a strange- looking plant. It sat in a bed of sand, boxed in on four sides by a clear plastic box. At its base the plant looked like a miniature bowling ball, bright red and pockmarked, bristling with long hairy spines. From its center grew a tall thin stalk that erupted in a hypnotic swirl of dazzling colors that climbed upward to wash over its leaves and onto a delicate flower at the end of the stem. It was the most amazing flower Alex had ever seen and he reached out to touch it.

"Stop!" Otis cried. "Don't go any closer!"

Alex jerked back his hand. "What is that thing?"

"It's called a Death Star," Otis said. "Indigenous to a single remote region of the Gobi Desert. One of the most poisonous plants on earth. Touch it and it'll make you sick, get pricked by one of its spines and it will kill you faster than a coral snake."

"What's it doing here?" Alex said, aghast.

"Saving the world," Cyd said.

"Oh that," Alex said. "I thought it might be something important."

"It's the key to all of Maury's research," Otis said. "It's how he made his discovery."

"What discovery?" Alex said. "How to grow better pot?"

"You want to hear this or you want to make stupid remarks?" Cyd said.

"How do you know Maury?" Alex asked Otis.

"Cyd introduced us."

"Go on."

"I've known Otis all of my life," Cyd said. "He can make anything grow. Not only does he have a green thumb, his whole body is practically green."

"I'm the tree that everybody wants to hug," Otis said modestly.

Alex made a circular motion with two fingers in a sign for them to speed it up.

"Maury needed somebody who could plant what he was trying to invent and make it thrive," Cyd said. "He tried doing it himself and his early versions all shriveled and died."

"Maury was kind of into secrecy, man," Otis said.

"Once he knew what he had he wanted it off campus, out of town and out of sight," Cyd explained.

"So why keep it a secret from me?" Alex asked.

"You could be working for Rxon," Cyd said. "We didn't know."

"And if I was working for the police you'd be under arrest right now. What you're doing here is illegal."

"There's a reason why Maury used Cannabis as the basis of his genome research," Otis said patiently. "The healing properties of the marijuana plant are amazing. It treats glaucoma, AIDS wasting, neuropathic pain, the spasticity associated with multiple sclerosis; it relieves chemotherapy-induced nausea, helps anorexia sufferers, improves movement disorders, asthma, allergies, inflammation, infection, epilepsy, clinical depression, bipolar disorders, anxiety disorder and it helps people dealing with dependency and withdrawal issues. It's a treatment for autoimmune disease, cancer, neuroprotection, fever and blood pressure disorders. It can relieve tics in people with obsessive compulsive disorder and Tourette syndrome. It's been shown to help prevent Alzheimer's disease, reduce arterial blockages and even help prevent certain types of epileptic seizures. In other words, if you're trying to genetically engineer a new drug, it's not a bad place to start."

"You're supposed to be a doctor," Cyd said. "What do you know about gene splicing?"

"I'm an E.R. doc. I know trauma. All I remember about DNA is that it's an acid and the parts of the DNA that carry the genetic information are called genes. They're like little computer chips with blueprints or recipes on them that tell a living organism what it is and how it's going to be built. I know you can take a gene with a desirable characteristic from one DNA molecule and splice it into the DNA strand of another molecule and come up with something that's theoretically better than the sum of its parts. Don't ask me to explain how it's done."

"You're oversimplifying it..." Cyd began.

"Which brings us to the Death Star," Otis interrupted. "It's resistant to everything. Nothing short of a forest fire can kill it and there aren't any forests where it comes from. Anything that attacks it only makes it stronger. The plant has a million defenses. It has the most astounding capacity to reinvent itself on the spot, to identify an invader and mutate a portion of itself into the thing that will kill it. It's a hostile plant, a killing plant, with the most seductive flower on earth. It wants you to touch it so it can kill you."

Alex was appalled. "So if you combined them wouldn't you get pot plants that are poisonous?"

"That's the beauty of genetic engineering," Cyd said. "You transfer the parts you want and leave behind the parts you don't want. Maury was able to manipulate the genomes of the plant cell, isolate the curative gene in the Death Star and transfer it to the marijuana plant, all without transferring the poison to the hybrid. The linkage maps of the two plants are surprisingly similar so it was easier than you might imagine—they practically have the same genetic makeup."

"Cannastar!" Otis announced with a sweep of his hand that encompassed the whole attic. "Glorious, genetically altered weed. Boil it into a tea and drink it and it turns the human immune system into a lean, mean, fighting machine. An army of soldiers are turned loose in the blood stream that can kill anything that attacks it from cancer to the common cold. What you see before you is the end of illness, the end of viruses and disease, the end of suffering as we know it. Instead of making you high it makes you well! You are looking at a whole new world here Alex, a world where people aren't sick all the time, where everyone is mostly healthy, where most illness is a thing of the past. That's what Maury died for and that's why we have to be so careful about who we tell."

In his growing amazement Alex forgot about his pounding head. "So in a way it's like a vaccination?"

"Only better," Otis said.

"Do you have any water?" Alex asked. Otis handed him a bottle of water and he downed half of it in one gulp. "I imagine Rxon was a little upset when they realized they'd paid to develop a drug that could put them out of business."

"What they paid for was for Maury to develop a cure for the common cold," Cyd said. "That was what he was working on. The rest just evolved from there. Rxon was fine with a cure for the cold, colds come back. What they weren't fine with was a permanent cure for practically everything else. It didn't exactly fit their business model."

"So to keep it quiet they murder the guy that invents it and steal his research," Alex said. "I imagine the rest of the medical community would have helped Rxon pull the trigger if they knew how much revenue this was going to cost them."

"No worries," Cyd said. "Once they destroy the research it's over and they win."

"Not necessarily," Otis smiled. "We still have the progeny. As long as we have the plants we have the seeds." He went over to one of the bushes and lovingly cupped a flowering seed pod in his hand. The tiny seeds in the pod were striped in the same kaleidoscope of colors as the Death Star. "See these? These are all we need. The seeds contain the genetic information so the plant can replicate itself—forever. You plant it and it grows and it makes more seeds! And it's a true hermaphrodite meaning it can fertilize itself." He paused and frowned. "Of course, you wouldn't want to swallow one or let any of the seeds get in the tea you're drinking because they'd make you sick. In and of themselves, they're a little poisonous."

"A *little* poisonous?" Alex said. "What's a *little*?"

Otis shrugged.

Alex was still skeptical. He was a scientist and as a scientist he wanted proof. "How do you know it works?" he said. "How much testing have you done?"

"There was all the usual testing on lab rats," Cyd said. "That was before Otis was diagnosed with pancreatic cancer."

"What...?" Alex said.

"Pretty much a death sentence if it hadn't been for Maury," Otis said. There was a profound sense of affection in his voice every time he said Maury's name.

Alex was incredulous. "You've taken the drug yourself?"

"Every day," Otis said. "I'm cancer free. Complete remission. There's only one catch."

"You're slowly poisoning yourself to death?"

"Nope. You have to keep taking it. Once the herb has hyped your immune system and turned it into an army of ninja warriors you gotta keep taking it or the effect wears off and you go back to being sick," Otis said. "Tell him about your cancer, Cyd."

"He doesn't need to know about that."

"She had breast cancer," Otis said. "Show the doctor your breasts, Cyd. The lumps are completely gone."

Cyd hesitated, then started to remove her sweater.

"Uhh…that's okay," Alex said, trying to hide his embarrassment. "So you take it too?"

"Twice a day," Cyd said. "Apart from getting a little buzzed, it's like drinking decaf."

Alex had goose bumps he was so excited. "This is a miracle. We have to tell everyone, get all the approvals, get it out so people can start…"

"That's the thing," Otis said. "They killed Maury to stop it, so what's to keep them from killing us?"

Just then there was a great pounding and splintering of wood downstairs and the sound of heavy boots on the stairs. The attic door burst open and a squad of drug enforcement agents wearing black DEA vests surged into the room all yelling at once and waving automatic weapons.

"Everybody down! On the floor! Hands behind your heads!"

Alex was slammed to the floor and his arms were wrenched behind him. Military boots stomped close to his head. The confusion of soldiers all barking commands at once sounded like a pack of baying hounds. Cyd screamed and kept on screaming until someone slapped a gloved hand over her mouth to muffle the sound. Otis was thrown down with a loud grunt. Alex turned his head, cheek to the floorboards, watching in horror as the agents started ripping up the plants and stuffing them in plastic bags.

"Nooooo!!!" wailed Otis. "Not the plants…!" Two men held him down while a third put handcuffs on him.

"You have the right to remain silent. Anything you say can and will…"

Alex felt his arms being ripped from their sockets as he was cuffed and hauled to his feet.

Across the room the officers were going through the attic like locusts, hacking down the Cannastar bushes, destroying and bagging the plants as fast as they could. Above the din, Alex could hear Cyd's frantic voice:

"Stop, please stop! Listen to me. You don't know what you're doing…!"

Alex turned to see that she was not in handcuffs and was being carefully helped to her feet by the squadron commander.

"Let us do our job, Ms. Seeley," the commander said.

"Then put me under arrest too. Why aren't you taking me in?"

"You're not part of the investigation."

"What do you mean…?"

"I'm just following orders, ma'am. Please step out of the way."

Alex overheard and it made him sick to his stomach. "What the hell's going on here?" he yelled. He was bobbing his head left and right to get a view of Cyd through the swarm of agents.

"How do you even know my name?" Cyd screamed.

"You can stop pretending, Ms. Seeley. We have all the evidence we need now."

Alex saw the shock and sadness on Otis's face as they were hauling him up from his knees.

The officer closest to Alex spoke in his ear: "We only want to question you, sir. Promise to behave yourself and I'll take the cuffs off."

Alex stood fuming as his handcuffs were unfastened. Rubbing his wrists, he realized Cyd had betrayed them, betrayed Maury, betrayed everything his friend had worked and died for. All he could think was that he wanted to strangle her.

"Lying twisted BITCH!" he bellowed and lunged for her throat.

A burly officer grabbed him and pulled him off her. "Don't move, don't move!" The officer growled, struggling to recuff him. "Gimmie your arm, godamnit!"

"What have you done?" Alex shouted at Cyd. "What have you done?"

"I can explain. It's not what you think..."

Otis was hauled off in cuffs and stuffed down the staircase. Alex was shoved in the same direction. He looked back from the top of the stairs and caught a final glimpse of Cyd. The commander was talking to her, trying to calm her down. She was crying and waving her hands helplessly at the devastation. One of the officers reached a hand inside the clear plastic box and started to pull up the Death Star.

"Don't touch that," she screamed. "You'll die if you do!

To Your Health

O tis pled not guilty, put up his mortuary as collateral and made bail the next morning. The judge cautioned him not to leave town.

On their way out of court Otis's lawyer told him not to worry, it was just a routine pot bust and a first offense at that. "The courts are being fairly lenient these days in cases like this," he said. They would sit down with the prosecutor and cut a deal. "You'll change your plea to guilty and probably the worst that'll happen is you'll get probation and a fine." The lawyer's assurances that all of this would go away fairly quickly did not have a calming effect on Otis. If anything, he grew more agitated.

"You'll probably lose your coroner's job, but I thought you might at least be a happy to hear that you're not going to jail," the attorney said.

"Hear what...?" Otis said, looking around anxiously.

"If you're looking for your friend Alex, they're probably done questioning him by now."

"That's not who I'm looking for..."

After grilling Alex for hours about his possible involvement in Otis's pot farm he was finally able to convince them he didn't know anything and they released him. He was headed for the exit when he passed Otis at the property window picking up his belongings. They walked out together, shaken and shattered.

"It feels like they murdered Maury all over again," Alex said miserably.

"They did," Otis said.

"So what do we do now?"

"We're screwed. End of story." He pushed the exit door open with a violent shove and a blast of cold air hit them hard.

Cyd was waiting at the curb with the motor running in the red rental Jeep. When she saw them come out of the courthouse she got out of the car. Alex grimaced going down the concrete steps, his back killing him from being manhandled by the police.

Cyd rushed up anxiously. "I didn't tell them anything, you have to believe me." Cold as it was, their stares made her shiver. "All I did was I gave them updates on Maury's research while I was in school."

"Gave who updates?" Otis asked indifferently.

"The people at Rxon."

Alex made a move toward her with clenched fists and Otis restrained him.

She rushed on breathlessly. "It's how I paid my tuition. I know that sounds horrible but it didn't seem that wrong at the time. I was broke and my cousin said… Okay, I was wrong. But the more they pressed me for information the less I gave them, so help me. I admit I'm the reason they knew about the discovery, but by the time they closed Maury down I'd stopped giving them information completely. I feel so guilty, I'm so ashamed, only I swear I'm not the one who told them about what Otis was doing or what he had in his attic."

Her pleas were met with silence. She stumbled after them as they continued on toward the Jeep.

"Listen to me, you two!"

"Get away from the car," Alex said as he got behind the wheel.

She turned desperately to her old friend. "Otis...!" she pleaded.

Otis squeezed into the passenger seat. "You heard him," he said as he slammed the door.

"I'm not like that. You know I'm not..." she yelled as they drove off. The Jeep disappeared up the street and she broke down sobbing.

IT WAS A SHORT DRIVE to the mortuary. Alex pulled into the driveway and switched off the engine.

"We can't just give up," he said. "I can't do that to Maury."

"We almost saved the world," Otis said. "And then we didn't. We're lucky to be alive is what I think. You come up with a plan, you let me know, all right?"

"Think," Alex said. "Who else could have known about it? Did you tell anyone, anyone at all?"

Otis got out of the car and headed for the house. "Later, man," he said. He couldn't imagine it was Eloise, not his Eloise, so he didn't even bother to mention her. He just hoped and prayed she would be there waiting for him when he got inside.

Three months before Alex Farmer's frigid arrival in Helena, when Montana was still warm and fine and the trees were still bright with fall colors, the local chapter of the Montana Garden Society was holding its monthly meeting.

The featured guest this evening was Otis Appleseed who stood addressing an enthralled audience of some thirty ladies and two gentlemen on the subject of hydroponic winter gardening. An entertaining and knowledgeable speaker, Otis was enjoying the audience as much as they were enjoying him. He had covered the various types of media available for this type of gardening, gone on to irrigation techniques, the different nutrient solutions that were available, and was just going over the cost and relative effectiveness of various types of grow lights when he was distracted by the adoring stare of a woman in the audience he had never seen before. His gaze kept returning to her as he spoke. In the middle of his big close where he was recounting the statistics on the amazing crop yields that can be achieved with hydroponics over conventional farming, the lady that had been staring at him with such adoration caught his eye and held it. He lost his train of thought and stood staring at her in silence.

"Sorry," said the rotund speaker, recovering himself. "All this talk about growing food makes me so hungry I can hardly think."

Everybody laughed and Otis finished to a big round of applause. Afterward, people crowded around asking him all manner of questions. When he had dutifully answered them as best he could and the crowd had moved on he saw that the woman who had been staring at him was still sitting in her chair with the same soft, sensual look in her eyes.

"Did you have a question?" he asked politely.

"Yes," she said. "Can I buy you a cup of coffee?"

The café and bar was in one of the many antique stone buildings on Last Chance Gulch. She introduced herself as Eloise Small and they sat at a table talking for what seemed to Otis like minutes but was actually hours. He was grateful for her endless, earnest questions about gardening and flower growing because it gave him something to talk about. His lively and passionate answers seemed to delight her.

There was nothing especially pretty about Eloise. She was a big woman with unremarkable features, glasses, dyed black hair cut in a perky style and a spider web tattoo on her neck. The spider in the center of the web had a single red dot on its back, the only color in an otherwise all black image. But taken all together she was gorgeous in a way only sensual women can be: warm, soft, vulnerable and inviting; a living, breathing, open invitation to get lost in the soft warm folds of her ample body. Otis fell immediately, hopelessly, utterly and completely in love.

For Eloise the attraction was simple: she had a thing for gardening and a thing for heavy men—they turned her on. Besides that she was obviously a bit of a Goth and a date with a mortician was more than a little appealing.

Country music was playing over the bar's sound system and it reminded her of Texas and home. "I want to dance," she said, extending a chubby hand. "Come dance with me."

Otis loved to dance but hadn't had the opportunity in years. He rose on nimble feet and followed her gracefully out onto the dance floor. She pressed herself against him and his mind went blank.

"You're really quite good. Where did you learn to dance like this?" she asked.

"You wouldn't know from looking at me but my nickname in high school was 'Lightfoot'."

She laughed gaily. "I believe it," she said and pressed closer. He felt a surprising warmth coming from her body almost as if she had on an electric blanket and was slowly turning up the heat. He tried to ignore it by making conversation.

She was in town on business, an accountant from Houston. Her boss was thinking of buying a company in town—one that would be a nice compliment to his existing organization—and had gotten her a job in the accounting department. She was supposed to keep her eyes open, spot any weaknesses or irregularities, and report back on the efficiency and effectiveness of the company's operation and its key personnel before they made a final decision on making an offer.

"Kind of like a spy," Otis said and felt the rheostat on the electric blanket go up a notch.

"Something like that," she said with a smile that had nothing to do with what they were talking about.

It turned out to be the best night of Otis's life. He awoke in her hotel room the next morning and thought he was dreaming until he rolled over and pressed his face to her neck tattoo. She smelled like...lilacs.

Eloise opened her eyes to find him smiling at her. "So when do I get to see where you live?" she asked sleepily.

"Right after breakfast. You hungry?" He kissed her and she responded and he felt the now familiar sensation of her body temperature beginning to rise.

"Starved. But first things first."

Eloise couldn't get over the enormous Victorian mortuary, couldn't stop admiring the overgrown rain forest that crowded the rooms. They were on the second floor when she spotted the door to the attic.

"What's up here?" she asked enthusiastically, opening the door. "I bet you're saving the best for last."

Otis was not subtle in pushing the door closed on her. "Just a lot of stuff you wouldn't be interested in." He could tell she was an honest person and hiding something from her felt like a breach of trust, but he had another trust that was more important that he couldn't violate, a secret that absolutely could not be told.

She looked disappointed, then brightened. "Can I see a dead body then?"

Eloise kept her hotel room since her company was paying for it and she didn't want them to think she wasn't focused on her job, but she spent every night from then on with Otis. For the rest of the fall and into early winter they were inseparable. Then one day she surprised him by walking in on him in the attic while he was tending the Cannastar plants.

"Far out!" she cried. "Why didn't you tell me? This is so cool!"

"I thought I told you not to come up here."

"Oh, don't be such an old grouch," she said, giving him a brief hug and a kiss and running up the rheostat. "When can we smoke some?"

"It's not ready yet to be harvested," Otis said mildly. He couldn't eat or sleep from thinking about her so he couldn't stay mad at her for that long either. He wished he didn't have to lie, wished with all his heart he could share his proudest achievement with the woman he loved. He would, he vowed, once they were married. He had bought a wedding ring and was planning on proposing over a special dinner that very evening.

ALEX DROVE AWAY FROM THE mortuary with the foul taste of Cyd's betrayal still in his mouth. Conflicting images of her clashed in his mind.

Otis rushed inside his to find his beloved. He was glad she hadn't been there last night when the police came—he didn't know where she'd gone—but after the terrible loss of the Cannastar he needed her now more than ever.

"Eloise!" he called as he came through the door. No answer. He went from room to room calling her name. She wasn't there. He tried dialing her cell phone and got a message that said it had been disconnected. He called the company where she worked. They had never heard of her. His hearse was parked behind his car and rather than taking the time to move it he jumped in the long white Cadillac and drove as fast as he could, fishtailing around corners on the slick roads, arriving at her motel and skidding sideways into the parking spaces in front of a row of rooms.

HURT AND ALONE, CYD WANDERED away from the courthouse. Her eye and lip hurt like crazy, but she hardly noticed. Down the block she saw a Starbucks. If ever she needed a cup of coffee, it was now.

A cowboy named Jesse Longbow, his greasy black hair hanging down below his hat, was just coming out of the Federal Express office next door. He cut in front of Cyd at the coffee shop door and did not hold it open for her. *Perfect,* she thought, tugging the door back open and following him inside. She stood behind him in line. The cowboy paid for his coffee and picked up his cup. As she stepped up to the counter she noticed his pockmarked face and cold dead eyes.

"Can I help you?" the girl at the register said.

Suddenly Cyd was staring at the cowboy's hand. She backed away in horror. On the back of his hand was a tattoo of a large black cross.

"Can I help you?" repeated the clerk, eyeing the growing line of customers behind Cyd.

Longbow turned and headed for the door. Cyd started shaking as she watched him go. She ran after him and saw him get into his truck and casually light a cigarette before starting the engine. On the side of the truck door was a familiar logo—the double-S brand of her cousin Sam Seeley's ranch, the ranch run by the Senator's son Ty. Too stunned to move, she realized she couldn't call the police without telling them what he had stolen from her. She stomped her foot in frustration and let out a furious scream as she watched him drive off.

WHEEZING LOUDLY, OTIS RAN UP the motel stairs to the second floor and down the hall to Eloise's room. A maid's cart was outside the door and he almost turned it over pushing it aside. A startled maid looked up from the bed where she was changing the sheets.

"Where is she?" Otis demanded. "The woman who's staying here, have you seen her?"

"Lady she check out late yesterday, Señor."

Frantic for some trace of her, Otis started tearing the room apart, opening all the empty drawers, throwing open the doors to the empty closet, looking under the bed, searching under the bathroom sink.

"Señor, maybe I help you find," said the frightened maid. "What you looking for?"

"I don't know!" said Otis. "Where's the stuff that was in the waste baskets?"

The maid pointed to a large plastic bag that was tied at the top and stuffed with papers. Otis tore it open and dumped the contents all over the floor as the maid fled the room. Otis fell to his knees, desperately digging through the pile, opening wadded sheets of paper before throwing them aside. He found nothing. Still on his knees, he buried his face in his hands and closed his eyes. When he opened them again he caught a glimpse of a large tan envelope that must have fallen behind the dresser. He reached underneath the chest of drawers with a groan, fished it out and tore it open. Inside was a pile of paid bills and old credit card receipts, all with the name Eloise Funk on them and a Houston address. *Funk? Funk?* he thought in a panic. *Her name is Small!!*

Otis rushed home, did a quick MapQuest search for her address in Houston and printed out the driving directions.

Three hours later, heartbroken and out of control, he was on a plane to Houston. Because there was so much of him to love, he had to buy two seats.

OBSESSION IN A MAN IS LIKE a wave that washes logic and reason out to sea.

It was after midnight, six days before Christmas, when Otis landed at the Houston airport. He rented a minivan and made his way onto the freeway. The traffic was light at this time of night and there were no delays.

The map directions led him past an endless urban sprawl to a remote suburb. He got off the freeway and wound through the streets, following the lefts and rights that MapQuest had given him, until he turned onto a darkened avenue and slowed to look for the house number. It was a run-down blue-collar neighborhood, once proud, decorated now in graffiti with old cars and trash piled up where the lawns used to grow. Otis stopped across the street from a modest duplex that had the only well-tended yard on the block. The house was dark and silent. A late-model four-door blue Honda in good condition sat in the driveway. He watched and waited.

The sound of someone grinding on the starter of a car that didn't want to start jolted him out of a deep slumber. The first light of day was just filtering through the smog. He sat up with a snort, rubbing at his eyes, in time to see a shiny black town car driven by a man in a white shirt and tie pull up to the curb in front of the duplex. Otis tried to scrunch down in the seat to make himself less visible, but it was like trying to hide an elephant in a cookie jar. The door to the duplex opened and Eloise came out wearing a business suit over a blouse with a high collar that hid the tattoo on her neck. Otis started to get out of his car, then stopped when he saw someone else coming out of the house behind her.

The driver of the town car came around to open the rear door as a young boy of nine or ten followed Eloise down the walk to the car carrying a school backpack. Otis was taken aback by the sight of him. The boy was completely bald in the milk-white way of someone who is going through chemotherapy. Eloise helped the boy into the lush leather interior of the car and got in after him.

Otis watched them drive off as he fumbled to start his engine. In his haste he pulled away from the curb without looking, and had to slam on his brakes to avoid plowing into the side of a lowrider car that was backing out of a neighboring driveway, its stereo shaking the earth with vibrations. The young bald-headed driver—a different kind of bald—shot Otis the finger. For his winter ensemble the youth had chosen a no-frills white undershirt accented by thick ropes of gold chain from Tiffany and diamond stud earrings by Cartier. Otis gunned the rental van around the angry driver and with a pounding heart sped after the town car.

The chauffer-driven limo was easy to follow in the early morning freeway traffic that was slowly starting to coagulate but was still flowing smoothly. After half an hour they turned off the freeway and drove at a faster pace down a broad industrial boulevard that ended at the entrance to an industrial park. Otis followed at a safe distance as they continued on past a dazzling array of tall glass high-rise office buildings. At the rear of the park, in the center of a sprawling 100-acre campus, towered the tallest building of them all.

The entrance to this private campus was marked by a low, modest sign on a knoll that was colorfully planted in flowers. Leaping over the sign, seemingly suspended in midair, was a Santa and sleigh drawn by a team of nine flying reindeer.

Behind the knoll rose three proud flag poles, the taller one in the center flying the American flag, the one on the left flying the flag of Texas and the one on the right flying a company flag with a logo on it. The logo was spectacular: a globe of the earth with the top cut off, the center scooped out and a stem added at the bottom to make the world look like a giant goblet. Overflowing the goblet, erupting from a decapitated world, was a cornucopia of prescription pills of all sizes and shapes that poured down the sides of the earth in candy- coated colors. Across the globe was written the word *RXON* with the right leg of the *R* extending down and a small line crossing the leg at the bottom to form the *x* like on a prescription pad. Under the graphic were the words *To Your Health!*—the company's message and wish for the world.

Otis hung back, following the limo as it wound through the beautifully landscaped grounds, continued on past a building the size of a small town with a sign out front that read *Pharmaceutical Manufacturing*, past a small fortress of a building with a sign that said *Security*, and stopped in front of a school with a playground full of squealing children. The low-rise structures, and others like them, all worshiped at the base of the gleaming glass and steel tower that rose from their midst like the mother of all mother ships.

The curbside sign in front of the school read *Wellness Center*. As he drew closer Otis was surprised to see that many of the kids in the schoolyard were wearing caps and scarves over their heads and that the ones that were bare-headed had bone-white skulls like the boy who was riding with Eloise.

The boy got out of the black car, tolerated a goodbye kiss, and ran off to be with his friends. The car moved on with only one passenger now in back. They passed a gymnasium with indoor and outdoor running tracks, tennis courts, pools, basketball courts, climbing wall, weight, cardio and aerobics rooms and a spa. The sign in front said *Employee Health Center* and the company motto—*To Your Health!*—was scripted in big letters on the outside wall of the gym.

Further on, the limo finally stopped and Eloise got out, walking briskly past a sculptured Roman fountain and through the gigantic front doors that framed the entrance to the main tower. Otis parked in guest parking where he could see the entrance, got out and tried to follow her inside, only to be stopped at the front door by heavy security. When he couldn't produce a pass they asked his name so they could check and see if he was on any of their lists. Otis said he had forgotten something and that he would be right back. He went out to his car to sit and wait. He was starving but dared not leave or look away from the busy front doors.

He waited all day, finally bribing one of the grounds keepers to go and get him some hamburgers. At five o'clock people started to leave the building and he saw Eloise come out just as the limo showed back up. The driver let her into the rear of the car and they drove back to the campus Wellness Center where she picked up the boy. Otis followed them out of the industrial park and back onto the freeway.

It was a long drive home, the freeway moving in starts and stops, but mostly not moving at all. Finally they pulled off and were back in the seedy neighborhood they had left early that morning. The driver dropped off his passengers and waited until they were safely inside the house before driving away.

Otis got out of his car, marched across the street, up the walk and rang the bell. When Eloise answered she gasped and tried to close the door on him.

Otis angrily pushed his way inside. "It's Funk, isn't it? Eloise Funk? Help me out here because I have a hard time with last names."

"Get out of my house! How did you find me?"

"Never mind about that. Why did you leave? Why didn't you tell me?" Despite his anger, Otis couldn't help noticing how much she looked like a frightened hen protecting her nest—a nest that was neat and clean and furnished with delicate antiques that clashed horribly with the macabre posters of Goth rock bands and vampire movies on the walls.

"You're scaring me," she said, backing away.

"How much did Rxon pay you? Do you know what you've done? Do you have any idea the damage you've caused?"

She staggered backward in horror, fell onto the sofa and buried her face in a pillow. "I can't lie. I can't do it any more," she sobbed. "I hate to lie."

Otis towered over her. "I'm not going to hurt you. Just tell me what happened."

A flood gate opened and the words poured out. "My boss made me do it. I didn't have any choice. He said if I refused, he was going to fire me and I was going to lose my health benefits and...oh God!"

"So it was all just some kind of game to get information out of me? To make me look like a fool?"

"No. Never. Don't think that. Maybe in the beginning, but..."

Otis saw her staring at something behind him and turned to follow her gaze. The boy with the bald head had come out of his room and was standing there looking at them, eyes wide with fear. Up close he was thinner and sicklier than he had appeared at a distance, his chalky skin traced in blood vessels that looked like red thread.

Hastily drying her tears with the backs of her hands, Eloise said, "Otis, I want you to meet my son. Elton, this is Mr. Appleseed."

Otis felt his anger melt away. "Nice to meet you," he said, reaching out a meaty hand to grasp the child's tiny fingers in his. The boy had to transfer the action figure he was holding into his other hand in order to shake. "Did you get your good looks from your mom?" Otis asked.

"I look better with hair," the boy said.

"Nonsense. Bald guys rock. How old are you?"

"Nine and a half." His bloodshot eyes were bright—too bright. He glanced down at the toy figure in his hand, then looked back up at Otis. "You look like the Hulk," he said.

"I know. The Hulk is cool, right?"

"The coolest. You want to hold him?"

"Thanks." Otis reached out and the boy reverently placed the green monster in his palm. "Your mom and I are just talking. Is it okay if I talk to your mom?"

"Sure. She's always saying she wishes she had somebody to talk to. Besides me, I mean."

"Why don't you go to your room and do your homework?" Eloise said. "We'll call you when we're finished."

"Mind if I hold on to the Hulk until then?" Otis asked.

Heading happily back toward his room, Elton said, "You can keep him. I've got two other ones. You can see the rest of my collection if you want when you're done."

"Cool."

When the child was gone Otis turned back to Eloise who was looking at him with a mixture of gratitude and alarm.

"That's some boy," Otis said.

"Yes he is. And he's dying of leukemia." Otis put his hand over his heart in devastation and sat down beside her. "I don't expect you to understand," she went on, "but I did it for my son, to keep him alive—that was my only reason. Not for the raise, not for the car and driver, not for the new house they promised me. If it wasn't for Elton I wouldn't even have considered it. I know it was a lie and I don't blame you for hating me. But you and me Otis, that wasn't a lie; that was real. And now I've lost you and I only have myself to blame."

"Something my size is hard to lose," he said thoughtfully.

"I'm so ashamed that I spied on you. I've never done anything like that before. It's not like me. I'm a whore is what I am. I'm a terrible person."

"We all make mistakes. What did you tell them? What is it you think you saw in my attic?

"I didn't know what you were doing up there, I still don't. I was supposed to find you, find out everything I could and report back every detail, no matter how small. I think they had someone following that Cyd Seeley woman is how they knew about you. I told them I'm not suited for this sort of thing. They said I was perfect. I told them I wouldn't do it and that's when the threats started. What was I going to do? I have my son to think about. I couldn't pay for one week of his treatments if I had to do it myself. I can't just stand by and watch him die without…" Her eyes grew large and rivers of dark eyeliner began to run down her cheeks.

"So you have no idea what it is you saw at my place?"

"You grow pot, right? I'm guessing a special hybrid kind that's like super powerful. I figured they wanted it so they could be ready when it's finally legalized—and it will be legalized, you know, sooner than you think. Then as usual they'll have the rights to the best drug on the market and they can sell it in a high-priced prescription like they do everything else."

Otis considered her logic. "Good thinking. Wrong, but good."

"I'm sorry, I'm sorry, I'm sorry. I never meant to hurt you. I couldn't stand the thought of never seeing you again, but they told me they had everything they needed and that I had to get out of Helena and come home immediately, right now, no questions asked. I was afraid if I didn't do what they said I'd be out on the street."

Otis believed her because he wanted to believe her, simple as that. Nodding absently, lost in thought, he was trying to make a decision. He only had so much of the dried Cannastar leaves left and no way to grow any more. His stash was hidden in one of the few places the DEA agents hadn't looked when they raided his house. It was a few months' supply at most. Cyd would get sick again, but she probably wouldn't die. He would. As an undertaker, death wasn't as awful to him as it is to most people. *We all die eventually*, he thought. *It's how we live that counts.*

"Call Elton back out here," he said.

She went to get her son. Otis pushed himself off the sofa and went into the kitchen where he took out a sauce pan, filled it with water from the tap, put it on the stove and turned on the gas. When it was boiling he took a packet of crushed green leaves from his pocket and dropped some in the water, stirring them slowly. Then he took down two mugs.

"What are you doing?" Elton asked, appearing in the doorway minutes later.

"Making tea," Otis said. "Want some?"

"I don't like tea."

"You might like this kind." Otis poured out two steaming mugs through a strainer, blowing on his and taking a tentative sip. "Mmmmm," he said. "Tastes just like chocolate mint. You like chocolate mint?"

"My favorite," Elton said. Otis handed him a mug and the boy blew on it before taking a small drink the way he had just seen his large friend do.

Eloise watched anxiously. "Is that medical marijuana? I've heard it can help."

"It's a special tea."

"I've never believed in homeopathic remedies myself."

"Here's the rest of the packet. When I get back home I'll send you some more."

"I don't see how a tea can help him. I'm just saying, you know? I mean, what does it do?"

"It cures leukemia."

Eloise was speechless. Her mouth worked open and closed but nothing came out.

"It's good, really good," Elton said, taking another sip. "Do I get to drink this all the time?"

"As long as it lasts," Otis said, then to Eloise: "Give him all he can hold for a week, then two cups a day after that, morning and evening."

"How...how is it possible?" she stammered. "If it's true, why would Rxon want to stop it?"

"They murdered the man who invented it, stole his research and turned you into something you're not so they could have me busted and destroy the plants. What does that tell you?"

"Then my boy is going to live? He's really going to get better?"

"Temporarily."

"I don't understand."

"I don't have that much of it left. Unless I can grow some more..."

"You'll find a way, I know you will," she cried excitedly. "Oh my God!"

"You can't tell anyone about this. If anybody finds out I won't be able to help him any more and he won't get well." He turned to Elton. "That goes for you too, son. Not a word, okay?"

Eloise looked at her boy, playfully pinched her thumb and index finger together, drew it across her sealed lips, turned an imaginary key at the corner of her mouth and threw it away. Elton nodded enthusiastically and the pact was sealed.

"To your health, then!" Otis said, raising his mug in a toast and clinking rims with Elton. The boy raised his mug in both hands and buried his face in it, smiling at Otis over the rim. The smile won his heart forever.

After Elton was in bed asleep, Otis and Eloise sat on the sofa holding hands and talking like teenagers in love, mindful of what they had almost lost, treasuring it all the more for having regained it.

She wanted to know more about the research that was stolen. He explained it was the complete records, the only records, of the Cannastar project his murdered friend Dr. Maury Bernstein had been working on and that without it there was no way to replicate the discovery. He went on to explain more about the healing powers of the drug, about getting arrested, about how the only existing plants had been summarily torn up and hauled off by the police. He left out the part about how he would die without it.

Eloise was not overly surprised to learn the truth about the company she worked for. "I never had a good feeling about them," she said. "That goes double for my boss."

"What's his name?"

"Dick Tremble."

"What does he do? His title, I mean."

"CEO. It's his company."

Now that Otis's obsession over Eloise had subsided, his obsession with the Cannastar came back with a vengeance. "I want to meet this Dick Tremble," he said grimly. "I want to meet the man that had Maury Bernstein killed and had me arrested. I want to know what kind of man would keep a thing like this from the world."

"You can't be serious."

"I want to get inside that building where you work."

Eloise looked flustered, then said suddenly, "I think I know a way."

"You do?" He wanted to kiss her.

"The company is hosting a Christmas party tomorrow night. It's for top management and their key assistants—that's me—and we can bring our 'significant others'. Do you want to be my significant other?"

Otis grinned broadly. "I do."

"I can leave a pass for you with security, that's no problem. Just to be safe though, we should come up with another name for you. Who do you want to be?"

"How about Charles Darwin?"

"How about Sergio Lancelot?" He laughed and saw that she wasn't laughing with him. "I hope I'm doing the right thing," she said. "You won't get me fired, will you?"

"Nobody ever got fired for bringing a date to a Christmas party."

Later, he would remember what he'd said and cringe.

"All right then, be there about six," she said. "I guess you know how to find us."

Otis raised one hip and fished in his pocket for his cell phone. "I have to call Cyd and Alex and tell them everything you said. Poor Cyd, she probably hates us. This changes everything."

Eloise smiled her sensual smile and stood, reaching out her hand. "That can wait," she said, motioning toward the bedroom. "First things first."

CHAPTER 5

Fear and Greed

Early the next morning Alex turned off I-15 at Wolf Creek and guided the rental Jeep up the narrow freshly plowed road that led to Cyd's ranch. Sunlight sparkled off the snow that was weighing down the branches of the trees. The road flattened out when he reached the rolling plane and he leaned forward and looked up through the windshield at the vast expanse of blue overhead. *The sky really is bigger up here*, he thought, *they weren't kidding.*

Otis had called him with the exciting news: Cyd didn't turn them in, it was his girlfriend Eloise. No, it wasn't her fault; she had been threatened and coerced. But he needn't worry because Eloise was on their side. In fact, she was taking him to a Christmas party tonight—at Rxon's corporate headquarters!

Alex was concerned. He told Otis to call him the minute he left the party. "And don't do anything stupid while you're there," he added before hanging up.

CYD ANSWERED THE DOOR IN A loosely tied bathrobe that fell partially open as she bent over to wrap a towel around her wet hair. Alex turned away in a supreme effort to avert his eyes.

"Otis already called me and told me everything," she said. "What do you want?"

Alex leaned in close to examine her discolored eye and puffy lip. "I came to apologize."

"Apology accepted. Now go away."

"I don't blame you for being mad," he said awkwardly, fumbling for something else to say. When nothing came to mind he realized he'd made a mistake in coming. "I'm sorry. Sorry I doubted you."

She was silent. "Wait," she said as he turned to leave. "I was about to have my tea. I can make some coffee."

He smiled gratefully. "Coffee would be good."

A huge and noisy fire filled the log cabin with heat. Alex had to take his jacket and sweater off it was so warm. Cyd went upstairs and came back down wearing baggy sweats. She went into the kitchen and returned minutes later carrying two cups. They sat down in front of the fire and she started angrily brushing out her hair.

"How could I have been so naïve to let them use me like that?" Cyd said.

"They took advantage of you. It could happen to anyone."

"The Cannastar is gone, Alex! Otis will die, millions of people will die."

"How much of it do you have left for yourself?"

"A little."

It made him angry to think of her breasts—her perfect breasts—being laid waste by cancer. "What if we went to the press and made it public?" he said.

"Without the research or the plants, what proof do we have?"

"There's always options."

"Like what?"

"We'll figure it out."

She stopped brushing her hair and laid down her brush. "You know what, you're right. This is bullshit. We're in over our heads, I know that...but they haven't beaten us yet and they're not going to beat us."

"No, they're not."

"I mean, fuck the bastards!"

"You bet," Alex said with an admiring grin. Cyd thought the grin made him look like a little boy—one that was always getting into trouble. She tried to smile back but it hurt her lip and she flinched.

"My money's on Otis at the moment," she said.

"Otis could get in a lot of trouble down there doing what he's doing."

"I know." She took a sip of her tea and studied him with new interest. "Tell me about L.A. It's one place I never wanted to go." He grew tense and tried to avoid her eyes. "Did I say something wrong?" she asked.

"The sailing is nice."

"You sail?"

"I live on a boat down there."

"I've always wanted to try sailing." She took another sip of tea. "Why did you quit the E.R., didn't you like being a doctor?"

"I didn't quit, I was asked to resign." She raised her eyebrows. "Long story," he said. "And yes, I love being a doctor. It was the kind of medicine I was practicing that I didn't like."

"How so?"

"I wasn't relieving suffering, I was just prolonging it. For me, the ER stopped being about medicine and became all about watching people doing everything they could to destroy themselves with both hands." She appeared to be listening so he went on. "I got tired of trying to save people who were going out of their way to die. I want to help people who want to live, not the ones that keep coming up with new and better ways to commit suicide—not that I'm any different as it turns out. It got to the point where I felt like I was just making it safer and easier for the bangers to bang, the junkies to shoot and the drunks to drink. That's not why I became a doctor."

"So why did they ask you to resign?" She saw that the question made him nervous.

"How did you meet Maury?" he asked.

He just changed the subject on me, she thought. It gave her an uneasy feeling. "My cousin is Senator Seeley," she said. "*The* Senator Seeley. He got me the job. It was the first time in my life he was ever nice to me."

"Interesting."

"Isn't it though."

The sunlight streaming through the window was making mirrors in her hair and he found himself staring at her. She was beautiful even with a swollen eye and a fat lip.

"Getting myself fired was a good thing," he said. "If I hadn't gotten out of L.A. when I did there's a good chance they'd be looking at my toe tag right now trying to figure out where to ship the body."

He fell silent and she got up and threw another log on the fire. Sparks shot up and tongues of flame licked around the log. She didn't know why she should feel so drawn to him, she didn't even like him that much. She sat back down and he smiled and she thought of the little boy again.

"You got out of a bad situation," she said. "That's what matters."

"Sometimes I wonder." He had been attracted to a lot of women before, but never like this. "What's it like living on a ranch in the middle of nowhere? Don't you get lonely?"

"It's Montana. I like the solitude. And I love to sleep and I sleep really good out here. At least I used to. What I miss is

Maury, having an exciting research project to work on, helping to grow something truly miraculous. I don't know...maybe I'll try farming next." She tried smiling again and this time it didn't hurt so much. "Like your last name—it's Farmer, right?"

"Don't let it fool you. I once had a fake tree that died."

"So what do you *like* about being a doctor, Doctor Farmer?"

He thought a moment. "Seeing a patient stabilized and out of danger, I think. That's a good feeling, knowing I was able to help save a life."

Suddenly there was a loud banging at the front door.

WHILE CYD AND ALEX WERE inside the cabin talking by the fire, the tiny silhouette of a lone horse and rider appeared on a rocky ridge overlooking the ranch. The rider squinted into the sun that was reflecting off a snow bank to watch a black one-ton Ford pickup with big tires come up the road, turn in at the ranch entrance, proceed down the dirt drive and stop in front of Cyd's house.

The driver stepped down off a chrome rail in butterscotch-colored ostrich skin cowboy boots, closed the door behind him and headed for the house. On the truck door was the distinctive double-S brand of the enormous Seeley ranch that surrounded Cyd's small spread.

The rider on the ridge pressed a spur into the side of the horse and laid a rein against its neck. The horse wheeled on its haunches and disappeared out of sight back over the ridge.

THE BANGING CAME AGAIN AS Cyd crossed the room and opened the door.

"What the fuck...?" she said.

The visitor brushed past her and entered the house like he lived there. Looking around, he saw Alex and extended his hand.

"We met at the fire," he said. "I'm Cyd's second cousin, Ty Seeley."

"Cyd told me who you are," Alex said, ignoring the outstretched hand.

"What are you doing here, Ty?" Cyd said, hands on her hips.

Ty tried to imitate his father's dangerous smile but with his undersized mouth he looked less like an intimidating bully and more like a butterball with lips.

"The family is concerned about you, Cyd. Everybody knows you can't afford this place and that you're about to lose it. I'm here to solve your problem, but before I do let me ask you a question. Would you rather be a wealthy botanist or a homeless rancher? I suggest wealthy botanist."

"I suggest you wipe that silly smirk off your face before I wipe it off for you," Cyd fumed. "Your family has been trying to steal this land for generations and I'm not going to be the one to lose it, especially to you."

"I can buy it now or buy it later from the bank," Ty shrugged. "Your choice."

"I got a question for you," Cyd said. "That Indian that works for you with the cross on the back of his hand—what's his name and how much did you pay him to mug me?"

Ty made little snorting sounds that Alex assumed was laughter. "You know, Cydney, I didn't want to have to do this, our being cousins and all, but you leave me no choice. Now I'm going to have to marry you."

IT WAS ALMOST DARK BY the time Otis drove his rented minivan back onto the Rxon campus, passing the entry sign and the flying sleigh where the nose of the lead reindeer was glowing red now, lighting Santa's way. The trees lining the road through the campus twinkled in a fairyland of white lights. Otis continued on and parked in the shadow of the futuristic tower that loomed overhead, casting a pall over the holiday cheer below. He got out and walked toward it.

The first time he was inside the tower Otis was too upset to notice any of the detail, but now he stopped and stared. The lobby was a vast crystal cave with soaring bundles of pointed glass spears that looked like clusters of stalagmites reaching up from the floor at bundles of stalactites reaching down from tho ceiling. High overhead revolved a hollowed-out world with the word Rxon across it, pouring forth an endless flood of tasty pills. The armed guards at the front desk had the grim look of a mercenary army. Otis approached and identified himself to one of the uniformed officers, a man bigger than himself and all muscle. The officer ran his finger down a list until he found the name that Eloise had given him, wrote "Sergio Lancelot" on a badge, and solemnly handed it to the guest.

Otis walked toward the elevators pinning on the badge, craning his neck to look up at the crystal spears that were pointing down at his head. He entered one of the express elevators and pushed the top button that said "Executive Dining Room". The doors closed silently and he heard a sound that reminded him of the vacuum tube at the drive-up window at his bank. The elevator launched and began to rise and the sensation of weightlessness turned his stomach. The ride was over in seconds. The doors whooshed open onto a loud, drunken, crowded Christmas party.

Otis stepped out into the room—its tall windows beautifully draped in holiday decorations—eyeing the serving tables that were laden with an array of roast beef, chickens, hams and turkeys that were being carved and forked onto plates. Steam tables stretched like railroad tracks into the distance with pans full of tamales, burritos, tacos, chili rellenos, enchiladas, frijoles, pizza, fried and baked chicken, chicken fried steak, NY steak, pork chops, beef noodles, mashed potatoes, fried potatoes with onions, liver and onions, yams, rice, corn, string beans, peas, vegetables, gravies, sauces and grits. A mountain of shrimp and another mountain of king crab legs overflowed a separate table. There were fruits and salads and a desert bar that exploded with colored and frosted delights. Bowls of eggnog were being replenished by bartenders in bow ties and Santa Claus hats. Otis was startled by the shouts and whistles that went up as gurneys piled with Texas barbequed ribs were wheeled out from the kitchen. Not a creature was stirring, not even a mouse, because they had all been caught, cooked and served up for Rxon's sumptuous buffet. Live carolers in Dickensian costume strolled through the throngs of partygoers singing holiday songs, somehow staying on-key despite all the noise and confusion.

"Sergio, Sergio," said a voice, which Otis ignored since that wasn't his name. "Otis!" came the voice again in a stage whisper. He turned and Eloise was standing there with a forced smile, two cups of eggnog in her hands, looking absolutely beautiful in a high necked black gown with a corsage of red berries and green ivy pinned over her heart.

"Darling!" she said, rising on tiptoe to kiss him, forcing a cup of eggnog into his hand and hissing in his ear: "Follow me out onto the terrace. I have something exciting to tell you."

The view from the terrace was like standing on the wing of an airplane looking down at the city. The distant sounds of the party and the carolers were carried away by the wind.

In her distraction, Eloise put her cup of eggnog down on the railing too close to the edge and it fell off, tumbling into the darkness, spilling Christmas cheer as it went.

"Oh, silly me," she said loudly for the benefit of anyone who might be listening. Looking around and finding no one within earshot, she rushed on: "Listen...my boss got a Federal Express package today. I opened it like I do all the mail and guess what?"

ELOISE'S SMALL OFFICE ADJOINED HER boss's large office and the connecting door between them was open when the Federal Express delivery arrived that afternoon. She was busy with other correspondence and only glanced at the packages... then one of them caught her eye and she snatched it up. It was addressed, as they all were, to Dick Tremble, CEO, Rxon Corporation, but this one was from Helena, Montana! She tore it open and pulled out the contents...just as her boss came walking into her office through the common door.

"I'll take that," Dick Tremble said. She looked down as he took the large stuffed manila envelope and CD wallet out of her hands and saw the handwriting that was scrawled across them both. It read: *"Property of Dr. Maury Bernstein"*.

OTIS SAID IN A TENSE WHISPER, "What did he do with them? Are they still in his office?" He was so excited that he knocked his own drink off the balcony. Eloise nodded and grinned. "Can we get to them? How do we get in there?"

"Easy," she said.

ELOISE LEANED FORWARD ACROSS HER desk and watched her boss verify the contents of the envelope and the CD holder, then walk quickly to a Flemish oil painting on his wall—an original that was worth a fortune—and swing it out to reveal a safe. He spun the dial, opened the vault and put the two items inside. He then closed and relocked the safe and swung the painting back in place.

OTIS CLOSED HIS EYES AND heaved a sigh. "So we're screwed."

"Nope," Eloise said. "I'm not supposed to know the combination, but I do. He's always having me hold things for him while he opens the safe and I've looked over his shoulder a thousand times. You may not know this about me, but I'm naturally kind of nosey." She smiled a devilish smile and Otis loved her more in that moment than he ever thought possible.

They went back inside, hurrying toward the elevators, and in their haste bumped straight into Dick Tremble who was talking with his good friend and old fraternity buddy, Riley Gray. The affable crew-cut lobbyist was home from Washington for the holidays to play a little golf and tag up with his boss—which among other things meant attending his Christmas party.

"Eloise!" boomed Tremble in a slightly intoxicated, baritone voice, bending to kiss his executive assistant on the cheek. "Merry Christmas, darlin'. Did you get your bonus check?"

Dick Tremble wore a Christmas tie that showed a grinning Santa riding in a sleigh full of pill bottles. He was a street fighter with a mean streak; a man who could do what needed to be done. His father had owned low-income apartment buildings and one of Dick's favorite things growing up was slapping people around who didn't pay their rent. He made his wealthy father very proud. Tremble had a full head of blond wavy hair, a pugilistic face to go with his personality and a permanently broken nose that was pushed slightly to one side—a trophy from his days as a middleweight boxer in college and in the Army. A narrow mustache barely masked a permanent sneer that almost looked like a permanent smile. He had married the plain-faced-big-breasted-long-waisted-not-very-bright-oversexed-granddaughter of Rxon's founder and that's how he got to be CEO.

"Yes sir, thank you very much," Eloise said in an effort to compose herself. "Mr. Tremble, I want you to meet my boyfriend. Sergio, this is Mr. Tremble, my boss."

"What do you say, big guy?" Tremble said, shaking his hand. "What do you do for a livin'?"

"I bury people," Otis said.

"Me too," Tremble smiled. "Fun, isn't it?" He turned back and resumed his conversation with the lobbyist before Otis could reply.

"Merry Christmas," Eloise said as she took Otis's arm and led him away. Her words fell on deaf ears. Tremble gave Otis the chills. He looked back over his shoulder at the two men talking, oblivious to the crowds of people that eddied around them. Beyond them were the heavily laden food tables. It was one of the few times in Otis's life that he didn't feel hungry.

"What about Elton?" Otis inquired as they waited for the elevator.

"I had my mother pick him up," Eloise said. "She's going to keep him overnight and bring him back to school in the morning."

They went down one floor and stepped out of the elevator onto a hushed and darkened floor of opulent, high-ceilinged executive offices. Eloise led Otis down a dimly lit hallway paneled in exotic Hawaiian koa wood and hung with expensive art and continued on through the door to her office. She crossed quickly to the door that connected her office with her boss's and eased it open. Otis followed her into an enormous suite that was more of a throne room with a view than an office. They walked soundlessly over priceless carpets past a shadowed wall filled with humanitarian awards, all with Dick Tremble's name on them, and on to the Flemish painting on the far wall. Eloise swung it carefully aside, fumbled with the dial and seconds later had the safe open.

Otis shivered in the dark.

Eloise reached inside the safe, pulled out the manila envelope and the CD wallet and handed them to Otis. They did a little victory dance together. Then she closed the safe, swung the painting over it and they snuck back out the way they had come.

Eloise fidgeted nervously in the foyer as they waited for the elevator, her heart pounding in her chest. The bell dinged, the doors slid open...and four snarling security guards stepped out and grabbed them by the arms. Eloise screamed and struggled, Otis tried to throw them off, but it was no use. They were handcuffed and taken into custody.

AFTER THE OPULENCE OF THE EXECUTIVE suites, the inside of the campus security building looked like a prison—cold, hard and hopeless. Otis and Eloise were shoved stumbling into one of the holding cells and the iron barred door was banged closed behind them.

"What are they doing with jail cells in a place like this?" Eloise said, looking around in terror at the windowless walls, the two thin mattresses on narrow bunks, the toilet with no lid.

"Let us out of here!" Otis yelled. A loud bell clanged and the lights went out and the cell was plunged into total darkness.

Sometime the next morning—it was impossible to tell when because their watches, along with their other belongings, had been confiscated—the lights came back on with another clanging of the bell and a mute guard brought them two bowls of watery oatmeal. An hour later they were taken out of the cell and ushered into the harsh glare of a concrete interrogation room lit from above by bare light bulbs. The guards shoved them down into two cane chairs in front of a bare metal table. Minutes later the door opened and Dick Tremble entered carrying Maury's research files and looking fresh as the morning. He dropped the manila envelope and the CD wallet on the table and sat on one corner, dangling his leg over the side. Otis struggled to get up but was pushed back down in his chair.

"Let me tell you 'bout mah daddy," Tremble began, adjusting an already perfectly knotted tie—not the one with the Santa on it—over a freshly laundered shirt. "He used to buy old buildings and turn them into apartments and while he was refurbishing them he'd put up signs that read 'Trespassers Will Be Hung'. What he was sayin' was that the common side effects of breaking and entering in Texas can be...unpleasant." His smile morphed into a sneer. "We aren't near as tolerant of criminals here in Texas as some of your liberal states up north."

Otis was boiling mad. "That research doesn't belong to you!" he said.

"Ah paid for it and it's in mah possession so under the law I'd say that pretty much makes it mine."

"Not when you commit murder and robbery to get it."

"You're a long way from home, Mr. Appleseed. Does the judge know you're gone?"

"What do you want from us?"

Dick Tremble drew the manila folder toward him with one hand and snapped his fingers with the other. One of the guards left the room and returned moments later with a shredder in his arms which he plopped down on top of the table and plugged into a wall socket.

"Ya'all need to understand somethin'," Tremble said. "You're fightin' a losin' battle here. It's over and you lost and if ah can't convince you of that, well, all I can say is, this is gonna get ugly."

Eloise's eyes were big as plates. "You're evil, pure evil," she said.

Tremble shook his head in disappointment, switched on the shredder and pulled a handful of research papers out of the envelope. "Eloise darlin'…ah'm gonna miss you, ah truly am."

"I used to think you were human at least," Eloise cried.

"People often make that mistake."

Seething with anger, Otis said, "You're looking at the most important thing since penicillin. This discovery is going to change modern medicine. It's going to change the world…"

"Ah had a chance to look over these papers," Tremble said, feeding the first of the documents into the shredder, "and you know what? There's nothin' here of any value."

The shredder happily ground up the paper. It took two guards to keep Otis in his chair. "This is genocide!" he shouted.

"This is why you're going to go home and forget you ever heard of Cannastar. You grew a plant that never existed, Mr. Appleseed." Tremble drew more papers from the envelope and fed them into the machine, continuing his methodical destruction of Maury's discovery.

"How can you want people to be sick?" Eloise whimpered. "How can you not want them to be well?"

"Capitalism is money and money is war," Tremble said. "Sometimes there's casualties."

The man was dangerous and Otis knew it. He had to bite his tongue to keep from saying, *That's the real religion, isn't it? Everybody on their knees praying to your God of Fear and Greed.* A sadness came over him. It was as if he were watching a house burn down with his loved ones inside. Suddenly it all was clear. *Your company is the bastard child of a country gone wrong,* he thought. *A creation of a government of the lobbyists, for the lobbyists, by the lobbyists; the product of a spineless, gutless, bone-lazy bureaucracy; the ultimate achievement of successful politics, not commerce.* He watched tearfully as the last of Maury's papers went into the shredder. *Your business is a rip-off, man. It's the criminal exploitation of a once-hopeful country, of people who were somehow betrayed by the very ones they elected to serve and protect them. You rob them blind so they can't see what you're doing and then they blindly go on helping you do it. You celebrate your success, but it's a celebration of mediocrity instead, of the glory of your capitalism mutilated and deformed by the bureaucratic disease of lethargy, apathy and incompetence.* Before he could stop himself he was speaking out loud: "The money you spend on politicians, lobbyists and advertising could cure half the diseases in the world."

Tremble laughed. "Words are turds, boy. You can spread 'em, but you can't spend 'em." He picked up one of the CD files that contained Maury's findings, held it up like he was tempting a dog with a treat...and gingerly fed it into the shredder where it was ground to shreds, then continued shoving CDs into the metal jaws until they were all gone.

Otis and Eloise sat motionless under the harsh lights, too stunned to speak.

"Well, that's that," Tremble said, brushing his hands with satisfaction. "Eloise, you need to pick up your brat from school and remember...we know where you live." Eloise made a small moan as he walked to the door. "And if ah ever hear that either one of you so much as mentions the word Cannastar again...

well…let's just say that murder is messy and complicated, which is why you're not dead already." He smiled back at them. "Ya'all have a nice day now, hear?"

OTIS AND ELOISE PICKED ELTON up from the Wellness Center and in a daze drove away from the Rxon campus for the last time. The boy sensed something was wrong and sat sullenly in the back seat.

In utter devastation, Eloise said, "Dear God." Her breath caught in her throat. "Dear God," she repeated. There wasn't anything else to say.

When they got home Elton went straight to his room.

Eloise turned to Otis. "What about his medications, his treatments? How am I going to pay for even part of what he…?"

"Don't worry," Otis said, taking her in his arms and stroking her hair. "It'll be all right. He won't be needing any doctors or anything like that…at least not for now."

"But what am I going to do? I don't have a job and…"

"You and Elton are coming home to Helena with me."

She looked up at him and tried to smile. The nightmare of the last 24 hours felt unreal, other-worldly, almost like it hadn't happened. Her house was the same, her son and Otis, they were the same, she was the same—and yet everything was different.

"I'll fix us something to eat," she said absently.

He wasn't hungry, but he let her do it because it gave her something to do. While she was in the kitchen he called Cyd.

"Where have you been?" Cyd said with relief. "We've been worried sick."

Otis could hear Alex in the background asking if he was all right.

"Not really," Otis said, and proceeded to tell them every-thing that had happened. Alex listened with his ear close to the phone. When Otis was done Cyd felt dizzy and had to sit down. She passed the phone to Alex.

"At least you're not hurt," Alex said.

"Put Cyd back on. I need her to do something for me."

When she came back on the line Otis said, "I want you to go over to my place and go in the coffin display room and look in the bottom of one of my coffins, the rosewood one…"

Otis finished giving her instructions, then told Cyd that when he was done helping Eloise pack up and put her things in storage he would be driving back to Helena with her and her son; that he'd be home in about two weeks.

Cyd hung up and told Alex that she had to go into town on an errand.

He said he would drive her.

CYD TIPTOED INTO OTIS'S COFFIN room while Alex wandered around the big house watering Otis's plants for him.

The stifling silence, the open coffins with their lace trimmed pillows and white satin liners, gave Cyd an eerie feeling. She found the rosewood coffin, gingerly fished around inside it and pulled out the liner as Otis had instructed. Underneath the liner was a false bottom. She opened it up and inside found a row of neatly tied clear plastic kilo bags of dried Cannastar leaves.

Suddenly she had an idea.

She snatched up one of the bags, shook it excitedly and held it up to the light. Nothing. She grabbed another and then another, repeating the process with each one. If there were any seeds left in the bottoms of the bags, just a few, it might solve their whole problem. She shook and inspected the last bag. Otis had done a good job of cleaning his stash and ridding the leaves of any of the colorful, poisonous little seeds. She couldn't find a single one.

Take two of the bags, Otis had said. *Overnight one of them down to me and keep the other one for yourself. And Cydney... try to make it last because that's all there is.*

With a sigh she replaced all but two of the bags, closed the false bottom and put the liner back in place. Three bags of Cannastar leaves remained in the bottom of the coffin.

Alex drove Cyd to the Federal Express office and afterward they went next door for coffee. Cyd couldn't help remembering what had happened the last time she was in the coffee shop, took one look around, and had to leave. Driving back to the ranch she called Betty Littlehorn to tell her they had retrieved the contents of the locker but that they had gotten mugged and Maury's papers had been stolen.

"Shit," Betty said. "Shit, shit, shit."

Later that night in Houston Otis got into bed beside Eloise, wishing with all his might that something would happen so that he could get his plants back from the police.

IN JANUARY, OTIS PLED GUILTY and was given a heavy fine and 14 years probation. The DEA was then free to destroy the evidence.

Agents in surgical masks and gloves built a bonfire in a three-sided cinderblock enclosure out behind their office. The heat was intense. Shielding their faces with their arms, they threw the bags of "pot" confiscated in the raid on Otis's funeral home onto the fire. The inferno roared to new heights as it embraced the dried greenery. It made a pleasant smell as the smoke rose in the still air and drifted into the winter sky. Blazing brightly in the center of the flames was a red spiny ball. When the ball got hot enough it exploded and, like a dying star, went out in a violent burst of color and light. The agents jumped back, startled at the sound.

CHAPTER 6

Seed for the Pot

The day broke clear and cold on the morning after Cyd shipped the bag of Cannastar down to Otis in Houston. The lone horse and rider again appeared on the ridge above her ranch and this time, with no unwanted visitors in sight, began a slow descent down the slope toward the house. Cyd's two horses trotted along inside the fence in greeting as the horse and rider passed close by their corral, a rifle tucked into a leather scabbard under the rider's leg.

The visitor dismounted and knocked on the front door, stomping her boots even though there was no snow on them. Cyd opened the door and to her surprise found Betty Little-horn standing on her front porch.

"Nice shiner," Betty said, taking off her coat as she came inside.

Alex knew by now that no matter the occasion in Montana, you offered the visitor coffee. Betty took a sip from her cup and hesitated, searching for the right words to begin.

"What is it?" Cyd asked.

"This isn't a social call," Betty said. "I don't know how to tell you this, but Maury left you something else."

"What do you mean *something else*?" Alex said.

"I wasn't supposed to give it to you unless everything got completely screwed up. I'd say this pretty much qualifies."

"Pretty much," Alex said.

Betty withdrew a small notepad from her pocket and handed it to Cyd. The corners were stained in blood. Cyd opened the cover and squinted at the barely legible handwriting. Alex leaned in to look over her shoulder.

"I give up," Cyd said helplessly.

The notebook read:

N47 18 32
W112 46 18
Rock/Trees—Log

Alex had a mental flash that took him back to Iraq.

Combat soldiers with flashlights were huddled around a topographical map on a dirt floor plotting their next movements while he, Alex, tried to keep some poor kid from bleeding to death in the corner of the filthy hut.

ON MAURY'S INSTRUCTIONS, AND OUT of a sense of self-preservation, Betty had not opened the notebook. Now she couldn't contain herself and had to look over Cyd's shoulder as well.

"What does it mean?" Betty asked.

"These are coordinates," Alex said excitedly. "Latitude and longitude! A specific location." Then in frustration: "Why in hell didn't you give us this before?"

"Because if I had you would have lost it just like you did everything else he left you. Maury died giving me this notebook and he told me to protect it. He said to hold it back, keep it as a fail-safe. He said, 'If this gets lost, everything is lost'. I was just following orders and keeping it out of harm's way until you needed it."

"You did good, real good," Cyd said, giving her a hug. "He hid something for us up there. Can you guide us? Can you take us to the place where Maury was killed?"

"Guiding I can do," Betty said. "Guiding is something I'm good at."

"Maybe we should wait and let things cool down a bit before we go rushing off," Alex said.

"Whoever's out there isn't going away," Betty said. "Now or later isn't going to make any difference, not if this is as important as you say it is."

"If I chicken out now, I'll never feel safe again," Cyd said.

The women were right. Alex was as anxious as they were to find what Maury had left them. He thought about all the things they were going to need if they were going to do this right. His military experience taught him if you want to come out alive, you go in prepared.

"You two get some food and water together," he said. "I'm going into town."

Cyd frowned. "Now? What for?"

"Didn't I read that fishing is like a religion in Montana? I need a fishing store, a good one."

Cyd looked at him like he was crazy. "You think this is some kind of vacation we're going on?"

ALEX WALKED RAPIDLY UP LAST Chance Gulch toward a building with a tall, Romanesque façade of hand hewn stone. The name 'Atlas' was chiseled into the building's round stone parapet five stories above the cobbled street—a street lined with tall narrow medieval style stone buildings built on postage-stamp size mining claims; a street that wandered like an old man's memory through Helena's past; a street where men once panned for gold in the gutters and in the mud of the wagon ruts.

Alex entered the Atlas building, passing under a colorful wooden sign hung from a granite arch that read:

THE MONTANA FISHERMAN
Fly Goods, Outfitters

Minutes later he came back out with his purchases: a roll of topographical maps, a scaled ruler and a digital hand-held Global Positioning System or GPS. He had also bought the warmest jacket they had in the store—one that actually fit. When he got back to his car he checked the GPS to make sure it was working, stuck it in his pocket, took out the coordinates he had copied down from Maury's notebook, rolled out the topo maps on the hood of the Jeep, found the right map and peered down at it. With his finger he traced up the latitude markings on the left side of the map. Where the tip of his finger stopped he drew a horizontal line straight across the map with his ruler. On the top of the map he moved his finger right to left, located the longitude Maury had given them and drew a line straight down...then examined the place where the two lines crossed. Tightly spaced elevation lines indicating steep terrain squiggled around barren peaks and along deep mountain valleys in dizzying swirls. It was a vast wilderness and they were headed into the heart of it. Before leaving town Alex made one more stop—a pharmacy.

Betty helped Cyd tack up her two horses and load the saddlebags with supplies. Cyd jammed a rifle into the scabbards on both saddles. She didn't know how long it would take to find whatever it was they were looking for or what would happen once they found it, so just to be safe she tied bed rolls behind the cantles on their two saddles. By the time she saw the red Jeep coming back down the drive, they had been ready to go for almost an hour.

Alex parked by the corral, got out and walked toward them. This was the part he'd been dreading. He didn't know what to expect, but he knew it was going to hurt. Cyd handed him the reins to his horse.

He hesitated, then confessed, "I don't know how to ride."

Cyd caught Betty's eye and rolled her eyes. "It's easy," she said, gracefully swinging a leg over her horse. "Just hold on and don't fall off."

"Your little horse has been climbing these hills all her life," Betty assured him. "All you have to do is stay out of her way and she'll take good care of you."

Alex groaned. There was a well-worn hat and a pair of chaps hanging off his saddle horn. Assuming they were for him he awkwardly buckled on the chaps and tried on the hat. To his surprise it actually fit. He zipped the roll of topo maps up inside his parka and with an effort managed to get on his horse.

They started off to the northwest, Betty in the lead on her spotted appaloosa and Alex bringing up the rear on the gray dun. Cyd rode in between them on her solid black gelding, her hair hanging long beneath a black cowboy hat, a red bandanna tied around her neck. Alex was so taken by the sight of her on her horse that for a moment he forgot he was bouncing along on the back of an animal that weighed over a thousand pounds.

THE THREE MEN THAT AMBUSHED Maury felt no need to hurry or follow too closely. Resupplied and freshly mounted, they had a pretty good idea where their three victims were headed and they weren't going to make the same mistake twice: this time they would be more careful; this time they would wait and watch and let their prey do the work for them before they made their move.

IT SEEMED TO ALEX THEY had been riding for days instead of hours. His back was killing him. The sky was still clear, the sun was out, no new snow had fallen and what was left on the ground was soft and wet. They were on a gradual trail that rose and fell and twisted, climbing steadily alongside the Dearborn. High above them the trees climbed ever steeper terrain until they were lost in the sky.

Betty led them to the place where she had left the trail with Maury to cross the river. She crossed the water and went up the bank on the other side. Cyd followed, urging her horse through the stream. Alex brought up the rear, lagging behind, shivering as he looked down at his mare's feet dancing over the shallow rocks where the frozen water flowed. His horse bounded up the far bank and knives of pain shot down his back. By the time he topped the trail and reached the clearing, Betty and Cyd were waiting for him at the spot where Maury had died. Cyd got off her horse and squatted on her haunches, tentatively touching the dark stains on the rocks and bowing her head.

Betty got down to stretch her legs and Alex followed, barely able to walk at first. They were about two miles north of the Continental Divide where it runs along the spiny ridge of Scapegoat Mountain.

"The police helicoptered me up here so they could investigate the scene," Betty said. "I only took them to here...said this was where we were shot at. I don't know what happened when Maury went up the trail, but I don't think he would have wanted me to take them there."

"You're right," Cyd said, grabbing a fist full of mane and making a little hop to catch the stirrup with her foot before swinging into the saddle.

Betty led them in the direction Maury had gone when he left her in the clearing. Alex had his GPS out now, checking their location as they went. Up ahead they could hear the river. When they got to the edge of a bluff he told them to hold up. A hundred yards below, the Dearborn was cascading furiously over big rocks and making giant icicles as it fell.

Alex looked down again at his GPS and with the flat of his hand pointed at a small meadow at the bottom of the hill where a rock the size of a house stood beside the river. Behind the rock was a stand of aspen.

"Down there," he said, wagging his hand at the location. "Right there. Betty, I want you to stay up here and keep watch."

Betty nodded and took up a position in the rocks where she could watch the meadow below and the trail they had just come up at the same time.

Alex urged his horse over the cliff, then gripped the saddle horn and held on for dear life as his horse slipped and slid down the slope on its hocks, skidding over the loose frozen earth.

MAURY SOMEHOW MANAGED TO MAKE IT to the bottom of the same hill in one piece. He rode across the meadow and dismounted between the rock and the trees. Standing on tiptoe, he untied the leather that held the collapsible camping shovel to the back of his saddle and unbuckled his saddlebags. Between the boulder and the aspens he dug a hole. When it was deep enough to cover the saddlebags he threw them in and stood back studying his work. It was the best he could do. He quickly filled the hole, patting the mound of fresh earth down with the back of the shovel when he was done. Then he spied a dead log and drug it over the top of the grave for good measure. From his parka pocket he took out a GPS similar to the one Alex would later buy, got a reading on the location and hurriedly scribbled it down in his notepad. Brushing the dirt and snow off his knees, he looked around for anything else he might have missed. Satisfied, he struggled back onto his horse and started back up the hill.

His horse was climbing in mighty leaps, breathing hard, and was almost back to the top when three riders came out of the trees on the trail on the other side of the river. One of them raised a high-powered hunting rifle and took careful aim. The target bounced around in his sites…as his finger closed on the trigger and the gun recoiled. The shot echoed up and down the river and the shooter's hand, tattooed on the back with a large black cross, levered another shell into the chamber.

The first bullet struck Maury in the shoulder and threw him forward in the saddle. His horse made one final leap to clear the top of the hill as another shot rang out and slammed into his back. The horse broke into a gallop with its barely conscious rider hanging off the saddle to one side.

The three riders realized they were trapped on the other side of the rapids and couldn't make it across. They wheeled their horses and angrily spurred them back downriver to find another way across.

CYD FOLLOWED ALEX DOWN THE HILL, leaning back and calmly sitting her saddle as her horse made its way down the slippery slope.

Alex dismounted by the huge boulder, took out his GPS and read the screen as he turned in a circle. The river was rushing loudly over the icy rocks, drowning out all other sound. A few paces behind the rock he took another reading: 47° 18' 32" North, 112° 46' 18" West—it matched exactly. He was practically standing on the log. Reaching down, he drug the deadfall aside. Underneath was a fresh mound of earth. He fell to his knees and began to dig with his gloved hands. Cyd dropped beside him and they dug furiously together. A foot down they found the top of the saddlebags.

"We got something!" Cyd cried.

Alex grinned. "Help me get it out."

They tugged hard. The saddlebags came free and Cyd triumphantly brushed away the dirt. Alex helped her hold them up so Betty could see.

From her hiding place Betty gave them a thumbs-up.

Alex opened one flap on the saddlebags and Cyd tore at the buckles on the other. Almost simultaneously they each pulled out two heavy leather pouches tied at the top with rawhide string. They fumbled with the knots. Cyd got hers untied first. She held the bag under her arm and poured out part of its contents into her hand, staring in wonder as a mound of tiny rainbow-colored seeds filled her palm.

"Holy crap!" she cried. "It's the Cannastar! It's the seeds!"

Alex opened his bag and peered inside. "Maury, you're amazing," he said softly.

"This is the answer! If we have the seeds we don't need the

research. The seeds can reproduce themselves. We've done it, Alex. Maury's miracle isn't lost after all."

"I'll feel better when we're off this mountain," Alex said, looking around anxiously. He quickly retied the pouches, stuffed them back in the saddlebags and threw them over his shoulder.

Cyd was too excited to think about being scared.

They mounted their horses and Alex led the way back up hill, his little mare climbing like a tree squirrel. Cyd's black gelding bounded up behind him. When they reached the top both riders were out of breath. Betty came out of hiding to join them.

"We found treasure!" Cyd beamed. Betty looked away with a forlorn smile. Cyd saw her sadness and reached down and put her hand on the woman's shoulder. "Maury didn't die for nothing, Betty. He did a brave thing. What he hid for us down there is important."

"Good to know," Betty said, impatiently swiping at her eyes with her sleeve. "I'll feel better when we're off this mountain."

Cyd caught Alex's eye. Alex adjusted the weight of the saddlebags on his shoulder with a look that said *I wish I'd said that.*

They went back down the hill to the clearing. Betty kept on going without looking back, descending the trail they had climbed earlier.

Alex called after her: "Hold up a minute!"

She turned and saw that Alex and Cyd had stopped their horses in the place where Maury had bled out. Alex was speaking urgently to Cyd:

"I've got a bad feeling. We can't go back down that way."

FOR A MOMENT ALEX WAS back in Iraq.

His squad had just left the hut with two men carrying the wounded soldier he was tending. The plan was to backtrack the way they had come and go around the village by wading through a field flooded with sewage. It was the only safe way to get through a section reported to be heavily mined with IEDs. Laden down with medical supplies along with his field gear, Alex walked ahead, retracing his steps exactly...or so he thought. He didn't usually go on patrol, he spent most of his time in the hospitals, but it was a bloody surge and three medics had recently been killed in explosions. They were desperately shorthanded and he had volunteered. Now he was wishing he hadn't.

Everything was mud-brown, the houses were all bombed out, the neighborhood destroyed. It looked like the end of the world—only worse. Alex was about to take a step when he stopped, staring down at a slight indentation in the dirt under his boot. Reeling backward he raised his fist and shouted for a halt. The team froze.

The probing took an hour once the ordnance squad arrived. They set off a terrible explosion—right under the spot where Alex was about to step. He watched from the distance, badly shaken. From that time on he was known as 'Dr. Bigfoot'. Alex didn't mind the nickname, it reminded him that someone or something was watching over him and that maybe death wasn't as random as it looked, that perhaps it wasn't arbitrary; that it might be a choice after all. The feeling of impending doom when he was about to put his foot down on the bomb was one of the worst he'd ever felt. He would never forget it.

AND THE FEELING THIS TIME was the same.

Cyd didn't know what to make of him, but he was so adamant that they shouldn't go down the trail that she believed him.

Betty spit tobacco juice from the corner of her mouth. She didn't believe in any of this candy-ass, touchy-feely, new-age psychic bullshit. "You two can catch up when you get cold enough and hungry enough," she said. "I'll be up ahead."

They watched her ride off.

Cyd frowned. "How long are we going to wait?"

Alex shook his head. He didn't know.

The minutes crept by. Cyd squirmed impatiently in her saddle. Alex was still staring in the direction Betty had gone. Then they heard the crack of a rifle shot from below. Their horses shied and Alex grabbed at his reins, trying to control his mare as she spun in a circle.

Moments later Betty came bursting out of the trees at a dead run, a bloody rip in her jacket sleeve, her arm hanging limp at her side. She reined in beside them, breathing hard.

"Maybe we should try another way down," she panted.

"What happened?" Alex said.

Cyd had her rifle out. "Anybody behind you?"

"Not exactly," Betty grinned, still trying to catch her breath. "They got what you might say, delayed."

Alex was still trying to calm his horse. "By what?"

"Grizzly."

BACK DOWN THE TRAIL THREE armed men had been lying in wait.

Betty came around the bend and one of them got overly excited and fired too soon. The bullet went through her arm and she cried out in pain.

The shot startled a giant grizzly bear that had been foraging upwind with her two cubs close behind where the three men were hiding. The cubs ran screaming for safety and the sow rose up on her hind legs, howling like hell. The would-be assassins turned to see Mother Nature herself in all her fury towering over them in an avalanche of teeth and fur.

Holding her arm and looking back over her shoulder, Betty saw the three men climbing trees faster than she had thought men could climb. They looked like monkeys on a string being yanked into the branches by an invisible hand, scraping their hide off on the bark as they went. One of them, a lanky cowboy with half his teeth, wasn't fast enough and the bear caught his foot and hauled him back down, slashing him to death with her oversized claws. Blood from his wounds sprayed the ground like it was coming from a garden hose.

"I like bears," Betty muttered to herself, spurring her horse up the trail. "Always have, always will."

FROM THE CLEARING BETTY HEADED OFF in the same direction she had taken to evade the attackers when Maury was killed and Cyd and Alex followed.

"Bear should keep the other two busy for a while," Betty said. The bullet wound in her shoulder was starting to throb and pain shot up her arm every time her horse jostled her in the saddle.

"Let me take a look at that arm," Alex said, calling to her from behind.

"It's broke, what more do you want to know?"

They rode swiftly and before long were at the place where Betty had turned off the trail onto the rocks to ride up to her cave. Alex made her get down so he could tend to her injury. This time she didn't resist.

The bullet had gone through without hitting any major arteries. He cleaned and disinfected the wound as best he could and wrapped it in gauze from a small first aid kit that Cyd had brought along. Then he tore up his shirt and fitted her arm in a sling. He told her it needed to be set and that she needed to get to a hospital for x-rays as soon as possible. The patient did not argue. Instead, she explained to them how to find the cave, pointing out landmarks under the sheer rock cliff above.

"You won't be able to see the entrance until you're right on top of it," she cautioned. "I'll head back down the mountain and leave a trail for them to follow. Those old boys are gonna be mighty pissed once that bear gets bored enough to wander off and they can come back down out of those trees. You two get on up there and hide. Protect what Maury left you, that's your job." She gritted her teeth as she got back on her horse. "I'll just mosey on along home."

"What if they catch you?" Cyd said uneasily.

"They won't catch me. They won't even see me. My grandfather was Crow Indian, you know, even if my mother was a Jew." Cyd put her hand over her heart in sympathy as she watched her go. Up the trail beyond the loose rock, holding her arm close to her side, they heard her fart.

"That's just in case they can't follow my tracks," she said as she disappeared into the trees. "They can follow my scent."

CHAPTER 7

Somewhere Safe

Smoke was being drawn back into the darkness of the cave toward an unseen exit far inside the mountain. Near the back of the dank cavern the gelding was munching grain and the mare was drinking from a small pool fed by a trickle of water that came out of the rock and made icicles as it ran down the stone. The horses seemed to know they needed to be quiet.

Alex watched Cyd turn sideways to get through the cave opening with a wide armload of deadfall, then drop the wood beside the fire he had built. She stood brushing loose bark from her arms, her freckled cheeks flushed from the cold. He thought she looked beautiful.

"What are the chances there's a bear sleeping back there somewhere?" he asked with a nervous glance toward the rear of the cave.

"Alex Farmer, I do believe you are afraid of the dark."

"I'm afraid of bears."

"This is more the kind of place where you find mountain lions."

"You mean like the one behind you?"

Cyd's eyes grew wide as she slowly turned...and heard him laugh.

"Jerk!" she said.

"What's for dinner?" He was rummaging through her saddlebags, trying to keep the pain off his face. The agony in his back was almost unbearable.

The beef and vegetable freeze-dried stew turned out to be delicious. Cyd brewed her Cannastar tea over the fire in one of their two metal pans and they sat on the stone cave floor on top of their horse blankets and bed rolls with their saddles as back rests. The saddlebag that contained the seeds lay safely between them. Cyd kept touching it as if she couldn't believe it was real. It filled her with hope. Beyond the fire, the mouth of the cave revealed a narrow vertical strip of brilliant stars.

Alex adjusted his sitting position, grimacing in pain.

"You all right?" she asked.

"Never better." He didn't know when or how it had happened, but he realized he was as passionate about the seeds as she was. Their eyes met and lingered. He couldn't look at her without wanting her.

She scowled. "So how do we keep the seeds a secret? How are we going to keep them safe?"

"I don't know. You got any friends around here?"

A long pause. He loved that it took her forever to say anything; it gave him more time to look at her. She brightened. "I do, actually. Not here maybe but...on the other side of here. Let me see those maps."

Alex unrolled the topos he had bought in town. Each map covered roughly 50 square miles and was divided into smaller grids of one square mile each. Cyd sat cross-legged on the blanket, pulling one out for the quadrant they were in and laying it side by side with the one for the quadrant directly to the west of them.

"This is how we go," she said, tracing a route west with her finger on the first map and working her way gradually north on the second map. "We follow this valley—see here?—and that connects with this valley, you see? We cross the river... right about here...and that eventually leads us to Pablo."

"Who's Pablo?"

"Pablo is a town. The seat of government for the Flathead Nation."

"You know someone there?"

"You might say that."She put her hand on his and a current of electricity went up his arm. "We need a place where nobody can find us, Alex. Somewhere safe where we can get these seeds in the ground."

"And you think we can just show up on an Indian reservation in the middle of winter and start a farm?"

"The only thing that grows on the Flathead Reservation is rocks—the land is worthless. The Salish used to be wonderful farmers until the white man kicked them out of the Bitterroot. They're a gracious people. They'll hide us until we can figure out what to do."

"I hope so because I think this cave has plumbing and heating problems."

Cyd looked away, lost in thought. A smile slowly lit her face. "The seeds, Alex! We have the seeds!" She leaned over, pulled him to her and suddenly kissed him. It surprised them both.

"Sorry," she said. "I tend to get overly excited sometimes."

"I admire that in a person." They were staring openly at one another, the pain of their longing exquisite. "You think you could get excited like that one more time?"

"Anything's possible."

She kissed him hard. Then breathlessly and furiously they kissed again...and again...and much later she fell asleep in his arms and the floor of the stone cave was one of the softest beds she ever slept on.

Alex couldn't sleep, but he dared not move for fear of disturbing her. His tortured back was so inflamed that he had to bite his lip to keep from screaming. He had the bottle of Vicodin out that he had bought at the pharmacy and was rolling it over and over in his hand. He had a lot of reasons why he shouldn't take them, all of them good. Unfortunately, his addiction had better ones. *Long hard day tomorrow,* he thought. *Got to sleep, have to sleep…this is what they're for… one can't hurt…not like I'm starting up again.* Then admonishing himself: *One hour at a time, one hour at a time.* Then: *Can't stand it…just one, one can't hurt.* Then: *No-no-no…I can't, I can't do it…*

Long into the night he fought away his demons. The fire had almost died down when she snuggled close…and awoke in the darkness and began to touch him.

"Ouch!" His back felt like it had a skewer running through it and he was being slowly burned alive over hot coals.

"Want me to stop?"

"I just rolled over on a rock is all."

"How nice," she murmured, moving her hand up and down.

Immediately afterward she was sound asleep again.

The pain was more than he could stand. He reached for the pills, eased off the cap, shook two out…and tossed them down his throat. And soon after a stillness and a calm came over him and in its warmth he felt his eyes grow heavy.

Out of the blackness something silky soft was nuzzling his cheek and hot breath enveloped him. Suddenly he was wide awake, staring up at the enormous muzzle of his horse who was nudging him with her nose. He tried to sit up and pain slammed him back down.

He heard Cyd laugh. "She's trying to tell you you're burnin' daylight."

"Easy for her to say."

Blinking rapidly as his vision cleared, he saw Cyd bent over a small fire blissfully brewing her tea and cooking powdered eggs and Canadian bacon. His head hurt from having slept so hard; it felt like his brain had collapsed.

"Coffee?" she asked.

He managed a smile as she handed him a steaming cup. It was the best night of his life, it was the worst night of his life, depending on which body parts you were talking about. He preferred to think about the ones that didn't hurt—not the fact that he had taken pain medication after having sworn to all that was holy that he would never take them again. *Just let me get through this,* he thought, *and then I'll go back to not taking them. No way am I getting back on this stuff.*

"You're probably wishing right now you could get your pants on and go home," she said defensively, mistaking his distraction for indifference.

"I am home."

"Well...I like what you've done with the place," she said evasively, glancing around at the cave that in the first light of dawn was no less dark and damp than it was the night before.

"Cyd," he repeated, drawing her down to him. "I'm home."

She looked at him, vulnerable and exposed, and her defenses came down and she let him in. She beamed broadly and gave him a kiss. "So you don't care if I go out and buy curtains?"

"I'll give you my credit card and you can clean out the whole damn furniture store if you want."

She laughed and Alex realized he was in love with her.

"Well, credit card or no credit card," she said, happily bouncing to her feet, "if you're not ready to go in ten minutes I'm leaving without you."

"How long will it take us to get there?

"Two days if the weather holds."

Inwardly, he moaned at the withering thought of what two more days of horseback riding would do to his back. Before they left the cave, while Cyd had her back turned saddling her horse, he took another pill.

Just until this is over, he promised.

IT WAS A LONG HARD ride over rugged terrain. The wind blew cold, but the sky stayed clear. Crossing the Continental Divide the trail was so steep and narrow Alex was afraid to look down. Cyd rode ahead of him on her coal black horse, steadfast and silent, her red bandanna a light leading the way. According to his GPS they were making less than three miles an hour.

The vastness of the land overwhelmed him. It was as if man had never existed—and in this place perhaps he never had. An eagle circled overhead, motionless on an updraft, rising almost a thousand feet in less than a minute. Once he saw a bull elk moving off in the distance, the width of his horns wider than the span of his rifle. Down valley wolf pups yipped in their den, hungry for the kill. The wind conducted an orchestra in the trees on a keyboard made of mountains. And the sky—always the sky—its pregnant belly swollen blue with light over a wilderness where life and death meant everything and nothing and in the end were all the same to something larger than a man could know.

They rode northwest along the southern boundary of the Bob Marshall Wilderness and after a long descent to the valley below crossed the South Fork of the Flathead River an hour before sundown. Alex had the feeling they were being watched and for the thousandth time that day turned in his saddle to look over his shoulder...but saw nothing.

They made camp at Big Salmon Lake next to a meadow where enough brown grass was still poking through the snow that the horses could feed. It was as safe a place as any to spend the night. They had been traveling almost twelve hours and had come a little over thirty miles. In war, in hospitals in the Middle East and stateside where he had worked, Alex was used to pushing himself beyond exhaustion. This was harder than that.

Dark storm clouds were building to the north as Cyd unpacked their things and spread out their bedrolls in the failing light. Alex had taken another pill along the trail, but the effects of it had worn off and the pain was getting worse by the minute. He saw Cyd on her knees digging a handline and a tiny can of corn out of her pack, then watched as she slumped forward in fatigue. He took the fishing gear out of her hand and helped her to lie down on the blanket.

"I have to catch us a fish for supper," she protested feebly.

"Why don't you let me give it a try. You sit here and rest."

"Just bait the hook with the corn and..." Her smile faded, her eyelids fluttered and she was asleep. Alex covered her with his blanket, laid her rifle next to her, picked up his own rifle and threw the saddlebags that contained the Cannastar seeds over his shoulder before heading down to the lake. He went no further than the edge of the water where he could keep an eye on her sleeping form.

To his utter amazement he caught a two-pound trout on his first cast. He hauled it in hand over hand, dragging it flopping and thrashing onto the shore, its sides almost as colorful as the seeds in the leather pouches. Cyd awoke an hour later to a warm fire and the smell of fish cooking on a stick over the flame. Suddenly she was famished. Alex cut up a potato and fried it in one of their pans and they feasted on greasy potatoes and trout, gingerly pulling the hot meat off the stick with their fingers and drinking from Cyd's flask of whiskey.

She smiled with a greasy mouth. "Thanks for dinner."

"If you like that, wait until you taste my pheasant."

She laughed and he reached over and wiped the corners of her mouth.

It was a fine party.

They lay by the fire with their bellies warm with food, he with his back against his saddle, she with her head in his lap, her dark hair spilling over his leg and onto the blanket. One of her hands rested lightly on the saddlebags that contained seeds. The pain in his back was relentless, but looking down at her face all he could think was that he had never been happier in his life.

The wind picked up and the flames of the fire bent sideways sending sparks into the air. Alex once again had the feeling they were being watched. He scanned the darkness. Beyond the fire the forest was restless, the surface of the lake unsettled.

"We should take turns standing guard," he said, checking to make sure his rifle was close at hand. "I'll take the first watch."

"I want to make love," she murmured.

Bending to kiss her he saw that she had drifted off to sleep. "Merry Christmas," he whispered. It was Christmas Eve.

Alex sat watching her slow steady breathing as the pain in his back grew worse. Finally he couldn't stand it any more, dug the bottle of Vicodin out of his pocket, tore it open, shook out two more pills and popped them in his mouth. As he was taking a swallow of water to wash them down he saw Cyd's eyes flutter open. Suddenly she was staring up at him, wide-eyed and fearful.

"What are you doing?" she asked. "What is that?"

"Just something for my back."

"Your back?"

"Pain pills."

Cyd sat up and grabbed the pill bottle out of his hand. "Let me see!" She squinted at the label in the firelight...then jumped to her feet, backing away in horror. "Oh no...oh no..."

"What's wrong?"

"These are what's wrong!" she cried and threw the bottle in the fire.

"Are you crazy?" He grabbed a stick, frantically digging the pills back out of the coals.

"I'm not going to be around someone who takes pain pills!"

"They're for my back. I was in a bad car wreck and all of this jarring on the horse..." She stumbled backward. He caught her by the arm, completely dumbfounded. "Cyd...what's this about?"

Appalled and disgusted, she broke free of his grip. "My mother died from an overdose of pain pills, you ass! She committed suicide with those fucking things..."

"I didn't know...I'm sorry. I won't take any more if that's what you want." Impulsively, he threw the bottle back in the fire...and immediately regretted it. "See? They're gone."

Cyd broke down sobbing. Memories flashed through her mind. Terrible memories:

Nine-year-old Cyd padding softly into her parent's bedroom to wake her mother because it's late and she's going to miss the school bus. Her mother lying in bed on her back. Cold and still and deathly white. Her father next to her on his back. Motionless. Staring up at the ceiling. Hyperventilating. Cyd shaking her mother by the arm, calling her name...then screaming: Motherrrrr! *Her father just lying there. Breathing fast. Cyd screaming at him through her tears to do something. Pounding on her mother with her tiny fists...then running to the bathroom to throw up. Seeing the empty pill bottle rolling around on the tile floor. That horrible bottle! Fumbling with the phone to call 911. Sobbing into the receiver...then paramedics, firemen, police—huge men—crowding into the tiny bedroom, trying to wake her mother up. Hearing their awful voices:* "...must of swallowed the pills and then slipped into bed...careful not to wake him up...just laid down beside the poor bastard and died without making a sound...damn." *A blur of bodies blocking her view. Rough hands restraining her.* "...she got in the last word after all, it looks like..." *and hearing them laugh.*

Cyd remembered how her father never showed any emotion after that.

Ever. How he never spoke of the suicide again. The little girl never got over it.

And neither did the adult.

"I have to tell you something," Alex said, jolting her out of her reverie. "I should've told you this before. Please come back and sit down..." She tearfully shook her head and refused to move. He took a deep breath and rushed on: "Before I came here I was in rehab...for taking pain pills."

"You what? And you're right back on them again?" She came at him and Alex thought she was going to hit him, but she brushed past him and started furiously packing up her things. "I am so out of here!"

With a wild heart he said, "Cyd, listen to me. It's not a problem..." Then watching as she saddled her horse, he desperately told her the story of the car wreck:

How it was one of those torrential downpours in LA; how the other car crossed over the line and hit him almost head on; how it demolished his back; how he laid in the hospital with the pain getting steadily worse until he didn't have a choice: if he ever wanted to get out of this place, let alone work again, he was going to have to take the pills. An innocent decision,

one that thousands of people make every day. The addiction…
it wasn't like he planned it or anything; he didn't set out to
become a drug addict. That's how it is with pain pills; they
sneak up on you until they own you…

"Fuck you!" she screamed.

He managed to talk her into waiting until morning to
leave, but she moved her bed to the other side of the fire. He
heard her crying herself to sleep.

Lying there afraid and confused, alone and miserable,
Alex thought about what he had just told her. He had lied—if
omission was a lie. He hadn't told her that his wife was in the
car with him.

The next day they awoke to thunder. To the north the pale
morning sky was under attack by jagged lightning strikes that
were electrocuting the air. The horses, tied to stakes in the
meadow, pulled back against their halters.

Strained and stifling silence hung between them as they
hurriedly packed to try and get on the trail and stay ahead
of the storm. Neither of them felt like eating. Cyd's tea was
brewing on the fire.

"I'm sorry about your mother," Alex said. "It must have
been rough."

She was so angry he didn't think she was going to answer.
Then heatedly: "Why are men so macho?"

"I'm not being macho." He paused with a self-effacing
smile. "Well…a little, maybe."

"Why didn't you tell me you were in pain?"

"You've got enough problems without having to listen to
mine."

She shook her head in exasperation, went to the fire and
poured out a boiling cup of Cannastar.

"Try this," she said, shoving the cup in his hand.

He looked down. "I don't want to take your tea."

"Fucking drink it, all right?"

"Okay, okay." He took a sip. "You think it might help?"

"Pot helps with neuropathic and neuromuscular pain. The Cannastar should amp that a thousand times over, especially if your injury is to the central nervous system, but who knows, it's only a theory. It's never been tested. Guess that makes you the guinea pig. Good luck with that."

The 'good luck' part didn't sound sincere, but at least she was talking to him, which was a start. He smiled and took a drink. It scalded his throat going down.

The storm broke at noon. Thunder exploded so close overhead that Alex ducked. They hurried off the mountain under a boiling sky, skirting the little town of Condon and crossing Highway 83 just as the sky opened up and it started to pour. Their horse's hooves sounded hollow clicking across the slick two lane blacktop. A trailer-tractor rig screamed by throwing sheets of water at their startled horses. Rain ran down off the brims of their hats and pattered onto their chaps. They reined in under a tree to let the squall pass.

Alex remembered the hellish nightmare of trying to get off the pain killers the first time. How he had fought the people who were trying to help him—how he wasn't willing to admit he even had a problem—and later, deep in the horrors of withdrawal, swearing that if he ever survived he would kill himself before going through this again. He realized if Cyd hadn't stopped him he would have been right back in rehab—or laid out on Otis's stainless steel table; that he had been lying to himself that he could handle it; that taking a few pills wouldn't make any difference and the minute he got to wherever the hell they were going he would stop. *Amazing what suckers we are for our own bullshit,* he thought. A feeling of gratitude welled up in him for what Cyd had done to wake him up—along with a stab of fear for what he might now be facing without the pills. Then he realized that today wasn't like yesterday, that he wasn't about to pass out from the pain, that it was actually tolerable at the moment. He tested it by cautiously shifting his weight. Miraculously, his spine no longer felt like it was being ripped out of his skin with hot tongs.

"Cyd, my back feels better!" he said, elated at the thought that the Cannastar might be working. "A lot better."

She was struggling with her emotions and didn't hear. What the hell was she doing with this man? "I don't know," she said in answer to her own question, staring up the trail through the driving rain. "I just don't know."

They were both shivering.

"How long before we're there?" he asked. Then when she didn't answer: "Hope your friends the Indians know how to build a fire."

"So now you're a racist on top of everything else?"

"Wanting to be dry is not racist!"

LATE IN THE AFTERNOON THEY reached the outskirts of the reservation. A light snow had begun to fall. They rode numb and silent past depressing hovels with old tires and garbage strewn in the yards, past worn-out single-wide trailers sitting bleached and broken on cinder block foundations. Cyd looked neither left nor right but rode steadily on, shoulders slumped, head down. Alex urged his horse up alongside her, but she did not look over.

The rutted road turned into a smoothly graded gravel road and the houses started looking better until they were riding through a sprawling subdivision of five-acre lots. The farther they went the more prosperous the homes became. Wooden structures turned into brick residences with swing sets, soccer nets and abandoned toys in the yards. Most of the houses had a large RV and/or an expensive boat on a trailer parked beside the garage. The pastures were fenced in neat rectangles and many had little barns where one or two horses were grazing or standing motionless with half-closed eyes. Cyd kept up the steady pace. Alex was beginning to think she might be asleep in the saddle.

And then they came to it.

Up ahead was a house of colossal proportions. It sat in the center of a ten-acre lot on a little denuded knoll and was a wonder to behold. It looked like it was made of large, white, flat-roofed cubes that had been jumbled together at startling angles to form a modern mosaic of glass and steel. Perhaps the architecture would have gone well in West LA or the Hamptons, but here on a Montana Indian reservation it was strange to say the least. The chaotic structure grew larger as they rode up a long drive that was bordered on either side by a clean white fence. Dogs began to bark as they approached. A garage with a dozen overhead doors flanked the near side of the house. On the far side was a separate cubical attached to the house by a long glass passageway. Mirrored walls could be seen through tall glass windows that reflected a hardwood dance floor. Ballet bars ran around the inside of the cube and above them, hanging down from the ceiling in graceful loops, were ropes of pine boughs decorated with Christmas balls.

The barking stopped as a robust man in shorts, sandals and a Hawaiian shirt opened the front door and stepped out into the falling show. He was about sixty, six feet tall, two hundred and twenty pounds and had a pony tail blacker than Cyd's horse. With his dark skin, high cheek bones and Hawaiian shirt he looked more Polynesian than anything else. When he saw Cyd he beamed broadly, spread his arms and let out what sounded to Alex like a war whoop. She jumped from her horse and ran into his arms where he scooped her up and tossed her in the air with the agility of a man half his age.

"Cydney! You stay away too long!" he shouted. "Skinny as ever, I see. My wife, she'll fix that. You brought a friend. What did you do to him, he looks terrible?"

"Clarence, this is Alex Farmer. Alex, I'd like you to meet Clarence Bigfoot."

Alex was taken aback by the last name. "Pleasure," he said, stiffly dismounting his horse. Clarence extended the arm that was currently holding up Cyd's bottom—he had to adjust her weight to keep from dropping her—and shook Alex's hand at an awkward angle. For a gregarious man in a loud shirt he had a surprisingly gentle handshake. Alex reached over to help him with his load. "You need a hand with that?"

"I got it," Clarence boomed, playfully carrying Cyd through the door and depositing her inside. "Come in, the both of you...Mary!" he called. "Guess who's come to visit?" Then in a stage whisper to Cyd: "Watch this; she'll have a heart attack."

There was a scream of delight as a tall willowy white woman in her mid-fifties wearing dance clothes, her graying hair pulled back severely into a bun, swept down the hall to give their guest a big hug. She kissed Cyd's cheek and head, then with a mother's adoration kissed her again as the two of them started chattering excitedly.

Alex, still outside on the porch, watched as a sullen wrinkle-faced old man dressed in insulated bib overalls appeared to take away their horses. It was a point of honor with the old man that he administer all things concerning the livestock on the estate. He and Alex had a small tug of war with the saddlebags that contained the seeds until Alex managed to get them away from him.

"We're having a Christmas party tonight," Mary was saying as Alex came inside, the saddlebags over his shoulder. "Robert is coming. Is that all right?"

Cyd hesitated. "Sure, I guess."

The entry hall was decorated with a Christmas tree big enough to have full size toys hanging from its branches. To make room for the tree, a modern sculpture of a human torso—its appendages rearranged in positions more suited to a body that had fallen from a roof—had been pushed to one side. Alex turned his head this way and that trying to make sense of it as they were ushered into a high-ceilinged living room where colorful oil and acrylic canvases of incomprehensible swirls and shapes rioted along the walls. Looking out through the floor-to-ceiling windows at the barren landscape beyond, Alex felt like a goldfish in a modern art museum on Mars. A gas log fire burned brightly behind a piece of fireproof glass that was mounted flush against a solid wall of cold hard marble. Alex stood with his back to it, but felt no heat.

"Quite a house you got here," Alex said in amazement.

Clarence grinned proudly. "Like it? My wife just got done redecorating it for the second time this year."

"It's...really something."

"How far have you come?" Bigfoot asked, eyeing their bedraggled, stressed and exhausted condition now with some concern.

"From Helena," Cyd said.

Mary was appalled. "At this time of year? In this weather?"

"It wasn't like we had a choice," Cyd said.

"Whatever kind of trouble you're in, you can tell me about it later," Clarence said, encircling their shoulders with fatherly arms and guiding them toward a clear plastic staircase that hung suspended from the ceiling by steel cables. "Right now you're going to have a hot bath and a good meal and tonight you're going to sleep in a real bed."

"If I'm not up in a week, come and get me," Alex said.

Clarence left them alone together in an upstairs bedroom to clean up and recoup before dinner. Cyd pushed a button and a drape descended like a theater curtain over a glass wall of windows, coming to rest above a window seat of gray concrete decorated with colorful throw pillows. Alex went into the marble bathroom and turned on the water in the whirlpool bath, then came back out while the tub was filling. Cyd was shedding her damp clothes and throwing them on the chair where Alex had hung the saddlebags.

"How do you know these people?" Alex asked, pulling off his wet socks.

There was a pause while he listened to the sound of the running bath water. "I used to be engaged to their son."

"You broke up with their boy and they still treat you like their daughter?"

"He broke up with me. Clarence and Mary are family," she said. "Just like Maury was family." Steam was coming out of the bathroom. She went in and locked the door behind her.

"Take as long as you want," Alex said through the door... wishing he was in there with her.

There was no response.

When she came out after her bath he was asleep on the bed. She shook him awake. He got up and went into the bathroom and she saw that he was bent in pain.

"I'll fix you some more tea when we go downstairs," she said in a flat voice.

He wanted to kiss her but restrained himself.

While he was letting the hot water jets massage his back she came into the bathroom and used the toilet like he wasn't there. He asked her where Clarence had gotten his money.

She said he was a software engineer; that he'd worked in Silicon Valley during the early '80s where he founded his own company. In the late 80's he sold the company for something like eighty million dollars, she said. Since then, among other things, he'd built a hospital and a school for his people and in his spare time started a new software business that did something—she didn't know what—for the defense department. It employed most of the people in the subdivision they had ridden through on their way to his house.

BIGFOOT'S FESTIVELY DECORATED DINING HALL had the acoustics of a racquet ball court. Cyd and Alex walked in and after three days of camping out, the smell of hot cooked food overwhelmed their senses. Friends and relatives milled about a stainless steel table that stretched thirty feet or more, its burnished surface piled with holiday fare. High-backed chairs made of metal rods and fitted with small black hard leather seats ran down either side looking like they required seatbelts for the rigid business of sitting—which may have explained why the guests seemed to be avoiding them.

Alex was introduced around to the guests. Most were baptized Roman Catholic with Christian names, but at family gatherings they used their traditional names. There was cousin *Hethonton* (Towering Antlers) and his two sons *Hebazhu* (Little Antlers) and *Heshabe* (Dark Antlers), otherwise known respectively as Doug, Tom and Bill Medicinehorse; uncle *Demonthin* (Talks As He Walks) and his wife aunt *Watewin* (Victory Woman); cousin *Shonge* (Wolf), his wife *Zitkala* (Bird), their son *Shongesabbe* (Black Wolf) and daughter *Zitkalatu* (Blue Bird). At least that was how the words sounded to Alex's ear. More were arriving by the minute and he smiled

and shook hands until the names all ran together in his head
and he gave up trying to keep them straight. Clarence Bigfoot
was known on these festive occasions as *Wekushton* (One Who
Gives Feast Frequently) and Mary was called *Donama* (The
Sun Visible To All).

Alex thought his hosts made the perfect couple. Mary
was dressed in a Santa Fe style skirt with a silver Concho
belt, red blouse and turquoise jewelry—the only person in
the room who had made an effort to wear anything even
remotely ethnic. She and her husband were clearly devoted to
one another—with the tacit understanding that she was the
boss. Perhaps this was born from the fact that she had been
a prima ballerina with the San Francisco Ballet—or maybe it
was just because she was not Native American and had been
brought up to believe that no man was her master—but the
understanding was clear nonetheless. Clarence was fine with
this. He doted on his family and preferred spending his time
thinking about his software business and his community
work rather than thinking up ways to order his wife around.
His egalitarian view of women rankled the other members of
his clan who held their tongues out of respect for the fact that
he was the richest sonofabitch in the valley.

While Alex was meeting everybody, Cyd went into the
kitchen and brewed him some of her tea. He drank it down
and felt the relief wash over him. It was like being released
from a torture device.

He noticed that someone had been staring at Cyd ever
since they walked in and now that someone was walking
toward them. He didn't usually give much thought to another
man's looks one way or the other, but even he could see that
this fellow could stop traffic with his clothes on; he was
gorgeous. He was about Cyd's age, same hair color, six foot
two, broad-shouldered and gifted with brilliant teeth and an

equally brilliant smile. Cyd introduced him as Clarence's son Robert. He shook Alex's hand without taking his eyes off Cyd. Alex took an immediate dislike to him.

"You a Flathead too?" Alex asked.

"We call ourselves Salish," Robert said, continuing to stare intently into Cyd's eyes. "It means 'The People'. My dad said you've been on the trail for days. How can you still look so beautiful?"

"Robert is a geologist," Cyd explained self-consciously. "We used to go together, but that was ages ago. He works for the different tribes now helping them develop the natural resources on their lands, oil and gas, that sort of thing." She was captivated by his stare. "We haven't seen each other in— how long is it Robert?"

"Two years, thirteen months."

That really is some smile, Alex thought. *I'd like to break his teeth for him.*

At the dinner table Alex sat on one side of Cyd, Robert on the other. Every time her former boyfriend made her laugh it made him mad. Down at the other end of the table, sitting next to Mary, was an emaciated girl about five years younger than Cyd who kept coughing into her napkin. She was a long-legged bird-like creature with tiny bones that looked like they might snap in a high wind. Her hair lay dull and lifeless against her skull. She had once been a striking beauty with flowing raven-black hair, prettier even than her mother had been at her age when Mary was an aspiring ballerina. Now she was pale and sickly and far too thin. Alex noted her condition, but mostly what he saw was her sadness. He asked Cyd about her.

"That's Robert's sister Tiffany. Her real name is *Washudse* which means Wild-rose, but she hates everything Indian." A pause. "She has AIDS."

After dinner Clarence offered Alex a cigar and they went out onto the terrace to smoke them. Alex was surprised after their long trip over the mountains that the cool air would feel this good. His host, dressed in different shorts and a different Hawaiian shirt—this one from his *Mele Kalilimaka* (Merry Christmas) collection—seemed invigorated by the cold as well.

"Bigfoot was my nickname in the military," Alex said, by way of making conversation.

Clarence nodded thoughtfully. "What does it mean?"

"It means I am careful where I step."

Clarence studied his house guest while puffing on his cigar. Alex wasn't sure he hadn't offended his host. Finally, the playful man with the pony tail said, "Careful Where He Steps. It is a good name. I think you wear it well."

"How do you say it in Salish?"

"I don't know, I only speak English."

For some reason they both found this funny and they laughed and in that moment they became friends.

It was late morning by the time Alex and Cyd made their way back downstairs to the kitchen. When they came in Lupe, the cook, was setting out large pots of water on the black granite counter top and pouring different kinds of beans into them to soak in preparation for making her famous 7-bean soup. Lupe was a good-natured Hispanic woman who looked like, and in fact was considered, a member of the family. She stopped what she was doing and cordially made them break-fast, informing them that Mary was in her studio teaching a dance lesson and that Mr. Bigfoot would like to see them in his office when they were done eating.

Cyd made them both tea. Alex accepted his eagerly. "You know what?" he said, taking a sip. "Along with the pain, I think this stuff is actually killing my cravings. You think it's possible Cannastar could cure addiction on top of everything else?"

"That sort of thing takes a lot of testing," she shrugged. "Why don't you round up a bunch of your fellow junkies and you can run a control group."

They walked down a glassed-in hallway not speaking to one another. Alex had the saddlebags over his shoulder. The hallway led to another of the seemingly endless cubes that made up the house. They stopped at a door that was slightly ajar and Cyd knocked softly.

Clarence, talking on the phone in his office, waved them in and motioned them into a pair of leather chairs in front of his desk. He wore yet another Hawaiian shirt, this one adorned with hibiscus blossoms. While they waited for him to finish his conversation they looked out the high wall of office windows across the infertile reservation at the snow-capped mountains beyond, dangerous and grand, that they had crossed the day before.

The office itself was a wonder of technological gadgetry. An array of computer monitors hung above a massive circular desk that was piled with jumbled papers. Bookshelves overflowed with technical manuals carelessly propped up by pictures of Clarence Bigfoot shaking hands with various politicians and celebrities. Prominently displayed was a photograph of Clarence arm in arm with a smiling President Clinton. Against one wall, between the door to the bathroom and a remarkably life-like, life-size bronze of an attacking bear, was a tall black gun safe with gold pin striping and a digital combination lock.

Clarence laughed at something the caller said. "Thanks for your help, Sam. See you at the fund-raiser." He chuckled again and hung up. "That was your cousin in Washington. The Senator is helping me with government financing for a new hydroelectric plant over in Missoula that's going to provide income for the tribe forever. It's amazing what a hundred thousand dollar campaign contribution will buy you. I told him you arrived here safe and sound and that I was taking good care of you."

"Fuck," Cyd said under her breath.

"Excuse me?" Clarence said, puzzled.

"I wish you hadn't said that," she said.

"He was worried about you," Clarence insisted. "He said you disappeared four days ago without a trace. They were afraid you might have gotten lost in the mountains or something. His son apparently sent men out looking for you. He was delighted when I told him you were all right." He saw that Cyd was still alarmed. "What is it, dear heart? Tell me."

"Sam Seeley isn't who you think he is," she said.

"He's your closest relative. He's only looking out for your best interest..."

Alex shook his head. "I'm afraid that's not all he's looking for."

"All right, out with it," Clarence said. "What are you two being so secretive about?"

Cyd picked up the saddlebags that were lying on the floor between their chairs. "We need a place to hide this," she said.

Clarence stood and came around his desk. "That's easy," he said, relieved that there was something he could do. He crossed the room to the gun safe, punched in the combination and swung open the door. Inside was his collection of frontier firearms, all in good working order. "How's this?" he asked proudly. "The man who sold me this safe said it was guaranteed burglarproof and fireproof."

Cyd kissed him on the cheek before reverently placing the saddlebags in the safe, doubling them over so they would fit inside. Clarence closed and locked the door and gave them the combination in case they needed to get into it when he wasn't around. Then he went back to his desk, sat down in his big chair and folded his arms across his chest.

"I'm waiting," he said.

"Maybe it's better if you don't know," Alex said.

"The seeds in those saddlebags can give your daughter her life back," Cyd said bluntly.

Clarence searched her face, trying to divine her meaning. "That would be...a miracle," he said. "Have you brought us a miracle, Cydney?"

They spent the next hour telling him everything that had happened. Clarence listened intently. When they were done he was at a loss for words.

"It's probably better if you let me tell Tiffany," Cyd said. "She needs to know there's a possibility it might not work."

"But it will," Clarence said excitedly. "I know it will."

"We'll see," Cyd said. "I hope so."

Clarence sobered. The more he thought about their story the more upset he became. "If your suspicions are true..." he said. "I mean, I knew Sam Seeley worked for the drug industry...Hell, he works for anybody who pays him, but never in a million years did I suspect...My God, what have I done?"

"Don't blame yourself, you didn't know," Alex said. "We were followed here anyway I think."

Cyd looked at him sharply. "Why do you say that?"

"Just a hunch."

"Careful Where He Steps I believe has good hunches," Clarence said. "What can I do? How can I help?"

"We need some place to go where we can't be found," Cyd said. "Somewhere nobody would think to look. The only way these seeds are going to be of any good to anyone is if we can grow them without getting killed or caught. I can't imagine where..."

"Nothing much grows around here," Clarence said. "Not on this land."

"We'll figure it out," Alex said. "At least we're safe for now."

"What does it feel like, to be safe I mean?" Cyd said, looking out the window. "I forget."

That afternoon Alex was still tired from the ordeal of his back pain and horseback riding and went upstairs to take a nap. Two hours later he awoke with a start. Rubbing his eyes, he went to the bedroom window and looked out. It had begun to snow again and the light was fading rapidly. Suddenly he saw something down by the swimming pool that made his stomach turn.

Cyd was just coming out of the pool house—a white cabana with double French doors on either end, full of outdoor furniture and pool toys stored for the winter—as Robert appeared and intercepted her beside the pool.

They stood talking, engrossed in conversation while steam rose all around them from the heated water. Impossibly large snowflakes drifted down and stuck to her dark hair and made her look like she was wearing a white veil in a snowy church. They were close together, too close as far as Alex was concerned, and there was an urgency to the way he was speaking to her. Cyd nodded solemnly. Then Alex saw her stand on tiptoe, kiss his cheek and gently caress the side of his face with the back of her hand before walking away.

Alex heard her come back into the house. He met her at the bottom of the stairs just as she was starting up.

"So what's up?" he said, trying to sound casual. She didn't respond. "I saw you and Robert by the pool. He looked pretty intense."

Seconds ticked by while she stared at him. Finally: "He wanted us to get back together. He said he'd made a big mistake in breaking up with me."

"What did you say?"

She smiled with her eyes. "You're jealous."

"I'm not jealous, I'm a doctor."

"What do you think I said?"

"I don't know…All I know is that I'm afraid of losing you."

She turned and walked slowly, deliberately up the plastic stairs. At the top of the staircase she paused with her back turned and said, "Just because I'm mad at you doesn't mean I don't love you."

His heart raced with joy. *It might turn out to be a good day after all,* he thought as he followed her up the stairs and down the hall. Neither of them suspected it might be also their last.

CHAPTER 8

Tagged and Bagged

It took a lot of convincing the next morning, but Tiffany finally agreed to come along.

Mary was going into Missoula to do some after-Christmas shopping and she was going to take Tiffany and Cyd along, subject closed. She didn't know what all the fuss was about anyway. What harm could there be in taking her two daughters to lunch? Cyd thought it might be the perfect opportunity to break the news to them about the Cannastar and have a calm discussion about it without freaking them out. Mary loaded Cyd and Tiffany into her new green Range Rover with the cream-colored leather upholstery—a Christmas present from her adoring husband—and waved goodbye to Clarence and Alex who stood on the front porch watching helplessly as they drove off.

Nervous about driving her new car to begin with, Mary was so excited to have both her girls with her that she didn't stop talking. As a result, the fifty-mile drive into town took an hour. Cyd was ambivalent about being back in Missoula. So much had happened there that was over, done, finished. The streets, the stores, the clubs and restaurants that were once so familiar now seemed like they belonged to someone else. The town was no longer hers. She was a stranger in a familiar place.

After they got there Tiffany came to life. Cyd wanted to try and reconnect with her before revealing her secret, so she helped her buy some new jeans and a couple of tops and actually got her talking and laughing. For the first time in a long time Tiffany felt like one of the girls and not like someone on the outside of her life looking in. She was still coughing her dry cough every few minutes, but the fever and the night sweats hadn't been so bad the night before, the diarrhea had subsided, her headache was gone and, for once, she had a little energy. *Maybe for a change the doctors got the medications right*, she thought.

She had once loved the ballet and tried very hard to live up to her mother's expectations. Mary was encouraged by her enthusiasm, her natural grace, her long strong body, and for a time thought her daughter might actually have the talent for the professional stage. That seemed like another lifetime ago. Tiffany no longer danced, no longer even thought about it. Much of her time was spent hating the boyfriend who had infected her—the cute football player who had slept with a hooker at a victory party so he could prove to his teammates that he wasn't gay. But she wasn't thinking about that today, this was a good day. She was out with her mother and Cyd and for a little while she could forget about who she was, what she had become and what her fate would ultimately be.

Seafaring memorabilia decorated the barnwood walls of the bistro where they ate. Their seafood salad lunch was served with a carafe of wine and when that was gone they ordered another. Cyd was biding her time; she knew that what she had to tell them would rock their world and she did not want to do it in a crowded restaurant. It was 2 PM by the time they left the cafe and headed home, drunk and happy.

Mary said she didn't feel like getting a DUI and asked Cyd if she would mind driving. Cyd was only too happy to oblige, Mary's driving made her crazy. The statuesque dancer with the graying hair tossed Cyd the keys and they went flying over her head and landed on the sidewalk.

"Oops," Mary said with a lighthearted laugh.

COYOTES TRAVEL IN PACKS AND are deadly hunters, lethal in their stalking skills. Typically one will jump out and startle the prey, spooking it so that it turns and runs straight into the waiting jaws of the others.

And that was how it happened.

Cyd followed Highway 93 north from Missoula through the 1.3 million acre Flathead Reservation, turning west at the town of Ronan onto Route 211. The deserted asphalt turned to gravel after they crossed the bridge over the river. A mile farther on, with nothing around but empty land, Cyd pulled over to the side of the road. Mary asked her why she had stopped and Cyd began telling them about the Cannastar.

Mary's screams of joy could be heard up and down the rural road. Then mother and daughter were peppering Cyd with questions, weeping with happiness at her replies.

Cyd kept trying to tell them that Cannastar was still experimental and that there was a chance it wouldn't work, but Mary and Tiffany were having none of it, especially after learning about Cyd and Otis's success with curing their own cancer. Cyd didn't tell them about the seeds or their dilemma over where and how to grow them. Her problems were her business and she felt a strong need to keep that part secret.

While they were talking a police car came up from behind and stopped. The occupants of the Rover didn't notice so the cruiser crawled around in front of them, its tires crunching gravel…and stopped again, blocking their way, hitting its siren one time to get their attention. The low moan scared the hell out of them.

The officer got out of the car and they giggled like schoolgirls. He walked toward them, hand on the butt of his holstered revolver, cigarette dangling from his lips, and their smiles faded. Cyd noticed that his uniform didn't quite fit right—the shirt was too big at the neck, the sleeves and pants too short. Then she saw the pockmarked face, the dead eyes, and she froze.

Back down the road a few miles an esteemed officer of the chronically understaffed Flathead Tribal Police Department lay dead behind some rocks wearing only his shorts and an undershirt, his limbs twisted and contorted in ways unnatural to a living body.

The uniformed policeman rapped on Cyd's window with his knuckles and she jumped, letting out a squeal. He rapped again, harder this time. On the back of his hand she saw the tattoo of a cross.

"Ma'am, would you please step out of the car."

Cyd jammed the Rover into reverse and floored it, throwing gravel as she rocketed backward down the road. When she was in the clear she slammed it into drive, cranked the wheel hard and spun a donut. The car fishtailed back the way it had come. The officer drew his gun and took careful aim…before jerking the barrel up again without firing. His orders were to kidnap, not to kill. He turned and ran for his car.

Cyd drove like a madwoman, trying to reach the main road where there might be some traffic and somebody to help. Mary and Tiffany were screaming, but Cyd didn't hear. All she could feel was raging anger. She rounded a curve going eighty miles an hour, wheels clawing for traction, almost going in a ditch before pulling it out at the last second. Up ahead was the bridge where the asphalt started. Two cars were parked across the road, blocking her path. She slammed on the brakes. The heavy four-wheel-drive vehicle skidded wildly on the gravel and looked like it was going to broadside the roadblock before coming to a halt at a sideways angle inches from the other cars. Men wearing ski masks and waving weapons swarmed the Land Rover.

IT WAS A LITTLE AFTER 6 PM by the time Clarence and Alex realized something was wrong. Clarence had been trying to reach Mary and Tiffany on their cell phones for the last two hours, but there was no answer. He tried one more time, then pulled out his laptop computer and turned it on, bringing up a program that he helped devolop for the military to track their top secret special ops missions.

Alex watched anxiously. "What is that?"

"It's like OnStar or LoJack only more sophisticated. It works anywhere in the world, no matter how remote. All my vehicles have it." He was punching keys, concentrating on the screen. "Gotcha!" he said, pointing at a red dot on a digital map. "They're in Polson. The car isn't moving."

"Where's Polson?"

"North of here about thirty miles."

"I thought they were going to Missoula. Isn't that south?"

"Maybe they changed their minds. Maybe they got a flat or the car broke down or something..."

They both wanted to believe that, but neither of them did.

Minutes later they were barreling down Clarence's driveway in his white Bentley and a few minutes after that they were crossing the river, speeding past the place where the kidnapper's cars had blocked the road. There was no sign of the struggle that had taken place there earlier.

It took them half an hour to reach the south shore of Flathead Lake. They entered the town of Polson with Clarence repeatedly glancing at the laptop on the console between them that showed the route his wife's car had taken. They pulled into the Safeway parking lot and saw Mary's Land Rover sitting off by itself in a dark corner. Clarence rocketed across the deserted lot, screeching to a halt beside the car and jumping out. A dog barked in the night.

Clarence jerked open the Rover's driver-side door and stuck his head in, the smell of new leather filling his nostrils. The car was empty. He slid behind the wheel and found the keys in the ignition. Alex got in the other side to look around. There were scuff marks all over the seats and dash. The women had been hauled kicking and screaming from the car, that much was clear. Clarence's cell phone rang, startling them both. The caller ID said it was Mary.

"Hello-hello? Mary, thank God! Where are you?"

A zombie voice: "Give us what they dug up in the mountains that the scientist hid there and you get the women back. Wild Horse Island. Skeeko Bay. Seven o'clock tomorrow morning."

"Who is this?" Clarence shouted. "Let me speak to my wife!"

"Any tricks or police and the bitches is history."

There was a click and the phone went dead.

Clarence turned to Alex with a panicked look.

EARLIER THAT AFTERNOON JESSE LONGBOW made a call to another number on Mary's cell.

"Tagged and bagged," the cowboy with the tattooed hand said. "We got three all together. What do you want us to do with the other two?" Silence as he listened. "It was the whole package or nothin'. We even got their car; it's a nice one, too." The angry yelling on the other end of the line made his ear red. "Sorry, boss. I didn't think..." He listened contritely as further instructions were given. "Yes sir, whatever you say sir," he said and hung up.

ALEX SAT WITH CLARENCE IN the abandoned Land Rover as wave after wave of fear washed through him. And with the fear came words, terrible words, telling him Cyd was going to die, that he would never see her again. He knew it was his fear talking, but he let it have its say. Then when it was done, when it had worn itself out flailing its arms in his face...he told it to fuck off.

"Where the hell is this Wild Horse Island?" he said. An urgent calm had settled over him, the same calm he felt in the emergency room when someone's life was in his hands and hanging by a thread.

Clarence pointed north up the lake. "A few miles that way."

"How do we get there?"

"The tribe keeps a couple of boats in the water year-round down at the marina," he said in a trembling voice. "We can use one of them."

They discussed calling the police and decided it was too much of a risk. *Any tricks or police and the bitches is history,* the caller had said.

"We need to go back to the house, get the saddlebags and tomorrow morning make the exchange," Clarence said.

"Cyd would sooner die than lose those seeds," Alex lamented.

"My wife and daughter are going to die if we don't cooperate."

"We'll cooperate," Alex said. "Then we'll see."

THE 24-FOOT PONTOON BOAT WAS basically a platform on floats with a canvas awning, plush seats and 18 cup holders. Alex threw off the dock lines and Clarence backed out of the slip, jamming the throttle forward when he was clear of the dock. The outboard motor screamed to life. It was 6:30 AM.

After receiving the phone call in the Safeway parking lot in Polson they had rushed back to Clarence's house, retrieved the saddlebags from the safe and returned to the marina on the south shore of Flathead Lake before dawn. Now as they sped across the lake, the faint shape of Wild Horse Island loomed darkly before them, its two thousand acres teeming with bighorn sheep, mule deer, songbirds, waterfowl, bald eagles, falcons and yes, three wild horses. The high whine of the outboard shattered the stillness of the freezing mist that lay on the water and the twin aluminum hulls left a wide, flat, foaming wake.

Clarence guided the boat into Skeeko Bay as Alex scanned the darkness.

"The irony," Clarence said in an effort to remain calm, "is that the Salish people used to pasture their horses out here to keep them from being stolen by other tribes. Now we come to this place to get back what was stolen from us."

"You got that right," Alex said.

They had been on the water twenty minutes when Clarence slid the pontoons up onto the sand and killed the motor. They looked up and down the shoreline in the early light. The beach was cold and deserted. They shivered impatiently.

Clarence poured coffee from a thermos Lupe had made for them before they left the house, offering some to Alex who shook his head and drank instead from a thermos of Cannastar he had brought to keep the pain in his back at bay. Clarence looked down distastefully at his coffee, tossed it out with a flick of his wrist and hastily screwed the cup back on the thermos. Nothing tasted good this morning.

Alex checked his watch. It was 7:05 AM. *They aren't coming,* he thought, then cocked his head at the faint sound of an inboard engine that was closing fast. The sound grew to a thunder as a fast speedboat rounded the point and headed straight toward them.

"Lock n' load," Alex said.

Clarence picked up the saddlebags that lay on the seat between them. Alex checked the rifles he had taken off their saddles and hidden under the seat cushions. Under another cushion were two antique revolvers, fully loaded, that Clarence was hoping he wouldn't have to use.

The speedboat landed fifty yards up the beach. There were six people on board: three armed men wearing cowboy hats and ski masks and three women who were bound and gagged with plastic garbage bags over their heads that were taped around their waists with duct tape. The prisoners were hauled roughly out of the boat and made to kneel in the sand. Faint moans and cries could be heard coming from inside the air-starved bags.

Alex and Clarence jumped from the pontoon boat and started up the beach. Jesse Longbow had the bottom of his ski mask pulled up over his nose so he could smoke. He took the cigarette out of his mouth, held up a hand and shouted for them to stay where they were. Clarence raised the saddlebags, offering them up with outstretched arms.

Longbow left one of his men to guard the women on the beach and brought the other one with him as he approached, striding up and snatching the saddlebags out of Clarence's hands. He dropped to his haunches, unfastened the buckles, opened a flap and yanked out one of the heavy leather pouches.

"You have the seeds, now give us the women," Alex demanded.

"Please…" Clarence said. "We've done as you asked."

The cowboy flicked his cigarette away and untied the knot in the leather string that bound the top of the pouch. Alex recognized the tattoo on the back of his hand from Cyd's description. He thought of that hand blackening her eye and splitting her lip and had to resist the urge to lunge at him and rip his throat out.

Longbow got the pouch open and poured out a handful of seeds in his hand.

Alex's eyes widened and his mouth went dry.

The seeds were not the tiny rainbow-colored ones from the Cannastar plant, they were beans!—black beans, red beans, pinto beans, white beans, Anasazi beans and lentils. Longbow put a few in his mouth, bit down and spat them out in disgust.

"Soup beans!" he snarled, drawing a hunting knife and slitting open the other pouches. Alex and Clarence watched in horror as more soup beans spilled out. Longbow looked up with a murderous smile. "Is this all they mean to you, your women?"

Alex's mind was racing. "That's it, that's all we found out there," he said hastily. "They might look like soup beans to you, but they're not…they have special qualities, special properties…believe me." He knew it was lame, but it was all he could think of to say.

"Here's what I believe," Longbow said in a barely audible whisper. "I believe you two just made a big mistake." He came to his feet and started back up the beach with the other man following close behind.

The third masked cowboy, the one guarding the women, raised his gun and pointed it at Alex and Clarence as his two companions headed for the speedboat and got in. He then hauled the women to their feet and began pushing them toward the boat.

Longbow held up his hand to stop him. "Leave them on the beach!" he ordered.

For a fleeting moment Alex had the wild hope they were going to leave the women behind until Longbow picked up an automatic weapon and opened fire. The bullets cut the three women in half. Their hooded bodies fell dead in the sand, blood pouring from the holes in the plastic bags.

"Let that be a warning!" Longbow shouted as the third man dove in the boat and they backed off the beach. The engine roared and the craft went flying across the water and disappeared around the point.

It was the longest fifty yards Alex ever ran. Stunned and horrified, he fell to his knees beside the bloody corpses, crying out as he tore frantically at the garbage sacks.

"Oh no...oh no...oh no," Clarence wailed as he dropped down beside him, clawing at the tape.

Then they were staring down without comprehension, unable to believe their eyes. The lifeless faces of three dead women looked up at them—the faces of three Mexican women they had never seen before in their lives. Alex's mouth worked open and closed but nothing came out. Clarence lowered his head, sobbing into his hands. Alex began checking the bodies for a pulse, moving as if in a dream, gently closing their eyes as he went. Then he fell back on his heels gasping for air and began to tremble. He felt like he was going to throw up.

In his grief Clarence said, "They're dead, that's what it means—Mary, Tiffany, Cyd—they're gone. If they were still alive they wouldn't have tried to fool us with these poor women."

Alex wasn't so sure. He had seen a lot of death in the E.R.; seen how often people went into denial claiming their loved one was somehow still alive when he had just told them they were gone. He wasn't in denial; he knew Cyd was still breathing. He couldn't explain it, but he could feel her. She was alive.

"I don't believe that," he said. "It's not true."

"You don't want to admit it," Clarence said. "Neither do I. Oh God…"

"It's a fear tactic," Alex said with growing conviction. "I saw it in the military and I saw the gang bangers in L.A. do it. It's what sadists do to break your spirit and get you to do what they want. If the exchange didn't work out, their plan was to scare us to death so the next time we'd hand over the real thing. This was a warning, I'm sure of it."

"Is it true…is it possible, do you think?"

"Tattoo Hand even said it, remember? He said, *Let that be a warning!* They plan on killing them all right, but not before they get what they came for."

"So where are the seeds?"

Alex shook his head. He didn't have a clue and that scared the hell out of him.

THE THREE KIDNAPPERS TRAVELED A long distance up the lake, their speedboat a scalpel slicing open the mirrored surface of the water…finally idling into the tiny tree-choked cove they had left from earlier that morning. Tying up to a dock, they scrambled out of the boat and started up a narrow path that led into the woods.

ALEX AND CLARENCE TOOK THE pontoon boat back to the marina, tied it up and headed for the car.

Clarence sat down heavily in the passenger seat of the Bentley and told Alex to drive. Alex got behind the wheel, but didn't start the engine. Not knowing where to go or what to do next was burning holes in his stomach. Clarence opened his laptop and began working the keyboard. Alex asked him what he was doing.

"Grasping at straws probably, but I want to see where they went yesterday and what stops they made." He turned the computer screen so Alex could see, explaining that his tracking system had a memory log and that he was rewinding it.

A road map of the area took up most of the screen. On it was a moving red line that tracked the Land Rover's progress along its route. The curser could be moved up or down to move the location of the Rover forward or back. Running down the left of the screen was a log that indicated the exact speed, time and location of the car at any point of the trip along the red line.

Clarence adjusted his reading glasses. "Here they are leaving Missoula at 2:04 PM," he said. "Here they turn onto Route 211 off of 93 and here they cross the river. Right after they cross the bridge they stop, you see here? That was at 2:40. They're stationary for six minutes and then they turn around. They go back to the bridge, but they're being chased. The Rover is doing over eighty miles an hour at this point, see that?" Alex watched with growing interest. "They stop again at the bridge and they're there for twelve minutes. Then they're moving again…going back to 93 and heading north. At 3:10 they go through Pablo and ten minutes later they're in Polson, but they don't stop there. They continue on, look here…" The red line went through Polson and continued around the lake, following the narrow twisting road. "They go another 18 miles until they come to this spot where they turn off the main road and go cross-country and finally stop…right here." The map indicated a remote location in the trees on a large tract of private land along the east side of the lake. "The Rover stays there for 16 minutes and then they drive it back to Polson. They abandoned it at 4:27pm in the place where we found it last night."

"That's it then," Alex said, pointing excitedly at the isolated location in the woods by the Lake. "That's where they are. They dropped the women off, probably left somebody there to guard them, and brought the Land Rover back to Polson. A second car must have picked them up from there."

Clarence motioned for Alex to drive. "Go, go, go!" he said anxiously. "I'll call the police and tell them to meet us there."

Alex started the engine and careened out of the marina parking lot.

A green four-door Chevy sedan driven by Jesse Longbow passed through Polson heading south just as the Bentley left the marina to head north. Alex and Clarence missed seeing Cyd riding in the front seat of the Chevy by less than a minute.

When Clarence called the tribal police on his cell phone to tell them about the abduction he told them where they were going and why. He also told him about the three dead bodies they had carefully covered with beach towels from the pontoon boat and left out on the island. The officer said he would see to the bodies, that he would report the kidnapping to the FBI in Missoula, but that his own men were at least an hour away, maybe more, and not to do anything until they got there. He said the reason they were so busy this morning was that one of their officers had just been found murdered out on Route 93.

RETURNING EMPTY-HANDED FROM WILD Horse Island, the trio of kidnappers followed the path through the woods until it came to a rundown summer cabin. The walls of the cabin were sheeted in delaminating plywood and insulated with wadded up newspaper from 70 years ago. It sat at the end of a rutted dirt road, buried in the trees, its rusted metal roof covered in snow and pine needles. In front of the house were the two Chevys, one green and one tan, used to barricade the road when the women were kidnapped. An outhouse sat behind the cabin on the edge of a cliff.

Inside the cabin, in a freezing bedroom with peeling yellowed wallpaper and bad smells, Cyd, Mary and Tiffany lay bound together on a sagging bed. Tiffany could not stop coughing. Her lips were cracked and blistered, her nose was running and she was burning up with fever. Mary was more frightened for her daughter than she was for herself.

The fourth kidnapper, the one left behind to guard the women, was named Tad. He was the smallest of the four and wore an enormous trophy buckle for bull riding that he didn't win. He opened the bedroom door to check on his prisoners, then closed it again as his three companions came storming in from outside. One look at their faces told him that things had not gone well.

The four cowboys stood crowded together in the small outer room of the cabin, a room that served as kitchen, dining room and living room all in one. The furniture consisted of a chrome legged Formica table with two plastic covered chairs to match, plus a sofa and arm chair with the stuffing coming out of the arms. Bookshelves laden with rows of dog-eared copies of Reader's Digest, carefully arranged by date, lined the walls and dozens of beat up VCRs were piled up on a dusty video player that was hooked to a TV with aluminum foil on the rabbit ears. A small fire burned in a wood stove, the smoke seeping into the room through rusted pinholes in a chimney pipe that ran through the ceiling.

Jesse Longbow flicked his cigarette into the kitchen sink, drew his hunting knife from the sheath on his belt and went straight for the bedroom. The three women screamed in unison as the door burst open. Longbow bent over the bed and cut Cyd free with a single slice of his knife, hauling her out into the living room by the hair and flinging her onto the sofa.

Cyd sat up defiantly rubbing at her wrists. "How was the trip?" she said. "You're home early."

Longbow smiled with empty eyes. "Who put the beans in them sacks? Was it you?" Cyd glared back at him. "You don't hardly seem surprised. It was you, all right."

She realized Alex and Clarence must have offered the saddle-bags up as ransom. A chill went through her and suddenly she was terrified that she might have gotten them killed.

"What happened?" she demanded. "What have you done to them?"

"I taught them a lesson," Longbow laughed. "One I'm guessing they won't soon forget."

Cyd lunged at him, lashing out with her nails and gouging his cheeks. "Fucking psycho!" she screamed.

Tad stepped up and backhanded her across the face. He had to stand on tiptoe to do it. The blow drove her back onto the sofa. Tad giggled as Cyd rubbed her jaw.

Longbow went on as if nothing had happened, blood trickling from the scratches on his face. "Listen to me carefully because I'm only going to say this once. Whatever was supposed to be in those bags, you know where it is. You tell me now or I start killing your friends." Cyd spat at him. "Bring me out one of them bitches," he shouted, turning to the two men who had been with him in the boat. The cowboy with the bald head and shaggy red beard was named Homer and the other, Louie, had a bulbous pitted nose, puffy eyes and two fingers missing from his left hand. "Move!"

Startled, the two men scurried into the bedroom and brought Tiffany out. Slender and frail, she squirmed and struggled with the last of her strength. Mary started to scream. They slammed the door on her, but she went on screaming, the sound muffled by the door.

"Leave her alone," Cyd cried. "She's sick. She needs her medication or she's going to die!"

Longbow grabbed Tiffany's hair, jerked her head back and laid the blade of his knife across her throat, pressing it into her sallow skin. "Then why don't I just put her out of her misery?"

"No wait! Stop!" Cyd said. "I hid the seeds. I can't tell you where, I have to show you. You'll never find them on your own"

"Not good enough." Blood began to trickle down Tiffany's neck.

Cyd was frantic. "I mean it. I'll show you. Otherwise, you'll never find them."

Longbow shoved Tiffany aside and sent her sprawling across the floor. She landed huddled and whimpering in a corner. "All right then," he growled. "Your friends stay here. If you're lying, they're dead. You got that? Tad, you're coming with me."

Turning to Homer and Louie, he added, "If we're not back by dark you two can have your fun with them before you kill them."

They looked at each other and beamed, revealing enough decay to put a dentist's kids through college. They didn't know what the rest of this was all about, but rape was something that had been on their minds ever since they grabbed the women up at the river.

The pint-sized cowboy put his face close to Cyd's. "I'm a trick rider by profession," Tad giggled. "How about on the way if I do some tricks on you?"

Cyd flared. "You lay one hand on my friends and I'm telling you nothing!"

"Fair enough," Longbow said, glaring at Homer and Louie and drawing his finger along the edge of his knife until a thin line of blood appeared on his skin. "Either of these low-lifes rapes your ladies before we get back and I'll cut their balls off myself. Nice and slow like." He smiled and licked the blood off his finger. "Think the two of you can remember that or should I write it down?"

Wide-eyed and fearful, they bobbed their heads up and down like bobble-head dolls.

Cyd was shoved out the front door and made to sit in the passenger seat of the green Chevy. Tad got in the rear, Longbow slid behind the wheel of the sedan and took off up the dirt road bouncing over the ruts. Tad sat in back pointing a large caliber revolver at the back of Cyd's seat, giggling every time the car hit a pothole and bounced him in air. The gun looked enormous in his child-sized hand.

CLARENCE LOOKED DOWN AT HIS computer and motioned for Alex to turn left off of Route 35 onto a gravel road. The Bentley's tires vibrated over a cattle guard, passing a faded sign nailed to a broken-down fence that read:

SEELEY LAND & CATTLE CO.
PRIVATE PROPERTY
NO HUNTING

Recent tire tracks leading to and from the paved road made dark muddy lines in the snow that covered the ranch road. They followed the lines, the road growing progressively worse the farther they went. Eventually they came to a terrible looking dirt road that was nothing more than two ruts leading off downhill to the right. The tire tracks they had been following turned right at the ruts and Clarence motioned for Alex to follow. The elegant Bentley bottomed out several times going down the same slippery road that Longbow had bounced up in the Chevy sedan less than half an hour earlier.

They reached the bottom of the hill and the cabin came into view through the trees, a thin line of smoke coming from the chimney. A tan sedan, the second car used in the kidnapping, was parked in front of the cabin. Alex coasted silently to a stop. Clarence pointed at the flashing target on his computer screen that indicated they had arrived at their destination.

Alex backed the white Bentley up the road to a flat spot and nosed it into the trees where it was all but invisible among the snow covered branches. They got out and softly closed the doors behind them. Clarence had his revolvers stuck in his waist band, Alex carried a rifle. They crept closer, their hearts racing. Alex looked over at Clarence and hardly recognized him. The Salish Indian with the pony tail had gone into a crouch and was moving soundlessly through the trees. He raised his hand and Alex froze. Peering through a screen of branches, they saw one of the kidnappers come out of the cabin and go around back to the outhouse. He had a shaggy beard, carried a rifle in one hand and a Reader's Digest in the other.

"What now?" Alex whispered.

Clarence motioned for Alex to go down to the house. "Stand at the corner and watch the door," he said. "Wait for me to make the first move. If anyone comes out, kill him. Can you do that, doctor?"

Alex quickly levered a shell into the chamber of his rifle, grim and determined. "You better believe it," he said.

They snuck down to the house. Alex pressed himself against the wall of the shack. An image flashed in his mind of watching a soldier in Fallujah kick open the door to a mud hut and seeing it blow his leg off. Inside the cabin he could hear the faint sounds of women crying and he softly flicked off the safety on his rifle.

Clarence slipped past him and continued on in a crouch until he reached the outhouse. From there he carefully placed his hands on the rotten wood, planted his feet and gathered his considerable strength under him. And then he made a sound that Alex had never heard before in his life and hoped he would never hear again. It wasn't Indian, it wasn't animal and it certainly wasn't human. It was the way Clarence had always imagined the real Bigfoot would sound if he ever met the monster in person. The blubbering bellow was so terrifying that Alex winced in pain.

Inside the outhouse Homer was tearing pages out of the Reader's Digest and wadding them up so they would be ready for use when he needed them. When he heard the inhuman howl coming from the other side of the wall his bowels let go all at once and he lurched forward, grabbing at his pants. At the same time Clarence gave a mighty heave, lifted the outhouse off its foundation and sent it rolling down the hill.

Louie, the kidnapper inside the cabin guarding the women, heard the sound Clarence made and for a horrifying moment thought it was the bear that had chased him and Jesse up the tree. Then he heard Homer's God-awful screams as the outhouse rolled down the hill and crashed onto the rocks below, splintering into a thousand pieces.

At the bottom of the cliff Homer lay wedged between the rocks, impaled on a splintered piece of wood that was sticking through his chest, drowning in his own blood.

Alex was waiting beside the cabin, the butt of his gun pressed to his cheek, as Louie came bolting out the door, waving his rifle like he was being chased. Alex sighted down the barrel...and squeezed. It was a clean shot between the eyes and the kidnapper was dead before he hit the ground.

The women inside were screaming. Clarence came running around the corner of the house with both pistols drawn and they burst into the living room together. The screams were coming from the bedroom. They rushed the door, banging it open.

Moments later Clarence was holding his sobbing family in his arms, trying to comfort them, crying along with them. Alex was frightened. He didn't see Cyd anywhere. He put a hand on Mary's shoulder, trying to ask her where she was.

Mary Bigfoot, her gray hair in tangles, turned from Clarence and flung her arms around Alex's neck. "Oh, thank you. Thank you, thank you, thank you. You saved my daughter's life!"

"Mary, where's Cyd? What have they done with her?"

Sobbing softly, Mary said the other kidnappers had taken her. "She was going to show them something, I don't know what. She said they couldn't find it without her. I think she was buying us time is all, trying to keep them from killing us. It had to do with beans or seeds or something. Does that make any sense?"

Alex had a flash, one of his waking dreams: Cyd was coming out of a white cabana beside a swimming pool with steam rising all around. Robert was intercepting her beside the pool, standing too close, speaking urgently...

He saw Tiffany struggling to sit up and bent down to give her a quick field exam—a procedure he had done many times before; one that required as much intuition as it did medical knowledge. He took her pulse, looked into her red-rimmed eyes, had her stick out her spotted tongue, felt her forehead and put his ear to her chest so he could listen to her ragged breath. He kissed the top of her head and stood up.

"She has pneumonia," he said. "You have to get her to a hospital immediately." He helped Tiffany to her feet, handed her to her mother, then turned to Clarence. "I know where they've taken Cyd. You need to stay with your family. I'm going to borrow that other car out front if I can find the keys."

"Where are you going?" Clarence asked.

"Back to your place."

"You think that's where they went?"

"I know that's where they went."

"I'll make a call and see if I can't get you some help."

Alex paused on his way out the door. "Out of curiosity, that sound you made back there. What did it do to the guy in the outhouse?"

"It made him fall off the cliff."

"While he was still inside that thing?"

Clarence nodded gravely.

"Shitty way to go."

CHAPTER 9

Cowboys and Indians

Longbow looked down at the Chevy's gas gauge and saw that he was almost out of fuel. He pulled into Joe's Jiffy Stop on the south end of Pablo just across the street from the Salish Kootenai College campus, lit a fresh cigarette, left the engine running and got out of the car. Tad stayed in the back seat pointing his gun at the seat in front of him. Cyd searched the gas station frantically with her eyes for any sign of help.

A '99 Ford pickup pulled into the Jiffy Stop and stopped facing the opposite direction on the other side of the gas island where the Chevy was parked. Tachini Pete got out of the truck, unscrewed his gas cap, swiped his card, inserted the nozzle and put the handle on automatic. He was good looking enough to be Robert Bigfoot's younger brother; a big, athletic engineering student with an engaging smile, shoulder-length hair and an academic scholarship to the college across the street. He'd been offered a football scholarship to play for the University of Montana Grizzlies but had to turn it down because of a bad knee. He smiled politely at the good-looking girl who was leaning forward, staring across the seat of the Chevy at him, then averted his eyes when he saw that she looked a little crazed. He noticed that the Chevy engine was running and that the guy pumping gas was smoking. He politely cleared his throat.

"Dude," Tachini said amiably, "how about putting out that cigarette and switching off your engine?"

Longbow ignored him and continued to pump his gas, the lighted cigarette hanging loosely from his mouth.

"Read the sign, okay?" Tachini said. "It says 'Turn off your engine' and 'No smoking'. You trying to get us all killed?"

Longbow looked up slowly and smiled. A long ash fell off his cigarette.

Tachini made a gesture with upturned palms and raised eyebrows that said *Well*? *I'm waiting.*

Longbow's smile widened.

"You think this is funny?" Tachini said, turning away in disgust and returning his nozzle to the pump so he could get the hell out of there. "Asshole."

"Hey?" Longbow said. Tachini turned. Longbow took the cigarette out of his mouth, fingered it...and flicked it in Tachini's face. The sparks burnt the boy badly and he howled in pain. "Happy now?"

Tachini lost his temper, bunched his fists and leapt across the island. Longbow took a wild swing at him. Tachini ducked and buried a fist in the smoker's stomach. Longbow gasped and fell to his knees, unable to breathe.

From inside the Chevy Cyd screamed, jerked open the door and ran around the car. Tad made a grab for her over the top of the seat but didn't even come close.

"I'M BEING KIDNAPPED! HELP ME!"

It took Tachini a second to realize what was happening. He got to his truck just in time to open the door so Cyd could dive inside. "Get in!" he yelled, glancing over his shoulder. "Hurry up!"

Cyd scrambled across the console and into the passenger seat. "They've got guns!" she shouted.

Tachini jumped in and fumbled with the ignition. Tad was running around the front of the Chevy to get a clear shot. Tachini's truck roared to life and rocketed away from the pump, tires smoking and burning rubber.

Tad leveled his gun at the back of the retreating truck and was about to fire when Longbow, doubled over in pain and gasping for air, batted his hand down.

"Hold up! We need her alive!" he wheezed, lurching into the driver's seat of the Chevy. He jammed the car in gear and took out after the truck. Tad had to run and jump through the window to keep from being left behind.

"You all right?" Tachini yelled, almost losing control of the truck as he hung a left onto Division Street and accelerated down the empty narrow two lane road.

"Better than I was," Cyd smiled.

Tachini looked over at her and grinned excitedly, thinking she looked better up close than she did at a distance. "Better put your seat belt on," he said, glancing in his rearview mirror, "this could get a little hairy."

"Appreciate the lift," she said, fumbling with her belt.

"Anytime, ma'am. Where would you like me to drop you?"

"How about that police station up there?"

They were coming up on the Tribal Law & Order station house doing about ninety with Longbow's Chevy closing fast. No squad cars were in the small police station lot at the moment; everyone was out dealing with the murder and the kidnapping. Tachini desperately slammed on his brakes to turn in and the truck began fishtailing all over the road. The Chevy caught the truck's rear bumper, rammed it and sent it into a slide. The pickup skidded off the road, hit the embankment and rolled, flipping end over end twice before coming to rest on its roof with gas spilling from its tank.

Cyd hung upside down inside the battered truck. She opened her eyes and through the broken window saw Longbow's black cowboy boots walking toward her. Tachini hung unconscious from his seatbelt on the other side of the cab.

Cyd was covered in cuts. She shook her head, trying to clear it. Longbow reached inside, a fresh cigarette hanging from his mouth, and unceremoniously sliced her seatbelt in half with his knife. She dropped hard onto the roof of the truck and he hauled her out through the window.

Tad rushed up to take her off his hands, twisting Cyd's arm behind her and frog-marching her back to the Chevy where he stuffed her kicking and screaming into the front seat. Longbow took one last, long drag off his cigarette as he studied the wreckage. His expression was dull and lifeless as he pealed the cigarette off his lip, held it between his thumb and middle finger and flicked it into the spilling gas. The fuel exploded with a whoosh, engulfing the truck in flames.

Cyd could hear Tachini's screams coming from inside the truck as the Chevy sped away. She looked back, tears streaming down and stinging the cuts on her face, crying out in devastation as the pickup was consumed by a giant fireball and a thick plume of black smoke rose into the sky.

BEHIND THE UPSCALE SUBDIVISION OF brick homes that Alex and Cyd had ridden their horses through when they first arrived at Clarence's house was a dirt fire-road that ran between the houses and the desolate rock and weed-infested land beyond. Longbow's green Chevy bounced along the dirt road, circling the subdivision until it came to a stop in back of the barren knoll where the modern cubes of Bigfoot's home stood out against a gray winter sky.

Tad prodded Cyd out of the car and she led her two kidnappers up the backside of the knoll. Her mind was racing with ways to avoid having to give up the seeds, but she kept coming back to the same conclusion: it was either this or get Mary and Tiffany killed. She was furious with herself for having put them in this situation.

Behind the main house was the swimming pool and behind that was the white pool house which was the first structure they came to coming up the back of the hill. Cyd led the way around to the front of the cabana, casting a desperate glance in the direction of the main house in the hope of seeing someone inside. Not even Lupe was around; the place was dead quiet.

Longbow and Tad followed Cyd into the cabana through one of the two sets of glass French doors. The heat was turned down to 50 and the place was crammed to the ceiling with summer things stored for the winter. A poker table and a pool table had plastic covers over them and dozens of seat cushions from the outdoor furniture were stacked on top in teetering rows. Dusty liquor bottles lined the glass shelves behind the bar. Round glass tables with holes in the center for umbrellas were pushed against one wall with a row of poolside loungers lined up in front of them. Balls and nets and blowup pool toys, slowly losing air, were piled on top of the loungers and tables. Along another wall rows of nested pool chairs were stacked in front of the showers and steam room.

Cyd hesitated, looking around, still trying to figure a way out of this.

"Quit stalling," Longbow growled.

Tad giggled, motioning with his gun for her to hurry it up.

She sighed and went over to the piles of outdoor seat cushions on the pool table, looking them up and down. Even

she couldn't remember which stack it was. Two days ago Cyd
had stood in this same place surveying the same cushions…

THEY HAD PUT THE SADDLEBAGS in Clarence's gun safe,
but Cyd couldn't shake the gnawing feeling that it wasn't a
secure hiding place; that if she left the seeds in there they
would lose them. Maybe it was just the paranoia she had lived
with for so long while protecting Maury's discovery, but at
the moment she didn't trust anybody. And if she was wrong
and moved the seeds and nothing bad happened, so what? No
harm done. The feeling wouldn't go away so that afternoon
while Alex was taking a nap and Clarence and Mary were out
with Tiffany somewhere, Cyd wandered through the empty
house looking for a better hiding place, eventually ending up
in the pool house.

She stood inside the lovely white cabana amid the piled
and crowded furniture wondering where she could hide
the seeds that nobody would think to look. She rejected the
showers, the boiler room—there weren't a lot of possibilities.
Then she saw the rows of stacked pool chairs and her eyes
moved to the waterproof seat cushions with the colorful floral
print covers that were stacked in uneven rows on top of the
pool table. She took one of the cushions down and studied it,
turning it over in her hands. A zipper ran along the back of
the cushion and around two of the corners. She opened the
zipper all the way, reached inside and pulled out the foam
rubber pad. Perfect!

Cyd walked briskly back to the house and entered Clarence's office. She went to the gun safe, punched in the
combination he had given them and removed the heavy
saddlebags. On her way back to the pool house she stopped

outside the kitchen, peering around the corner to see if anyone was inside.

The darkened kitchen was cool and still and spotless with everything in its place like one of those fancy kitchens in the glossy designer magazines. Lupe was the only live-in help; the rest of the staff lived elsewhere on the reservation. Cyd guessed that Mary had given the woman the day off after all the work she had done preparing and supervising Christmas day dinner yesterday.

Cyd opened the door to the big walk-in pantry and went inside, closing it behind her before switching on the light. She searched the stacks of built-in drawers until she found the one that contained the boxes of plastic bags, taking out one that said 'Gallon Zip-Lock Bags'.

She opened the saddlebags, removed one of the four large leather pouches and untied the rawhide string. Holding the plastic Zip-Lock open, she began pouring the tiny rainbow-colored seeds into it. Nervous about spilling even one seed, she felt like she was pouring gold dust. The Zip-Lock held about half of what was in the pouch and she took another from the box, filling it full as well, then repeated the process with the other three pouches until she had 8 one-gallon plastic bags bulging with Cannastar seed and four empty leather pouches.

She realized she needed to refill the pouches with some-thing and looked around. On one of the upper shelves she saw a neat row of glass canisters containing the soup beans that Lupe used to make her 7-bean soup. She pulled them down one by one and poured them into the leather pouches, tying off the tops when they were full and returning them to the saddlebags. The empty glass canisters she put back on the shelf.

Lupe's collection of reusable canvas shopping bags hung from a hook inside the door. Cyd took two of them down and filled them with the plastic bags of seed. She then left the shopping bags sitting on the pantry floor while she went back to the office to return the saddlebags to the safe. Returning minutes later to the pantry, she retrieved her two shopping bags and carried them out of the kitchen.

Struggling out the back door, down the steps and around the pool deck with a heavy shopping bag hanging from each hand, she waddled toward the cabana.

Once inside the pool house she started unzipping the removable seat covers and pulling out the foam rubber pads. Into each cushion cover she inserted two plastic Zip-Lock bags of Cannastar seed, flattening them out as best she could before rezipping the seat. Then she put the four cushions containing the seeds back in the stacks of regular cushions, slipping one each into the center of four different stacks. When she was done she tossed the four foam rubber seat pads and the two empty shopping bags into the boiler room and closed the door on them.

Coming out of the pool house she ran into Robert. He had been over at a friend's house watching football, but couldn't keep his mind off Cyd. All he could think about was getting her back. Seeing her yesterday at Christmas dinner with that tall skinny doctor, seeing how beautiful and feisty she was, made him realize what a mistake he'd made in breaking up with her. He came back to his parent's house to find her and tell her that he loved her.

And now she was telling him gently that she loved someone else and he was feeling like a fool.

TAD HAD BEEN EYEING THE pool table in the cabana ever since they came in. Finally he couldn't resist, brushed past

Cyd and threw off the piles of seat cushions that were stacked on top.

"Man, I always wanted one of these," he said, scattering the cushions. "How about a game of nine-ball, Jesse?"

"You guys are a couple of real geniuses," Cyd said.

"And why's that?" snarled Longbow, smacking Tad upside the head to get him to settle down.

"You didn't have to do that," Tad whined, rubbing his scalp.

Cyd bent in disgust and started searching through the scattered seat cushions that were now all over the floor. "Just keep that idiot away from me if you want me to find what I'm looking for," she said.

ALEX PULLED UP IN FRONT of Clarence's house in the tan sodan, got out carrying his rifle and ran to the door. It was locked. He started around the back following the jagged line of the jumbled cubes, eventually coming to the chain link gate to the pool area. To his relief it was unlocked. He opened the gate and went through. From there he could see the cabana on the far side of the swimming pool and the people moving around inside.

CYD FOUND ONE OF THE four seat cushions that contained the seeds and handed it to Longbow. He looked confused.

"Unzip it and we can all go home," she said.

The cowboy undid the zipper, jerked out one of the plastic bags, opened it and plunged a tattooed hand inside. Beautifully colored seeds sifted through his dirty fingers.

"This is it?" he scoffed. "This is what all the bullshit is about?"

"Pretty much," Cyd said. "What could a bunch of seeds be worth, right? Why don't you just give them back to me and we'll forget the whole thing."

He studied her while he lit a fresh cigarette off the stub of his old one. Suddenly, viciously, he drew his knife and started stabbing the cushions on the floor that Cyd hadn't searched yet.

"Stop that!" Cyd shouted.

Longbow smiled with tobacco stained teeth. "You saying there's more?"

"I might have missed a couple," Cyd admitted shakily. "Let me keep looking."

Alex was just outside the pool house doors now. He could hear them inside talking and thought if he could somehow get the kidnappers to come running out he might be able to pick them off one by one like he had done at the cabin. On impulse, he leaned his rifle against the building, picked up a landscaping stone from one of the flower beds, held the rock over his head like a big medicine ball...and heaved it through the French doors.

Tad wheeled and fired at the shattering glass. The bullet went wide and struck the wall. Longbow pulled his gun and they both started firing wildly. In their distraction they forgot about Cyd. She picked up a pool cue, crept forward and broke the fat part of the stick over the top of Tad's head. The tiny man crumpled in a heap. *Shit, I killed him,* she thought as she turned and ran for the French doors at the other end of the room. Longbow saw her, aimed, then spun back around as a second rock came crashing through the doors.

The last time the pool man was out to clean the pool he left a long poled leaf skimmer leaning against the wall of the cabana. Standing to one side, Alex grabbed it and started waving it frantically in front of the opening. Longbow saw something moving outside the door and emptied his gun at it.

Alex snatched up his rifle and sighted down the barrel as the other set of French doors flew open...and Cyd came running out!

Cyd saw Alex pointing his gun at her. "Don't...!" she screamed.

Alex exhaled, lowered his rifle and motioned frantically for her to run behind the cabana. She bolted around the corner of the building and he went the other way. They met breathlessly in the back, falling into each other's arms.

Alex knew it would only be a matter of seconds before Longbow was reloaded and running after them. He pointed two fingers at his eyes, then pointed left and right for her to help him watch the corners of the building. A second later Longbow appeared at the corner closest to him and then ducked back as Alex fired. The bullet struck the corner of the building and dug a gaping hole.

Below them was the barren hill. They were exposed with no place to hide and no place to run if Longbow came charging back around the corner and Alex couldn't drop him with the first shot.

Then from the bottom of the hill they heard the thunderous sound of roaring engines and blaring horns. Cyd and Alex looked in the direction of the noise and couldn't believe their eyes.

Stampeding up the knoll on all sides was an armada of pickup trucks overflowing with armed tribesmen. Over a hundred trucks were making the charge loaded with men standing in the beds waving guns and firing them in the air. It was an army, an invasion, an attack of wild-ass, kick-ass, drunk-ass Indians, charging the knoll from all directions. Clarence's son Robert stood in one of the truck beds leading the charge.

Alex smiled at Cyd with his crooked grin. "I was beginning to think we might have a problem here."

She laughed nervously as Longbow appeared again and fired. The bullet sounded like a mosquito whizzing past her head. Alex fired back and the cowboy turned and ran, shooting wildly at the advancing enemy.

Trucks were coming up the hill from all directions—Fords, Chevys, Dodges, GMCs, Toyotas, Nissans, Hummers, Mazdas and Suzukis of every size, age, color and description, turbo chargers screaming, tires throwing mud and gravel. The entire house was suddenly surrounded by a circular wall of pickups. Four hundred guns dismounted, leaping from the trucks with whoops and shouts as they stormed the house. They wore boots and jeans, plaid shirts, cowboy shirts, sports jerseys and baseball caps, but the effect was no less fearsome had it been war paint and feathers; this was one scary bunch.

They ran Longbow from one end of the compound to the other, flushing him out of first one place and then the next as they tightened the circle. Finally they had him cornered by the swimming pool. He ran up and down the pool deck like a snarling animal, pointing his gun this way and that...then stopped in his tracks with nowhere to turn, breathing hard, the circle of men closing in on him.

Robert stepped forward and advanced on the fugitive. The cowboy backed up, then stopped when the crowd of men behind him took a step forward. He grinned slowly, opened his mouth, inserted the muzzle of his gun...and pulled the trigger. There was a *click*, but nothing happened. The pistol was empty.

Robert reached out and with one finger pushed him in the pool. A whooping, cheering touchdown roar rose up from the pickup cavalry as he hit the water. The men around the pool howled with laughter as the angry kidnapper flailed his arms trying to stay afloat. Then Longbow discovered to his embarrassment that the pool was only 4 feet deep and this had the rescuers laughing so hard they were leaning on each other for support.

Just then Tad stumbled out of the pool house half blind, head reeling from where Cyd had split his skull. The crowd parted to let him through and he staggered drunkenly straight into the pool, wailing loudly and sputtering water as he surfaced. The crowd broke out in fresh convulsions of laughter watching him thrashing about.

Cyd and Alex were in a state of shock. They fell desperately into each other's arms. Tears of relief were streaming down her cheeks. It was over, it was actually over. They kissed...until an urgent question occurred to her and she broke away.

"How did you find me? How did all these men get here?"

"Ask Robert," Alex said. "I think he's trying to impress you."

Cyd went over to Robert who was standing nearby, stood on tiptoe and gave him a grateful kiss. "I'm impressed," she said.

Robert made a call on his cell to tell the police to come and get the outlaws they had captured in the pool. The dispatcher told him what he had told Clarence earlier in the day: It was going to be an hour or more before they could get there and not to do anything until they did. Robert said he wouldn't dream of making a move without them.

Cyd suddenly remembered that Mary and Tiffany were still in danger. Alex assured her that everything was all right, that they were safe. She wanted to know what had happened, but before he could tell her another fear occurred to her.

"We have to get the seeds out of the pool house," she said, low and urgent. "Otherwise, the police are going to show up and confiscate them for evidence. Too many people know about them already."

Alex nodded and they slipped away. The pickup truck crowd was busy keeping an eye on the prisoners in the swimming pool and congratulating themselves with handshakes and back slaps and didn't notice that Cyd and Alex were gone.

Cyd retrieved Lupe's shopping bags from the boiler room and scurried about loading them up with the bags of Cannastar seed while Alex called Clarence on the pool house telephone. Clarence picked up immediately. They were at the hospital in Kalispell. They had just gotten there and the doctors were still with Tiffany. All he knew was that she was alive and relatively stable. Alex told him what had happened and that he and Cyd were okay. Clarence was saying how relieved he was when Mary came on the line and asked to speak to Cyd.

The two women cried together happily as Mary told her what Alex and Clarence had done to rescue them. When Cyd hung up she was staring at Alex in a curious way.

"What?" Alex said.

"She said you saved their lives. And for the second time since I've known you, you saved mine."

"Three women got killed because I didn't have the seeds," he said. "Why weren't they in the safe?

"I moved them."

"What the hell for?"

"I had a bad feeling, okay? I was being cautious."

"Your feeling got three innocent Mexican women killed."

"And a fine young boy as well," she said sadly. "But if I hadn't done what I did, three other women you know would probably be dead instead. Not to mention the countless thousands of people who might get a chance to live now because the seeds didn't get lost."

Alex thought about what she said. It didn't make the murders any easier, but she was right. "If we can do some good with those seeds, if we can save some lives with them, then maybe it was worth it," he said.

"How's your back?" she asked, torn between loving him for what he'd done and hating him for being addicted to pain pills.

"Never better," he said.

"Don't lie to me."

"If you're offering, I could use a cup of tea."

Pale-eyed, freckle-faced and scratched up, she looked at him and smiled the way she had at Big Salmon Lake in the light of the campfire before she caught him taking the pills. It reminded him of how much he loved her.

"I think that can be arranged," she said.

THE NEXT MORNING CYD AND Alex brought a thermos of Cannastar tea to Tiffany at the hospital in Kalispell in the hope she'd be well enough to drink it. Clarence and Mary, who had been there all night, greeted them when they arrived. The antibiotics were helping, but Tiffany was still alternating between fever and chills. Alex examined her chart. As he'd feared, it was pneumocystis pneumonia—the worst kind.

It broke Cyd's heart to hear Tiffany cough and hear her troubled breathing. Clarence and Mary stood at the end of their daughter's bed watching anxiously and it broke Cyd's heart all over again to see the painful looks on their faces. "I can't promise anything," she said, unscrewing the top of the thermos and pouring out a cup of Cannastar, "but I'll try."

Cyd put her hand under the sick girl's head. "Tiffany, can you hear me?" She opened her eyes and managed a weak smile. Cyd raised her head and put the cup to her lips. "Drink this Tiff, it will make you better."

Cyd fed Tiffany the tea in tiny sips until she fell back exhausted onto the pillows. The tea in the cup was only half gone.

Just then an officious nurse came in and demanded to know what was going on.

"GET OUT!" Clarence commanded.

"I'm calling the doctor is what I'm doing," said the nurse, retreating in a huff.

Clarence put his arm around his wife. "Keep the faith, honey."

"Faith is all I've got left," Mary said. "How else could I stand here thinking a cold remedy is going to cure AIDS?"

"It's like putting your immune system on steroids," Cyd assured her. "If it cured me and cured my friend Otis, it can cure Tiffany."

"How much of it do I give her?" Mary asked.

"As much as she can drink for now. I'll keep making you fresh thermos bottles. I don't have that much with me because I didn't think we were going to be gone that long, but I have more at home that I can send you when I get back."

Mary took the cup from Cyd's hands and got Tiffany to take another sip.

TWO DAYS LATER TIFFANY'S CONDITION had improved to the extent that they could bring her home from the hospital. The doctors said she was making a remarkable recovery. Mary was beside herself with joy. It was New Year's Eve.

After Longbow was captured and they had retrieved the seeds from the pool house, they had put them back in

Clarence's gun safe until they could figure out what to do next. They were standing now with Clarence in front of his open safe discussing their options—or rather lack of options—when Mary walked in. She wanted to see these seeds that had almost gotten them killed and that were responsible for her daughter's rapid recovery. Cyd reached inside the safe, took out one of the Zip-Lock bags and handed it to her.

Mary looked down in amazement at the colorful bag of Cannastar seed. "So they're just seeds? You just plant them in the ground like any other seeds and they grow?"

"Except if we try to go in the farming business around here it's going to be like taking a stroll in a firefight with a target on our backs," Alex said.

"We stopped the kidnappers, but we didn't stop the people who are trying to stop us," Cyd explained. Mary gingerly handed the bag of seeds back to her. "The other problem is money," Cyd went on, returning the bag to the safe. "Even if we could find a place to do it, starting a Cannastar farm of any size is going to cost a small fortune. I can't even afford the mortgage on my ranch I'm so broke."

"And the longer we stay here, the more we put you in danger," Alex said. "We need to leave."

"You're my guests and you're not going anywhere," Mary said. "Nobody's going to intimidate me in my own home."

Clarence flushed at the thought of losing his wife again. "Have you forgotten what they did to you and our daughter and Cyd?"

"Who's 'they'?" Mary said. "Who are these people exactly?"

"The drug companies," Alex said. "Rxon in particular."

"I don't understand," Mary said.

"If Cannastar gets into the hands of the public, if people have access to it, then most of the drugs on the market are going to become obsolete," Alex said. "The only reason these drugs exist in the first place is because of illness and disease. If you take away the illness and disease, the drugs go away and that means the drug companies go away. These corporations are run by some of the richest, most powerful men on earth. Along with the rest of the medical community, they own the Congress and they own the government. The drug companies would start World War III before they let us put them out of business."

Mary was furious. "Are people really that vicious and destructive and vile? How could anyone be that self-serving and cruel?"

"Conscience doesn't have anything to do with it where money is concerned," Alex said. "Most of the ways corporations make money today used to be illegal. And for good reason."

"So what do we do now?" Mary said.

Cyd put a comforting arm around her shoulders. "We make sure that Tiffany gets well, that's what we do."

Mary thought a moment. "We'll pay for it!" she said suddenly.

Clarence was perplexed. "Pay for what?"

"Everything," Mary said excitedly. "If it's going to make Tiffany well, if it's going to help the other Tiffanys out there, we'll give you all the money you need. You figure out what to do and how to do it and we'll foot the bill." Clarence cleared his throat. Without looking at her husband, Mary said firmly, "Isn't that right, dear?"

"Yes…of course," said the soft spoken man who could roar like a Bigfoot, thinking out loud. "Anything. We have more than we can spend, more than I can count, actually…It keeps accumulating all the time." The enormity of what he might be able to accomplish with his money was just beginning to dawn on him. This could be the greatest public service project he'd ever done. He always wondered why he had gotten so rich. He thought it was so he could do good for his people, but maybe it was more than that—maybe it was a lot more. "This...this could really be something," he said enthusiastically. "Something wonderful..."

"It's settled then," Mary said.

Cyd hugged Mary with tears in her eyes, then turned and flung her arms around Clarence's neck. The gesture startled him. She kissed his cheek and it unnerved him even more.

Alex shook both their hands. "When you folks step up, you really step up," he said admiringly. "You do realize we could spend an awful lot of your money and accomplish nothing."

"We'll take that chance," Clarence said.

Robert had come in and was leaning casually against the door sill listening to the conversation. "Atta boy, Pop," he said.

Clarence, who at heart was a humble man, was embarrassed by his own generosity and tried to change the subject. "I hear my son has a new name," he said.

"Clarence..." Mary warned. She had lived with her husband's cornball sense of humor for too long not to know what was coming.

"Cyd, Alex, do you know what my son's new name is?"

They both shook their heads.

"Dances With Pickups!"

Alex sputtered and laughed. Mary looked exasperated and batted the remark away.

"Thanks a lot," Robert said.

"It is a good name," Clarence said, smiling proudly at his son. "He wears it well, don't you think?"

MUSIC IS A LANGUAGE THAT everyone speaks.

It was 8 PM and the gravel parking lot outside the Snake Snot Saloon in Pablo was already full with many of the same pickup trucks that were part of the cavalry charge up Bigfoot's knoll. Robert, Cyd and Alex had to park out on the street it was so crowded. Walking toward the bar, Alex glanced up at the marquee. It read:

Happy New Year!
THE CUSTER BUSTERS BAND
Tonight Only

He turned to Cyd. "Custer Busters?"

"Little Big Horn?"

"Oh."

The place was packed with more cowboys than a rodeo on the 4th of July. Crowds of men were marching their ladies around the dance floor, parading them in time to a two-step. Tables jammed with people and covered in beer bottles surrounded the dizzying swirl of dancers. They stood three deep at the bar. Balloons hung from the ceiling and feathered plumes and confetti streamers and sparkly New Year's signs decorated a sea of cowboy hats.

Robert seemed to know everyone in the place and after what had happened at Clarence's house everyone seemed to know Cyd and Alex. They were greeted with cheers and applause, chairs were shuffled and they were quickly wedged into the ongoing celebration. The men at their table were all from the pickup cavalry. Cyd and Alex were introduced around to their laughing, giggling, hollering wives and girlfriends who were excited to meet the couple they had heard so much about.

For the benefit of the newcomers, enthusiastic lies and exaggerated war stories were retold about what had become known as "The Great Swimming Pool Massacre". As it turned out, it was not two cowboys that were captured in the pool three days ago but more like twenty—or was it thirty?—all of whom had to be subdued with nothing more than fists and knives. It was a brave band of warriors who had won honor and glory for the tribe that day at Bigfoot's house; the stuff of legend.

A cocktail waitress was making her way between the tables. She was sexy as a pear with an ass that Betty Little-horn, had she been there, might have described as "three axe handles and a snoose box wide". Watching her maneuver with her tray of drinks was like watching a farmer plow a field of boulders; she cut a wide, uneven swath.

The waitress was known as Puffin, but it was a subject of some debate whether that was her first or her last name. She wore a midriff shirt and low cut camouflage pants that hung off her hips with lace on the rear pockets. She bent over a table to set her tray down and Alex could see her butt crack as well as a tattoo that stretched all the way across her backside. In elaborate 2 inch tall letters it read:

$$\mathcal{TROUBLE}$$

The boys followed her warning sign around with hungry eyes and most were of the opinion that the size of the tip should at least equal the size of the tattoo. Since having it done, Puffin had been able to buy herself a new car and had moved herself and her young daughter into a new house.

Cyd saw that Alex and Robert both wanted to dance with her and said loudly, "I should warn you two...I don't dance."

"The two-step is easy," Robert said. "Quick-quick, slow—slow. That's all there is to it."

"No friggin' way. You're not getting me out there."

The *Custer Busters* had one great gift: they could imitate almost anybody who had ever made a hit record. It was like having all the legends and icons of country music, living and dead, together on the same stage at the same time. They were playing a well- known song and Alex could have sworn it was the original band playing.

Robert stood, tugging Cyd to her feet. She reached back and downed a shot of bourbon before allowing herself to be towed out onto the dance floor where she stiffened the minute he took her in his arms.

Robert smiled and said, "It's easy, just relax and follow me. Quick-quick, slow—slow. Follow my step."

She immediately stepped on his foot. "Sorry, sorry. Can I sit down now?"

"You're doing fine. Much better...see? You're a natural."

Cyd tried to relax, but it was like rigor mortis had set in. A couple who could really dance caught her eye and she watched as they glided by like they were on rails...then suddenly realized it was Alex! One of the girlfriends at the table had asked him to dance—a pretty young thing with blond hair and huge eyes who could dance like one of those willowy bean poles Cyd had seen on the TV dance shows. *Where the hell did he learn to dance like that?* Cyd thought, grimly concentrating on her steps. *Well, if he can do it, so can I.*

"Cyd?" Robert said.

She looked up from staring at her feet to see Robert's handsome face looking down at her. "I'm sorry," she said. "Did I step on your feet again?"

"Not at all. Actually, I think you're ready for one of my mother's ballet classes."

"That's the liquor talkin'," she said, glancing again at Alex as he went by. He and the blond were drawing a lot of attention to themselves.

Robert looked at her sadly, knowing he had blown it. "You really do love him, don't you?" he asked.

"Who?"

"Alex. You're in love with him." She dropped her head so he couldn't see her face. He gently lifted her chin. "Cydney, I do believe you're blushing."

"I don't blush."

When the dance was over they made their way back to the table. The ubiquitous Puffin brought more beers and after a few more songs the band began a waltz and another of the girlfriends at the table asked Alex to dance—he was very popular—but he politely refused.

"May I have this dance," Alex said, offering Cyd his hand.

"Don't make me, I'm terrible."

"You're beautiful, come on."

Cyd turned to the woman beside her, a jolly, middle-aged housewife who had befriended her when she first sat down and confided, "He thinks I'm beautiful."

"Go on, honey," encouraged the mother of three in a motherly way.

Robert watched as Cyd rose and followed Alex out onto the dance floor. Alex put his arm around her waist and they began to sway slowly to the music.

"Alex, what good is Clarence's money if we don't have a plan?"

"Don't worry. Whatever happens, we'll always have Pablo."

"Very funny." She looked away, then quickly looked back, studying him with her head to one side. "Alex Farmer, you're a romantic."

He smiled. "It's true. How about you?"

"How about me what?"

"Are you a romantic?"

"No way," she said with innocence in her voice and trust in her eyes. A smile lit her face. She had never allowed herself to feel this vulnerable with another man before. It was a thrilling sensation—like a bungee jump before the fall. She looked up at him and her eyes swam brightly. Without realizing it she was waltzing perfectly.

Alex grinned. "I thought you said you couldn't dance."

"I can't," she said, marveling at what she saw.

Robert stood at the bar watching them dance, sad for what he had lost, glad for what they had found. It was as if her feet weren't touching the floor. He realized she had never looked at him the way she was looking at Alex.

CHAPTER 10

The Worst Kind of Lies

Senator Sam Seeley received a call from the Montana Attorney General that his son Ty had been arrested for murder and was being extradited to Polson. Sam called his pilot and told him to fuel the plane and by late that afternoon the Citation was in the air and he and his wife Annie were on their way back to Montana.

Lake County District Attorney Lydia Stone was an aspiring Native American screen writer and this case—*The Great Swimming Pool Massacre*: *Based on a true story*—was finally going to get her through the door and launch her career...*if* she could win a conviction. It looked easy, but it was the easy ones that always fooled you.

Jesse Longbow knew he was going to get the death penalty. It didn't matter that there wasn't enough evidence to charge him in the murder of the scientist he had killed in the mountains. There were witnesses to the three murders out on the island, a witness to the kid he had torched in his truck in Pablo and forensics had matched the bullets in the dead cop they had found beside the road to his gun. He was toast.

Most of what the witnesses told the police was true. Cyd said that she, Mary and Tiffany had been kidnapped for ransom. Alex and Clarence confirmed that Longbow was not satisfied with the ransom they brought him out on Wild Horse Island. Cyd confirmed that as a result, Longbow decided to rob Clarence's safe and that he took her with him as a hostage and to show him where the safe was and how to get into it. Cyd said if she hadn't cooperated they would have killed Mary and Tiffany, which was also true. The police assumed that when the witnesses referred to such things as ransom and safe robbery they were talking about money. The witnesses let them go on thinking that.

As far as District Attorney Stone was concerned, something didn't add up. Why did this Longbow character keep talking about seeds and strange little colored ones at that? Was he crazy? Obviously. But not that kind of crazy; he wasn't delusional. The story was bizarre. It was just a feeling, but it felt like somebody was lying. In fact, now that she thought about it, it felt like everybody was lying. If Longbow was after something other than money—*Why the hell would he kill all these people over a bunch of seeds?*—then he had to be working for somebody else. Who was he working for, that's what she wanted to know.

The detectives that got the D.A. her answers told her they wanted a royalty when she sold her screenplay. It wasn't that hard. They simply gave Longbow a choice: he could face execution or he could look forward to maybe getting out of jail some time before he died of old age. Death was inevitable, it was just a question of whether he wanted to drag it out or hurry it up. Longbow didn't even have to think about it; he could have won an Olympic medal he flipped so fast. He worked for Ty Seeley, he told them, he was getting paid by him, he was just following orders.

Bingo, thought District Attorney Stone after she listened to the tape and read Longbow's written confession. *Hello Hollywood, hello.*

TY SEELEY SAT IN CUFFS at a table in an interview room in the Helena jail awaiting the Lake County van that would take him to Polson. He looked like a navel orange in his orange colored jail jumpsuit. Across from him was his Attorney, Milos Shedlock.

Milos was the best criminal defense attorney in the state. Sam called him the minute he heard his son had been arrested. In the early days Milos had helped put Sam Seeley in office and they had been close friends ever since. The attorney had a skinhead haircut and a demonic goatee, but mostly what he had was style. The retired Navy Seal was a real snake charmer when it came to hypnotizing a judge and jury. He was not troubled by the things that trouble most people, things like right and wrong. Societal morality was for amateurs and in that sense he was a lot like his clients. What he loved was the game, beating the game, taking the law and putting his knee on its neck and breaking its back. Justice was a pawn to be sacrificed in the name of victory. The rewards for being the best at making certain the worst of the worst went free were remarkable; he was extremely rich. Mainly what he specialized in was defending wealthy drug dealers, but occasionally he would defend a murderer—if the poor innocent man could afford it—which in this case was no problem thanks to his old friend Senator Sam or *Uncle Sam* as he called him.

Even Milos didn't realize how easy this case was going to be. He went into it blissfully unaware that he would soon be saying to Sam, "I'm almost embarrassed to be taking your money." And Sam Seeley, in turn, would reply, "Milos, you could show up in court with your dingus hanging out and you wouldn't be embarrassed."

The more Ty talked the more hyper and agitated he became. "This Longbow, he's crazy, man," he told his attorney. "He's a disgruntled employee is all he is."

"That's good," Milos said. "We can use that."

"That's right. I fired him. I don't know what he was doing out there kidnapping and murdering people. I mean, what the fuck, man. It's my word against the word of a goddamn murderer who's trying to avoid the goddamn death penalty. You call that proof?"

Milos laughed. "You should have been an attorney, Ty."

"Well, I'm not taking the fall for this, you can bet on that."

"What do you mean?"

"You know exactly what I mean. The police are asking me who *I'm* working for and by God…" He suddenly buried his face with his hands. "…oh, fuck me!"

The charm went out of Milos' smile and he looked like a boa constrictor about to drop out of a tree onto an animal and swallow it whole. "As your attorney I'm advising you to say nothing and let me do all the talking," he said evenly.

Ty was clearly terrified. "All I'm saying is you better do something about this, counselor, because they're not putting me on death row for something that wasn't even my idea."

THE PRESS DESCENDED ON POLSON like a school of piranha, gnashing their teeth and tearing off bits and pieces of scandalous fiction that they would report as fact. A Senator's son had been arrested in a sensational murder and kidnapping case and the tabloids and TV talk shows were in a feeding frenzy over the lurid and shocking details.

Ty Seeley's arraignment at the Polson courthouse where he would enter a plea and bail would or would not be set was scheduled to begin in thirty minutes. The courtroom was already jammed.

Annie Seeley sat anxiously on one of the hard wooden courtroom benches, staring straight ahead, her gentle smile twisted in pain. Cyd was crammed in next to her, holding her hand. Without Cyd at her side she probably would have fallen to pieces. Alex was wedged in next to Cyd on her other side. She was as glad for his presence as Annie was for hers.

"I don't understand any of this," Annie said in a small voice. The gracious silver haired southern lady with the youthful eyes looked tired and fragile. "What earthly reason would Ty have to kidnap and murder people—especially you, Cydney. Oh my darling girl, I am so sorry. Are you sure you're all right?" Cyd squeezed her hand and gave her a reassuring smile. "He wouldn't have any reason for doing this," she went on. "Not for money, at any rate. He's wealthy in his own right. Anything he wants, he just has to ask." She shook her head stubbornly. "I don't believe any of it, not for a minute. This is all a monumental mistake."

Cyd took a deep breath. "Annie, there's a lot you don't know. It's not about money."

"Whatever do you mean, dear?"

"I...I shouldn't tell you. Not here. Ask me later."

Down the marble hallway from the courtroom two officers stood guard outside the closed door to a private conference room. Inside, Sam Seeley was meeting with his son. The stubby defendant was dressed in a suit, tie and ostrich skin cowboy boots and was shackled to a chair. It was a secure room and he was with his father, a United States Senator, so the guards outside the door were not concerned. Nonetheless, the muffled shouting from inside the room grew so loud that one of the officers opened the door and stuck his head in to make sure everything was all right.

Both Ty and his father were red-faced with anger. Sam Seeley smoothed a blue and white silk tie over a powder blue shirt and tucked it back inside the jacket of his immaculate suit, thanking the guard politely for his concern and assuring him that everything was fine, he was just explaining some things to his bone-head son. The guard nodded knowingly and withdrew from the room, closing the door softly behind him.

Back in the hallway the muffled sounds from inside the room once again grew heated. The two officers exchanged glances and the one who had looked in the room rolled eyes.

Minutes later the door opened and Sam Seeley stormed out. "Ever wonder why you had kids?" he said to the officers, pausing to compose himself.

The guards, both with children of their own, were in complete sympathy with the Senator and felt they had a common bond with him.

Ty Seeley shouted at his father from where he was still handcuffed to the chair:

"Just do it and do it fast or you know what's going to happen!"

Sam turned slowly and with clenched teeth said, "I told you, it's being handled."

The hearing began on schedule. The bailiff announced "ALL RISE!" There was a noisy shuffling of feet as the judge entered and took her seat. *A stinking Indian woman for a judge in the murder of three women, the kidnapping of three more, the murder of an Indian kid and an Indian cop,* Ty thought. *I am so screwed.*

Milos Shedlock sat next to Ty at the defense table looking confident and dangerous. Sam Seeley was in the first row behind the defense. Several rows away his wife Annie sat up straight, clutching Cyd's hand. District Attorney Lydia

Stone, flanked by her two best prosecutors, smiled from the prosecution table at her old friend, Judge Whitefish. The judge returned her smile with the smallest of nods. *I'm so screwed*, Ty repeated nervously to himself.

Judge Whitefish quickly dispensed with the preliminaries, read the charges and asked the defendant, "How do you plea?"

"Not guilty, your honor," Ty Seeley said in a clear voice.

Just then the courtroom door opened and another attorney from the prosecutor's office walked in, moving rapidly down the aisle to the prosecution's table to huddle with Stone and her staff. They talked in hushed whispers while the judge glowered impatiently.

When the huddle broke up District Attorney Stone was hanging her head. She looked up, sighed heavy and addressed the court on an unsteady voice:

"Your honor, the prosecution is forced to drop all charges."

"Approach the bench!"

Both attorneys dutifully complied.

The judge looked down sternly. "Now will someone please tell me what is going on here?"

Milos seemed to be thoroughly enjoying himself. He smiled at the limp D.A. with his best boa constrictor smile.

"The witness for the prosecution has been murdered, your honor," said Lydia Stone.

"He was your whole case, I take it?"

Lydia nodded miserably.

The judge motioned with her head for the attorneys to return to their seats, then banged her gavel.

"Case is dismissed," she said. "Mr. Seeley, you are free to go."

The courtroom erupted in noise, reporters ran for the exit, Ty turned and grabbed his father in a bear hug and Annie collapsed weeping into Cyd's arms.

IN THE UNSPEAKABLY VIOLENT WORLD of the *narcotraficantes* (drug traffickers), Angel Ramon Ayala was the *Jefe de Jefes* (Boss of Bosses). He fancied himself the king of Mexico—which wasn't far from the truth—and had probably killed more people than AIDS. It didn't seem to matter. This charming homicidal psychopath was known and loved throughout Mexico for his work with sick children. A devoted family man who had slaughtered countless families, a devout Catholic who had tortured priests, a builder of hospitals and schools who had blown up entire villages for revenge, this almost mythical *Jefe de Jefes* was affectionately known as Don Bueno, a corruption of the name of the patron saint of sick children, Saint Beuno Gasulsych. Many *narcocorridos* (ballads of the drug traffic) had been written and sung about him.

Chalino Garza, better known as *El Cirujano* (The Surgeon), had the good looks of a moray eel with a face that looked like it was molded from lumpy clay and left half finished. He earned his nickname by being good with a knife—so good that he had turned murder into an art form. Like many artists however, he had an ego problem: he was proud of his creations and wanted people to know who had executed them. As a consequence, he got caught. Up until then, and for most of his distinguished career, The Surgeon worked as a valued assassin for Don Bueno.

They had brought The Surgeon up to Polson from the Montana State Prison in Deer Lodge as a witness in a separate murder trial that was scheduled to start that same week. It was a case involving a rival drug dealer that Don Bueno wanted put behind bars and The Surgeon, who had nothing to lose, was only too happy to oblige his old *Jefe* by providing the necessary testimony.

To his bewilderment, The Surgeon was awakened in the middle of the night, taken from his Polson jail cell and ushered into a brightly lit interview room. Once inside the room, shielding his eyes from the glare, he discovered that Milos Shedlock had come to call. They shook hands warmly. He liked his former attorney even though Milo had failed to get him off and his trial had ended in a sentence of three consecutive life terms. He didn't hold a grudge. Hell, there were so many witnesses to his 'artwork' that The Pope himself couldn't have gotten him off. And it wasn't a total loss. He had finally received the public acclaim he deserved for his artistic talent.

Milos nodded to the guard that everything was all right and the guard left them alone. The defense attorney got straight to the point, telling the prisoner he needed a small favor. In return he was willing to offer money, a lot of money. *El Cirujano* stared back impassively—he already had money. Milo offered him unlimited drugs to sell in prison. The stoic stare didn't change—he already had drugs. Milo offered a cushy job in the prison infirmary where he could be around lots of sharp scalpels. A smile flickered at the corners of The Surgeon's mouth and he gave a minute nod and the bargain was sealed.

Milos slid the flat of his hand across the table and The Surgeon covered it with his own. Milo withdrew his hand and The Surgeon was left holding a plastic box cutter with a retractable razor blade the size of a flat carpenter's pencil inside.

The next day, in the showers of the county jail, they found Jesse Longbow dead. A Smiley Face had been drawn across his neck in a thin red line that ended at a perfectly severed carotid artery on either side. One eyeball had been popped from its socket, adroitly cut and scooped and left to hang on the outside of his face. The thumb of a hand with a tattooed cross on the back was stuffed into the empty socket. And a box cutter had found its way down the shower drain. It happened so fast that no one saw who did it. Later, some jailhouse wag would observe that it was one of the better crucifixions he'd seen in almost two thousand years.

Art, in its many forms, has many different admirers.

WHEN ELOISE ARRIVED BACK IN Helena with Otis and her son, a startling thing happened: she gave up Goth. As a mortician's wife, death wasn't a game any more, it was real—it was a business and businesses have a way of taking the fun out of a hobby so Goth got put away in the happy place where youthful daydreams go.

They were married in Las Vegas. It was a little out of the way to swing that far west on their drive north from Houston to Helena, but Otis was in no hurry and he wanted Elton to have a chance to see some sights he would probably never get a chance to see again. So he pointed Eloise's blue Honda west on I-10 and, looking like an inflated air bag wedged behind the wheel of the small car, drove his new family along the southern route all the way to Arizona. At I-17 he turned north, went through Phoenix and then Kingman and turned north again onto Hwy 93 which took them to Hoover Dam.

While the boy was ogling the sights, Otis and Eloise stood in the warm winter sun looking down the sweeping face of the dam. Otis had been putting this conversation off, dreading the thought of it, but the truth had to be told. Before they went any further with this relationship he wanted Eloise to understand exactly what she was getting into. The Cannastar plants were gone and there was no way of getting them back. Once the remaining bags of dried tea leaves ran out, he and Elton would die…slowly and painfully. If they had more Cannastar they would probably live long and healthy lives, but that was not the case. What they had at best was a reprieve, a stay of execution. In the end Eloise would be left alone with not one loss but two.

It was the hardest thing he ever had to say.

Eloise looked over the edge at the dizzying drop below. "It's a long way down," she said. "You want to jump?" He shook his head; he was afraid of heights. "Then we're not going to die today, are we?" He shook his head again. "The future is something we make up, Otis. We're always so upset about it and it hasn't even happened yet, you know? It doesn't exist. Making up bad things that might or might not happen and then being miserable all day over them is just another way of telling lies. The worst kind of lies. And the irony is, having something to lose and being willing to lose it is what makes what you have worth having. What I have right now is you, Otis. I love you. We can spend our time living or we can spend it dying, it's a choice. I choose happiness. So here's what you're going to do..." His own thoughts came back to him: *We all die eventually. It's how we live that counts.* Eloise pressed herself against him and the thermostat on her amazing internal furnace went up. "You're going to marry me and if you say no I'm going to throw you off this dam myself." Otis was speechless. "Don't think for a minute I can't do it either," she added, "I lift weights."

And that was how they got engaged.

They drove up Las Vegas Boulevard gawking at a midway of lights where the circus was always in town and the ring-toss and the dart throw had been replaced by sophisticated electronic games, but the carnies still took your money, the clowns still laughed down at the rubes and the oversized Panda still stayed on the top shelf, a prize too high for anyone to reach. Elton, who to his mother's delirious delight was actually looking and feeling better, pointed excitedly to all the G-rated rides that wrapped around the X-rated hotels. When he heard he could ride every one of them if he wanted to, the boy smiled like he hadn't smiled in years. She noticed he was even starting to get his hair back. His head looked like the fuzz on a new tennis ball.

They checked into the Wynn, made an appointment at the hotel wedding chapel and before the night was out Eloise Funk, alias Eloise Small, became Mrs. Eloise Appleseed.

ANNIE, THERE'S A LOT YOU don't know. That's what Cyd had said. Annie Seeley couldn't get the remark out of her mind.

Clarence Bigfoot loaned Cyd and Alex a truck and horse trailer so they could haul their horses back to Helena. When Cyd walked into her house the red message light on her phone recorder was blinking and the digital readout said she had two messages. The first was from Otis:

"Hey, Cyd. Hope you weren't too bored while I was gone. Guess what? I got married! Call me so you and Alex can meet my new bride."

The other was from Annie:

"Cydney, dear. We're staying over at the ranch for a few days. That thing you said to me in court before the hearing started is very troubling. Can you please call me and maybe we can get together and talk? You did say to ask you later. I hope that's all right." She left her number.

Cyd returned both calls. She congratulated Otis, told him she was looking forward to meeting his new wife and said she had good news of her own. No, she hadn't married Alex, why would he think that? She didn't want to talk about it on the phone, it was too much to explain, but boy was he going to be excited. She said she'd meet him tomorrow morning at 10 at his place.

Next she dialed the Seeley ranch, praying Annie would pick up. She did. Annie was glad Cyd wanted to get together, happy that she was willing to answer her questions, but was curious why on earth she wanted to meet at a funeral home of all places. Cyd said she would try and explain everything tomorrow morning, asked if she could be there around 11 and asked Annie to please trust her until then. They hung up and Cyd thought, *I just hope I can trust you.*

CYD AND ALEX CAME THROUGH the front door of Otis's foliated mortuary with Cyd wheeling a carry-on suitcase behind her. A friend of Otis's who owned another funeral home in town, Crane Stevens, had come over while Otis was away and faithfully watered his plants for him. Without Otis around to keep things trimmed back, the place was more overgrown than ever. Alex wondered aloud if there was a Mayan pyramid hidden under all this greenery somewhere.

Otis greeted them with enthusiastic hugs. He was still heartbroken over what had happened in his attic and had not been able to make himself go up there since he had been back.

A large woman with dyed black hair and a boy with very little hair of his own came down the stairs. There was something immediately sensual about the woman and something immediately likeable about the boy. Cyd and Alex met, and instantly adored, Eloise and Elton. Eloise, of course, knew all about them from what Otis had told her and couldn't stop gushing about the effects of the Cannastar on her son.

Otis made tea and he and Eloise listened on the edge of their seats while the harrowing stories were told of finding and digging up the seeds, the ride over the mountains, meeting Bigfoot and his family, the kidnapping, the murders, the rescue...and Ty Seeley being allowed to go free after Longbow was murdered in jail. When they learned that eight one-gallon bags of the seed had been recovered they leaped for joy and cheered like they had been the ones to push Jesse Longbow in the pool. Cyd wanted to know where so many Cannastar seeds had come from and Otis explained that he had harvested them for Maury, but that he had no idea what the scientist wanted with them. He assumed he was using them in his lab for more research.

Otis was so excited over the idea of growing more Cannastar that he couldn't stop talking. "We'll grow it for ourselves, we'll grow it for everybody in the world!" he cried. They would begin again and this time they'd do it right and not get caught. Idea after idea poured out of him about where and how to grow the seeds—none of which were any good. Every time he thought of something that might work he found a reason to reject it. He would jump up with an inspiration, then sit back down again when he realized it was too risky or wouldn't fly. Finally he fell back in his chair exhausted and frustrated.

Eloise smiled quietly. Her son and husband were going to live, that's all she knew and that's all that mattered. Somehow, the news about the seeds didn't surprise her one bit. She was telling Otis that he would think of something, that a solution was out there, soothing him the way you would sooth an agitated hippopotamus, when the bell over the front door rang and a small figure walked in bundled in an elegant fur coat and hat so that only her nose was showing.

"Annie!" Cyd cried.

The matriarch of the Seeley dynasty took off her coat, scanning the entry and parlor of the funeral home with a gardener's eye, gasping at its splendor. She had never in her life seen exotic plants like these grown with such success, especially in Montana. The magnificence of the indoor rain forest momentarily distracted her from her anxieties.

Otis introduced himself, and from that moment on they were great friends. It was thirty minutes before Annie came up for air from asking Otis questions about how he had achieved this or that with his unusual plants. Reluctantly, she turned to the subject of why she had come.

They went into the kitchen and sat around the table. Annie accepted a cup of chamomile tea but didn't touch it. She needed information. Her husband and son were lying to her, she could tell. The way she could tell was by the way she felt when they answered her questions about what had happened. Instead of making her feel better, their replies made her angry. What really sent up a red flag was when she asked about these strange seeds she'd heard about, the ones the murdered kidnapper kept insisting he'd been hired to steal. Even if he hadn't said he was working for their son, the seeds would have intrigued her; seeds were her life. Sam told her she was crazy if she believed the seeds existed, even crazier if she believed Ty had anything to do with it. It made her so mad when he said it that the top of her head almost blew off. She would never have been so rude as to say so in polite company, but privately she called it her *Bullshit Meter*. It was how she knew that something was terribly wrong.

She asked Cyd, "So dear, tell me please. All this talk about seeds, is it true? The man who was murdered in jail who wouldn't stop talking about them, was he crazy? If the seeds exist, what are they? What do they do?"

Annie sat motionless as Cyd and Otis told her everything, right from the beginning, starting with Maury's research. Otis and Eloise then told her what had happened down at Rxon headquarters in Houston. And why. Annie jumped as if touched by a cattle prod at the mention of the name Rxon; she knew of her husband's involvement with them. Otis told her about the hydroponic garden in his attic, about being arrested and the Cannastar plants getting torn up and confiscated. He explained that it all came down to the drug companies, to Rxon in particular and their frantic efforts to destroy anybody and anything that might threaten their cash flow and never mind that Cannastar could change medical science, change the medical industry, change the way people lived and died forever.

Cyd said, "This is a dangerous game, Annie. Your husband and the people he works for at Rxon know we have the seeds. That means this is the last time we can meet or even talk about it. I don't want to put you in danger too."

Annie was overwhelmed. It was too much all at once. She shook her head and refused to believe it. Her world and her whole belief system were being challenged.

Eloise drew her son to her side. "Mrs. Seeley…"

"Please Eloise, call me Annie." Her voice distant and vague.

"My son Elton here was dying of Leukemia. Look at him. Does he look all that sick to you?"

Annie absently stroked the boy's fuzzy head. "Is it true, honey? Are you really sick with Leukemia?"

"Not any more," the boy said happily. "Otis gives me this tea to drink every day and now I'm getting better." His smile widened. "Have you ever been to Las Vegas because it's really cool?"

"Yes darling, I was there once."

"I had pancreatic cancer," Otis said. "Cyd had breast cancer."

Annie was dumbfounded.

"We're both in complete remission thanks to the Cannastar," Cyd said.

The elderly woman turned to Alex, visibly shaken. "What about you? What are you dying of?"

"Curiosity."

"I beg your pardon?"

"I'm curious how a woman like yourself—how anyone—could be so brave and strong and have so much heart as to sit here and listen to what we've been telling you without getting up and storming out."

Annie smiled weakly. "I thought about it," she admitted. Cyd took her hand. "What... what about these seeds?" Annie asked, heartened by Cyd's touch. "What do they look like? Can I see them?"

Cyd got up, retrieved her carry-on suitcase from the other room, brought it into the kitchen and unzipped it. Inside, neatly packed, were eight bulging plastic zip-lock bags of Cannastar seed. The reason she had brought them with her was because she knew just where she wanted to hide them: the coffin that had kept Otis's bags of Cannastar leaves safe during the raid. She took one out and handed it to Annie.

Annie turned it over in her hands. "May I?" she asked, indicating she wanted to open the bag.

"Of course," Cyd said, opening the zip-lock for her.

Annie dipped her hand in and ran it through the colorful seeds, letting them sift through her fingers. A look of wonder came over her face and her eyes filled with tears. "My God," she said. She tried to reclose the bag, but her hands were shaking. Cyd gently closed it for her. Annie laid her head on her arms and began to sob.

"Annie, don't," Cyd said, putting her arm around her.

"My husband, my son, they're not murderers..." She looked up with tortured eyes. "They couldn't be!"

"I'm sorry," Cyd said.

"It's a lie, isn't it? My marriage, my life. All one big fat lie!"

Cyd tried to calm her. "The only thing that isn't a lie is you, Annie. You're one of the truest people I've ever known."

"And look where it's gotten me!" She was frightened. "What do I do now? Where do I go, what do I do?"

They talked on into the afternoon. Otis was still having his business calls forwarded to his friend Crane Stevens' mortuary and so did not have any funerals scheduled for this week. Until yesterday, when he had to appear in court, he didn't even know if he was going to go to jail or not. To his immense relief it had all worked out. All he had to do now was not get caught growing pot for the next 14 years.

Cyd tried to get Annie to lie down, but she wouldn't hear of it. They tried to get her to eat something and she wouldn't do that either. Alex finally got her to take some fluids. Crushed and betrayed, the more she talked the angrier she got.

"My son isn't bright enough or ambitious enough to come up with anything like this. Not on his own at any rate. His father was pulling the strings like always." Saying it out loud inflamed her. "Sam turned Ty into a murderer! My husband is a murderer!"

"I wish I could tell you different," Alex said gently.

"Well, he's not going to get away with it," Annie fumed. "Not if I can help it."

"Are you going to divorce him then?" Eloise asked.

"Pshaw. We southern ladies don't get divorced, we get even. The question is how..." Suddenly she brightened. "You people say your only problem is a safe place to grow the seeds? Maybe I can help with that."

"You can't be involved," Cyd said.

"That's for me to decide. I've never heard of anything so intriguing or enthralling in all my life as this Cannastar of yours and I have the perfect place to grow it!" They looked at her skeptically. "Where, you might ask? I happen to have the most beautiful new greenhouse in the world. It's absolutely huge. State of the art. Otis, you're going to love it."

"Me? How am I going to love it?"

"Because you and your wife and son are going to move back east with me and together we're going to grow some righteous weed. Right under the old fox's nose. What do you think of that?"

"I think you're crazy," Cyd said. "I can't go back there. Your husband knows what I look like, what Alex looks like. He or Rxon or both are going to be sending other people after us, after the seeds. We can't be seen hanging out at your place."

"Then you'll have to wait and visit me after dark, won't you?" Annie said. "Sam doesn't know what Otis looks like. If he sees him around I'll tell him I hired him to help me grow my orchid hybrids. Oh Otis, you'll be perfect. I've seen what you can do. You're the only one for this job, you know you are."

Eloise clapped her hands like a happy chipmunk.

Annie rushed on: "Sam is never around anyway. He spends most of his nights in Washington with his whores." She pronounced it *whoors*. "When he is around he doesn't pay me the least attention and couldn't care less what I do. He told me flat out he wouldn't be seen dead setting foot in my greenhouse—any greenhouse. He wouldn't want anyone to think he was a farmer, you know. As a fifth generation rancher he hates farmers."

Alex Farmer said, "I knew there was something about him I didn't like."

Annie's world was shattered and it hurt more than she could bear. She wanted revenge and she wanted to set things right. *If I can help to heal the world, maybe I can make up for my pathetic, miserable, wasted life,* she thought. "I want to help," she said. "Oh Otis, please? Won't you say yes?"

Everyone looked at Otis who had turned pale. He mopped his brow with a handkerchief. "I guess…I guess if I'm going to do this I should start looking for somebody to buy my business," he said.

"Bravo!" Annie said, turning to Cyd and Alex. "As for the two of you, I suggest you start working on distribution."

"Distribution?" Alex said.

"I don't know that much about dealing drugs," Annie said, "but I do know, if you're going to grow something illegal, you're going to need to find a way of selling it to the public."

Alex couldn't believe the words coming out of this demure little lady's mouth. But she had a point. Even if they could grow it, how were they going to distribute it?

WHEN SHE LEFT THE RANCH the next morning to go back to Virginia, Annie could not bring herself to say goodbye to her son. Ty didn't notice. On the flight home, enveloped in one of the plush leather seats aboard their Citation, Annie was so disgusted with her husband that she couldn't bear to look at him. Sam didn't notice either.

Then somewhere over Iowa Annie smiled to herself and had to cover her mouth to keep from laughing. Her bright blue eyes darted furtively left and right. She had a secret, a wonderful secret, and it was a pretty good pain pill all things considered. Safely stowed in the cargo hold of the private jet, buried among her other luggage, was an extra carry-on bag. She knew that her sadness would catch up with her sooner or later, but right now mad was easier than sad and she wanted to be mad.

Cyd, Alex and Otis discussed it and after much deliberation came up with a plan. They agreed that the most likely target, if anyone were to come after the seeds, would be Cyd and Alex. The last place Sam Seeley or anybody else would think to look for them was in Annie Seeley's luggage. So they divided up the stash. Annie would take four bags of the Cannastar seed with her on the plane and Otis would take four bags with him when he drove back east with his family. This way, if either of them got busted, they would still have a backup.

Annie was amazed at the feeling of satisfaction it gave her knowing that Sam Seeley was being so helpful in the orchestration of his own downfall. To think that she was going to be able to take part in defeating that pig of a husband of hers and maybe even a big corporation! It was a guilty pleasure that gave her the chills—so much so that she had to remind herself that she was *also* doing it to help mankind. And she would be helping to grow a whole new species of plant.

Now that was exciting.

And more dangerous than she could possibly imagine.

CHAPTER 11

A Love Too Far

Cyd and Alex lay warm and close under a down comforter as the first light of day streamed into her bedroom and cast a dusty shaft of light across her log bed. Even if Alex had known he was about to lose her, there was nothing he could have done about it.

Two weeks had passed since Annie flew back to Virginia. Ever since she made the suggestion that they *start working on distribution* they had puzzled over a solution and were no closer now than when they started. The problem of how to publicize an illegal product that a mega-corporation wanted destroyed was daunting enough, but getting it out into the hands of an entire nation without getting murdered or arrested seemed impossible.

Otis and his family had left yesterday for the East Coast. Once he got set up at Annie's, it would take him another four months or so to grow a new crop of Cannastar, so there was still time to solve the marketing and distribution dilemmas, but if people didn't know about it and didn't have access to it, all the Cannastar plants in the world weren't going to do anybody any good.

Last week they had gone to visit Betty Littlehorn who was still recovering from the bullet wound in her arm, but was healing nicely. The injury had kept her from working and as a result she was in dire financial straits. "A one-armed farrier is about as useful as a one-armed paper hanger," she complained.

Betty gave them both a lopsided hug and invited them in for coffee on the condition that they wouldn't tell her what they were up to and that they wouldn't ask her to hide anything else for them. "Not that we didn't kick their butts," she said, spitting into a Styrofoam cup.

Cyd and Alex lingered under the covers, luxuriating between asleep and awake, as the morning sun continued to flood the bedroom. His back still ached—he could feel the injury down there lurking in the dark—but the Cannastar was keeping the pain and his pill addiction at bay. He rolled over and buried his face in her hair, inhaling deeply. Her warm smell made him dizzy. Cyd's arm lay outside the covers and he idly ran his finger down its length, watching the fine silky hairs stand up. She looked at him and he saw the wonder in her pale gray eyes. They kissed and the taste of her that morning was a memory he would have to carry with him a long time.

Cyd made tea and they sat across from one another at the kitchen table. She stretched and yawned. "Tell me about Iraq," she said. "What was it like?"

Alex closed his eyes and sighed as images flashed through his mind. "The faces," he said. "I remember the faces of our troops. The vacant stares. The empty looks on the crippled, broken kids I had to send home to shattered lives. I couldn't fix them; I couldn't fix any of them. If they weren't wounded on the outside they were wounded on the inside, you know? Emotionally. It was like they had lost their souls and all that was left were these empty shells." He shuddered and tried to block out the pictures. "And the blood…so much blood. I still have nightmares. Bodies without arms and legs pouring blood into the sand. Endless, pointless, mindless rivers of black blood soaking into the desert. I try to stop it and I never can." He paused and shook his head. "Sorry...can we talk about something else?"

She reached across the table and covered his hand with hers. "Sure," she said. "What do you want for breakfast?"

"I'm not hungry."

They talked on about this and that while Cyd fixed herself something to eat. When she was done eating she made coffee and they went into the living room.

"Tell me about your ex-wife," she said. "How long were you married?"

A jolt of fear went through him. This was the moment he'd been dreading. He knew the subject would come up sooner or later and now that the time had come to tell her he didn't know if he could go through with it. *Please let her understand,* he thought, just as the phone rang.

Cyd got up and went to the kitchen to answer it. As she listened her face grew red. Then silently she held the receiver out to Alex, her eyes filled with angry tears.

THE HULKING 45 FOOT MOTOR home towing the blue Honda toad exited the Interstate and pulled into a RV park in Madison, Wisconsin, its windshield and front end covered in bugs. In the luggage area under the motor home, safely hidden behind one of the bulkheads, were four bulging zip lock bags of Cannastar seed.

Otis hit a series of switches and the luxurious home-on-wheels leveled itself on the concrete pad while four slides whooshed out of the sides of the coach and expanded the interior. It was the end of their second day on the road and two or three days from now they would be in Virginia. Eloise and Elton were filled with excitement and anticipation.

When Otis told his friend Crane Stevens that the Appleseed Funeral Home was for sale Crane jumped at the chance and the deal was consummated in a week. Crane had always wanted to expand his mortuary business and this was the perfect opportunity. With part of the proceeds from the sale Otis bought the motor home and for the first time in his life had something to drive that he could actually fit into comfortably.

That evening at the Madison RV park, Otis got a call on his cell. He answered and as he listened his face fell.

"Not really, man," he said and hung up.

"Who was that?" Eloise asked.

"Cyd."

"What did she want?"

"She wanted to tell me she kicked Alex out. That he went back to L.A." Eloise gasped. "She asked me if I agreed with her that we're better off without him."

BACK IN CYD'S KITCHEN EARLIER in the day, Alex stood talking on the phone while Cyd listened, tears of rage streaming down her cheeks. When he hung up all the color was gone from his face.

"I...I have to go back to L.A. for a while," he said.

"When were you going to tell me you were still married?" Cyd demanded. "On our wedding day?"

"It's not what it sounds like."

"Are you saying your wife wasn't in a coma and now that she's awake you're not going back to her?"

"She was in a persistent vegetative state. The doctors said she would never wake up. They told me I should let them pull the plug."

"I'm surprised you didn't do it yourself on your way out the door. You abandoned her the same way you're abandoning me!"

"Cyd, please. There's a perfectly good explanation..."

AFTER FOUR YEARS OF MARRIAGE, Alicia Farmer was barely speaking to her husband. She had not let him into her bed in over a year. He had tried repeatedly to get her to talk to him or go to couples counseling, but she would always refuse, flaring angrily at the slightest suggestion that they try and work out their problems. They worked different shifts on different floors at MLK so he rarely saw her at the hospital. At home she was a distant stranger and Alex's patience was wearing thin.

But tonight for some reason she was different. Alicia was her old smiling sensual self, flitting around the house getting dressed for a party they had been invited to that was being given by one of the doctors she worked with. She was wearing a skintight dress that fit her like a latex glove and he felt the old familiar stirring in his loins for her. Could it be that the worst was over and they were finally going to get back to being a couple? He had his fingers crossed.

Alicia sat at her dressing table combing out her voluminous blond hair and humming softly to herself. She asked him to help her with the clasp of the diamond necklace he had bought her for her birthday. Bending to fasten it around her neck, smelling her perfume, he wanted her so badly he could barely restrain himself.

"What's come over you?" he asked.

"Some people just know how to please a girl," she said gaily.

Alex smiled. If he'd known that expensive jewelry was going to make her this happy he would have bought out the store and given it to her a long time ago.

The party was at the home of Anton Learner, a doctor at MLK that Alex barely knew. He had been surprised when the man stopped him in the hospital corridor and was so friendly and cordial in inviting him and Alicia to the party that he and his wife were throwing this weekend. Dr. Learner was a towering black man who looked more like a NBA basketball player than a renowned orthopedic surgeon. Alex was so taken by his toothy smile and gregarious personality that he accepted the invitation without thinking.

Learner lived on the strand in Manhattan Beach in a house with seven balconies, each with a sweeping view of the Pacific. A valet took Alex's black BMW at the front door as there was practically no parking on the narrow street. He and Alicia entered the house and were greeted warmly by both Anton and his gracious wife Natalie. Alicia and Natalie looked so much alike that other than the fact that one was black and one was white, Alex would have sworn they were twins. The house was overflowing with people from the medical field, many of whom Alex knew from the hospital. Before long he found himself having a good time with old friends.

Alex was off in a corner talking shop with his boss, the head of the ER at MLK, when he realized he hadn't seen Alicia in over an hour. He excused himself and went looking for her, wandering through the crowd, poking his head outside to see if she was on one of the balconies. Finally he had to take a leak. All the bathrooms seemed to be occupied so he kept climbing staircases until he was on the top floor where he found a restroom door that wasn't locked. He opened it to

find Alicia on the counter top with her legs spread and Anton
Learner between them.

Alicia came running out the front door of the house with
her clothes in disarray just as the valet was bringing Alex's
BMW around. It had begun to rain and water was coming
down in sheets. Alex got in the car and took off just as she tore
open the passenger door and threw herself into the passenger
seat. They both were soaking wet. Alicia's hair was plastered
pathetically to her face and her mascara was running.

"You have no right to embarrass me like that!" she yelled.

Alex slid around a corner on the wet pavement and accelerated up the block. He was so mad he couldn't speak.

"I want a divorce!" she shouted. "You're boring and stupid
and I hate you!"

Alex clenched his hands around the wheel. "How long
have you been seeing him? Is this the first time or is it an
affair?"

"We're in love, you ass. He's going to leave his wife and
we're getting married!"

"HOW LONG, I ASKED YOU?"

"A goddamn year! Maybe more if it's any of your business!
What do you care anyway?"

The rain was coming down harder as they pulled onto
the freeway. She started flailing at him with her fists and he
shoved her away. He could see almost nothing through the
windshield. All that was visible was a blur of tail lights in
front of him and the white line flashing by on the black wet
concrete. He didn't know how fast he was going and he didn't
care. All he wanted was to get home and get away from this
woman that was ragging in his ear and flashing her finger-
nails at him and breaking his heart.

"You're my wife!" He swerved to avoid a car that cut him
off and laid on his horn. "How could you do this to me?"

"I won't be your wife for long, Mr. 'I-Don't-Have-A-Specialty'. Anton and me, we got plans and they don't include you!"

"God *damn* you!" Alex shouted and slammed the steering wheel with his fist. Alicia jumped and shrunk back. "God damn you both you no good, counterfeit, lying whore!"

He sped up, cutting in and out of traffic. Through the driving rain Alex saw the traffic up ahead begin making wild moves, swerving from lane to lane, diving for the shoulder. He started to hit the brakes and for an instant all he could see was a pair of headlights, going the wrong way on the freeway, coming straight at him…a blinding light.

Then nothing.

HIS BACK WASN'T BROKEN AND the MRI showed only minor damage, but the pain was unbearable. The pain pills helped.

While he was still recuperating in the hospital he struggled into a wheelchair and wheeled himself down the hall, into the elevator, down another hall and into the room where they had Alicia on life support. She looked so calm and peaceful lying there with her long blond hair combed out over the pillow that if it weren't for the breathing tube down her throat he would have thought she was just resting.

As far as he knew, Anton Learner never came to see her.

ALEX FACED CYD WITH A RACING heart. Standing in her kitchen and seeing the hurt on her face was worse than being in the car wreck.

"Alicia wanted a divorce," he said. "She was seeing someone else. It was an accident. It was raining…"

Cyd laughed bitterly. "You're a drug addict, you're married and you're running back to her. Don't let me stop you. I am such an idiot."

"I don't love her, I love you," he said, reaching out for her.

"I trusted you. I believed you," Cyd shouted, backing away. "Get out of my house!"

"What about the Cannastar? You need me for that."

"I don't need you, I don't need anybody!"

"I think you want this relationship to fail. I think you can't wait for it to be over." The minute he said it he regretted it, but he was hurting too much to take it back. "All men are traitors, isn't that what you believe? You're so sure that everyone you love is going to leave you that you can't wait to be right about me being the latest one. I'm not running away Cyd, you are. You think it's so much safer to be alone. Well it's not, it's just lonely. I have to go back to LA and clean up this mess. Then I'll be back. If you'll just calm down and listen a minute you'll see…"

"I can't do this," she said, shaking her head. "It's too much. It's too far to reach…AND YOU LIED TO ME!"

"Cyd, please. I admit I was afraid to tell you, afraid you wouldn't understand. I was afraid of losing you…"

She grabbed a rifle from the gun cabinet and pointed it at him. "GET…OUT!"

ALEX DROVE AWAY FROM CYD'S ranch feeling worse than he had when he woke up in the hospital after the wreck. He realized he didn't have any Cannastar for his back pain. He didn't care.

After the wreck that put Alicia in a coma, Alex sold his condo in Santa Monica and bought a sailboat in Marina Del Rey. He lived on the boat for a year while his life spiraled out of control. Now that Cyd had kicked him out, the boat was the only place he had to go.

Alex's plane from Helena landed at LAX and he took a cab from the airport to the marina where he'd left the beater of a car he'd bought after his BMW was totaled. He paid off the cab and got into a lime green sedan with dented fenders and rusted out rocker panels that he had affectionately named "Slime". His intention was to drive straight to the nursing home and see Alicia. He turned the key, but the battery was dead and Slime wouldn't start. Suddenly he was exhausted. Alicia could wait. He took his pack back out of the car and headed down the gangway.

It had been less than two months since he'd seen his sailboat, but it seemed like two years. The decks, rails and rigging were filthy from the air pollution, but otherwise the yacht was just as he'd left it. A storm was blowing in from the northwest and the boats in the marina were all heaving in their slips and straining at their dock lines. Halyards rattled against a thousand masts and sounded like a thousand wind chimes. He went aboard intending to go below, but instead sat down in the empty dirty cockpit and stared out at the choppy water thinking about Alicia. A feeling of dread came over him.

Alex had named his boat the *Pequod* because in the poetry of Whitman and the prose of Emerson and Thoreau, a ship at sea is sometimes a metaphor for the soul and because he too was obsessed, not in a self-destructive search for revenge against a white whale, but for revenge against the madness that had destroyed his life. He thought he had survived that madness, or at least eluded it when he found Cyd, but it had found him again.

The *Pequod* was a 25 year old, 48 foot, center cockpit cutter and she was as fine a cruising boat as he could ever hope to own. As a medical student he had dreamed of sailing to the remote islands of the South Pacific and bringing decent medical care to the people there, but the dream had withered and dried and now was stored in the attic of his mind covered in cobwebs.

He grew cold and hungry from sitting in the cockpit and went below. He was going to open a can of soup, but instead laid down on his messy bunk intending to close his eyes just for a moment...and woke up the next morning with a storm howling in the rigging. He sat up and pain shot down his back. Edgy and depressed, he pulled on his clothes. He didn't want breakfast, he wanted pain pills. He went up to the parking lot and ran into another live-aboard sailor he knew who had a pair of jumper cables and together they managed to get Slime started.

The nursing home where Alicia was being cared for was just off Beverly Blvd. near Cedars-Sinai Hospital. Driving to it through the flooded Los Angeles streets brought back painful memories of the night of the accident. He parked Slime in the nursing home parking lot and entered the facility with a knot in his stomach. When he entered Alicia's room she was sitting propped up in bed, staring out the window, looking like a gaunt skeleton with good bone structure.

"Alicia, it's me," Alex said. She turned slowly from the window. "You're awake, I can't believe it. How are you?"

She looked past him as if he wasn't there, straining to see if there was anybody else out in the hall. "Where's Anton?" she asked in a raspy voice. "Has he come yet? Did you see him in the lobby?"

"I don't think he's around," he said, trying to remain calm. "Was he supposed to be here?"

"I haven't heard from him yet, but he'll come, I know he will. I have to get my hair done. Have you seen my makeup?" She struggled weakly to get out of bed. He gently eased her back onto the pillows as a nurse bustled in. Alicia sat up expectantly, then fell back in disappointment.

"You would be Dr. Farmer," the nurse said cheerfully. Alex nodded. "We start physical therapy this afternoon. We're very excited, aren't we?" she said to Alicia who stared back at her with a blank look. The nurse smiled at Alex. "I'll check back later after you two have had a chance to talk."

Calling after her Alicia rasped, "Tell Anton which room I'm in!"

"Has anyone else been in to see you?" Alex asked.

"Just my stupid sister. She says I have to come and live with her. She didn't believe me when I told her I'm going to live with Anton. He's divorcing his wife, you know."

"Do you remember anything at all about the night of the accident?"

Another blank stare.

Alex looked out the window in dismay. When he turned back she had closed her eyes. It was hard to look at her in such an emaciated condition. "It's good to see you, Alicia," he said.

Her eyes fluttered opened. "What?" she said absently. "Oh yeah…you too. You better go now. You can't be here when Anton gets here."

OTIS DROVE INTO AN RV park outside Arlington, Virginia and parked on a concrete pad under a shade tree next to a small lake. The next day he unhooked Eloise's blue Honda and went to find Annie. Eloise stayed behind researching the internet and making phone calls. She wanted to find a good school for Elton as soon as possible.

Otis followed the directions Annie had given him, driving for miles past rolling hills littered with baronial size mansions.

Eventually he came to an ivy covered stone gatehouse sitting discreetly just off the road in the shelter of some trees. He pulled in and identified himself to the guard who called the house. The wrought iron gates swung open to let him pass and he drove through feeling like he was entering Buckingham Palace. He followed a narrow winding lane lined with majestic American Elms until a Georgian mansion came into view through the trees. He decided he was wrong, it wasn't Buckingham Palace, it was Balmoral Castle—a rural retreat for royalty, a country home befitting a king and queen.

Annie was waiting for him under the porte-cochere and couldn't have been happier to see him if he had been Falstaff himself come to stay. She got in his car and they drove down to the greenhouse by the lake, circling the golf course size lawn.

Once inside the glass domed conservatory, Otis walked around with his mouth open, incredulous at what he saw. Finally he had to sit down, staring up in awe at the state-of-the-art facility.

"You could grow a national forest in here," he muttered.

"It's all yours, my dear, yours and mine," Annie beamed. "Are you ready to kick a little Cannastar?"

A MONTH LATER ALICIA MOVED in with her sister Beth Gun and her Korean husband in Rancho Cucamonga. Beth was a born-again Christian of indefatigable devotion and energy who home schooled her four children, including the one with Down syndrome. She had inherited none of Alicia's beauty and instead been born with a large head, a round face and short limbs. Despite her constant activity, she was 80 pounds overweight. Her husband was a hardworking gardener named Gi Gun who was half her size and spoke very poor English, but who doted on his family. One wall in every room of their home was a picture gallery dominated by different portraits of a tortured Jesus surrounded by framed pictures of the Gun family dressed all in white taken at various outdoor church functions.

Alicia was walking now with the help of a cane and had put on a little weight. Alex helped move her from the nursing home into her sister's house and a few days later drove the two hours on the crowded freeways to visit her. During the long drive in bumper-to-bumper traffic he had nothing else to do but stew in his guilt and remorse. He couldn't explain why, but he felt the accident and his wife's infidelity were his fault. The more he thought about it the more his back ached until, stuck in traffic and breathing smog and exhaust fumes, he screamed out in pain and anger. He screamed until he was hoarse and his throat was so dry he couldn't speak. He downed a bottle of water and then had to pee so bad he couldn't stand it. There was no way to pull off the freeway so he peed in the empty water bottle. *A doctor who's been to Iraq and spent 5 years patching up gang-bangers in east LA is nothing if he isn't resourceful*, he thought with relief.

It was late morning by the time he pulled up in front of Beth's house. He found Alicia sitting on her suitcase on the front porch wearing a heavy coat even though the day was warm and sunny. She had on too much makeup and her hair was dry and frizzy and stood out from her head like she had been struck by lightning.

"Alicia honey, what are you doing out here?" he asked as he came up the walk. "Aren't you too warm in that coat?"

"I keep calling and he doesn't answer so he must be on his way," she said anxiously, peering up and down the street. "Probably he's late because the freeways are jammed."

"The traffic was pretty bad," Alex agreed.

Just then Beth came out of the house looking distressed and harried, her stubby arms sticking almost straight out from a black T-shirt with a gold framed painting-on-velvet picture of Jesus on it.

"I've had it," she said. "I thought I could do this and I can't, not with everything I have on my plate. She's scaring the kids. I mean look at her, she's crazy. All she does is talk about this Anton character all day."

"I'm sorry," Alex said.

Beth put her hands on her ample hips. "You're her husband. Why aren't you taking care of her?"

Alex hesitated. "It's either this or the home," he said.

"Then it breaks my heart to say this because she's my sister and all and I love her, but she can't stay here any longer. I've prayed on it and that's my decision."

"I understand," Alex sighed, turning to Alicia who was anxiously clutching her purse. "Honey, would you like to move into a nice nursing home out this way so you can be close to your sister?" He glanced at Beth. "I bet she'll come visit you all the time."

"Of course I will, sweetheart," Beth said.

Panic crept into Alicia's eyes. She had always been flighty, unstable and spectacularly beautiful. Now that her looks were gone she had turned into a helpless bird, flapping her emotions like injured wings.

"Maybe he doesn't know I'm getting a divorce and that's why he hasn't come. Maybe he doesn't have Beth's address. If I move will you tell him where I've gone? When you see him at the hospital, Alex, you have to tell him, all right?"

"If I see him I'll give him your address," he said.

Shaking her big head as she went back in the house, Beth said, "Good thing she was a nurse and has good health insurance is all I can say. KIDS! BREAK TIME'S OVER! GET OUT YOUR MATH BOOKS!"

Alicia motioned for Alex to come closer. He bent down so she could whisper in his ear. "Bitch never liked me because I'm the pretty one," she said.

THE NEW NURSING HOME WAS just off the freeway in Ontario, a few miles from Beth's house. Alicia had a sunny room that looked out on a courtyard of grass and flowers, but she spent all day every day sitting in the lobby staring hopefully at the front door, growing more and more morose as the days wore on. Sometimes when Alex came to visit she would barely acknowledge him. Every time he went to her room he had to fight the urge to ease the pain in his back with the array of prescription drugs that Alicia kept in her bathroom.

Then one day as he sat with her watching a basketball game on the lobby television while she stared at the front door she suddenly turned to him, pulling at his arm.

"I wasn't such a bad wife, was I?" she asked. "Do you hate me for being so awful?"

Alex hesitated. "Part of me will always love you, Ali."

"Then you understand how I feel about Anton. It's like we're kindred spirits, you and me. I'm glad you're not mad at me."

But he was.

On his way home he tried phoning Cyd. He had tried calling her countless times over the past several weeks but could never get an answer. The phone rang three times and this time she picked up.

"Cyd, it's me," he said. "Don't hang up..."

Click.

ANOTHER WEEK PASSED. ALEX WAS in the galley of his boat at the marina making dinner when his cell phone rang.

Alicia had committed suicide.

When they found her all the mirrors in her room were broken. And most of her pill bottles were empty.

THE FUNERAL TOOK PLACE AT FOREST Lawn in Glendale.

Alex sat through the graveside service staring at Alicia's flower draped coffin suspended over a terrible hole in the ground, his face a blank. Beth, dressed in black with a Bible in her lap, sat next to him holding his hand. Her husband and their four children sat beside her on folding chairs. Most of Alicia's co-workers from the hospital had come. Alex received their condolences in silence. At some point he realized that Anton Learner was not among them.

When the ritual was over and the minister had said his piece, Beth's husband took their children on a tour of the gardens, pointing out the unusual varieties of plants and trees to try to take the bitter taste of death out of their mouths. Beth guided Alex away from the grave and they strolled silently along the peaceful pathways of the cemetery with life in all its splendor bursting from the somber ground all around them. They came to a bench that overlooked a pond with a sparkling fountain and sat down to stare out at the tranquil water and the graceful swans gliding by. Marble angels watched modestly from a distance.

"She's with Jesus now," Beth said bravely, wiping at her eyes. "She's at peace with God."

"Whatever," Alex said. The pain in his back was unbearable. And something was wrong with his own eyes. A pressure was building behind them and his head felt like it was about explode.

"You have to forgive her," Beth said. "Forgiveness is the only path to salvation."

"You don't have any Vicodin on you, do you?" he asked, the pressure behind his eyes growing worse. He checked himself and found that he wasn't the least bit upset. And yet there was this welling up in his chest, this terrible and confusing force that was trying to get out. Then inexplicably, he was crying. He couldn't hold it back. He tried and it only grew worse until he was wailing so hard he couldn't breathe.

Beth took him in her stout motherly arms, rocking his long frame back and forth. "It's all right, it's all right," she said. "Let it out, sweetheart."

He felt like something or someone had taken over his body and he couldn't control it. He was sobbing harder than he had ever sobbed in his life. Beth continued her steady cooing and it somehow gave him the courage to cry harder. He had resisted it for so long and now he didn't want to stop. He wanted to cry forever.

"We all miss her so much," Beth said. "At heart she was a good person."

"I don't know who she was and I don't miss her at all," Alex said through his tears. "I didn't kill her, that's all I know. It wasn't my fault." He choked, gasping for breath. "It wasn't my fault!"

"Of course it wasn't your fault. It wasn't anybody's fault. Thank you, Jesus."

"But I thought it was, don't you see? I didn't know it and it was eating me alive." Overwhelmed with relief, he cried, "She's gone and I didn't do it!"

"Nobody said you did. That was Satan in you talking." She fished a wad of tissues from her pocket and handed them to him.

"I was addicted," he said, blotting at his eyes only to have them fill again. "To her, to the sex. I was obsessed. I lied to myself about who she was. I didn't want to know the truth, all I wanted was my sex fix. Jesus!"

"Amen!"

He laughed. "I didn't betray her, she betrayed me. She did it to herself and I'm not to blame!" He seized Beth's hands and squeezed them hard. "It wasn't me! Do you have any idea what that means?" The revelation brought on another wave of tears and he wept again.

Beth lifted her oversized head to the heavens. "Thank you, Jesus," she prayed. "Thank you for the healing."

"Thank you, Alicia," Alex cried. Beth looked at him and then they both were laughing, laughing through their tears.

THE CATHARSIS WAS MORE OF a miracle than Alex realized.

He went home to his boat that night and slept eleven hours straight. It was late morning when he opened his eyes and lay blinking up at the California sun that was flooding his cabin. He stretched and sat up, swinging his feet to the cabin sole before remembering that this movement always shot bolts of pain down his back and into his legs.

Since he'd stopped drinking the Cannastar tea, getting up had been the hardest part of the day. The pain kept him bent over until he could hobble up the dock to the showers and let the scalding hot water limber him up.

He stood slowly, carefully...girding himself for the inevitable agony...until he was completely erect. He gingerly swiveled his shoulders, then his hips. Nothing. He bent over and touched his toes. He sat back down on his bunk and stood up quickly. It was gone! There wasn't any pain!

"SON OF A BITCH!" he shouted.

His back felt like it had his whole life, limber and strong. He bounded up the ladder to the cockpit. Hanging onto one of the shrouds he balanced himself on the rail and shouted out across the channel:

"SON OF A BITCH!"

Alex grabbed his shaving kit and towel from below and strolled up the dock to the boat-owner's showers, delighting in every step. He felt like he had unexpectedly been let out of jail. He thought about running up the gangway but decided not to press his luck.

Standing under the shower, enjoying water that for once wasn't taking his skin off, he realized how mad he had been. The emotional pain had mysteriously disappeared; the anger, the guilt, the sadness had all vanished and it had taken the physical pain with it. The way he could be sure was by how good he felt now that it was gone.

And all it took was a good cry.

Now why was that so hard? he thought.

CHAPTER 12

True North

Alex had never wanted anything so much in his life. He wanted it more than he ever wanted Alicia, more than he ever wanted the pain pills. The feeling was stronger than any obsession, any addiction. It was love. He loved Cyd and he wanted her back.

On his return trip to Helena, Alex had to change planes in Salt Lake City. Looking around the crowded airport at all the people engrossed in their computers while waiting for their flights, he got an inspiration. He still had no idea how they were going to distribute the Cannastar, but he thought he might know how they could publicize it. Now all he had to do was get Cyd to talk to him. No easy task.

He landed in Helena and rented a Jeep, a silver one this time, and arrived at Cyd's ranch about sunset. Driving past the corrals he was puzzled to see so many new horses in the pens. He parked and got out and walked toward the log cabin. It was no use calling her, confronting her face to face was the only way. He thought if he could tell her everything that happened in LA it might help to soften her attitude toward him.

He knocked on the door. It opened…but it wasn't Cyd who answered.

"Well suck a man blue," Betty said, looking Alex up and down. "You're a sight for sore eyes."

"I'm not sure Cyd is going to share your enthusiasm," he said.

"What Cyd doesn't know won't hurt her."

"Why, where is she?"

"Gone," Betty said. "You want to come in?"

They sat at the kitchen table—the table he had shared so many times with Cyd—drinking Betty's god-awful coffee.

"When did she leave?" Alex asked.

"Few days ago."

"Where did she go?"

"Back east."

"Where back east?"

Betty shrugged. "Better if I don't know certain things."

Alex closed his eyes in frustration. "So you're taking care of the place, I assume?"

"I live here now."

"Live here?"

"Had to sell my place. Couldn't afford it anymore. Cyd said I could move my operation over here in exchange for taking care of the ranch while she's gone."

"What about the mortgage? I thought she was about to be foreclosed on."

"Friend of hers over in Pablo paid it off. Told her she could pay him back when she had the money. Wish I had friends like that."

"Bigfoot!" Alex exclaimed.

"The Abominable Snowman is rich?"

"He's not a snowman, he's an Indian."

"Don't that beat all," Betty grinned. "We Indians have all the money."

Alex asked if it would be all right if he went upstairs to make a private call.

"You got a place to stay?" Betty said, calling after him.

"I'll get a motel in town," Alex said, climbing the stairs.

"You can bunk here if you don't mind the sofa."

"The sofa is where I came in," he said.

CLARENCE ANSWERED THE PHONE AND was thrilled to hear from Alex who immediately started questioning him about Cyd, asking him if he knew where she'd gone.

"Sounds like Careful Where He Steps has stepped in it this time," Clarence said with a chuckle.

"That would be an understatement," Alex said.

"Annie Seeley will know where to find her."

"Do you happen to have her address and phone number?"

"I'll get it for you. You going after her?"

"What do you think?"

"Good boy."

A pause. "Clarence, I need to ask you something. We need to tell the world about Cannastar. I think what it's going to take is a grass roots campaign. People spend half their lives at their computers, I saw it at the airport. We need to get the word out on all the blogs and websites and search engines, on Twitter and Facebook and YouTube, on all the places where people go every day. Can you help? I wouldn't have a clue where to begin. The danger is that nobody can know where the information is coming from. If Rxon finds out who's doing this they'll shut us down in a heartbeat."

Clarence said excitedly, "Don't give it another thought, my boy. Of course I can set up an Internet campaign for you. I could get somebody elected President of the United States and nobody would know who did it. I'd be honored if you would consider me your Wonk."

"Wonk?"

"You really don't know anything about computers, do you?"

CYD DROVE SLOWLY THROUGH ONE of the seedier sections of Harlem, past decrepit buildings and shuttered warehouses covered in graffiti, looking for an address. Abandoned cars and piles of garbage littered the curb. Listless junkies and wasted whores watched from the shadows, staring out with hungry eyes at the passing car.

As she continued on the street grew more crowded until the sidewalks were teeming with life. Up ahead under a streetlight an armored black Cadillac SUV was parked in a red zone directly in front of an old movie theater. A tall lighted cross was suspended from the roof and the words *Jesus Saves* and under that *Baptist Church* were spelled out on the marquee. Newer model cars lined the street and as she drew closer the prostitutes and drug dealers faded into the raucous crowds going in and out of the clubs and restaurants on either side of the church. Cyd pulled up and double parked beside the SUV. It was being guarded by grim black men wearing black suits and expensive jewelry who bristled and stepped from the sidewalk to surround her car when she stopped.

Cyd lowered her window. Her hair was pulled back in a long pony tail and she wore a dark business suit with a straight skirt. She looked like a business executive on her way to a sales meeting.

"I'm here to see Reverend Hutstader," she said nervously.

A big black head leaned in the window and scanned the inside of her car, then grinned with gold teeth. Cyd recoiled from his breath.

"Never heard of him," said Gold Teeth. He pulled his head back out and called to his friends. "Yo, check it out. Ya'all ever hears of a Reverend Hutstader?"

Vicious laughter. A pretty white girl showing up in a neighborhood like this at night in an expensive car like the one Annie had lent her—a red Jaguar convertible—was like parading a lamb in front of a pride of lions.

Cyd jerked the door handle and flung the car door open, forcing her admirers to take a step back with their hands on their guns. *I can't believe I'm doing this*, she thought.

The man who had leaned in her window stepped in so close that once again she was gagging on his breath.

"Look, fuckstick," she said. "Take me to The Hut or I'm going across town and see Lenny Shapiro and then the good Reverend is going to slice off your balls and feed them to you in a red wine sauce for running me off and not giving him first shot at a product that's going to blow meth and crack right off the street." Lenny Shapiro was the other big drug dealer in New York and Hutstader's sworn enemy. An armed truce existed between the two organizations that was tenuous at best.

Cyd's courage was failing and she started to shake. Gold Teeth hesitated…then motioned for his men to escort her into the church.

THREE DAYS EARLIER, CYD WAS having coffee in a boutique coffee shop and book store in a quaint little village near Annie's Virginia estate when an article in Rolling Stone Magazine caught her eye. It was written by a brilliant and courageous—some would say drug-addled and deranged—investigative reporter who took perverse pleasure in risking his life to research human interest stories about dangerous people in politics and businesses that thrived beyond the fringes of polite society.

This particular article was about a simultaneously loved and feared preacher named Ishmael Hutstader, pastor of the Jesus Saves Baptist Church in Harlem, who was known to his many followers as Reverend Ishmael and to those in the drug trade as "The Hut". Of all the conflicting stories about him, nobody disputed the fact that his community work had helped transform major sections of Harlem and turn ravaged ghettos into thriving neighborhoods. The beneficiaries of his largesse did not seem concerned that his good works might be funded by the very thing that created the horrible neighborhoods to begin with: a narcotics and prostitution ring that was alleged to be one of the largest in the State. Though often vilified in the so-called legitimate press for his entrepreneurial misdeeds and arrests, Ishmael Hutstader had never been convicted of a major crime. To the folks north of roughly 110th St. and south of 155th St., this colorful and fiery preacher was a good and pious man.

The manic author of the Rolling Stone article had also spent tense days with Lenny Shapiro, Hutstader's arch rival, who in a candid moment suggested that the Reverend was a predatory pimp and pusher devoid of conscience or morals. When informed of the remark, Hutstader pointed out that even Jesus had his critics.

What impressed Cyd the most about the article was The Hut's purported vast network of drug dealers that stretched well beyond the borders of New York City.

INSIDE THE CAVERNOUS movie-theater-turned-church, the choir was practicing on stage. Heavenly voices rang out to the gilded rafters and the great curved balcony in rock and roll glory.

Cyd was patted down by a pair of rough black hands with rings on every finger. She was made to unbutton her jacket and lift her blouse to show she wasn't wearing a wire. They found she was carrying a bag of weed, which they confiscated. One of them made a terse call on his cell to someone who had to check with someone else. Seconds passed. The approval finally came and he grunted and hung up.

Cyd was escorted down the aisle between the theater seats to a side door that opened onto a backstage room where a wooden staircase and a freight elevator led to the rectory. Her guards marched her up four flights of stairs, the freight elevator being for the exclusive use of the Reverend. Arriving breathless, Cyd stepped inside a penthouse and gasped.

The smell of fresh baked goods and dark rich Middle Eastern coffee filled her nostrils. Flamboyantly dressed men and women lounged around on down-filled sofas. Recessed lights highlighted an extensive collection of African art and crude antique weapons on the walls. Persian rugs covered the floor. The disorienting sights and smells made Cyd feel faint.

Dominating the room and weighing in at over 400 pounds, the Reverend Ishmael Hutstader sat behind a massive desk on an elevated platform, attended by more groupies than a rock star. He was wearing flowing black robes and a benevolent smile. A gold cross hung from a gold chain around his neck. The cross was smaller than the original but not by much. He looked like the CEO of hell. His pudgy fingers wandered over a large platter of French pastries, hovering indecisively before selecting an éclair and popping it into his mouth whole. His tongue darted out and wiped the fleshy pillow of his lips in one efficient swipe.

Cyd shuddered and took a deep breath.

"Praise God," Hutstader said. "The Lord has sent me a heavenly body. Speak, Heavenly Body. Do you bring a blessing or a curse?"

"I'm...I'm here to offer you a business proposition, Reverend Hut. One that will make you the best loved... minister in New York."

"Call me Ishmael," the Reverend said, motioning graciously for her to come closer while indicating the platter on his desk. "Pastry?"

"No...no thank you. I'm too frightened to even think about food."

Hutstader laughed and his jowls and chins jiggled. "Good," he belched. "I like this one." She noticed that he spoke without a trace of a black accent where on the CDs of his bombastic sermons she had listened to on the drive up she could barely understand a word he said. "Now for the record we are a legitimate organization engaged in honest trade for an honest profit. Heaven forbid your proposal involves anything illegal."

"What I have to offer you isn't legal or I wouldn't be here," she said. "And it's dangerous, very dangerous, which makes it all the more profitable."

The Reverend laughed again, then quickly sobered and waved away the groupies, leaning forward and peering at her like she was an éclair. One of his body guards unceremoniously dropped the baggie Cyd had brought with her onto his desk. Hutstader opened it and took a deep breath.

"Marijuana isn't anything new, child, even if it does smell like chocolate."

"It isn't marijuana."

"I'm glad to hear that. I don't tolerate drugs in my establishment."

"Oh, it's a drug all right. Only instead of making you high it makes you well."

"Well? What do you mean well? We're all healthy here!"
Everyone laughed on cue.

"What I mean is, it cures cancer," Cyd said. "Among other things."

Even Hutstader couldn't contain himself at this one. He threw back his head and bellowed with laughter. His minions laughed with him. When he stopped they stopped. Silence hung in the air as Hutstader's face darkened. Cyd rushed on:

"We need underground distribution and you have a distribution network. What could be sweeter?" Cyd picked up the baggie and boldly dumped the contents out on his desk. The dried green leaves went everywhere and Hutstader's eyes grew wide. The bodyguards lunged forward, but he held up his hand to stop them.

"Explain yourself woman or you could find yourself working out of a crib on Lenox Avenue strung out on heroin."

"And you could find yourself the hero of the American people."

He folded his arms over his belly. His hands didn't quite meet. "Go on."

"Cannastar is a genetically engineered herb invented by a scientist who was murdered for his efforts."

"Who would do a thing like that?" he asked skeptically.

"Rxon Corporation. If this gets out and people start using it nobody is going to want to buy their drugs. They'll try and kill anybody who gets in their way. The law thinks it's pot so if you don't get murdered trying to sell it you'll get arrested. We can grow it, but we have no way of getting it into people's hands. Once the world knows about Cannastar there's going to be a demand for it the likes of which even God has never seen. You'll be the richest Savior on earth."

"I am but a humble servant of the Lord Jesus Christ," he said, charging his boilers and gathering steam for a righteous sermon. "I am a tool in God's hands! A lump of clay to be molded by His will! It would be a sin for me to presume to be a savior, a sin in God's eyes and damnation on my soul. Praise God!"

A chorus of amens rose from the faithful who apparently were so imbued with the rapture that they couldn't keep their hands off each another. There was enough sex going down here to make Caligula blush.

Cyd flared. "And would God object if you broke the law selling a drug that's going to do somebody some good for a change? Would He object if you were universally loved for doing His work?"

Hutstader regarded her thoughtfully. "How much THC does it have in it?"

"None. Very little. It's not for getting stoned..."

"So it's like oregano or catnip? It's for cooking and for the cat to scratch?"

"Mr. Hut—Ishmael—you don't understand..."

"I understand perfectly. I will pray on it." He leaned back in his chair and closed his eyes. "I would hate to find in my prayers that you are not who you say you are."

It was a threat and shivers went down her spine. "Please don't be concerned," she said, scribbling something on a scrap of paper and shoving it across the desk to him. "This is my phone number, Reverend Ishmael. Call me after you've had a chance to think about it. You won't regret it."

The Reverend reached for another pastry, then paused and slowly looked up. His mask of religious piety fell away revealing a violent cruelty she hadn't seen before.

"Go with God," he said.

Shaken, she turned and started for the door. As she was going out she heard him say to his body guards in a chilling voice, "Don't none of you niggers let no more crazy bitches like that in here."

CYD DROVE AWAY FROM THE Jesus Saves Baptist Church humiliated and discouraged. The fear she had kept at bay during the interview rose up and overwhelmed her. She was trembling so badly that she had to pull over to the side of the road and stop. That night, huddled under the covers in a cheap motel, she cried herself to sleep. The next morning she took a shower, but she still felt dirty. She was on the Pennsylvania Turnpike on her way back to Virginia when her cell phone rang.

The call was from Joe Angolia.

LATER THAT EVENING CYD SLIPPED into Annie's darkened greenhouse. The grow lights had been turned off for the night and stars twinkled through the hexagon panes of glass in the overhead dome.

A whispered voice: "Over here."

Cyd followed the sound, shouldering her way through a forest of thousands of maturing Cannastar plants that were already taller than she was with jagged edged leaves the size of elephant ears. With Annie's modern high-tech facility at his disposal Otis had been able to experiment with light, humidity, temperature and nutrients to fine tune the ideal hydroponic growing environment for the Cannastar. As a result, the plants were thriving in a way even he hadn't thought possible.

Cyd found Otis and Annie in the dappled darkness next to a potting bench that ran along one of the eight glass walls. At the sight of her friends she burst into tears. They tried to comfort her, but she pulled away, castigating herself for being so stupid as to think she could get a notorious drug dealer to distribute the Cannastar.

Otis wiped his hands on his voluminous apron and took her in his arms.

"What was I thinking?" she wept. "I am such an idiot. I am so lame! How could I be so naïve to think that a notorious drug dealer would help me? The way he looked at me..." She trembled. "I am so creeped out!"

"That was a really brave thing you did," Otis said.

"I don't know what to do," Cyd said furiously. "I'm out of ideas."

Annie kissed her cheek. "You'll think of something, dear."

"I was fool enough to leave my phone number, can you believe that? Now I'm getting phone calls from shitheads like this Joe Angolia who called me. He talks a mile a minute in this raspy voice like he's the Godfather or something. He claims he runs a hedge fund and if I'll come to his New York office and prove to him that Cannastar really works he'll pay me a million dollars. He probably operates out of a dumpster and rapes virgins for a living."

"Actually, he's the real thing," Alex said, stepping out of the shadows. "And your idea of getting drug dealers to distribute the Cannastar was pure genius."

Cyd jumped backward and bumped into the potting bench. "WHAT ARE YOU DOING HERE? You scared me to death!"

"Sorry."

"He arrived just before you did," Otis said. "He said you might be a little upset at first. I was the one who told him to hide when you came in. I was going to break it to you gently."

"Cyd, he's here to help us," Annie said.

"I missed you, man," Otis said, giving Alex a bear hug.

"We all did," Annie said.

"Bullshit," Cyd said.

"You two need to stop being so silly," Annie said.

"You guys have done an amazing job," Alex said, looking around admiringly. "How do you keep the Senator out of here?"

"He doesn't know I exist," Annie said, turning to Otis and taking his arm. "I think we should give these young people a little time alone, don't you? Do you feel like taking a look at the tulips and pansies I've started or is it too late?"

Otis grinned. "It's never too late for tulips and pansies."

Cyd turned on Alex the second they were gone. "I thought I told you to stay away from me!"

Alex smiled in that infuriating way he had of looking like he knew something you didn't. All he really knew was how much he loved her.

"No can do," he said.

"So now you're stalking me?"

"A lot happened in LA, Cyd. I have all kinds of things to tell you..."

"You're like a stray dog," she said. "You won't go away."

"We need to talk about Joe Angolia. I grew up with him. He's one of the biggest mobsters on Wall Street."

Cyd threw up her hands. "You really are something, you know that? Now you're telling me you're mob connected?"

"Not me. Him."

"So the mob is after me? Terrific. Thanks for the heads up."

"We need to go see him together."

"And why is that?"

"I don't know. Because I'm fun to have around?"

THE AMTRAK RIDE FROM UNION Station in Washington DC to New York City took a little over 3 hours. During the trip Alex made repeated attempts to try and talk to her but all Cyd did was stare out the window and ignore him. He didn't mind. He was content to be with her even if she wasn't speaking to him. A feeling of excitement was building inside him, a sense that despite the horrendous challenges they faced, they would figure it out. She was not alone any longer—and neither was he.

"Love is a lie that horny men tell," she said, suddenly turning away from the window. "I trusted you, Farmer. That was really hard for me. I don't think I can do that again."

Alex laid his head back and closed his eyes. "I understand," he said with a quiet smile.

She made a furious growl and turned away. He had to be the most exasperating, annoying, irritating man she had ever met.

THEY TOOK A CAB FROM Penn Station and arrived in the financial district in lower Manhattan around noon. The cab left them standing at the curb in the shade of giant skyscrapers.

"It's that one," Alex said, pointing at a building that was so tall they couldn't see the top. As they started toward it he said, "Yea, though I walk through the valley of the shadow of commerce, I will fear no evil."

Cyd was noticing the way he walked. "You're not limping," she said. "And you're walking straighter."

"It's part of what happened when I was away. I'm not in pain any more."

"How nice for you," she said, shoving the heavy glass door open indifferently and entering the building ahead of him.

They got out of the elevator on one of the upper floors and walked down the corridor. The name on the elegant ten foot tall double doors at the end of the hall read *True North Partners*. They pushed open one of the doors and went inside...

only to find the reception area deserted. The front desk had no pens or papers, no clutter—not even a phone. Another set of double doors led to the inner offices and Cyd stuck her head inside calling, "Hello? Anybody here?"

No answer. Then from far away a faint voice:

"Come to the back, please."

Motioning to them from the far end of the room was a harried secretary who sat at a desk jumbled with papers and phones. They walked toward her past a trading floor that had dozens of desks, each with an array of monitors for actively trading the markets. Except there was no one at any of these desks either. An eerie silence hung over the deserted work stations.

"Can I help you?" said the secretary as they approached, her voice echoing in the deserted room.

"We're here to see Joe Angolia," Cyd said, looking around uncomfortably.

"Whom shall I say...?"

"Cyd Seeley."

"Of course. Ms. Seeley. If you'll just have a seat..." She picked up a phone and buzzed her boss.

Minutes later they were ushered into a huge corner office with a jaw-dropping view of Ground Zero, the Hudson River and New Jersey beyond. There were no decorations on the walls and no furniture in the barren room except for a circle of chairs in front of a chaotic desk that was crowded with computer monitors. Behind the desk a high backed leather chair was turned facing the view so that they could not see who, if anyone, was in it.

"Freakin' crazy, that's what Hutstader said you were. I don't have time for crazy," said the chair in a nasal voice. The "you" came out *youse*. "Me, I'm crazy for even talking to you." The chair spun around revealing a tiny, hook nosed, pallid man sweating into his Armani suit. He regarded Cyd with cold intelligence, then shifted his attention to the other person in the room...and exploded with delight. Joe rushed around the desk and he and Alex embraced, hugging and laughing in a happy reunion.

Cyd looked on incredulously. "Fuck me," she muttered under her breath.

"Joe, I want you to meet the girl I'm going to marry. Cyd Seeley, this is Joe Angolia."

Joe pumped her hand admiringly, talking so fast she could barely follow. "I had a feeling. I get these freakin' voices in my head, you know? They always know what's up. So you're not crazy, I'm not crazy, nobody's crazy—I knew it. Cyd Seeley and Alex Farmer, I'll be damned."

"Just so we're clear," Cyd said. "I'm not marrying anybody."

"Sit down, sit down," Joe said with a staccato laugh. "Lately I've been thinking about you, Alex. Thinking about you a lot..." Suddenly a coughing fit overtook him. He snatched open a desk drawer and began pulling out Kleenex and coughing up blood.

Alex rushed around the desk, took Joe's forehead in his hand and patted his back. The coughing eased. Alex took his pulse, reaching for more tissue to mop Joe's perspiring face. In the drawer beside the Kleenex box he saw a hand gun. Joe saw what Alex was looking at and quickly closed the drawer.

"...and here you are," he wheezed.

"Take it easy," Alex said. "Try to breath."

"I'll be all right in a minute," Joe said.

Cyd poured a glass of water from a pitcher on the desk and gave it to Joe who nodded thanks and drank it down along with a couple of pills he shook out of a prescription bottle. Alex went back and sat down and Joe started up again with his mile-a-minute chatter.

Alex interrupted him. "I have some bad news," he said. "I don't know if you heard...but Maury is dead."

Joe looked at him quizzically, then fell quiet. He rose and went to the window, looking out with red eyes and blowing his nose. Alex explained what had happened to their childhood friend and how Rxon was behind it. When he finished Joe was fuming.

"So this Cannastar, that's the reason they killed him? They must be really afraid of this stuff." He paused to think. "BASTARDS!"

Watching Joe's reaction to Maury's death softened Cyd's opinion of him. His sadness brought up her own grief. "Rxon wanted to bury Cannastar so they buried him," she said. "I...he was somebody I loved very much."

"We all did, kiddo, we all did," Joe said. "Him and Alex... they were like the only two friends I ever really had." He brightened. "So this weed that Maury invented, it isn't a myth? It really works?"

"What have you got that's making you so sick?" Cyd asked.

"Let's see it," Joe said. "Show it to me."

Cyd remained motionless. "That tub-of-guts Hutstader, how do you know him?"

Alex cleared his throat. "Cyd, maybe you better let me handle this..."

Joe gave Alex a dark look. "You love her, so you're probably not a good one to ask, but do you trust her?"

"She's the most genuine person I've ever met," Alex said, looking at Cyd.

Cyd frowned. She didn't like the way this conversation was going.

"Hutstader is one of my clients," Joe said.

"Your client is a drug dealer?" Cyd said.

"They're all drug dealers," Joe said. "Distributors, I should say."

Cyd slumped in her chair. "Fuck me," she muttered again.

JOE ANGOLIA WAS A LEGENDARY market trader whose money making skills were reputed to be almost superhuman. His peers on Wall Street would have been shocked if they knew the real source of his income.

His hedge fund, True North Partners, didn't actually make any money, but paid out huge profits using its client's funds. What distinguished its customers from those who had gotten bilked by other phony hedge funds was that True North's investors knew exactly what was going on and heartily approved. The reason was that the hedge fund's distinguished roster of wealthy clients had a common problem: as the top one hundred wholesalers of illegal drugs on the east coast they all needed to launder vast sums of money.

Hedge funds operated outside the rules and under the radar so washing all that drug money through the books was easy. True North was deliberately structured to be as complicated and confusing as the almost nonexistent law would allow. And because the laws prohibiting such things had long since been abolished, they were able to own all the other related, interwoven companies that made it possible; i.e., People's Capital Bank, its trading desk and even the two trading companies through which they anonymously placed their trades. Anyone investigating the company would need a sharp knife and a lot of elbow grease to cut through the tightly woven corporate infrastructure and get to True North's smelly interior core—and even then they probably couldn't find it.

WealthHouse handled the equity and currency trades and PT Hastings cleared their commodity trades. Both companies were legitimate and both were extremely profitable. The only thing that wasn't legitimate was the money they made for True North Partners.

Money rushed into True North's customer trading accounts from successful, electronically verifiable market trades in short selling, leveraged program trading, swaps, arbitrage and derivatives—trades that never happened. The electronic profits from these trades were electronically transferred into the customer's bank accounts in People's Capital Bank. The money was then shown to have been paid out to the customers. As a result the actual cash, which was already in the hands of the drug dealers to begin with, was immediately available to be legally spent or invested in legitimate enterprises. The bank's books balanced and the money was sanitized and washed, clean as a freshly laundered shirt.

The accountants that cooked the bank's books called these *Garbage Accounts*—as in *garbage in, garbage out*. With the exception of the Jesus Saves Baptist church, a nonprofit organization, True North's clients dutifully paid their income taxes on their "profits".

And Joe Angolia got rich. He had a penthouse overlooking Central Park, a house in the Hamptons, his own jet airplane and he owned half an island in the Caribbean.

What he didn't have was his health.

Ishmael Hutstader had called Joe to discuss his "investments"—code for the amount of "profit" he needed to show this month—and while they were talking happened to mention this crazy bitch that had come to his church wanting him to distribute some kind of weed that was supposed to cure cancer and didn't even get you high. He only mentioned it because the incident somehow still bothered him and he couldn't get it out of his mind. He was puzzled when Joe became agitated and demanded to know how he could get in touch with this person. Hutstader found Cyd's phone number in his waste basket and gave it to him.

Joe called Cyd immediately.

Desperate men will sometimes do desperate things.

"DON'T LOOK SO SURPRISED," Joe said.

"I'm not surprised, I'm thrilled," Cyd said. "This means your *distributors* can start selling Cannastar."

Joe said nothing.

"I should warn you," Alex said. "Once corporate America and the government find out it's on the street, things are going to get ugly."

"You criminalize something that people want and you're going to create a black market for it," Joe said. "The more illegal it is, the more they want it."

"Exactly," Cyd said. "Think of it as a new income stream. A whole new way for your clients to make a shit-load of money."

"No question," Joe said.

"You'll be getting in on the ground floor," Alex added. "You'll *be* the ground floor."

"True."

Cyd couldn't contain herself. "So you'll do it then? You'll go in the Cannastar business with us?"

Joe sighed and shook his head. "I wish I could help you, but it's out of the question. There's no way."

Alex was stunned.

"He doesn't believe us," Cyd said miserably.

"Maury invented it and Alex says it's true, so absolutely I believe you," Joe said. "That's not the problem. The problem is I can't ask my people to get involved in something this controversial, this high profile. Drugs are big business and Cannastar is a game changer. I can't even imagine what a stir this would create. My clients would end up getting a lot of unwanted attention and that would not be good. National, Federal, local cops—they're all way too interested in us to begin with. Upsetting the status quo would mean risking everything. I'd recommend it to my people and they'd go for it, believe me—they trust what I say when it comes to business—but my hands are tied. It's too risky, I'm sorry."

Cyd felt a calm come over her. This man was the key to everything and she wasn't about to take no for an answer. "What do you think is going to happen to all the people who are terminally ill if you don't help us?" she asked.

"They'll die, same as always," Joe said.

"Same as you," she said.

"Now wait just a minute..."

"I'm guessing whatever it is you have, you don't have long to live." Another coughing fit caused Joe to grab for more tissues. "What kind of cancer?" Cyd asked.

"Lung," Joe coughed. "Inoperable."

"Bummer," Cyd said.

"But Cannastar will fix that, right?"

"You'd likely get your health back in no time."

"Then I don't see a problem..."

"Oh there's a problem all right," Cyd said. "Cannastar isn't available to the public."

Joe turned red. "I'm not the freakin' public! I'll pay whatever you want. One million, two million, name your price!"

"It's not for sale," Cyd said. "Not for any amount of money."

"Tell her, Alex. Don't let her do this..."

Alex shrugged. "My hands are tied."

"NOBODY SAYS NO TO JOE ANGOLIA!" His shout brought on another bloody coughing fit.

"Either I get distribution or you can go fuck yourself," Cyd said.

"Try to understand…" Joe pleaded.

Cyd stood and started for the door. "Have a nice life," she said. "What there is left of it."

Alex got up to follow.

"ALL RIGHT, ALL RIGHT," Joe yelled. "What if I put it out to a couple of my distributors and we'll see what happens?"

"I assume your distributors are all in the east?" Cyd asked. Joe nodded that they were. "All right then. I want the whole east coast or nothing."

"I can't, I just can't…"

Cyd tossed her head and went out the door.

Following behind, Alex said, "I used to think you had the biggest balls in New Jersey, Joe. When did you go and get yourself castrated?"

"WAIT!" Joe said. "Let me think, let me think." He turned in his chair to stare out the window. When he turned back around he was mopping his brow. "This could get me killed, you know."

Cyd said from the doorway, "Dead if you do, dead if you don't. Do we have a deal or not?

"Deal," Joe said weakly, extending her his hand. She crossed the office and they shook on it. His hand felt wet and clammy.

"For Cannastar to work you have to keep taking it," Cyd said. "That means if you go back on your word, the Cannastar goes away."

"Okay, okay," Joe said. "You got what you wanted, now give it to me for God's sake."

Cyd smiled and took a baggie out of her pocket.

IT WAS RUSH HOUR AND Penn Station was insanely crowded.

Cyd and Alex stood waiting for the train to take them back to Washington while noisy crowds streamed past them. The experience with the preacher and now the hedge fund manager had given her a new confidence. She had discovered things about herself she didn't know existed and she was glowing inside. Then a troubling thought occurred to her and the glow went away.

"What's wrong?" Alex asked.

"Publicity," she said. "How are we ever going to let people know it's available?"

"It's handled," Alex said.

"How so?"

He told her about his internet idea and what he had cooked up with Clarence—how before long everybody would know about Cannastar. It was a brilliant plan and for a moment she forgot that she hated him.

"No shit?" she said.

"No shit."

CHAPTER 13

El Diablo

With the good came the bad and with the bad came the beautiful.

It was spring and Annie Seeley's estate was Pandora green. The high walls of English Ivy were chartreuse with new growth, acacia trees mushroomed with shade, white flowering dogwood blossoms popped like popcorn balls and tulips and pansies rioted everywhere.

A convoy of three rented box trucks rolled through the entry gates of Annie's estate at midnight and followed the winding drive until they came to the greenhouse that sat dark and silent beside the shimmering lake. Men in dark clothes and skull caps got out and rolled up the rear doors of the trucks.

Otis and Annie stood excitedly to one side as a mountain of overstuffed black garbage bags were taken from the greenhouse and silently loaded onto the trucks. Growing and harvesting this much Cannastar had not been difficult. The time consuming part was curing it and removing all the poisonous seeds before it could be bagged for transport. But it was a labor of love so the work was neither painful nor boring—it was fun. The two farmers watched proudly as the rear doors rattled down, engines started and the trucks moved back up the drive and disappeared into the night.

The first crop was shipped and a new industry was born.

THE IP ADDRESS OF THE CANNASTAR website, located somewhere in Russia at the moment, kept moving around Eastern Europe. The site was getting more hits than a free porn site. Even Clarence was amazed. The promotional campaign, targeted exclusively at the east coast for now, was succeeding beyond his wildest expectations. People were clamoring for the product and everybody was talking about it.

The website's FAQ page gave very specific instructions on how Cannastar was to be administered and cautioned that it might not be appropriate for all people for all things. Common side effects, it said, included robust health and a disease free life. Visitors to the site were urged to give this organically grown transgenic miracle a try with colorful animation that read:

See Your Local Drug Dealer Today!

And they did. By the thousands. With soaring hopes and urgent hearts people flooded from their homes to the streets, from the suburbs to the ghettos, from their arm chairs and canes and sickbeds, from their cancer and disease and despair, in search of a local pusher. The demand was overwhelming. Otis and Annie were working day and night and still they couldn't keep up.

DONALD "DUCK" DONALDSON GOT HIS nickname because of the way he combed his hair. He had worn it in a "Duck's

Ass" or DA for over fifty years and he wasn't one to give up on a style just because it had gone out of fashion. But other things in his life were changing that he couldn't control and as a result he hadn't slept in a week. His wife was dying of lymphoma and he had just lost his job as a diesel mechanic that he had held for over thirty years.

Duck left his home in Stroudsburg, Pennsylvania in search of Cannastar for his wife and an hour later arrived in Allentown. In his hand—a hand permanently stained with grease and oil—he clutched a piece of paper where he had hastily scrawled the address of a reliable drug dealer that his neighbor had given him. He didn't know whether all the hype around this stuff was true or not, but he was desperate and doing something—anything—was better than sitting around feeling helpless and scared.

The drug dealer turned out to be a friendly enough fellow who told Duck he wished he could help him, but that he had sold his last bag of Cannastar two days ago. Duck asked where he could look for more and was directed to the dealer's cousin in Newark, some three hours away. As of this morning the cousin supposedly still had some left.

Duck arrived at the cousin's house around dark only to be disappointed once again. After that he drove from neighborhood to neighborhood, getting out and walking the streets, stopping everyone he met and asking if they knew where he could find a drug dealer. When people learned that he was looking for Cannastar they were very helpful, but every dealer he talked to told him the same story—they were out and they didn't know when they'd be getting any more.

Late that night he found himself on a bus bench in a gangbanger neighborhood, desolate and alone, agonizing over what he was going to tell his wife. His head was in his hands when someone tapped him on the shoulder. He looked up to find himself eyeball to eyeball with a mixed race boy of about ten who was waving a fat baggie of dried green leaves in his face.

"Yo, Homes, what up?" the kid said. "Brothers say you lookin' to score."

"I'm looking for Cannastar, not Marijuana," Duck said.

"What it is, Homes. Three hundred bucks."

"That's three times the going rate!"

The kid gave him a look of disdain and turned to go. "Whatever, yo. Last bag in town. Don't need no white-ass bitch punkin' me for it."

"No wait. Please. I'm sorry. Here you go..." Duck shoved three hundred dollars at the boy who tossed the baggie at him and ran off.

When he got home he and his wife followed the directions on the web site, carefully boiling a measured amount of leaves into a tea. They were encouraged when it didn't make her high. She drank it morning and night and a month later she died. The bereaved husband took what was left of the baggie to the neighbor who had told him about it in the first place, telling him bitterly how it hadn't worked.

The neighbor smelled the bag. There was no chocolate smell.

MEANWHILE, POLICE WERE BEING CALLED in to handle the traffic jams on once-deserted streets where only junkies lived. Some street corners got so busy that the hookers could barely make a living. A rising tide of sick and dying were abandoning their doctors and pharmacies for the open air markets of the ghettos.

The medical community saw the growing danger and descended on Washington like fire breathing dragons. The heat was intense. Clamoring voices rang out from drug companies, insurers, hospitals, medical-supply firms, health service companies and health professionals. Their protests echoed in the ears of senators and representatives until the halls of Congress sounded like a zoo at feeding time. This abomination had to be stopped; it needed to go away before it got out of control.

Law enforcement agencies on the national, state and local level were called in to find and eradicate the source of this noxious weed. Investigations were launched. Arguments broke out over whether it was being grown inside or outside the country. One day no one had ever heard of it and the next day everybody was trying to score some. An agonized DEA agent, frustrated over the lack of leads, said, "It's like it's arriving here on cargo ships from Mars." Search and destroy teams were put on alert to be ready to move the minute the source was discovered.

SAM SEELEY AND HIS LOBBYIST friend Riley Gray were in the Senator's office in Washington on a conference call to Houston. Sam had been fielding angry calls from his biggest campaign contributors all day, but this one was by far the worst.

The speaker phone on Sam's desk rattled as Dick Tremble screamed, "THIS THING IS TURNING INTO A CLUSTER FUCK! WHAT THE FUCK AM I PAYING YOU FOR? I WANT THIS CANNASTAR STOPPED! NOW DO YOUR FUCKING JOB OR I'LL PUT SOMEBODY IN THERE WHO CAN!"

And that was just some of the nicer things he said.

Sam Seeley needed time to think and plan. He wasn't all that concerned. He had the full weight of the United States Government behind him. Hell, he *was* the United States

Government. All he needed was a little break to work this thing through. With that in mind he decided to do something he hadn't done in the middle of the week in a long time. He left Washington and went home to Virginia.

WHEN THE SENATOR ARRIVED BACK at his estate he noticed all the activity going on down by the lake. *More f'ing nonsense with her stupid plants*, he thought as he went into the house. But it went on all day—every time he looked out the damn window he saw people coming and going—so that evening, when Annie came back up to the main house tired and dirty from a long day of work, he asked her what was going on down at her greenhouse. His unexpected visit took her off guard, but she quickly regained her composure. She had carefully rehearsed her response should anything like this ever come up.

"My greenhouse, you say?" she said, stalling for time as she took off her gardening hat.

"No, that Epcot Center of yours that you moved up from Orlando. Yes, your greenhouse. What are you doing, running a truck farm?"

"Oh, that's my new business," she said, bright and breezy.

"What kind of business?"

"Gardening, dear. What other kind of business would it be?"

"It needs to make money before you go calling it a business."

"Oh I'm making money, all right. Scads of it."

"I find that a little hard to believe."

"This gentleman I hired to help me, he developed the most amazing hybrid plant. It's really caught on. People everywhere seem to want it."

Sam lost interest and began opening and reading his mail while he talked. "Caught on, you say?" It was the power bill that caught his eye. He handed it to her. "Then how about you start by using some of your "profits" to pay the bills? You're using enough electricity to light a city."

She looked at the bill and swallowed hard. "My goodness… I had no idea. Of course I'll pay for it. In fact, I'm making so much money I'm thinking of building a second green house."

"Like hell you will. What do you think you are, a farmer?" He said *farmer* like it was a dirty word.

"As a matter of fact, that's exactly what I am," Annie said. "A very successful one, I might add."

"You don't say. Well maybe I should have a look at this growing operation of yours. If it's all that successful I'll put some of my people on it."

For a moment Annie was at a loss for words. "You'll do nothing of the sort," she said. "You have your world and I have mine, so unless you want me to start paying unannounced visits to you and your *whoors* in Washington I'll thank you to keep your nose out of my affairs."

This was the second time today somebody had challenged him and he didn't like it, especially coming from Annie-The-Church-Mouse. It frightened him more than he was willing to admit it. "You live in your little dream world," he said. "What do you know about what goes on in Washington?"

"I know enough to ruin your chances for reelection." He stared at her in stunned silence. "And as for my new greenhouse, I'll build it in the trees where you won't have to look at it. Other than that, I'll thank you to mind your own business."

The Senator was boiling with rage. "You do that," he sputtered, storming out. "And while you're at it, why don't you move into it?"

"I would," she said sweetly, "but I live here and you don't. Oh, and the next time you come to visit, I'd appreciate a call first."

The door slammed behind him.

WITH SAM SEELEY OUT OF THE picture, at least for the time being, the work progressed smoothly. Annie's contractor, Jim Toomey, broke ground on the second greenhouse. "Cannacot II" Annie called it.

On a whim, Cyd decided to cut her hair. She came happily bouncing out of the beauty salon with a short and sassy haircut that made her feel like a new person. When she got back to Annie's everyone was busy working in the greenhouse. It was a beautiful day and she didn't feel like being indoors so she went down to the lake for a swim. The water was freezing and she quickly climbed back out, the mud squishing between her toes. Alex found her sitting on a bench in her underwear vigorously drying her hair with a towel. Beyond where she was sitting the glassy surface of the lake reflected a perfect upside down picture of the dense greenery that surrounded it.

Alex stood behind her thinking she didn't know he was there. It took him a minute or two to get used to the new haircut. She looked so cute he wanted to kiss her—which of course was impossible.

"You look like a summer day at the beach," he said.

"Sit down," she said coldly. "We need to talk."

He sat beside her. The tension between them was like a rubber band that was stretched too far.

"We need to expand," Cyd said. "The east coast is only the beginning."

"Otis and Annie can't grow half enough as it is," he said. "We can't service the territory we've got."

A long pause. "Like I say, we need to expand."

"Joe Angolia called," Alex said. "He wants to see us."

"About what?"

"I don't know, but it sounds urgent." He touched her arm and she pulled away. "Cyd, can we talk about us?"

"Why, do you want to tell me more lies? Do you need more stories to tell your friends back in LA?"

"Everybody I know in LA is dead."

"Lucky you. A life without friends." She stood up and pulled on her jeans. "If we're going to New York, let's go."

"A life of crime with the woman I love," he said with a wry smile. "Lucky me."

SAM SEELEY PUT RILEY GRAY in charge of the campaign to poison people's hearts and minds against Cannastar and Riley hired Griffin Gant, the infamous Republican strategist and dirty trickster, to get it done. Gant was a horrible human being who couldn't be killed with a stake through his heart. He had no chin and his shoulders sloped away from his neck at a sharp angle so that he looked like a pointed arrow. Calling him evil was like calling Adolph Hitler ambitious; the word was too kind and left too little to the imagination.

"Cancer is bigger business than war," Riley lamented.

"Don't worry," Gant assured him, "It's not going anywhere. War is here to stay and so is cancer."

CYD AND ALEX TOOK THE train back up to New York and arrived in Joe's office at lunch time. Joe was at his desk, glowing with health and wolfing down a hero sandwich. He greeted them with his mouth full, motioning for them to sit.

He was wearing a sweat suit and looked like he had just come from working out.

"You training for the New York Marathon or what?" Alex said.

"New lease on life thanks to youse guys," he said. "This freakin' Cannastar is freakin' amazing."

"So I've heard," Cyd said.

"Thanks for coming," Joe laughed. "Good news. Guess who wants to see you?"

"The State's Attorney General?" Alex said.

"Angel Ramon Ayala. Don Bueno they call him. Head of the biggest drug cartel in Mexico."

"I hope you told him we're not available," Alex said.

"Price of success, price of success," Joe said. "He's sending his plane for you. You need to be at Washington Dulles at 7am tomorrow morning."

"What if we don't want to go?" Cyd said.

"I wouldn't advise that," Joe said. "Besides, this man could get you distribution for the rest of North and South America."

THE MEDIA GOT WIND OF the growing storm around Cannastar and, with the behind-the-scenes help of Griffin Gant, began to raise "concerns". Experts from a variety of institutions appeared on the various news and talk shows voicing similar sound bites.

Kenton Krill, a long haired geneticist from one of the Ivy League universities, told CNBC that "to turn an untested, unproven, genetically engineered who-knows-what loose on the world without the research to show that it does not create a risk of contamination is the height of irresponsibility."

"Are you saying this thing could start an epidemic?" asked the interviewer.

"All I'm saying is that we don't know what it is," the geneticist said.

On MSNBC the next day Ashit Patel, a representative from a Middle Eastern pharmaceutical company, told a noontime panel in a sing-song voice, "In the drug industry, when the technology advances far too rapidly relative to the science, that is a sign we need to stop, slow down and take another look. Before a new drug is released onto the market we are obligated to work closely with the FDA to accumulate hard evidence as to the risks and hazards of the particular drug. These checks and balances are in place for a reason and need to be respected."

Bud Sweet was the crew cut, bug-eyed deputy director of Plant Diagnostics for the Department of Agriculture. Before going to work for the government he was on the board of directors of Farmacopia, the international producer and marketer of food, agricultural, financial and industrial products. He came on Good Morning America and made some alarming remarks:

"Once you insert a gene into a plant, the question is, will it escape into other plants? The unintended consequences can be devastating. There is a criminal lack of any caution going on here." Sweet was asked if he could be a little more specific. "Plants like Cannastar cross pollinate actively and easily," he said. "It's surprising how quickly something like this can spread. Someone has put a rogue gene into a plant—marijuana in this case—that you can't control and that won't die! Once it gets going you can't get rid of it."

On the Today show an expert in transgenics, Ira Lundski, said, "This is a potentially dangerous event. We are going too fast. No one, to my knowledge, has run any clinical trials on Cannastar. There is no risk assessment—it's being defined by a few outsiders. This is a system of irresponsibility and, in my opinion, an invitation to disaster."

An Oklahoma farmer named Dave Grow was interviewed on CNN. He explained, "A 'volunteer' is the farmer's nightmare. It's something that is seeded on the wind and is growing in another field. Cannastar volunteers *are* going to cross-pollinate other crops." He turned ominously to face the camera. "That means this poison could get in our food supply. It can't be stopped. We could be looking at the beginnings of a plague of biblical proportions."

His neighbor 30 miles away, dressed in bib overalls and a Sooners baseball cap, echoed Grow's concern:

"If God had wanted us to have it He would of growed it Hisself."

CYD AND ALEX SAT COCOONED in elegance listening to the muffled rush of air as the Falcon 2000DX Jet flew them from DC to Mexico at a speed of Mach .80 and an altitude of 40,000 feet. An attractive stewardess cleared away the delicate china on which they had been served a sumptuous meal as the plane began its descent. The jet swooped out of the sky and landed on a short, high altitude runway that had been built by scraping the steaming jungle off the top of a mountain.

A helicopter was waiting to take them the rest of the way. The chopper skimmed the canopy of an impenetrable rain forest in a ten minute ride that ended at the base of a roaring waterfall named *Cola de Diablo* (Devil Tail Falls) where it hovered, then rose straight in the air 2,000 feet up the face of the cascading water. When it cleared the rim of the waterfall they were staring directly into the chiseled eyes of a one hundred foot tall white marble statue of Saint Beuno Gasulsych, legendary grand-nephew of King Arthur himself, who was serenely placing the severed head of Saint Winifred back on her body and miraculously bringing her back to life.

Beyond the statue lay a broad denuded mesa, surrounded by jungle, and beyond that, at the back of the mesa, rose jagged cliffs where the upper half of *Cola de Diablo* thundered down. When the waterfall reached the rear of the mesa it formed a great pool that split into two natural rivers that curved for 3 miles around either side of the plateau and provided a natural moat that entirely surrounded the compound of the feared drug lord, Don Bueno. The rivers rejoined beneath the feet of Saint Beuno where, from the base of the statue, *Cola de Diablo* fell off the cliff and continued its journey to the sea.

Around the six mile perimeter of the compound, strategically placed and manned by heavily armed militia, were mobile ground-to-air missile launchers. But that was not the amazing part. Within the moat, dwarfing a massive Spanish hacienda in the center, was an amusement park that was somewhat smaller than Disneyland, but no less elaborate or fanciful. Children were everywhere, hundreds of them from all over Mexico, swarming the park and grounds. It was like another Neverland up north, but without the nefarious sexual overtones; a place where no one ever grew old. There was a terrible reason for this. Most of the kids here were terminal. And the boys and girls of Don Bueno's Mexican Wonderland served another purpose. No army of *Federales* or enemies was going to come charging in here bombing and shooting up the place with so many sick kids around. They provided a dome of protection more bullet proof than any bullet proof glass.

The helicopter landed on a replica of the great stone slab of the tomb of Saint Beuno where to this day, in far off Wales, people still brought their sick children to lay them on his actual tomb in hopes of their healing.

Spanish guitars and Peruvian flutes haunted the air as security guards with bulges under their coats came forward to escort Cyd and Alex to the hacienda. Following along in stunned silence, Cyd looked up in awe at a looping, death-defying rollercoaster that made the ones in Vegas look like they were built with Legos.

"Fuck me twice," she said under her breath.

"I'd settle for once," Alex said with a grin.

She shot him an angry look as they entered the magnificent home of Angel Ramon Ayala, a.k.a. Don Bueno, and were ushered into a living room the size of a Cabo San Lucas hotel lobby where every wall was hung with pictures of beloved children who had passed on from one terrible disease or another.

Don Bueno, built like a muscle car and reputed to have a nuclear temper with the firing pin filed down, was dressed in a silly pirate hat and eye patch and was engaged in a mock sword fight with a dozen screaming kids. Cyd and Alex watched in amazement from the other end of the room as the attacking horde easily overpowered the one-eyed buccaneer and ran him through, sending him sprawling to floor, piercing his body again and again and squealing with delight while spilling his mock blood all over his $8,000 rug. When he saw that he had visitors Don Bueno miraculously recovered and shooed the kids from the room with a mighty roar.

As he approached he took off his hat and they saw that the eye patch was not part of the costume. A ragged scar ran over the top of his bald head and down beneath the eye patch, giving him an appearance far more frightening than if he had left the hat on. A little girl was clinging to his pant leg with one hand and staring up at the visitors with enormous eyes.

Don Bueno studied Cyd, then asked abruptly, "Do you have any children?"

Cyd hesitated. "I don't want children."

"You are not Catholic, *Señorita*?" She shook her head no. He continued to study her. She felt like a bug under a microscope. "*No importa*," he concluded. "Does it work?"

"Does what work?"

"Guess," said the Don.

"Yes," she answered.

"And does it work on children?"

"As far as we know."

"Winifred here was born with Down syndrome," he said, stroking the hair of the child that was hanging adoringly off his leg. "Will it cure that?"

"No," Alex said. "It won't."

"And you would be Dr. Farmer?" Alex nodded. "Well, Dr. Farmer, what *does* it cure?"

"Primarily viral and infectious diseases and the uncontrolled growth of malignant cells in the body."

"May I see it?"

Cyd handed him the baggie she had brought with her.

He turned the zip-lock full of seedless Cannastar over and over in his hands, holding it up to the light, opening it and sniffing it, taking a bit out and tasting it. "This is a good thing," he said, then bellowed, "A GOOD THING!" He laughed when his guests jumped and just as quickly sobered. "Come with me," he said, scooping Winifred up and handing her off to a nanny who appeared out of nowhere. He charged out of the room and they followed behind in confusion.

Don Bueno led them down a flowered path and through the glass doors of an adjoining building shaped like Noah's Ark. Inside, the hallways were braced with wooden ship's timbers to look like the inside of an old ship. Going down one of the hallways they went through a set of double doors and found themselves in an immaculate hospital ward of fifty beds, filled with boys and girls and decorated with colorful animals cavorting over the walls. Gentle nurses were tending to the children.

"What do you think, Doctor? A beautiful infirmary for you to in work, no?"

"I'm no pediatrician," Alex said. "What's wrong with these kids?"

"They are dying. Sooner rather than later I fear." His face darkened and he scowled. "So now you prove it."

"Prove what?" Cyd asked.

"That it works, of course! That this so-called genetic invention of yours does what you say it will do. I give you one month." The room full of emaciated children were all staring at them.

Cyd was overwhelmed. "We can't treat all these kids with one bag of Cannastar," she said.

"Then you shall have more!" the drug lord boomed. "Tell me where to send it—I send the airplane."

ELOISE'S HUMBLE BLUE HONDA LOOKED out of place on the tarmac at Washington Dulles next to the Falcon Jet. She opened the trunk of her car and a uniformed pilot politely helped her remove an overstuffed garbage bag. She watched as the black plastic bag was loaded onto the plane, then got back in her car and quickly drove off.

Minutes later the Falcon was in the air and headed home and a new international threat had begun and the game of drug trafficking was forever changed. Government agencies were set up mainly to handle drugs being smuggled into the country, not out of the country.

"TERRIFIC," CYD SAID TO ALEX, looking out at the dense jungle that surrounded the thatch roofed, tile floored, open air bungalow that was to be their temporary home. "I feel like we won a one month all-expense paid vacation to Devil's Island."

"I thought the Devil had horns," Alex mused. "I had no idea he ran a children's hospital. The guy's a one man Make-A-Wish foundation."

"I have a wish," Cyd said. "Get me the hell out of here!"

AFTER TWO NERVE-WRACKING WEEKS of making certain that the test group of dying Mexican children consistently drank their tea, Cyd and Alex were starting to see some results.

It was the end of another long day in the 50 bed hospital ward and Cyd was watching Alex minister to the children, marveling at the special connection he seemed to have with them. The kids adored him...she didn't know why. They left the air conditioned hospital together and stepped out into the hot sticky night, heading for their bungalow.

"You're a good man, Farmer," she said.

"So why do you hate me?"

"Maybe I don't."

"Then come on a boat ride with me this evening."

To his surprise she said yes. "I'll make us a picnic dinner," she said.

A little while later they walked through the amusement park's central plaza heading for the river boat ride. The plaza was a spaghetti western replica of a Mexican village complete with a fountain in the center and an adobe church at one end where every day *banditos* were shot from rooftops and colorful *fiestas* were celebrated to the frenetic strains of mariachi music. But it was night and the *piñatas* had all been burst and the push carts were covered until tomorrow where once again they would overflow with joyous sweets and fruits free for the taking.

They continued on to the dock where an attendant in an explorer costume and a pith helmet was waiting. He helped them into one of the electric fringe-topped river boats that were used to take the kids on rides around the mesa-top mote that encircled the compound and cast them off. If the jungle ride at Disneyland was the real thing, this is what it would look like: a real jungle with real jungle sounds complete with creatures swimming by that were not mechanical. They ghosted away from the firefly lanterns on the dock and drifted into the darkness where they were immediately engulfed by the surrounding jungle and the dissonant sounds of wild animals crying out at the tops of their lungs.

Humid air lay over them like a blanket. Alex manned the tiller and Cyd plucked a white orchid from a branch and stuck it in her dark hair before lying back contentedly, lounging on the seat cushions, but definitely *not* trailing her hand in the water.

"Thanks for being here with me," she said. "I couldn't have done it alone."

"*No problema*," he said. They drifted along saying nothing, listening to the night sounds and breathing the pungent smell of the undergrowth. Finally he said, "Do you think you can ever forgive me, Cyd?"

She was silent so long he didn't think she was going to answer. They were rounding a bend with the sound of rushing water up ahead when at last she said, "Tell me about LA."

Alex negotiated a small white-water rapid, then let the boat glide through the calm pool below as he told her of his wife's madness and her obsession with another man. He told her how Alicia had died from an overdose of prescription drugs, remembering too late that Cyd's mother had died the same way.

She lay quietly in the dark. He couldn't see her face.

He told her of his crushing guilt. He spoke of his tears, of the peace that was on the other side of the pain, and how it had healed him.

"Pull over," she said.

"Say again?"

"Stop the boat."

He nosed the bow into a bank where the trees came down low to the water.

In a halting voice she said, "I loved you and I didn't give you the time and space to do what you needed to do. I... I'm sorry."

"You can make up for it by marrying me."

"You're funny."

"I know."

"And conceited."

"It's all an act so you won't know how much you're breaking my heart."

"I...I don't mean to be cruel. It's just that sometimes you piss...me...off!"

"I seem to have that effect on people I love."

She watched him while the jungle howled and screamed. "Oh, fuck it," she said, throwing her arms around his neck and kissing him passionately.

When they parted he said, "Is that a yes?"

"Yes, what?"

"That you'll marry me."

"Shut up," she said, kissing him more passionately than before.

They made love on the seat cushions in the bottom of the boat in the stifling heat while the monkeys called the news across the treetops until all the creatures of the jungle knew that every now and then even humans can get it right.

"I thought you were somebody and you're not that some-body at all," Cyd said, looking up at him. "I'm glad I was wrong."

"Me too," he said.

Cyd was in love and this time it was for real. The next two weeks were an erotic blur of daytime tea parties and night-time sex. They made love on every sheeted, carpeted, tiled and padded surface in their bungalow. If sex was an Olympic sport they would have medaled in gymnastics and marathon. They didn't have tails or they would have been swinging from the trees. The monkeys heard the jungle sounds coming from the human habitat and thought that maybe a whole tribe was in there having a mating ritual.

The two lovers lay spent and naked on a lounge chair on their outdoor patio. They looked like they had been making love under water they were so drenched.

"Sauna sex," Cyd panted. "My new diet and exercise program."

"You might be on to something," Alex said, flopping onto his back on the adjacent lounger. Cuddling was out in this heat. "One of his goons told me that Don Bueno wants to see us at the *hacienda* at eight in the morning."

"What for, I wonder?"

"Either he wants to thank us or kill us, it could go either way."

DON BUENO CAME CHARGING ACROSS his living room and gave Cyd and Alex robust bear hugs. They suffered his embraces in silence.

"*Mi personas que hace milagros!* (My miracle workers!) So now we make a deal, no?"

"Deal?" Alex said. "What kind of deal?"

"The children are much better. They are all getting well! This Cannastar, it works!" He kissed the St. Beuno medal he wore around his neck. "I want exclusive distribution. I am the only one who sells it, agreed?"

"Maybe," Cyd said.

"Western hemisphere, Eastern hemisphere—I help children around the world and I get richer than Carlos Slim and Bill Gates combined! We grow it all right here in Mexico!"

"Not so fast," Cyd said. "We control production." *He can kill us*, she thought, *but it's not like marijuana or cocaine—without us he can't get his hands on it.*

The jagged scar that ran over his head and down to his eye began to pulse red. "If you are worried about quality control *Señorita*, I can assure you…"

"That's not my concern. I'm worried if someone like you gets complete control they can blackmail the world with it. I won't let Cannastar become another illegal drug that people are killing each other over."

"What are you suggesting?" Don Bueno asked. He looked like a pot that was about to boil.

Cyd took a deep breath. "You can have exclusive distribution. That's easiest for us anyway. But we grow it in the United States."

"Such an operation is expensive. Don Bueno, he will pay for it."

"No," Cyd said, a little too quickly. "I don't think I want to owe you money."

"You can do this alone then? Without my money? Without my protection? *Es muy peligroso*. (It is very dangerous.)"

"Don't worry," Cyd said, "we can handle it."

Alex was staring at her like she was crazy. "Cyd, maybe we should listen to what the man is saying…"

"Look," Cyd said, focusing on Don Bueno's one good eye. Alex's words from last night—*It could go either way*—echoed in her head. "We're on the same side here. It's just as important to us as it is to you that everybody in the world can buy Cannastar."

Don Bueno looked at her like he was aiming a gun. "How many tons a month are you going to be able to provide me?"

Cyd hesitated. "However many you want," she said. "Give us six months to a year to get set up and we'll supply you with as much weight as you can sell."

Don Bueno nodded thoughtfully. "And this is a promise? Without fail you will deliver?"

"I promise," Cyd said. "Without fail."

Alex was inwardly horrified.

Don Bueno turned away before spinning back around. *"BUENO!"* he shouted. Then stepping in so close that Cyd could see the stitching in his satin eye patch he added, "Sadly, many of my friends who did not keep their promises to me are *muerto* (dead)."

Cyd and Alex exchanged looks.

Don Bueno leaned back and laughed his explosive laugh. *"Pero, no importa.* FIRST WE TAKE THE ALAMO, THEN WE TAKE LA...NO?"

AN HOUR LATER THEY BOARDED the Falcon Jet for the trip home.

"Are you crazy? Are you suicidal?" Alex said the minute they were airborne. "What were you thinking telling him we could grow that much Cannastar?"

Cyd stared peacefully out the window. "Something will turn up," she said. "It always does."

"How many greenhouses do you think Annie can build?"

"I suppose two is the limit."

"Jesus!"

CHAPTER 14

A Matter of Opinion

O n CNBC the cheerleaders of illusion were encouraging investors to position for the start of a new bull market in pharmaceuticals as well as medical products and services. In fact, Rxon's east coast profits were in the toilet and the region's doctors, hospitals and insurers were suffering. The propaganda war against Cannastar had to be stepped up. The smear campaign wasn't smart and clever, it was vicious and mean—which was why it was so effective.

In the world of broadcast journalism, Sux News was as popular as guns. One of the network's widely viewed talk shows was hosted by the gorgeous Monica Stains. Her success in treating her own ovarian cancer with Cannastar—it was gone, completely and totally disappeared!—should have been headline news.

It was her first day back at work after being off for a month with her illness and Monica was once again the picture of health. Overjoyed to once again be the center of attention, she made Cannastar her lead story and opened with an important announcement:

"Unsubstantiated rumors are circulating that a number of deaths have been attributed to the use of this Cannastar weed that's been appearing on the streets. While these rumors are still unverified, the American people should be warned that a potentially dangerous drug has been unleashed and is being sold as a magic cure-all for cancer and God knows what else." She pushed her amazing hair away from her amazing face with one finger and tucked it behind her adorable ear. "Does that make any sense to you, because it makes no sense to me. Personally, I wouldn't touch it with a ten foot pole."

The media picked up the sound bite that Cannastar was a deadly drug and repeated it over and over until everybody had heard it enough times to know it was true.

"There have been rumors of Cannastar deaths," said Joel Potts, the blustering, swaggering, Bible-thumping talk show host who followed Stains. Tears welled in his eyes for the victims.

Later that night Sux News flashed another urgent bulletin. "Reports of widespread Cannastar deaths are still being veri-fied," the newscaster said, while at the bottom of the screen the streaming headline read:

Reports of widespread Cannastar deaths!

As shocking proof of the growing menace, they played a taped interview with Donald "Duck" Donaldson confirming the fact that Cannastar had killed his wife.

The message was picked up and championed by the popular radio show host Quinton Queen who sat in his over-sized chair stoned out of his mind on prescription drugs, his little pig eyes burning like coals in his bloated face, and announced to the world that Cannastar was a terrorist plot to take over America.

"Who are these people who are trying to shove this Canna-star crap down our throats?" Queen demanded. "Hippies turned terrorists is who they are! The Green Panthers of the 21st Century hell bent on turning you and your children into drug addicts. These criminals are using fear tactics to tell us that we're going to die if we don't start using their drug. Well, I don't know about you, but when somebody tries to force something down my throat it makes me mad!" He took a drink of water because the new pills he was taking were giving him cotton mouth. "Let me ask you something. Are you willing to stand by and let this happen because I...AM...NOT! Do you have a gun? I hope you do and I hope it's loaded because let me tell you something friends, these people are coming and they're coming for you!"

The US government ordered scientific studies to determine if Cannastar was dangerous and if so, how dangerous. DNA tests were run to discover the genetic makeup of the alien herb and it was found to contain, apart from marijuana, elements of another illegal plant. Their worst fears were confirmed when a Death Star was located in China and flown to the United States where they began overdosing hundreds of rats with injections drawn directly from the center of its spiked red ball. The rats started dropping like flies. Results showed that 100% of the rodents had died, proving conclusively that Cannastar was a deadly drug.

Senator Sam Seeley came on national television to assure the American people that Congress was dealing with the problem. With the grave authority of his high office and the comforting demeanor of a benevolent grandfather he assured a concerned nation that the United States government was doing everything in its power to protect its citizens from this threat.

"Americans have a right to know the truth and the truth is disturbing," the Senator said. "Recent scientific government studies confirm that we have a national drug emergency on our hands. To deal with this crisis and to avoid further tragedy

I have today, by emergency decree, had Cannastar added to the list of Controlled Substances and declared a Schedule I drug based on there being no accepted medical uses for the narcotic, its high potential for abuse, and there being no established medically supervised safety standards for its use. In plain English that means it is a deadly poison and anyone caught possessing, using or growing it will face the severest penalties allowable under the law. The criminals responsible for the proliferation of this noxious hazard are going to go to jail for a very long time, I assure you."

Ken Hammerman on MSNBC was as smart as he was tall—and he was *tall*. Before wadding up his script and throwing it at the camera in disgust he said, "The government is turning into a police state in defense of the drug companies. Have a nice day."

Quinton Queen, in another of his inspired diatribes, raved, "Some say these are the seeds of change, I say they're seeds of destruction! They don't want you to get well my friends, they want you to buy their drugs. They want to turn you into zombie junkies like themselves!" He paused to let his rhetoric sink in. And to take another pill. Refreshed, he went on: "I say what any patriotic American would say: Death to these Islamics who are perpetrating this horror on the American people!"

Fred of the Fred Show said, "You want to know what you get from taking Cannastar? You get to live! Is that so terrible? If these right-wing treasonous anarchists get their way with their nut-case lies they are going to succeed where the destroyers of 9/11 failed!"

The labor unions, their ranks decimated by a growing number of members who were sick and dying from incurable diseases, argued, "This is a destruction of our social fabric! Look at the people Cannastar is putting out of work!"

The Mormon Church issued an alert for the bishops in all their Wards to watch the backyards and farms for any telltale signs of people planting these "seeds of revolt".

Meanwhile, thousands of wildly enthusiastic blogs from the east coast were crisscrossing cyberspace with people espousing the successes they were having with Cannastar. Lives were being improved, lives were being saved and friends and families of the terminally ill were ecstatic. Across the country, people were clamoring for the drug.

Harry Noud was a balding former economic advisor to a dead president and the snappiest dresser on CNBC. He hosted a late afternoon panel show where news and information that might affect the markets was discussed and where, despite persistent evidence to the contrary, he was never wrong.

The topic under discussion on Noud's show tonight was genetically engineered plants in general and Cannastar in particular. One of the panelists, Horace Lake, was an expert in plant biotechnology from the University of Iowa. The soft spoken, wispy haired young researcher was trying politely to make a point: "The modern farmer has vastly increased his crop yields with transgenics. They get better weed control, better crop yield and lower costs. There is no evidence of any negative effects..."

He was quickly shouted down by the other panelists.

"What if we created another plant that could kill this Cannastar?" Noud asked another guest. The Iowa researcher stood his ground, interrupting the moderator: "You're talking about the terminator gene," he explained. "Creating more technology to get rid of a bad technology is a little like hiring a bobcat to get rid of the domestic cats—there are unintended consequences. For example, bobcats like to eat small dogs as well."

The other panelists agreed wholeheartedly that a terminator gene was a fine idea. Noud quickly changed the subject and when they came back from commercial break, Horace Lake had been replaced by a Republican congressman.

Across the land growing hordes of hicks, fattened on the madness of the negative propaganda, crowded the parade route as America's right wing radio and television hosts paraded their sound bites up and down Main Street on floats of fear, pitching their shit over the side to a sea of hungry hands that reached out for the lies and gobbled them down like poison candy.

The permanently pissed-off stoner on HBO said on his talk show, "The lunatics over at Sux News, the fake news station, have come out against Cannastar. I know, I've said they're a propaganda network that panders to the mentally deceased, but for once I agree with them. Why would anyone want to smoke Cannastar? I mean, what's the point of getting well if you can't get high?"

Brooke Balls, with her tomboy haircut, radiant smile and radiant skin, hosted a talk show on RSN, the Reality Show Network. In rebuttal to the Cannastar critics she protested to the camera, "BUT IT WORKS! I haven't had the sniffles since I started taking it and I used to get a cold every six weeks." She smiled, ironically amused, and asked, "What are these people thinking? Hello! Cannastar is the solution to healthcare in this country!"

The short guy over at Comedy Central's World News Headquarters reported, "Now that people are starting to take Cannastar, the AMA is recommending that doctors start holding bake sales to help cover their overhead."

The hyper host of the comedy show that followed the short guy's show said, "People who drink this Cannastar poison are starting to come down with life threatening cases of joy and happiness. America won't stand for it, I tell you!"

The late night comedian with the big chin and the big car collection said, "I put Cannastar in the gas tank of one of my cars. It didn't help the gas mileage, but the car definitely stopped smoking."

The folks over at Sux News, however, were just getting started. "Coming up, a report on the Cannastar plague that is sweeping our nation," said Karen Ho, the Asian news anchor who looked like a hostess in a strip club. "But first these words from our sponsor, The Rxon Corporation."

THE FALCON JET TOUCHED DOWN at Washington Dulles, taxied to the Executive Terminal where it let Cyd and Alex off, then throttled up and with a whining scream taxied away again for takeoff.

Alex rented a car and he and Cyd drove to the RV park outside Arlington where Otis was staying. Eloise had just popped her famous home-made Lasagna into the oven when there was a knock at the door of their motor home. She opened the door and with a delighted squeal threw her arms around the necks of the visitors. Otis joined in and Elton shook hands with the guests in a very adult manner.

Seated in the living room, Otis and his family listened in awe as Cyd and Alex told them the stories of the children of the jungle and the Mexican Disneyland on *Cola de Diablo*— and how they were now in partnership with a one-eyed homicidal maniac with a soft spot for kids who was perhaps the biggest drug dealer in the world.

"Cool," Otis said.

Eloise sang, "Oh beautiful, for spacious skies, for verdant waves of Cannastar…"

"You don't see a problem here?" Alex said. "Like how do we keep Don Bueno from hunting us down and having us killed if by some off chance we can't grow enough Cannastar to supply the world?"

"Let me show you something," Otis said, bouncing out of his TV lounger and leading them outside where he pulled open a door to one of the cargo bays under his bus. Inside was a storage area crammed with burlap bags. "A little trick I learned from Maury," he said. "Paranoid hording."

Cyd whistled softly. "There must be a ton of Cannastar seed here."

"Half a ton, anyway," Otis said. "So that means we're half way there. Now all we need is the dirt to plant them in."

"A few thousand acres where nobody is going to notice what we're doing," Alex said. "That shouldn't be difficult."

Otis was studying them with curiosity. They hadn't said anything, but they didn't have to. "I'm glad you two made up," he said. "You were wearing me out."

Cyd and Alex looked at one another and smiled, and she gave Alex a kiss.

"So what's in the other cargo hold?" Alex asked. "More seed?"

Otis pulled up the door to the second storage compartment. The bay was stuffed with black garbage bags full of dried Cannastar leaves. "These are for the free clinic," he said.

"Free clinic?" Cyd asked.

"The one me and Eloise started in DC while you were away."

Off and on they had discussed the idea of free clinics to dispense Cannastar, but the economics of altruism had stopped them. Charity is expensive, and up until now they hadn't been able to afford it.

Eloise called them back inside for dinner. Over lasagna, bread and salad, Otis explained that Eloise was really the one who had made the clinic happen. Her idea was to train people at this clinic so they could open up other clinics.

"Part of what Otis makes from growing Cannastar we intend to invest in making sure it's available to everybody," she said. "You wouldn't believe what a big hit the clinic is. I can barely keep it supplied."

"And I'm the poster boy," Elton bragged. "Everybody that comes there wants to be like me."

"And they will," his mother assured him, giving him a proud hug. "The problem is, I don't know how I'm going to be in two places at once tomorrow. The clinic wants me to drop off more Cannastar because they're almost out and I need to be at Elton's school to talk to his counselor about putting him in an advanced math class. And after that I have to be at his soccer game."

"I'd be happy to do it," Cyd said. "I'd like to see the clinic anyway."

"Would you mind?" Eloise said. "I'd really appreciate it."

Cyd asked Alex if he wanted to come along.

"I'll see it another time," he said. "I want to go visit Annie and tell her about all the kids' lives she helped save down in Mexico. She needs to know what a good job she's doing."

Otis frowned. "Don't tell her about the deal you cut with this Don Bueno dude. You'll just overwhelm her and make her feel guilty because she can't grow all the Cannastar we need."

"I don't mind going alone," Cyd offered.

Cyd and Alex spent the night in Arlington and the next morning drove back to the RV park where Otis loaded a big bag of Cannastar into the trunk of the rental car for Cyd to take to the clinic. Annie had bought Otis a white Ford pickup so he could get back and forth to work at the greenhouse and haul the farming supplies he was always buying. Alex got into the truck with him for the trip to Annie's and waved to Cyd as she drove off.

Eloise, getting ready to drive Elton to school in her Honda, called from the motor home door: "Don't anybody be late because I'm making pot roast tonight!"

The pot roast would go uneaten.

THE BOMBED-OUT NEIGHBORHOOD WAS as bleak and gray as East Berlin before the wall came down. Cyd couldn't believe a place like this could exist this close to the nation's Capital.

She didn't need an address to spot the clinic. Up ahead, hundreds of people were crowded around the door to an old brick warehouse. A disorganized line stretched around the block, spilling into the dreary street and blocking traffic.

Cyd was forced to park a block away. Pulling over to the curb she marveled at the miracle she was witnessing, at the hope and faith she saw on the faces of the chronically and terminally ill who stood waiting patiently for their twice-daily measure of Cannastar.

It was exciting to watch. The idea that all of these people could suddenly be returned to health was overwhelming. It brought back all that she had been through—the suffering, the fear, the struggle and the pain—and made it all worthwhile.

She got out of her car still amazed at what they had created and went around and opened the trunk where she pulled out the large black garbage bag that Otis had put in there. Her hand was on the trunk lid to slam it closed when she looked up and saw the riot vans pull up. Dozens of armored trucks rolled to a halt and squads of police in bulletproof vests jumped out armed with clubs and shields. They began immediately dispersing the crowd, bullying them out of line with pushes and shoves, as a bus with barred windows appeared to haul away the volunteers working inside.

Vivid memories of the horrid raid on Otis's attic flashed through Cyd's mind. She stood watching, the bag of Cannastar forgotten in her hand, as the people in the street began to resist, meekly at first, then more forcefully as the policemen's clubs came out and shouts and rocks began to fly.

A bullhorn, blaring above the din: "By order of the commissioner this is an unlawful assembly for the purpose of engaging in the distribution and use of illegal drugs. You are hereby ordered to disperse immediately or face incarceration."

"Incarcerate this!" shouted a young black man, throwing a rock. The kid had a major league arm and the rock struck a black shirted policeman in the helmet, knocking him down. The tear gas came out and instantly the whole scene was engulfed in billowing clouds of stinging burning haze. Then windows began to break and the looting began.

Absorbed in the horror, Cyd did not see the squad car that had pulled up alongside her. The siren made a moaning growl and she jumped a foot.

"Move along, please," the car said over its loud speaker. "This is a crime scene, move along."

Cyd remained frozen, too traumatized to think. A cop got out of the car with his hand on his gun. The image of Jesse Longbow in a murdered tribal policeman's uniform flashed through her mind. She struggled to collect herself.

"What's going on, Officer?"

"Ma'am, I'm going to need you to show me the contents of your bag."

Cyd looked down and realized what she was holding. "Oh, this is just some old clothes I was taking to the clinic."

"The clinic is an illegal drug operation, not the Goodwill. Open the bag now please."

Cyd hesitated...as shots were fired from somewhere in the boiling crowd. The officer jumped back in the squad car and it sped off in a burst of speed to be swallowed up by the escalating riot.

Cyd tossed the bag of Cannastar back in the trunk, slammed the lid and hurriedly got behind the wheel. Tears were streaming down her cheeks. People—the sick and dying along with the volunteers—were being hauled out of the warehouse in handcuffs and prodded aboard the bus with nightsticks. Crying uncontrollably, Cyd fumbled with the keys, started the car and made a screeching U-turn.

LATER THAT SAME DAY TY SEELEY showed up at his parent's house in Virginia for a surprise visit and recognized the fat guy working for his mother in her greenhouse.

Cyd had arrived grief stricken from her experience in DC that morning and was inside the greenhouse being consoled by Annie and Alex. Otis was sitting on a bench outside the greenhouse trying to get over his upset. He was going to have to tell Eloise that the clinic was gone and he knew she would take it hard. Rubbing his temples, he looked up and saw a round figure in ostrich skin cowboy boots walking toward him down the great slope of lawn from the main house. The little doughboy with the tiny mouth looked vaguely familiar. Their eyes met and they recognized each other at the same time. Ty was the one who had Cyd and Maury followed initially and had himself sat across the street from Otis's funeral home to see who they were spending so much time with so he was intimately familiar with what Otis looked like.

Otis came rushing into the greenhouse shouting for Alex, Annie and Cyd to hide!

It was too late.

Ty entered the glass domed conservatory and stopped, mouth ajar, gaping at the illegal crop of Cannastar pushing up toward the light. Then he saw the three people standing with his mother and a sadistic grin spread over his face.

"Would you look at this," he cried. "Would you goddamn look at *this*! My own mother! This is unbelievable! You're the ones. You're the criminals that have been growing this shit. I got you, by God, I got you good."

"Leave," Annie whispered, her voice rising to a shrill scream. "LEAVE HERE THIS INSTANT!"

"When Dad finds out he is going to tear this place to the ground and you along with it!"

Otis and Alex picked up shovels and started toward him as if to bury him. Despite his bravado, Ty began backing away. They made a grab for him and missed. Ty turned, bolted from the greenhouse and ran for the house.

Annie stood staring after her son with her hands pressed to her cheeks in horror. "I'm sorry," she sobbed. "I'm so sorry. What have I done?"

They took her in their arms and held her, rocking her back and forth, while up at the main house Ty flew through the door looking back over his shoulder. He rushed to the den and quickly dialed his father's private number.

Sam Seeley listened impassively as his son related the news. When he was finished Sam hissed, "Just sit still." Anyone overhearing the tone of his voice would have feared for their lives. "Don't move! Don't do a thing until I get there."

"They're going to pay big time," Ty raved excitedly. This was a feather in his cap, a big feather, and it was going to score him a lot of points with a lot of people. "I'm calling the cops!"

"You do," Sam said, "and I'll cut off your nuts and feed them to the dog."

ANNIE DIDN'T KNOW WHERE TY was, somewhere in another part of the house waiting for his father to come home, she supposed. Since her son had accosted her in her greenhouse she had come up to the house and taken a long hot bath to calm herself. Now, dressed in a pretty summer frock, she stood at the window of her drawing room, surrounded by crystal vases of cut flowers, staring out at one of her colorful gardens and feeling considerably more composed.

Sam Seeley burst into the room shouting and cursing, waving his arms like the house was on fire. Which, in a manner of speaking, it was. "What have you done to me? Have you lost your cottin' pickin' mind? Are you trying to destroy me?"

"Mind your blood pressure, Sam."

"I'll mind it after you're fitted for a straightjacket and locked up in the loony bin!"

"I was only trying to help, you see. So many people are relying on me."

"Tell it to the judge."

"Excuse me?"

"You heard what I said."

"Very well," Annie said, smoothing the front of her dress. "I'll tell him that every bit of Cannastar that's been sold from Maine to Florida was grown in your backyard, how about that? I'll tell him that it was your idea and that I was just being a good wife in following my husband's instructions. I suppose I'll have to go to jail for a while. With all the legislation and hype you've created over this, I wonder what they'll do to you?"

Sam Seeley's face turned heart attack red. "I'll deny it," he sputtered, spittle running from the corners of his mouth.

"You do that," she suggested. "Everybody knows you're a greedy hypocrite, Sam, but I bet they'll be surprised to find out how greedy and hypocritical you really are." The idea amused her and she laughed. It sounded like tiny bells.

"You won't be laughing when I'm done with you!" he said defensively.

"Imagine," she said, "the Senator that's been protecting the American people from this deadly Cannastar menace has all along been the one growing it and selling it. I can't wait to see the headlines."

He was cornered and he knew it. "I'll tell you one thing," he said, snatching up a vase of flowers, "your little garden party is over and your associates are going to jail!" He smashed the vase to the floor. "How do you like that?"

Outwardly, Annie remained calm; inwardly, she was terrified for her friends. "I don't want you coming around here any more," she said.

"What?"

"Stay away from my house. I mean it or you'll be explaining to the whole country why your wife is divorcing you for forcing her to commit this heinous crime."

He reached for another vase, but she beat him to it, snatching it away and weighing the heavy crystal in her hand. She was small, but all the gardening work had left her in good shape. She pitched it violently at his head. He ducked as the vase whizzed past him, shattering against the wall. He stumbled back and she picked up another, feeling she had the range now. "I told you to get out and I mean it! And you can take your worthless, murdering leach of a son with you! I never want to see either of you again!'

Fuming and bellowing Sam backed out the door, slamming it behind him. The remaining flower vases rattled on their tables. Annie stood staring after him...then burst into tears. She was no longer a miracle worker, no longer America's pharmacist and grower of good health. That phase of her life was over. And so was her marriage.

IT WAS ON EVERY TELEVISION station and in every newspaper:

Cannastar epidemic stopped in its tracks!

The location of where the illegal drug had been grown remained a mystery. In the interest of national security, no one from the government was talking. The rumor was that in addition to a Cannastar farm, it was also a meth lab and that there had been a terrible explosion, obliterating everything. The important thing was that the persons responsible for trying to turn Americans into drug addicts had been identified and a nationwide manhunt was underway for their capture.

Pictures of Cyd, Alex and Otis flashed on TV screens across the nation and were reprinted in all the newspapers. The National Enquirer had all three of them on the cover with a headline that read:

Health Drug Heroes On The Run!

Meanwhile, Sux News reported that Dick Tremble, the CEO of Rxon Corporation, had made a $1 million dollar contribution to cancer research in the name of the victims who had lost their lives to Cannastar.

They fled.

Otis, Eloise and Elton had some tense hours until they could get off the Interstate. Now they were sticking to the back roads, heading west. Up ahead, Otis could see Alex and Cyd in Eloise's blue Honda keeping about a quarter of a mile distance between themselves and the lumbering RV. They were running interference; their job was to be the decoy in case of trouble.

CHAPTER 15

Cash Crop

T he fugitives escaped across state lines, across the eastern states, and into the heartland, the Midwest, the bread basket of America. They returned to the land. And Iowa almost became a narco state. This is how it happened:

The dawn was at their backs and still hours away when they crossed the Mississippi river at Dubuque and entered Iowa on Highway 20. A hundred miles further on, the lights of Waterloo came and went in the night. They were running… with nowhere to run. Up ahead, Cyd and Alex's taillights were leading Otis through the dark. In the rear of the RV he could hear his family sleeping softly. He didn't mind at all driving at night; he liked the quiet. He could feel the unseen farm land swelling around him, bursting with life.

The sun comes up early in Iowa because the curve of the earth is the only place for it to hide. The road continued to unroll in front of the onrushing RV like velvet carpet going from black to gray in the growing light. Soon Otis could see the sections of land laid out around him in perfect squares as if the world was a grid of checkerboard green. Driving into the dark side of the dawn he could sense the crops throbbing in the ground, eager for the light, pushing up from the soil. He wasn't sleepy; he had never felt more alive. As the sun came up he rolled down his window and inhaled the sweet smell of the earth and it filled him with joy. He didn't need food; he could live off this air. Rich and moist, it smelled like home and like the earth he felt fecund.

His cell phone rang, startling him out of his reverie and nearly giving him a heart attack. It was Cyd. She was starving and if she didn't get coffee and breakfast soon she was going to get very, very angry.

"I'm just passing a sign that says, 'Fort Dodge, 20 miles'," he said.

"Make it so, Number One."

THE EARLY BIRD RESTAURANT IN Fort Dodge was a pickup truck café like any other, rich in smells of fried food and coffee and rich in another way as well: it was where old friends met every day to make old fashioned, long-winded conversation, mostly boring bullshit same as anywhere, but the stuff of life nonetheless. And if you showed up in anything but a pickup you probably weren't from here.

The weary travelers parked their two vehicles beside the restaurant and got out. Alex stopped them as they were heading for the entrance.

"Okay, let's have them," he said, holding out his palm and wiggling his fingers. "Hand over your cell phones."

Bleary-eyed and groggy from the road, they did as he asked. Alex began angrily breaking them in half and tossing them into the dumpster beside the building.

"What the hell are you doing?" Cyd said.

Alex took his own phone out of pocket and broke it in half as well. "From now on we use only disposable cell phones with prepaid minutes that can't be traced and when we use one we destroy it. Otherwise, it's like leaving a trail of bread crumbs for them to follow." Alex saw the horrified looks on Cyd and Otis's faces. "You only made one call," he assured them as they went inside the café. "It probably doesn't matter."

The Early Bird was packed and noisy and they had to wait a few minutes for a group of farmers at one of the round tables to pay their bill and leave before the table could be cleared and they could sit down. The owner and waitress, Mabel Nash, who looked old as rock and nearly as craggy, gave them a surprisingly sweet smile, dumped menus on their table and mutely filled their cups with coffee before rushing off to tend to her other tables. Elton immediately adored her because his cup got coffee in it too.

The front windows of the café looked out across the two lane blacktop at the boundless fields beyond. CNN was on the TV on the shelf behind the lunch counter, but no one was watching because the working men and women at the booths and tables and on the stools found the food, the conversation and the *Fort Dodge Messenger* far more interesting than some fool from Washington or Wall Street telling them how good the economy was. They knew different. The residents of this commercial farming hub, bisected by the beautiful Des Moines River and surrounded by some of the most fertile farm land on the planet, knew their crops and loved their country, but most lived with a feeling, gnawing, new and unspoken, that they were no longer safe.

The hungry travelers ordered ham, bacon, sausage, eggs, potatoes, toast and a mountain of hot cakes and ate like field hands, wolfing it down and chasing it with a gallon of coffee. Cyd was wiping the grease off her face when she looked up and saw their names and faces flash across the television screen. She couldn't hear the sound, but the crawl said:

"Reward Offered for Capture and Conviction"

She put her napkin over her mouth and said, "We need to leave. Now."

"I'm not finished yet," Alex protested.

"Okay," Cyd said. "You want to be Thelma or Louise because any minute we're going to have to run, I can feel it."

"I'll be Thelma," Alex said, looking anxiously left and right with just his eyes. "She was the tall one, right?"

No one in the restaurant had looked at the TV and no one had looked at them, but it was like they were all staring at them. Cyd could feel their eyes on the back of her neck. She gulped the last of her coffee and started to stand just as a large breasted, thick-waisted woman with a tightly curled perm came up to their table and stood over them nervously wringing her hands.

"Excuse me," she said. "You're them, aren't you?"

"Them who?" Cyd said defensively.

Otis grinned and extended his hand. "Otis Appleseed," he said.

The woman shook his meaty paw as if he were a movie star. "Oh my gracious," she said, too overwhelmed to think of anything else to say. "Oh my gracious." She turned and over her shoulder to no one in particular, still holding Otis's hand, said, "Would you look who's come to town."

Dead silence.

Then a clap, a single sound like a gunshot, followed by another and yet another, gaining in tempo as others joined in until the whole restaurant was applauding, rising to their feet as they clapped and cheered.

Cyd sat dumbstruck, Alex looked amazed, Otis was thrilled and Eloise was clapping along with them.

"Why are they all doing that?" Elton asked, looking around in confusion.

Alex tousled his hair. "I think they're trying to say welcome to Iowa, son."

"Does that mean we're not being arrested?" Cyd asked incredulously.

"Not today," Alex said, smiling and acknowledging the applause. "At least not at the moment."

A farmer, weathered as a Halloween corn stalk and with the bluest, saddest eyes Cyd had ever seen came over to their table, introduced himself as Abe Robinson and asked if he could sit down. Otis told him to pull up a chair and when he did he was immediately joined by almost everybody else in the room. Eager friendly faces crowded around, peppering the bewildered travelers with questions.

Mabel Nash went to the front door, quietly locked it and put out the closed sign.

Alex sat back enjoying the show. He couldn't help admiring how sociable Cyd was being and how much everyone seemed to like her. Of course the ever-lovable Otis was the center of attention and Eloise proudly deferred all questions to him. But Elton had his own audience. It seemed he had a knack for storytelling. With impeccable timing and appropriate dramatic pauses, he was offering a lengthy rendition of how he had cured himself of cancer. When asked about his part in all this Alex smiled and said, "Me, I'm just an itinerate doctor trying to keep the lady he loves from getting tarred and feathered for selling snake oil."

After thirty minutes or so of disjointed explanations of how Cannastar worked, and most importantly how the rugged weed was grown, many were asking where they could get some for themselves and their families. Abe Robinson leaned over and whispered something in Alex's ear. Alex relayed the message to Cyd who whispered it to Otis who nodded agreement. Abe stood up and announced:

"Everyone please, could I have your attention?" He was a quiet, stoop-shouldered man, patient and proud, who liked virtually everyone just as they were and so was loved just as he was. He was always saying he wasn't that smart, but when he spoke people listened. He was fiercely religious, tenacious as a wind-bent tree, and did not blame God for the recent death of his wife.

Abe cleared his throat and the room fell quiet. "What do you say we give these young folks a break before we talk them dry? It's a dangerous situation they're in. What they're trying to do is important and I don't think any of us want to see them arrested."

Cyd mouthed, "Thank you."

He went on. "Maybe I'm the only one worried about this, but what do you think is going to happen if you go out and tell everybody you know who you met here today?"

"They'll all go to jail," offered the lady with the perm.

Widespread murmurs of agreement.

"Probably that's right," Abe said. "And me along with them because they need to get off the road for a while and I'm taking them home." Eloise looked at Otis and a smile brightened her face. "I don't know the legal words for it, but that makes me guilty too. So my question to you is this: how do we protect them...and me?"

"I suppose you're suggesting we keep our mouths shut," said a big bellied, red faced farmer. "I guess there's a first time for everything."

Everybody laughed and a bond was formed among farmers who had known each other all of their lives who suddenly had a vested interest in five strangers who had just come to town. It was a conspiracy, an agreement, a trust; their lips were sealed.

Abe nodded curtly. "Lord willing, something good will come of this. That's all I have to say."

An unctuous redheaded scarecrow of a bookkeeper who lived with his mother and worked for the grain elevator in town that was owned by Farmacopia got off his counter stool and came over to take Otis's hand, pumping it vigorously up and down.

"I think I speak for everyone here when I say welcome, welcome, welcome," the scarecrow said. "We're all so happy to have you in Fort Dodge, yes indeed. If there's anything I can do, anything at all, please don't hesitate to call." He took a little metal box from his pocket, opened it, carefully selected one of his business cards and handed it to Otis. "Wilfred Baines is the name, grain's my game."

The man gave Cyd the creeps.

REVOLUTIONS WOULD BE A LOT more fun if nobody got hurt.

Simon Bolivar, the European educated, democratically inspired Venezuelan aristocrat who united most of Latin America under his presidency before dying in disillusionment, is reported to have said, "All who served the Revolution have plowed the sea." Perhaps if he had plowed an Iowa corn field things would have turned out differently. Because another revolution was coming and, nascent and vulnerable as it was, if it were to take root it could uproot the world. Which was why it had to be stopped.

In a state with over 90,000 farms, Abe Robinson's farm was bigger than most since he had borrowed against his 320 acres to buy 320 more. He wanted a full section so he could grow more feed corn for the government subsidized ethanol program. Now his Adjustable Rate Mortgage, predatorily known as an ARM, was eating him alive. His payments had doubled from what they were in the beginning, they were scheduled to go up again and he was six months away from foreclosure. He didn't know how he could work all his life only to end up homeless, but that was what was happening.

Abe led the Honda and the RV along a rural dirt road that divided his section of land from his neighbor's, turned in at a battered mail box with a yellow tube under it for newspapers and in a cloud of dust continued on down a rutted drive toward a huge white weather-beaten farmhouse in the middle of his fields. The house had been built by his wife's grandparents who had raised twelve kids there.

He passed the house and stopped in front of a great ramshackle barn with peeling red paint sides, got out and put his weight against the heavy barn doors to slide them open before motioning the Honda and RV inside. The cavernous interior of the barn was cool and dark and smelled of manure and hay. Otis rolled to a stop behind Cyd and Alex, switched off the RVs ignition and breathed a sigh of relief. They got out to help Abe close the barn doors, then followed him to the house

"Sweet," Elton said, looking around at the empty land that showed no sign of the fugitives ever having come this way. The rich soil was plowed in deep unplanted furrows that led away from the house in every direction. The only sounds were the birds and the insects.

They entered the house through a torn screen door to a service porch that led to the kitchen. Apart from the puce colored walls and the fifty year old stove and refrigerator, the worn out linoleum floored kitchen was the same as it had been before the farm got electricity. In the center of the floor was a long rectangular table covered in a flowered oilcloth where four generations of hungry farmers had been fed.

Abe led them through to the living room and up the stairs. It was a sad house, cold and lifeless, despite the brightly painted walls. The living room was a shocking shade of yellowish orange and furnished with twenty-three swivel chairs that sat in a circle, each a different color that clashed with the next and bought at a terrific discount over several months back in 1950 when the local dime store was going out of business and being replaced by a super center. The paint was purchased at different times throughout the early '50s, also at great savings, during a time when the stores didn't have paint mixers and had to guess at what the customers might like and then sell the colors they didn't like at a loss. Brenda Robinson knew a bargain when she saw one and considered herself lucky to have been able to buy such pretty colors on sale for less than a dollar a gallon. Decorating was her hobby.

Otis and Eloise were given their own bedroom, Cyd and Alex another and Elton a third, each with a warm soft bed and a fifty mile view of absolutely nothing. Cyd stood looking around in alarm at the not-quite-chartreuse walls of their room as Alex unpacked.

"I have a car in LA that's almost this same color," Alex said, not looking up. "Her name is Slime."

"How lovely."

That evening Eloise made supper. Cyd helped, but since she couldn't cook it was mostly Eloise's doing. In the year since Brenda Robinson had died it was the first time anyone had used the kitchen. Abe looked around the table at his guests laughing and talking as they ate and his eyes grew moist.

"Thanks for having us," Eloise said.

"It's a big place," Abe said stiffly. "No sense letting it go to waste. Have some more lemonade." He filled Eloise's glass from a big pitcher. "Wife made lemonade in this pitcher for forty years before she died." He paused, looking up at the purplish-brown walls. "She was sixty-two. The cancer got her."

"I'm so sorry," Cyd said.

"You know, I served my country for five years during Vietnam and when my wife got sick, there was nobody to help her. No insurance, no government, no nothing. If your Cannastar had been around last year maybe…" his voice trailed off. In his distraction his eyes wandered to the kitchen television that was always on and always tuned to Sux News. He reached over and turned up the volume as the same pictures of Cyd, Alex and Otis appeared that had been on CNN earlier in the day. The announcer was saying that the Federal government had stepped up its efforts to apprehend the fugitives. They cut away to a sound bite from an impromptu speech Senator Sam Seeley had given earlier in the day on the Capital steps. In grave stentorian tones he said, "These criminals who have harmed so many innocent Americans with their poisonous drug must and will be punished."

Eloise gasped as Abe switched off the TV. "I've been thinking," he said. "This hybrid plant of yours. Where does it grow?"

"Anywhere it wants, pretty much," Otis said. "It's not overly sensitive to temperature. All you need is sun, water and some place to plant it."

"I got six hundred and forty acres of arable land," Abe said. "Not that it's any good without seed."

"I might be able to help you with that," Otis said.

Alex was skeptical. "You can't just plant a square mile of Cannastar out in the open where everyone can see it."

"Sure you can," Abe said. "No problem."

"I'm all ears," Alex said.

"Exactly," Abe said. "Ears of corn. Rows of it—dense as fog and twice as thick."

"And in between the corn you plant the Cannastar!" Otis said excitedly.

"Couldn't spot it from a hundred feet up in a crop duster," Abe said.

Cyd started to say *fuck me*, but bit her tongue.

As an afterthought Abe asked, "Can you make any money with this Cannastar?"

"Boat loads," Cyd said.

Abe nodded. "Then we should get to bed. Farmers have to get up early."

Cyd went upstairs, brushed her teeth and climbed between the covers with Alex, but she was too excited to sleep.

ABE'S CORN SHOULD HAVE BEEN in the ground weeks ago, but it wasn't. His fields lay fallow, waiting for a crop that wouldn't come. Devastated by the loss of his wife and the impending loss of his farm, he had lost heart. But sometimes the heart is only sleeping, waiting to be revived, in the way that fields in winter only look like death.

Otis wandered out among the furrows trying to calculate how much space to give the Cannastar so that it would remain hidden and at the same time not get crowded out by the corn. He stooped to pick up a handful of earth and put it to his nose, inhaling deeply. The smell made him feel like anything was possible.

A month later Otis stood in the same spot looking down at green sprouts that were poking up through the ground. Cyd and Alex were beside him, tanned and freckled from working in the fields. "There was nothing...and now there's something," Otis marveled. "I'll never get over it."

Everyone they met that first morning at the Early Bird knew about the project. They kept dropping by Abe's farm to see how the secret experiment was coming along and offer endless advice. Sometimes Abe's driveway was lined with pickups. He had to stay on his tractor and keep well away from the house to get any work done.

For obvious reasons Cyd, Alex and Otis could not leave the farm, but Eloise and Elton could come and go as they pleased. Eloise did all the cooking and shopping and scrubbed and cleaned until the house looked like a home again. Eager voices, tired and hungry, filled the kitchen every night. Elton would start school in the fall, but for now his new best friend was Abe and he spent every spare moment riding with him on the tractor. At dinner one night he announced that when he grew up he wanted to be a farmer.

"All I can say is, don't borrow any money if you can help it," Abe said.

"Don't worry, I won't have to," Elton said. "I'm going to be rich from growing Cannastar."

After dinner that night Alex and Otis wandered into the living room together. Otis was saying how thrilled he was to see the Cannastar thriving in a natural environment even though he didn't think it was going to be quite as potent as the plants they grew hydroponically. Out of the corner of his eye he spied a row of dog-eared Burpee seed catalogues on a bookshelf. He squeezed between two of the colorful swivel chairs to take a few down and thumb through them. On the shelf beside the catalogues was a framed picture of a young soldier in uniform that Alex hadn't noticed before. The face looked vaguely familiar. He picked it up and was examining it just as Abe walked in.

Alex said, "I think I know this boy. What's his name?"

"Cal Robinson," Abe said. "He was my son."

"Was?"

"Iraq war. He's buried next to my wife. How could you possibly know him?"

Alex felt a chill go through him. "I kept him alive inside a mud hut after an IED blew off his leg."

Abe was shocked. "He wrote me about you. You saved his life."

"How did he die?"

"Suicide. Six days before he was scheduled to be shipped home." The farmer's hands were trembling.

"He was a fine brave soldier," Alex said, shaken by the coincidence.

"I know."

Cyd came into the room talking on one of the throw-away cell phones Eloise had bought for them in town. She held the phone out to Otis. "I called Annie so she wouldn't worry about us," she said. "She wants to talk to you."

Otis moved to the other side of the room and turned his back for privacy. "Annie!" he cried. "Oh my God, how are you?" Listening. "No, no we're fine, don't worry. We're back in business, can you believe that?" He held the phone at arm's length to keep Annie's excited squeal from hurting his ear. She asked where they were. Before answering he had to remind himself that Annie's phone was not a security risk—nobody was looking for her. "Iowa," he said.

"I miss you all so much," Annie said. "Since you left I've been so bored and lonely in this big house all by myself. I suppose you have all the help you need."

Otis tried to duck the remark. "We don't need any help."

"You're a terrible liar, darling."

"Sorry," he said sheepishly. "It's just that what we're doing here is growing illegal drugs right out in the open. It's too risky for you to get involved."

"You can't scare me. I'm too old to be frightened of anything. And growing Cannastar is as much a part of me as it is of you."

"I know, but…"

"I have my own airplane, you know darling. I made Sam sign it over to me along with the house, some rather large investments and a number of big bank accounts."

"How did you manage that?"

"Hush money. It's how you get divorced without getting divorced."

"Cool."

"I'm calling the pilot as soon as I hang up. I'll be there in a jiffy. Have you got some place for me to stay?"

"We got more bedrooms than a Holiday Inn."

SO ANNIE CAME AND THEY were once again a team.

Eloise watched the Citation CJ4 appear out of the sun and with barely a whisper touch down at the Fort Dodge airport. Annie deplaned and told the pilot to go home but to stay close to the phone. Eloise loaded Annie's pile of Gucci luggage into the back of her Honda and they drove out to the farm.

Cyd, Alex and Otis came out of the house when they heard the Honda coming down the driveway and were standing in the gravel drive waiting when Annie got out of the car. They hugged and kissed as Abe drove up in his tractor. He got down and he and Annie met. It was fusion at first sight. They started talking not from the beginning of anything but like they were picking up in the middle of a long running conversation. The others watched in amazement as Annie confidently took Abe's arm and together, chatting like old friends, they walked out into the fields so she could admire the flourishing farm.

At dinner that night Abe and Annie remained engrossed in one another. It was like they were the only two people at the kitchen table. Cyd looked from one to the other and realized in amazement that their eyes were almost the same startling shade of blue.

Abe picked up a platter of pork chops and offered them to Annie. "Annabelle, would you like another?" She smiled and shook her head. "How about some more potatoes then?"

"Abraham dear, I'm fine. You wouldn't want me to spoil my figure."

Is he blushing? Cyd thought. *I actually think he's blushing."*

"I didn't mean…"

"Of course you didn't, darling. Would you care to take the air with me after supper? It's such a lovely evening and I would so enjoy the company."

Cyd cleared the table as Abe fumbled to help Annie on with her sweater. They went out the door absorbed in an animated conversation about farming. Abe was explaining how the maize they were growing to hide the Cannastar was really a transgenic plant as well, genetically engineered from a virus resistant strain of corn from the highlands of northern Mexico.

"Part of the genome from the Mexican Maize that coded for resisting against the virus was incorporated into the existing strain of our commercial corn," he said. "The result was corn that's resistant to a virus that used to devastate crops here in the US."

Annie hung on his every word, smiling up at him, not so much listening to what he said as feeling what he was saying. He was a good and decent man, a lonely man. They had much in common.

Over the summer and into the fall Annie's boundless energy energized them all. Laboring right along side of them, she was as happy as she had been working in her own greenhouse. The effect on Elton and Abe was transformative. For his part, Elton grew jealous and wouldn't tell his mother why he was sulking. It was because Abe was spending all his time with Annie and ignoring him. As for Abe, Annie had done what none of them could do; she had brought the widower back to life. He looked and acted 20 years younger and went about his chores with a vigor that amazed everyone.

Although they had just met, the friendship between Annie and Abe did not seem new, it seemed old. It was as though in another life they had agreed to meet again in this one when they needed each other the most. Otherwise, without a shared history and without sex, how could you explain it? They both had emotional baggage from this lifetime that they were carrying around, but as each day passed they moved more and more of it into storage where it could stay safe and dry and not be so much underfoot.

IT WAS ALMOST THANKSGIVING AND the Cannastar was finally ready for harvest. The six hundred and forty acres of feed corn that had so successfully hidden the Cannastar all summer with its tall stalks and broad green leaves was ready for harvest as well, brittle and dried to the color of wheat. Otis looked out his upstairs window to admire his crops. His breath stopped and blood started pounding in his head. Poking up above the dead looking corn were thousands of lush green Cannastar bushes, flourishing in the sun in colors of emerald and jade and bursting with rainbow seeds.

They were exposed!

Otis rushed downstairs in a panic. Everyone followed him outside and they stood looking helplessly out over the fields.

"We need to get it in fast," Otis said. "Right now, today."

Cyd was paralyzed. "How the fuck are we going to harvest a square mile of Cannastar all by ourselves?"

Just then there was a lot of noise and honking as a convoy of pickups came rumbling down Abe's driveway. Cyd's first thought was that they were being busted and she flashed on The Great Swimming Pool Massacre. When she saw their friends from the Early Bird piling out of their trucks and waving farm tools in the air she beamed. They were here for the harvest. The women had brought food and Eloise helped them carry it into the kitchen. This was going to be a hungry day.

The eager army of harvesters descended on Abe's fields, shouldering their way through the sheltering corn where they began to dig trenches around the jagged leafed Cannastar bushes, pulling the nine foot tall plants up by the roots and loading them onto carts so they could be hauled to the barn. There was no combine harvester to separate the Cannastar from the corn—it all had to be done by hand.

Abe's barn was colossal in size. Otis was inside directing the stacking of the Cannastar plants, piling them up like Christmas trees in one corner and working his way out. He was as upset as he had been this morning looking out his bedroom window, that hadn't changed. Dark rings spread out under his arms. As fast as the bushes were brought in he stripped them of their seeds, loaded them into flower sacks and tossed them into the RV. He wasn't being careful, he was abandoning ship. He had the feeling they were coming—the cops, the DEA, whoever—it was just a matter of time. He had to get the seeds away from here. It was almost lunchtime when he looked out of the barn and saw they had only cleared a small portion of the land. He realized with a sinking heart that this was going to take days.

Alex, pulling on a Cannastar plant, drew his arm across his forehead and glanced up to see the wrinkled smiling face of Mabel Nash on the other side of the same bush pulling with him.

"Once a farm girl always a farm girl," she said, perspiration rolling out from under the band of her straw hat. She looked happy. So did the rest of the farmers down the row they were working in who were sweating into their shirts and laboring like migrants workers. The only difference between them and the illegals normally employed by the farming industry was that instead of getting paid next to nothing they were making exactly nothing.

"Isn't this exciting?" a voice behind him said. Alex turned and saw Annie grinning up at him, her face flushed and dirty.

"You never looked more beautiful," he said.

"Why thank you, dear. This is so much better than sitting at home worrying about how you all are doing. Now I can see for myself how much trouble you're in."

On the other side of the wall of corn and Cannastar separating their row from the next, Alex heard the shutter of a camera click. He shoved aside the stalks and branches in time to see a redheaded beanpole of a man covertly taking pictures of the Early Bird farmers with a small digital camera. He gave Alex an oily groveling smile and tried to slip the camera back into his pocket. Alex stepped through the corn row and grabbed it out of his hand.

"I'm sorry I am, so sorry if I've offended you," the book-keeper said, reaching out for his camera. "I'm only making a record of this momentous event for posterity. May I have my property back please?"

Alex dropped the camera on the ground and smashed it under his heel. "Uh-oh," he said. "Must have slipped."

"I don't understand, sir, I don't understand! Wilfred Baines is just trying to help."

"If you want to help, grab a shovel," Alex said, turning his back and walking off. Eloise rang the lunch bell.

Picnic tables that had not been used in years were lined up under a big tree in the backyard and piled with meat, potatoes, gravy and white bread. The harvesters sat on opposite sides of the tables under a waning fall sky, laughing and talking, powering down fuel for an afternoon of brutal labor that would be interrupted only at four o'clock when the women brought sandwiches, cake and coffee into the fields for an afternoon snack.

Men and women who had looked gaunt and slow at the Early Bird were moving like excited children. They could all feel it swelling in their breasts; they were part of something bursting from the land that was bigger than themselves. It felt somehow like they were taking their country back from the banks that had blown it for everyone, from a democracy that had been nationalized, from the bondage of credit card corporate America. Impossible as it seemed, the industrial revolution was being followed by an agricultural revolution. Accidently on purpose, the farmers had joined the growing storm that Maury, Otis, Cyd and Alex started—a grassroots rebellion against a medical industry that had the American people by the balls and was holding them hostage for a ransom that kept going up. What they dug out of the ground that day was hope for the future and for the first time in a long time they didn't feel helpless and afraid.

Elton, who had been working in the fields right alongside the adults, had his mouth stuffed with fried chicken and was eyeing a layer cake that was just coming out of the kitchen. "This is the best party ever," he said to his mother. It came out *Thth ith the beth party ever.*

Eloise grabbed at his hands in alarm. "They're bleeding, son. What did you do?"

"I lost my gloves," Elton said indifferently. *I Loth my glovth.* "Abe said he'd get me another pair after lunch."

"Don't talk with your mouth full."

Alex looked across at Cyd who was up the table sitting with a group of farmers who were all trying to talk to her at once. She caught his eye and smiled. It was the best smile in the world. And it was all for him.

Eloise took a plate of food out to Otis in the barn. She found him madly stripping and bagging seeds. "Honey, you have to eat something," she said. "Come inside the RV and sit down. Take a break."

He acted like he hadn't heard. "Can you get me another sack? They're right over there."

FIVE DAYS LATER THE CROP was in, the barn was overflowing with Cannastar bushes and the RV was overflowing with seed sacks. Otis should have been relieved, but he wasn't. The feeling that something terrible was about to happen wouldn't go away. He didn't know where he was going to put the RV, but he knew he had to move it. He backed out of the barn, drove down the driveway and into town, cruising around until he saw the airport sitting all by itself in the middle of a deserted corn field. *You want to hide something, hide it in plain sight,* he thought, following the arrows for long term parking. He pulled into a space that overlooked the empty runway and called Eloise to pick him up.

THE EARLY BIRD CREW WORKED in shifts over the next month to help Otis dry and clean the Cannastar leaves. Thousands of large black garbage bags were being stacked to the rafters, filling the barn until the growing pile was bulging out the hayloft door and the place looked like a city dump.

A mountain of roots and stems and branches from the Cannastar plants that they couldn't use was piling up behind the barn. Otis decided to burn the evidence and lit a bonfire. As he watched, a great plume of fragrant smoke rose into the air as if to shout, *Here we are, come and arrest us!* He panicked and began running around trying to put it out. Abe came along and saw Otis desperately throwing buckets of water on the fire.

"If you're trying to make it grow, watering it won't help," he grinned, chewing on a straw, "Around here, when we want to burn off a field, we generally use kerosene."

The crop was in and the work was done. Alex called Joe Angolia in New York, again using one of the throw-away phones, only to find out from his beleaguered secretary that her boss had been indicted for securities fraud and money laundering and had fled the country. Alex was so stunned he couldn't speak. He hung up feeling sick to his stomach.

Rousing himself, he quickly tried to call Don Bueno using a special number he'd been given, waiting anxiously while it rang. To his relief the drug lord finally picked up. Don Bueno sounded distant and removed until he found out that the first harvest of Cannastar was ready for shipment and then he started shouting in Spanish and wouldn't shut up. Finally in English he said, "How much you got for me? How much?"

"I don't know how many tons exactly. A lot."

An explosive stream of Spanish expletives followed that, loosely translated, meant *El Jefe de Jefes* was pleased. The next day a big cargo plane, part of a fleet of surplus military aircraft that Don Bueno owned, arrived at the Fort Dodge airport and the day after that Abe Robinson went into the bank and paid off the mortgage on his farm. It was a proud day.

ON DECEMBER 22ND, ABE THREW a Christmas party for his house guests and their friends from the Early Bird.

The house was jammed with people. For the first time since his wife died, all 23 chairs in his living room were filled. Abe beamed at Annie with pride. His home, once again, had a lovely hostess.

Wilfred Baines was the only one of the Cannastar pickers that Abe had not invited to the celebration. It was because of what Alex and Cyd had told him. The bookkeeper hadn't been much of a help anyway. All he had done was stand around bothering people, telling anyone who would listen how Alex had broken his camera.

When Baines found out he wasn't welcome at the party he made a call to the Federal Drug Enforcement Agency in St. Louis to see if a certain reward was still being offered.

At the party every harvester received a black plastic bag full of Cannastar leaves as a thank you present with the promise of more to come in the spring. They couldn't have been happier if it had been bags of money. Word got out about how much money Don Bueno had paid for the Cannastar crop and suddenly there wasn't a farmer in the room that didn't want to grow it himself. Elaborate plans and hand-shake agreements were made. It appeared that next year a significant portion of Webster County would be in the illegal drug business.

Otis groaned thinking about how much work was going to be involved once all of these farmers started growing it at the same time. Then he thought about what was going to happen when farmers in the neighboring counties found out how much money there was to be made in the Canna-star business and he had to sit down from exhaustion. His paranoia soon kicked in and he realized it didn't matter. They wouldn't be around anyway.

Cyd laid her head contentedly on Alex's shoulder. Her hair was warm and smelled of flowers and her touch was electric.

"Remember where we were last Christmas?" she asked.

"Before or after you found out I was taking pills?"

"How are you doing with that, by the way? You haven't said anything about your back in a long while."

"I can barely remember it hurting at all. My problem at the moment is how the hell do we get off this farm? If it wasn't for you I'd be going stir crazy."

"Interesting you would say that. I'm so restless I'm about to come out of my skin."

"What do we do?"

"I don't know," she said. "We can't stay here forever."

Forever came the next morning when Abe got a call from Mabel Nash down at the Early Bird. Her restaurant was full of DEA agents up from St. Louis whispering about the big raid they were going to pull off today.

CHAPTER 16

Window Rock

Chaos. Confusion. Fear. Everyone shouting and running in different directions at once, grabbing up their belongings. Cyd helping Annie with her bags. Alex outside tossing their stuff in the back of Abe's truck as fast as he could.

"Put those things *in* something!" Eloise screamed at Otis who was grunting down the stairs with an armload of clothes. He charged back upstairs to find a suitcase.

Eloise turned to Elton who had begun to cry. "It's okay, honey. We're just going on a little trip is all."

"I don't want to leave. Why do we have to leave?"

Abe sat slumped at the kitchen table, his hands in his lap, staring straight ahead. Annie came in and stood over him anxiously.

"Abraham, I've called my pilot. My plane will be here any time. We have to go."

"I can't leave," the farmer said. "This is my home."

"I have a home too and I'll go back to it one day, but for now we need to leave or we'll be arrested. You don't want that to happen, do you?"

"You go on. I'll be all right."

Annie sat down stubbornly beside him. "Then I'm staying too. We'll go to jail together."

He turned to her in alarm. "You can't go to jail. I won't allow it."

"Never you mind about me." Cyd came charging past them on her way through the kitchen and Annie caught her arm. "Darling, would you mind getting my bags back out of the truck? I won't be going with you."

Abe blinked rapidly and stood up. In a loud clear voice he said, "Annabelle, you're coming with me and I don't want any argument! We're getting out of here this instant."

"Yes, dear."

Alex was waiting behind the wheel of Abe's four door truck with Cyd beside him. Eloise started for the barn to get her Honda and Otis called her back, telling her to leave it. She did as he asked, looking back sadly over her shoulder as she opened the rear door of the truck and got in. Otis squeezed into the front seat and put Elton on his lap. The only ones still in the house were Abe and Annie.

Excruciating minutes ticked by. Alex blew the horn and still they didn't come. He opened the truck door to go look for them just as they came out of the kitchen. Annie was holding Abe's arm as he dried his eyes.

He had been saying goodbye to his house.

THE PICKUP FISHTAILED OUT OF ABE'S drive, jostling the passengers who were packed shoulder to shoulder inside. Their jumbled pile of belongings in the bed of the truck bounced around like salvage from a flood.

"Where do we go to wait for the plane?" Alex yelled.

"My RV is out at the airport," Otis shouted back. "We can wait inside."

They sat tense and mute as Alex drove to the airfield. He pulled into long term parking and parked next to Otis's motor home. Everyone got out and scrambled into the RV. Otis closed and locked the door behind them, pulled down the window shades and flopped into his chair, breathing hard.

The wait was excruciating. Frightened and nervous, huddled together like refugees, they kept imagining strange sounds and peering out through the blinds to see if the Feds had surrounded the bus.

Finally Alex looked out the windshield and pointed excitedly as a small silver winged jet touched down. "Saddle up!" he said. "Our ride is here."

They drove the RV and the truck out to the plane, constantly looking over their shoulders. No one at the sleepy little airport seemed to notice or care that they were leaving. While the pilot had the aircraft fueled, Otis loaded the bags of Cannastar seed into the belly of the plane. When he was done there was no room left for luggage and the pilot, concerned about the weight, said the only thing more they could put on board was themselves.

Everything they had brought from the house got thrown back in the bed of the truck and Otis and Alex got into the two vehicles to put them back in the parking lot where hopefully they wouldn't be noticed for a while.

"We're losing everything!" Eloise moaned as Otis prepared to drive away.

"We got what matters," Otis said through the open window of the RV.

Annie, holding Abe firmly by the hand, said in a calm voice, "My darlings, we can always buy more underwear when we get to where we're going."

"Where's that?" Cyd said.

Nobody answered.

"Back in a minute," Otis said and drove off.

Minutes later he and Alex came walking rapidly back from the parking lot.

"Everybody on board," Alex said. "Let's go!"

The pilot pulled up the steps, secured the door and settled himself in the cockpit. The engines whined to life and the jet taxied away, pausing a few moments at the end of the runway before the pilot released the brakes and the wheels began to roll.

The Citation rotated off the airstrip and they were gone, thundering into the open sky. Otis let out a sigh of relief that sounded like an exhale from the blow hole of a whale. The plane rose quickly, banking in a wide circle over Fort Dodge. Abe looked out the window at his farm below, suddenly pressing his hand to the glass in anguish. His property was black with cars and men who were swarming his home and fields like locusts. He turned away with a tragic look.

Captain Charles "Futz" Webber headed southwest before turning in his seat to call back to the main cabin. "No rush Mrs. Seeley, you got 2000 miles to make up your mind, but do we have a destination yet?" He spoke with the calm assurance of a man who had flown combat missions in two wars and logged over 20,000 hours at the controls of jet aircraft. He was a gray-headed, good natured, somewhat paunchy ladies' man with faraway smiling eyes whose home was in the cockpit of a plane. Senator Seeley had been the only private employer he ever worked for that he didn't like. He couldn't understand how a classy lady like Mrs. Seeley could be married to such an arrogant little prick of a husband.

"Patience darling, patience," Annie called back to him.

Elton sat in the co-pilot seat next to Futz. The boy's upset over their exodus from the farm was gone. What occupied him at the moment was the dazzling array of colorful glass screens that flashed in front of him. He decided then and there that he didn't want to be a farmer any more; he wanted to be a pilot.

The six escapees sat in the cabin of the Citation looking dazed and confused.

"This is so depressing I feel like I'm back in the funeral business," Otis said.

"We could go to Don Bueno's in Mexico," Cyd said dejectedly, "but the minute we landed there he'd own us."

Eloise started to cry and Otis put his arm around her.

Alex looked up suddenly. "Annie," he said, "does this thing have a telephone?"

"It has several, dear boy. Just open that little door there in the cabinet beside your seat."

Alex fished out the phone, dialed a number and waited for an answer. "Clarence, its Alex!" he said.

Clarence Bigfoot, sitting at his circular desk in his house on the Flathead Reservation, heard the stress in Alex's voice and his delight turned to concern. "Where are you?" he asked. "Are you okay?"

"No, we're not okay," Alex said. "Just listen. We need to find the biggest Indian reservation in the country. It has to be remote and isolated."

"I take it you need to hide."

"That would be an understatement."

"You're talking about the Navajo Nation," Clarence said. "I can't help you."

Alex's heart sank. "But Robert can."

TWO HOURS LATER ANNIE'S CITATION was on final approach to a 7000 foot runway that stretched like a highway to nowhere along the high desert floor. Elton, back in the cabin now with his mother, looked out the window at the desolate lunar landscape that was rushing up toward them and said, "It looks like we're landing on an alien planet."

"That's good. An alien planet is good," Alex said.

The jet whistled down, laid two smoking strips of rubber on the concrete and taxied to a tiny terminal under a bright warm winter sun. They had arrived in Window Rock, capital of the 26,000 square mile Navajo Nation, a sandy speck of a town that lay perched like a baked and scaly lizard on the northern Arizona/New Mexico border.

The engines shut down, the pilot opened the door, and they came down the steps where they were greeted by a handsome smiling Indian with outstretched arms.

"Robert, what in the hell are you doing here?" Cyd cried, hugging him happily.

"I work here," Robert said.

"Doing what? I can't believe it's you!"

"Helping the Navajo develop their natural resources. You wouldn't believe the oil, gas, coal and uranium they have around here."

Shaking hands with the ex-boyfriend he hoped he'd never see again, Alex said,

"I've never been so happy to see anyone in my life."

"Let's get you into town. Pop says you're in trouble."

"When are we not?" Cyd said with a wry smile.

Otis refused to leave the plane. "I'm staying with the seeds," he said.

Annie assured him the plane and the pilot were going nowhere until they figured out what to do.

"Or until we have to run for it again," Otis said.

THE QUALITY INN IN WINDOW ROCK was a southwestern looking motel with large comfortable rooms. Cyd and Alex lay in bed that night staring up at the ceiling. The corn crop idea to hide the Cannastar had been a dangerous failure, and the fact that they were safe for the moment was little consolation.

"What now?" Cyd asked angrily.

"I can't shake the feeling that we're here for a reason," Alex said, lost in thought.

"We tried, you know? We really tried. This can't be all there is, it just can't."

"I agree."

"It feels like we're under a net that's about to drop on our heads."

Alex sat up in bed. "What did you say?"

"About feeling trapped?"

"No. The net. What kind of net?"

"I don't know. The kind that dolphins get caught in, I guess."

He quickly kissed her forehead. "You're a genius!"

"I am?"

Alex fumbled for his cell phone.

"Who are you calling?"

"Clarence."

"It's the middle of the night…"

"Hello, Clarence? Sorry to wake you…No, Robert met us at the plane. Everything's fine. I need your help with something else…"

Clarence switched on his night light, smiling to himself. "This better be good."

Alex said in a rush, "When I was in Iraq we had camouflage nets that we used everywhere. Tan mesh ventilated cloth with fake shrubs on it. If you were flying over you couldn't tell there was anything down there but desert. You could hide a city under one of those nets and nobody would know. I need you to use your military contacts to find out the manufacturer for me."

Clarence thought a moment. "Actually, I know these people. I set up a computerized testing program for them. The latest version of that netting is some kind of amazing stuff. Did you know during WWII in Burbank, California they used something similar to hide the aircraft plants from Japanese war planes?"

"Will you call them for me? We're going to need a lot of it."

"Who's paying for it?"

"You."

"That's what I was afraid of."

Alex hung up and dialed another number.

Bemused, Cyd asked, "Who are you calling now?"

"Robert."

"I figured there must be somebody you hadn't woken up yet."

When Robert answered he told him to hold on a minute. "Get everybody in here," he said to Cyd, holding the phone against his ear with his shoulder while scribbling some notes. "We have a lot to talk about."

Cyd went padding down the carpeted hall in her stocking feet softly knocking on doors. Alex finished his conversation with Robert, broke his cell phone into pieces and threw it in the trash.

THE NEXT MORNING ROBERT CONTACTED Harvey Lawrence on Alex's behalf. The president of the sovereign Navajo Nation was reluctant to meet with the uninvited visitors until Robert told him who they were and what they were running from.

"I have heard about this Cannastar," Lawrence said. "I would like to know more."

That afternoon Robert brought Alex, Cyd and Otis into Lawrence's office. This was the most important sales pitch of Alex's life and his stomach was in knots.

Harvey Lawrence got up and came around his desk to greet his guests. He was a slender, salt and pepper haired man, intelligent and affable, with high cheekbones and narrow eyes. He wore pleated dress slacks and a Navajo shirt. Cyd thought he looked like a middle aged male model. Books on economics, law and business were crammed into his bookcases and priceless Indian artifacts were displayed everywhere as if in an effort to combine the best of the old with the best of the new.

The President motioned for them to be seated. Under his gracious exterior Alex sensed there was an iron will. *This guy is not going to be an easy sell,* he thought.

Lawrence seemed to be particularly taken with Otis and wouldn't take his eyes off him. It was as if he had seen him before and couldn't think where. Then it came to him. "You are the medicine man," he said. "I had a dream about you. You were standing in the middle of a forest you had grown on land where nothing would grow."

"I'm no medicine man," Otis said self-consciously, "but I can grow a garden in a desert."

"Sometimes a man is reincarnated many times in one lifetime until he becomes who he is supposed to be," Lawrence said. "Tell me, Medicine Man, how is this garden of yours grown?"

Otis explained how Cannastar could be grown hydroponically on top of barren soil. "The problems," he said, "are evaporation and keeping the water supplied with enough nutrients."

The president was fascinated. "Water is not something we have a lot of around here," he said.

"If you do it on a large enough scale you're going to need holding tanks for the water you truck in and generators to run the pumps." Otis said.

"How effective is this method?"

"You have year-round sun here so we can get three crops a year," Otis said. "Twice the number of plants can be grown per acre than if they were planted in the ground and they grow faster and healthier without the danger of soil borne diseases...not that anything could kill a Cannastar bush."

"The United States government and Western medicine are afraid of you," Lawrence said. "They will send their airplanes to search. Your healing garden will stick out like Central Park in a sand box."

Alex explained about the camouflage nets and how they worked. "If the Garden of Eden had been under a camouflage net the devil himself couldn't have found it." The President laughed. Encouraged, Alex went on: "The Cannastar will love the indirect light under the nets..."

"Please understand, Dr. Farmer. I have agreed to nothing. How do I know this illegal drug of yours even works?"

Cyd told him about all the people on the east coast who had been cured by the Cannastar and how they were clamoring for more.

"I am more interested in firsthand experience. Do you know anyone personally who has been healed?"

"I'll answer that one," Otis said. He described how Elton and Cyd had been cured, then told his own story. Alex spoke of how the Cannastar had helped him deal with his pain and addiction.

Watching the President's stony face, it was impossible to tell what he was thinking. He shook his head. "It's impossible," he said. "Such a thing could never be distributed on a mass scale."

Cyd knew this was going to come up sooner or later. She bit her lip and told him about Don Bueno. The President's face hardened. Rushing on, she explained about the children of the jungle and saw that he seemed to relax a bit.

"This guy Don Bueno runs the biggest drug store in the world," Alex said. "He's on every street corner from Wasilla, Alaska to Tierra del Fuego. Probably he's crazy and probably he's a saint, maybe both. He's taken on distribution of the Cannastar the same way he took on all those kids. He seems to regard it as his moral duty, his purpose in life, to cure everybody he hasn't killed yet."

The President laughed lightly and it was Alex's turn to relax. "How about transportation?" Lawrence asked. "I can't have trucks leaving the reservation filled with contraband."

"Don Bueno has airplanes that can be in and out of Window Rock before you know it," Alex said. He paused before going on. "Mr. President, we need the use of some extremely remote land. We need help setting up the camo nets. We need water trucks and men to drive them and we're going to need a lot of help tending and harvesting the crops. In return for this, the Navajo Nation will receive ten percent of the net profits."

"You're not asking us to put up any money? A growing operation like the one you describe would be very expensive."

"My dad is paying for all the nets," Robert said.

"And my friend Annie Seeley is putting up the rest of the money," Cyd said.

"The Senator's wife who's with you?"

Cyd hesitated. "Yes."

President Lawrence peered at Alex. "Twenty percent," he said.

He's negotiating! Alex thought. *We got him!* "Fifteen percent," he said.

"Done."

Alex reached out his hand to shake on it, but the president did not respond.

"I will meditate on it," Lawrence said. Alex tried to keep his disappointment off his face. "And then I must present it for approval to the 88 member Tribal Council. Their quarterly meeting is in two weeks."

Cyd said without thinking, "You couldn't get 88 people to agree to go to the same movie together."

ON THE WAY BACK TO the motel Robert told them they should not be discouraged. "All things considered, I thought the meeting went rather well," he said.

It was Christmas Eve once again.

THE WEATHER WAS UNUSUALLY WARM for the first week in January, even for Window Rock.

The Navajo Tribal Council building was a beautiful ultra-modern structure designed to look like an abandoned adobe fort. Inside, the Cannastar petitioners—Alex, Cyd, Otis, Eloise, Elton, Annie, Abe and Robert—sat as invited guests in the back of the big meeting room watching anxiously as members from all 110 chapters of the far flung reservation filed in and filled up the auditorium.

The Navajo had suffered a lot of infighting during many long and confusing years of changing leadership, but according to Robert, they had put their tumultuous past behind them and for the time being were enjoying a period of relative peace and cooperation.

The Speaker, elegantly attired in turquoise jewelry, was a jowly man with wide-set eyes and a drooping black mustache.

He brought the meeting to order and moved the assembly through a tedious agenda of routine business. Finally, it was time for the president to speak. Harvey Lawrence rose to his feet and walked to the podium. He had deliberately leaked word of what he was going to talk about and the news had spread rapidly. The room was charged with anticipation.

Much to Cyd's surprise, it was an impassioned speech. After patiently explaining what he knew about Cannastar, its healing properties, and the pros and cons of growing it on the reservation, he said:

"On portions of our reservation we have found four great natural resources that serve both the white man's nation and our own. Less than 10% of our land is good for planting. We have an opportunity to add a fifth valuable resource that can be grown on otherwise useless land.

"The Dineh understand about natural medicine. In our history, songs, prayers and ceremonies it is part of our culture, part of our way. The Holy Ones have brought us a Medicine Man. I believe he is here to heal the Navajo Nation and, in gratitude, I believe the Navajo must in turn help to heal an ailing world.

"Our faith in the Great Spirit assures us that our Indian nation will live forever, but that alone is not enough. We must participate in our own survival and this participation must not be a selfish act. Our people did not make the Long Walk for nothing; they made it to bring us to here. There is a reason we are thriving, a reason we have created the miracle of this Cannastar that has been brought to us. It is part of the old ways. Something new out of something old. *The Ones Who Can Not Be Seen* have shown us our path—a way to honor our past by growing our future. Mankind has lost its way and is no longer connected to the earth. In helping them find their way back, we are helping ourselves.

"It will not be easy. There are many dangers. White men have tried often to destroy us with laws that serve only themselves. They were not successful then and they will not be successful now! We are a sovereign nation and our laws are not their laws." He raised his fist in the air and a battle cry rose from the crowd. "I will send a prayer in the four directions for the success and safety of this great enterprise."

Tumultuous applause. Everyone talking at once. Like the Iowa farmers, mainly what they were so excited about was the prospect of an ongoing supply of Cannastar for themselves and their families.

IN THE SPRING ALEX ASKED Futz to take him for a short ride in Annie's Citation. About 60 miles north of Window Rock the jet swooped low over the empty desert. All that could be seen in any direction was sand, rock, sagebrush and cactus. Far to the north, the 27 million year old volcanic silhouette of Shiprock rose almost 1,800 feet out of the sand like a mysterious sphinx guarding the prehistoric lands of the Anasazi.

Alex peered intently out the window as the jet banked in a tight turn over a specific tract of land. To his infinite delight what he saw below looked as barren, desolate and arid as the rest of the landscape. The jet made one last low pass over the area before heading back to the airport. Otis stepped out from under the camouflage net and waved. It was as if he appeared out of nowhere.

Underneath the camo nets an army of Navajo workers were laboring in the Cannastar fields. Many looked up as the jet went over and smiled. They had built an invisible circus, pitching tents over a four square mile area of pancake flat desert. The netting was supported on long sturdy poles and anchored with support cables that were attached to stakes driven deep in the ground. The ventilated netting gave protection from the rain, snow and relentless sun without blocking the light.

A breeze was blowing through the open sides of the netting and it felt like air conditioning on Cyd's bare arms. Stretched out before her was row upon row of Cannastar bushes growing out of water-filled wooden troughs fed by miles of black poly irrigation pipe. Transportation under the nets was by quad and dozens of the little four wheeled vehicles rumbled up and down the rows. Separate camouflage nets hid the pumps, water storage tanks and generators and another net hid five single-wide mobile homes where the seven Cannastar conspirators and their pilot were now living.

President Lawrence had little trouble finding volunteers to help set up the massive project—it seemed everyone wanted to help. The Navajo regarded Otis as a shaman because of his expertise at growing the Cannastar, and treated him with great respect. Otis was baffled by his new status and found it a little disconcerting.

Futz began dating a beautiful Navajo woman named Dawn and would have stayed in Window Rock even if Annie wasn't paying him. Dawn had a daughter named Feather who was Elton's age and the two of them became best friends. Feather was teaching Elton the way of the Dineh and together they formed daily hunting parties that roamed the countryside in search of adventure.

"The Grow", as they called it, had been successfully launched and Don Bueno's planes would soon be making midnight trips in and out of the Window Rock airport.

The sound of the jet with Alex aboard faded overhead, and Otis went back to helping Annie and Abe supervise The Grow. They stood together looking out proudly over a sea of tightly packed Cannastar plants flourishing under the camouflage nets. It was a magnificent sight.

Then Cyd decided she needed a vacation and that was when the trouble started.

THE IOWA CROP OF CANNASTAR produced enough of the drug to open up a single region but not enough for the entire country. Don Bueno decided to start with the West Coast. The new product created a remarkable phenomenon among the thousands of violent drug dealers and gangs in California and the illegal drug business was changed forever.

Any good enterprise looks for ways to grow its business and expand its product line, but Cannastar offered more than a new income stream. It brought new pride and new meaning to the lives of countless streetwise entrepreneurs. It gave them a cause, a purpose, a reason to be right; it offered a dignity that hadn't existed before.

As a result, a new morality sprung up and a tenant was added to the already rigid code of criminal ethics. Just as child molestation was an unforgivable sin, so now was killing and gouging people over Cannastar. In marketing a cure for disease they were helping to heal their customers, not kill them. It felt good and decent and right.

Cannastar distribution became a unifying cause and the act of dealing drugs gained stature. It became almost a noble profession. For the first time since it began, the drug trade had something to believe in that was life-affirming and grand. Pushers and perps alike had a reason to do something honorable, get rich doing it and still not have to get a real job. There was profit in it for the little guy. Not only could the street dealer help his neighbor instead of killing him, he could help himself. It was capitalism at its best.

And the doctors, hospitals, drug companies and insurers—the medical profession with the government comfortably in their pocket and all the rules, laws and regulations either thrown out or rewritten in their favor—had in their hubris done something good after all. A common side effect of their greed was to produce an astonishing transformation in the drug culture and its legions of murderous criminals. Thanks to Rxon's megalomaniacal efforts to stop it, Cannastar was healing the world in a way even its supporters never imagined. It was curing a societal cancer. Instead of destroying the world, the drug dealers were now saving it.

To be certain, tattooed felons and gang bangers did not become nice guys, heaven forbid. The *gangsta* life was, thank goodness, safely intact. But Cannastar brought out the good in them and they were changed. The LAPD reported a remarkable and baffling drop in violence.

Meanwhile, California being what it was, people went absolutely crazy for the new drug. They couldn't get enough of it. Celebrities were buying it for their pets.

The medical community felt like a jilted lover. Doctor's offices and hospitals were starting to look as lonely and deserted as the Arizona desert, the health insurance business was in crisis and Rxon's drug sales were tanking.

Dick Tremble, Rxon's CEO, pulled out all the stops.

A representative from American Medical Association, or AMA, went on national television with a statement denouncing Cannastar. "Research has shown that death is a common side effect of this drug," a spokesman in a white lab coat said. "Patients who do not follow their doctor's advice are gambling with their lives. Take only drugs that are prescribed for you by your physician."

Given that the bullshit belied their experience, people weren't buying the spin. The medical profession grew desperate and began haranguing their congressmen and lobbyists to *DO SOMETHING!*

Nebraska senator Berkley Buyoff came on SUX News and said, "Addiction is a terrible thing. Do we give meth and heroine to people just because they want it? We do not! And your government is not going to stand by and enable these Cannastar addicts by giving them their drug either. This is America, not Amsterdam!"

The *Let Us Pray* evangelical church of Greenville, South Carolina called Cannastar "the devil's weed" and advised their followers to shun it at the cost of their very souls.

Senator Sam Seeley was once again the lead story on the evening news, denouncing Cannastar as "the seeds of destruction." He looked into the camera and with a vicious twist of semantics took his relentless rhetoric to a new height:

"This drug is a killer and the people who grow and distribute it pose a threat to national security. The three terrorists primarily responsible for its proliferation are still at large." Familiar pictures of Cyd, Alex and Otis popped up on the screen as he read off their names. "Anyone having knowledge of their whereabouts is urged to contact the Federal Drug Enforcement Agency immediately."

THE FIRST HARVEST WAS IN and The Grow became the best paying job on the reservation, employing hundreds of Navajo. With so much new product on hand Don Bueno was able to open up the rest of the country. It triggered a frenzied escalation of the war on drugs. The shit storm around Cannastar was reaching hurricane strength and the AMA and Rxon were showing signs of going into cardiac arrest.

For Cyd, isolated as she was from the outside world in Window Rock, the national turmoil over Cannastar wasn't real. All she knew was that she was bored senseless and needed a change.

Confronting Alex one night in their trailer she said, "I'm outta here."

"What do you mean?" Alex said.

"I mean I can't stand it anymore. I need a break. I want to drive into Santa Fe and go to some restaurants, look at the art galleries, soak up some culture. I've never been and I've always wanted to go. I'd love it if you came with me."

"It's not safe, honey."

"Alex, our job here is done. Otis, Annie and Abe are running The Grow. Don Bueno is doing a better job of distribution than Wal-Mart could. There's nothing left for us to do."

"We can't go anywhere and you know it."

"I'll tell you what I know. I know I'm not going to live the rest of my life on an Indian reservation. Come on Alex, please? Take me to Santa Fe. We deserve a little R&R after everything we've been through."

"You've got cabin fever, I understand. I've got it too. I just …I don't think it's wise…"

"Please, please, please?" She stood on tiptoe, pressed herself against him and kissed him.

He couldn't deny her. What man could? Reluctantly, he said, "I'll see if I can borrow Robert's car tomorrow."

Cyd squealed in delight and started throwing her things in an overnight bag. Unfortunately, where she was going, she wouldn't even be able to take a toothbrush.

CHAPTER 17

Run!

Early the next day Cyd and Alex left Window Rock in Robert's SUV, drove through Gallup and Albuquerque, turned north and arrived in Santa Fe around midmorning. A restaurant with an outdoor log veranda overgrown with flowers caught their eye and they parked and went inside. Seated on the patio, surrounded by the adobe charm of the oldest capital city in America, they enjoyed a Mexican food brunch. The architecture of Spain and Old Mexico was all around them, making Cyd feel like she was on a real vacation.

In an effort to disguise himself Alex had grown a ruddy beard. It tickled Cyd's face, but she kind of liked it. Her disguise was dark glasses and a baseball cap that only served to make her look cuter and more mysterious.

He was nervous; she was so excited she couldn't sit still. "Come on Alex, relax," she said gaily. "Let's have some fun."

He managed a smile, but couldn't stop looking over his shoulder.

After lunch they wandered through the historic downtown plaza peeking in shops, then turned toward Canyon Road, a narrow street that wound uphill with over 100 little art galleries and studios that sold some of the most expensive southwestern art money could buy.

Cyd danced delightedly in and out of the galleries until Alex got tired of following her around and sat down to study some sculptures that caught his eye. Cyd was already out the door. "I'll be up the street," she called merrily.

"Um-hmm," he said, resting his feet as he continued gazing at the works of art. He decided all his worry had been for nothing and had begun to relax when he realized he had been sitting there looking at the sculptures for quite some time. He got up and went outside to find Cyd.

A few doors up the street Cyd was inside another gallery, absorbed in the beautiful art that was on display. The gallery owner, Grace Slyly, came up and began explaining to Cyd something about the painting she was admiring. Grace wore her graying hair in leather wrapped Indian braids that did a pretty good job of disguising the fact that she was from Cleveland.

Cyd had taken off her dark glasses when she came into the shop because Grace's things were so lovely and she wanted to see them better. She told the shop owner she was just looking, but for some reason Grace decided Cyd was a buyer and wouldn't leave her alone, going to great lengths to offer information about the works of the various local artists she represented. Cyd was having a wonderful time listening to the monologue and getting an art lesson. What she didn't realize was that the minute she walked in Grace had recognized her and sent her assistant into the back room to call the authorities.

Alex was making his way from gallery to gallery searching for Cyd when half a dozen police cars screeched to a halt in front of the Slyly Gallery and several more pulled into the alley in back. Armed men jumped out and surrounded the

store while a man with a bullhorn crouched down behind the
door of his squad car and blared, "Cyd Seeley, this is the Santa
Fe police. You are ordered to come out with your hands up."

Inside, the color ran out of Cyd's face. Out of the corner of
her eye she saw the gallery owner backing away. Grace made
it to her cash register where she retrieved her hand gun. Not
knowing what to do or which way to turn, Cyd started shaking
as the voice came again:

"Come out immediately! This is your last warning!"

Cyd made a move to go out the back door and Grace raised
her gun, blocking her way. Cyd heard someone screaming…
and realized it was her.

Down the street Alex heard the scream and bolted toward
the sound, only to be restrained by the heavy arm of a police
officer who yelled at him to stay clear of the area. He watched
helplessly as Cyd appeared in the doorway with her hands up,
then gasped as she was forced to her knees, handcuffed and
roughly hauled away.

ALEX WAS SHOUTING INTO THE phone and had to repeat
himself several times before Clarence understood that Cyd
had been arrested.

His voice stuck in his throat. "I'm chartering a plane,"
Clarence said. "I'll be there in a few hours."

As soon as Otis heard Alex's voice he knew something
was wrong. He held the phone away from his ear so Annie
and Eloise could hear as well. Eloise started crying when she
heard what had happened.

"Alex, listen to me," Otis said. "Do not go near that jail.
Get back to the reservation as fast as you can."

"I'm not leaving her, I can't…"

"You're not thinking straight, man."

"It's my fault, Otis. I should never have brought her here."

"Never mind about that. You have to get out of there now!

Annie took the phone out of Otis's hand. "Alex darling, I'm on my way to Santa Fe. I'll try and stay as close to her as I can. Your job is to return here this instant, do you hear me? We don't want to lose you too."

"Tell Robert I talked to his dad," Alex said miserably. "The two of you need to meet him at the Santa Fe airport as soon as you get here."

ON THE FLIGHT OUT ABOARD a chartered Gulf Stream, Clarence Bigfoot was able to reach a friend in Washington who made a few phone calls on his behalf. By the time he landed in Santa Fe Clarence had already hired Santiago Vazquez, a local defense attorney who specialized in drug cases.

Cyd was booked into the Santa Fe jail and an hour later DEA agents arrived from Albuquerque to question her. It was a brutal and frightening interrogation. She was told that if she gave up her fellow conspirators and revealed where the drugs were being grown she might receive a lighter sentence.

"Come on sister, what's it going to be?" snarled one of the angry agents. "You want to spend the rest of your life in prison or just half of it?"

Cyd glared at him until he looked away. "Lawyer," she said softly.

"What?"

"I want a fucking lawyer, are you deaf?"

That evening Clarence, his son Robert and Annie met with Vazquez in his Santa Fe office. The attorney wore cowboy boots, a turquoise bolo tie and a pony tail that was shorter than Clarence's, but just as black. He regarded his worried clients gravely. "Given how badly they want her and how hard they've been looking for her," he said, "I'd say the chances of her being released on bail are zero, zip, nada."

Cyd spent the next two days in a jail cell. The longer she sat and stared at the bleak walls the more terrified she became. Vasquez came and went several times and tried to be as encouraging as possible. Each time after he left she cried.

Alex hadn't slept since he got back to Window Rock. Eloise was feeding him, but he didn't eat much. He had never felt more helpless in his life. They had arranged to call Annie for an update and he walked over to Otis's trailer so they could talk to her together. The moon shining through the camouflage netting overhead lit his way.

Otis opened the door, Alex came in and Eloise poured him some tea. At least they didn't have to ration the Cannastar now. Abe was running The Grow, which was fortunate, because Otis was almost as useless as Alex.

They sat at the kitchen table while Otis punched Annie's number into his disposable phone. He was relieved when she picked up. Alex and Eloise looked on anxiously.

"How are you all holding up?" Annie asked.

"We're not," Otis said. "Tell me something good."

"All right, I will" Annie said. "I think I have a plan."

"She has a plan," Otis said. Alex and Eloise held their breath.

"Don't get your hopes up yet," Annie said. "Cyd's arraignment is set for tomorrow morning and I won't know until then if my little scheme has worked or not. Call me at ten and every hour after that until I pick up."

An hour later Sam Seeley returned his wife's call. Annie listened to him gloat over Cyd's capture for less than a minute before she cut him off.

"Sam, I need to say something and you better listen." She waited quietly until he stopped fuming. "I want the charges against Cydney dropped."

His laugh was almost a shout. "It's too late for that," he said. "I couldn't make that happen if I wanted to."

"Then I'm going to the tabloids," she said. "I'm going to tell them how you enslaved me and turned me into a criminal; how you forced a helpless old woman to help you grow your illegal drugs. I'll say you thought you were above the law and that you thought you could get away with growing it in your own greenhouse because that's the last place anyone would think to look."

The Senator exploded. "What the hell did I give you all that money for? You said you'd keep your mouth shut! You said that would be the end of it if I paid you off!"

"I lied. I'll ruin you, Sam, I swear."

"I can't make this go away. It's too big now. It's impossible."

Annie hesitated before going on. "Then I want her out on bail. I want Cyd out of jail this instant."

There was a long silence. "I'll see what I can do," he said and hung up.

ALEX SAT MISERABLY ON THE edge of the bed he shared with Cyd in their trailer out at The Grow. The longing he felt for her that night was more unbearable than his back pain had ever been. Faced with losing her for good, an agonizing collage of pictures swirled through his mind:

Cyd in her truck at the airport, Maury's body, Otis, Cyd's ranch, the fire…the Cannastar in the mortuary attic…Betty… Cyd on horseback in the Montana wilderness….digging up the Cannastar seeds that Maury buried…being attacked…that first night together in the cave and their desperate escape over the mountains...Clarence and his preposterous house and taking pain pills again...Cyd, Mary and Tiffany kidnapped...the rescue and the Great Swimming Pool Massacre...and dancing at the Snake Snot Salon. Alicia's suicide...his guilt and pain and sadness...his desperate journey to find Cyd again...her courage and tenacity...the paradox that was Joe Angolia...his office, then...Mexico! *Oh God, Mexico*! he thought...the river, the jungle, the bungalow and their marathon love making...He buried his face in her pillow and inhaled her smell, trying to will her back into existence...Don Bueno and his insane amusement park for all those sad and beautiful children...Annie, wonderful Annie and her brave greenhouse...Running down the midnight roads to Iowa and Abe and the faithful farmers of Fort Dodge...the desperate flight to Window Rock and The Grow, the glorious, life giving, life affirming Grow and...Santa Fe! "Oh God," he prayed aloud, "don't let me lose her again."

THE US COURTHOUSE IN SANTA FE was made of stone, cold and indifferent, even in the warm morning light. Cyd sat with her attorney, Mr. Vazquez, at the defense table. Behind her in the courtroom she could feel the anxious eyes of Annie, Clarence and Robert on her. US Attorney Findley Ovid Fisk sat at the other table with two ambitious junior prosecutors.

The bailiff stood abruptly. "All rise! US District Court is now in session, Chief US District Judge David Young presiding!"

The black robed judge came in and took his seat, awkwardly adjusting the donut he sat on. Judge Young's principal virtue was a monumental arrogance that supplanted his limited intelligence and made it almost irrelevant. The fringe of hair that circled his bald head made him look like a Franciscan monk. He listened impassively as the charges were read and the attorneys argued about bail.

Mr. Vasquez said, "If it pleases the court, my client has absolutely no criminal record. She's never even gotten a speeding ticket. Ms. Seeley is a botanist and an outstanding researcher who, for some reason, has been singled out for persecution in a corporate and political witch hunt that bears no relationship to anything concrete or factual. Not a single shred of evidence exists to link the accused to this crime. We move that she be released on her own recognizance."

Mr. Fisk rose and ceremoniously buttoned his suit coat. "Your honor," he began, "Ms. Seeley here is responsible for unleashing on the American public a ghastly drug more dangerous than nerve gas. Her heartless greed has killed thousands already and the death toll is rising as we speak. This is a national epidemic, and she holds the key to identifying her fellow conspirators and locating the source of this poison. A carrion eater on a busy freeway is less of a flight risk than she is."

Fisk sat down and smiled confidently at his junior associates. *The next time this bitch sees the light of day is going to be in the next century,* he thought.

The judge banged his gavel. "Bail is set at two hundred thousand dollars."

Annie, who had been holding her breath, exhaled loudly.

Fisk exploded out of his seat. "Your honor, surely you'll want to reconsider…"

"Sit down, Mr. Fisk. I've made my ruling."

"But the government…"

"ONE MORE WORD AND I'M HOLDING YOU IN CONTEMPT!"

It was done. Fisk sat with his mouth working open and closed, too stunned to move, while Cyd was led back to jail until Clarence could post her bond. Clarence, Annie and Robert were hugging and Annie was crying. They waved triumphantly and Cyd smiled back, weak with relief.

THE NIGHT BEFORE CYD'S ARRAIGNMENT Judge David Young received a phone call from the distinguished Senator Sam Seeley, whose endorsement he had failed to attain in his desperate bid for the vacant US senate seat in New Mexico. The judge would have given his left nut to be elected senator and the polls showed he was losing badly. He was puzzled and delighted that the Senator would be calling him so late at night.

Sam didn't waste any time getting to the point. "Judge Young, are you ready to play Let's Make A Deal?"

"Go on," Young said carefully.

"It's simple. I want the Seeley woman out on bail."

"I thought…"

"Never mind what you thought. This guy running against you is kicking your ass. You don't stand a chance."

"I'm fully aware…"

"You're not aware of anything. This broad needs to get out on bond. If she does, you will get unlimited funding for that senate seat you want so much. And you'll win, trust me. If she stays in jail your opponent is going to win. Simple as that. What's it going to be?"

The honorable Judge David Young didn't even have to think about it. "See you in Washington, Senator Seeley."

"Yes you will, Senator Young."

FUTZ LINED UP ON THE Window Rock runway and brought the Citation in smooth and hot.

Alex, Otis, Eloise and Abe, accompanied by Robert who had driven his car back from Santa Fe, waited eagerly as the jet taxied up. They had decided that the safest way to bring Cyd home was to fly her back. At least this way she couldn't be followed.

The engines shut down, the door opened...and Cyd appeared, rushing down the steps and into Alex's arms. They covered each other in kisses. Tears of joy ran down Alex's face and he hugged her until she couldn't breathe. He had never been so grateful for anything in his life. Annie and Clarence emerged from the plane and they all embraced. Even Futz was moved to tears. Clarence put his arms around Cyd and Alex and she smiled up at him bravely, her dark hair dirty and matted from her ordeal in jail.

"Clarence, thank you for everything," she said. "I'll pay you right back, I swear. Alex and I are making plenty of money off The Grow. In fact, I almost have enough saved up to buy back my mortgage from you..."

"Keep it," Clarence said. "You're going to need it."

"What do you mean?"

"We'll talk about it tomorrow. Right now you need to get some rest."

When they got back to their trailer out at The Grow, Cyd fell on the bed fully clothed and pulled her knees up to her chin. Alex watched her lying there and carefully laid down beside her. She was staring at the wall with red eyes and a forlorn look. He put his arm around her as she began to weep. They lay together for hours while he held her, rocking her softly, as wave after wave of the trauma washed over her.

 The next morning when Cyd got out of the shower she was smiling again. They had breakfast, picked Clarence up at the Quality Inn and brought him out to see The Grow.

The big Salish Indian walked between the flourishing rows of Cannastar under the camo nets wearing his trademark shorts and loud Hawaiian shirt, staring in awe at what they had accomplished.

"I couldn't be more impressed if it was the streets of heaven you were showing me," Clarence said.

"The Navajo say the Great Spirit had something to do with it," Alex said.

"They would know," Clarence said.

"Before you two go all airy-fairy on me you should know that this was Otis, Annie and Abe's doing," Cyd said. "And yours, thanks to the camo nets you bought."

Clarence gave her a stern look. "And now it's over, Cyd. It's time for the two of you to go."

"That's impossible," Cyd said. "We can't just…"

"You must leave and leave quickly. I mean it."

"I was thinking the same thing," Alex said.

"So far it's just been talk," Clarence said, "but they are saying that the three of you are a threat to national security and they are doing everything they can to have you put on the list of known terrorists. If you show up for trial and that happens, you become an enemy combatant and the army will take you away. That means they can torture you for information, Cyd. There is no habeas corpus, no court of appeal, no liberties, no democracy and no America. They'll waterboard you—something as barbaric and brutal as anything ever devised by man. You will talk no matter how much you think you won't. You will tell them anything and everything they want to know and be glad you did. They will find out about this place and everybody involved will be arrested which means the Cannastar will be lost and everything you've done will have been for nothing. Is that what you want?"

Cyd's eyes grew huge and she shook her head.

"Then run! You don't have a choice. The two of you need to get out of the country as quickly as possible."

"What about passports?" Alex asked.

"I'm working on that," Clarence said.

THAT AFTERNOON CYD TOLD ANNIE she and Alex were leaving.

"Good," Annie said sadly. "I'm glad."

"I'll miss you like crazy," Cyd said.

"You'll always be my daughter wherever you go," Annie said, kissing her cheek. Cyd started to cry. "Before you go, I have a confession to make. I hope you won't think too badly of me, but Abe and I have moved into the same trailer together."

Cyd was flabbergasted. "You go, girl," she said, hugging her happily. "What's it like?"

"Like riding a bicycle," Annie grinned.

ABE AND ANNIE STOOD TALKING that evening in their trailer. The Iowa farmer was a foot taller than her, but somehow they fit together just fine.

Abe said unhappily, "If Alex and Cyd are leaving, maybe I'll go back to the farm for a while."

Annie took one of his calloused hands and held it between her slender palms. "I think it's still too dangerous," she said. "These are your crops now too, Abraham. Yours, mine and Otis's. We have a job to do. Otis can't do it alone."

"Aren't you homesick, Annabelle? I know I am."

"I have an idea," she said excitedly. "How about if we take a little vacation?"

"Where would we go?"

"I'd love to show you my place in Virginia. It's only a few hours by plane."

"Is it fancy? You know fancy places make me nervous."

"It's just a big farm, darling. Not as big as yours, of course. I can't wait to show you all the things I grow. You'll love it, wait and see."

THE NEXT DAY CYD AND Alex met Otis and Eloise out at the building site of their new house in Window Rock.

Otis was heartbroken when he heard the news. "Good thing we don't need you guys any more," he said.

"It's you and Eloise I'm worried about," Cyd said.

"You know you can't leave the reservation," Alex said.

"Don't worry about us," Otis said, smiling at Eloise who looked at him contentedly. "We're happy right where we are."

"I'm so excited," Eloise said. "I've always wanted to build a Santa Fe style house and now I'm actually getting to do it."

Cyd and Alex shuddered at the mention of the name Santa Fe.

Just then Elton and Feather, flushed from their latest adventures, bounded up onto the wood subfloor where the others were standing. When Elton was told that Cyd and Alex were leaving he ran to them and Alex lifted him up.

"When will I ever see you again?" he asked anxiously.

"I don't know," Alex said.

"Probably when Cannastar gets legalized," Otis said.

"When will that be?" the boy asked.

"It could be a while," Cyd told him. "Someday."

"Someday soon?'

"Someday," his mother said.

TWO DAYS LATER CYD AND Alex were with Clarence at the Quality Inn when a Fed Ex truck arrived with an envelope for Clarence. He ripped it open, inspected the contents and handed Cyd and Alex two new passports.

Alex looked his over closely. "It looks real," he said.

"It ought to be," Clarence said. "The guy that made them for me is the same guy that makes them for the CIA."

"How did you get our pictures?" Cyd asked.

"Mary still had digital shots of you on her camera from when you and Alex visited us last year." He reached in a drawer and handed them two more packages.

"What's this?" Cyd asked, opening her package and taking out a blond wig.

"Try it on," Clarence said. "You too, Alex"

Alex put his wig on and they stood laughing at themselves in the mirror. Alex's new hair hung down below his shoulders.

"We look like a hippie and a hooker," Cyd giggled.

"Now you can go shopping for the things you need for the boat and hopefully not get recognized," Clarence said. "When are you leaving?"

"Futz is flying us out to the west coast first thing tomorrow," Alex said.

"I'll say goodbye then," Clarence said, extending his arms.

Cyd cried as he hugged her.

AT THE WINDOW ROCK AIRPORT the next morning Otis, Eloise, Elton, Annie, Abe, Clarence and Robert stood on the tarmac and said their final farewells as Cyd and Alex boarded Annie's Citation. So much had happened and there was so much to say that they said very little. Otis bit his lip and Annie waved bravely as the plane taxied for takeoff, made a thundering run down the runway, left the ground and disappeared into the western sky.

"God speed," Clarence said.

RXON'S JUGULAR VEIN HAD BEEN cut and the company was bleeding to death.

Dick Tremble realized he was losing the war and made a desperate attempt to file a patent on Cannastar based on the fact that legally he was the owner. If everybody wanted it that badly he would get it legalized and sell it for a thousand dollars a cup. Unfortunately, all the research documents and paperwork had somehow been lost or stolen so there was no way to verify his claim or even that Cannastar had ever been invented.

A year from now the medical industry's criminal exploitation of the sick and helpless would be at an end, Rxon's campus would be overgrown with weeds, the windows would be broken out and the buildings would be deserted. Around the base of the corporate tower legions of vines would be sprouting from the ground and creeping up the sides of the monolith, leading the way for others to follow in a determined effort to do what they did to the Mayan pyramids.

And alone in the tower, Dick Tremble would be sitting at his desk staring at a pharmacy size bottle of sleeping pills and a large glass of water, contemplating the unthinkable.

CYD FELL IN LOVE WITH Alex's sailboat the minute she saw it. The cutter's long lines and low profile made the boat look fast and strong and safe even sitting in the slip. Cyd went below deck to see where she would be living, descending the ladder and scanning the interior with her eyes. It looked like home and smelled like adventure.

Slime was parked in the marina parking lot. Alex opened the door and Cyd got in so they could go to the store.

"Nice car," she said.

"I thought you'd like it," he said.

One of the first things Cyd did was change the name from *Pequod* back to the one the ship had been christened with 25 years ago when she was launched. Alex and Cyd stood on the dock admiring the new gold leaf lettering on the stern that spelled out *Volunteer*. It was as if the boat had renamed herself now that she knew her purpose.

Every day they spent on land they risked discovery and they hurried to be gone. Dozens of repairs had to be made to the boat before they could leave. Alex marveled at how handy Cyd was, especially with a paint brush.

They had fun running around buying everything they would need to spend months at sea if necessary. Every time Cyd looked at Alex in his hippie wig she couldn't help smiling. Alex actually thought she looked pretty good as a blond but was always happy at night when she went back to being a brunette.

Cyd was in a grocery store buying last minute supplies when some dust or pollen got in her nose and she started sneezing. A harried housewife with three children in tow came up to her thinking she had a cold and whispered, "I know where you can get some Cannastar if you need it."

"That's okay," Cyd whispered back. "I think I already have some."

After a long night's work with only two hours sleep, the day finally came. Cyd cast off the dock lines and Alex backed out of the slip for the last time. They motored slowly out of the harbor in a low hanging fog past thousands of boats rocking silently at the docks. When they cleared the breakwater the sun came out, the fog burned off and they ceremoniously threw their wigs overboard.

Alex raised the sails and the boat shuddered as she came alive. The ocean rippled with the first sign of wind and they ghosted in the direction of Catalina Island. Alex didn't want to alarm Cyd with his concern, but he kept looking around for any last minute assault by an overzealous Coast Guard boat coming at them at high speed.

Hidden deep in the hold, sealed in waterproof bags, was hundreds of pounds of Cannastar seed. Their intention was to plant the Cannastar wherever they went so that it could be spread around the world. The slender physician would fulfill his lifelong dream of doctoring indigenous populations on remote islands, and the Montana cowgirl planned to study the exotic flora that grew in the faraway places they visited.

Off the west end of Catalina they turned southwest toward the southern latitudes. The sails rustled and flapped, then filled and began to draw as the wind freshened and backed into the north. The *Volunteer* heeled as she picked up speed, her bow plunging into the white and boiling waves, the ocean hissing by under her lee rail.

The sea quickened their blood. Cyd stood at the helm and the wind blew back her hair. Alex put his arm around her and they smiled, then turned to squint into the distance. They were in the wind, they were on the wind, reaching for a distant shore, for a place unseen, unknown and yet to come.

About the Author

Stephen G. Mitchell lives in a remodeled Victorian in Helena, Montana with Beverly, his lifelong companion. He as been a sales trainer, Wall Street trader, builder/developer/contractor, cowboy, skier and sailor. A lifetime student of the human condition and a professional neurotic, Mr. Mitchell is one part novelist, one part investigative journalist—a teller of wild-ass tales, most of which are true.